Evan S. Connell was born in Kansas City, the locale of the two novels which appear in this volume, in 1924. He has written not only several other novels but also short stories, poetry and essays of great distinction. His history of General Custer and the Battle of the Little Bighorn, *Son of the Morning Star*, is also available in Picador.

Mrs Bridge
and
Mr Bridge

Evan S. Connell

PICADOR published by Pan Books

Mrs Bridge first published 1959 by The Viking Press, Inc
First published in Great Britain 1983 by Sinclair Browne Ltd
© Evan S. Connell 1959
Mr Bridge first published 1969 by Alfred A. Knopf, Inc
First published in Great Britain 1983 by Sinclair Browne Ltd
© Evan S. Connell 1969
This combined Picador edition first published in
Great Britain 1987 by Pan Books Ltd,
Cavaye Place, London SW10 9PG
9 8 7 6 5 4 3
© Evan S. Connell 1987
ISBN 0 330 29325 7

Printed in Great Britain by
Richard Clay Ltd, Bungay, Suffolk

Mrs Bridge   7

Mr Bridge   195

Mrs Bridge

To
Barbara
and
Matthew Zimmermann

But where is what I started for so long ago?
And why is it yet unfound?

Walt Whitman

1 Love and marriage

Her first name was India – she was never able to get used to it. It seemed to her that her parents must have been thinking of someone else when they named her. Or were they hoping for another sort of daughter? As a child she was often on the point of inquiring, but time passed, and she never did.

Now and then while she was growing up the idea came to her that she could get along very nicely without a husband, and, to the distress of her mother and father, this idea prevailed for a number of years after her education had been completed. But there came a summer evening and a young lawyer named Walter Bridge: very tall and dignified, red-haired, with a grimly determined, intelligent face, and rather stoop-shouldered so that even when he stood erect his coat hung lower in the front than in the back. She had known him for several years without finding him remarkable in any way, but on this summer evening, on the front porch of her parents' home, she toyed with a sprig of mint and looked at him attentively while pretending to listen to what he said. He was telling her that he intended to become rich and successful, and that one day he would take his wife – 'whenever I finally decide to marry' he said, for he was not yet ready to commit himself – one day he would take his wife on a tour of Europe. He spoke of Ruskin and of Robert Ingersoll, and he read to her that evening on the porch, later, some verses from *The Rubáiyát* while her parents were preparing for bed, and the locusts sang in the elm trees all around.

A few months after her father died she married Walter Bridge and moved with him to Kansas City, where he had decided to establish a practice.

All seemed well. The days passed, and the weeks, and the months, more swiftly than in childhood, and she felt no trepidation, except for certain moments in the depth of the night when, as she and her new husband lay drowsily clutching each other for reassurance, anticipating the dawn, the day, and another night which might prove them both immortal, Mrs Bridge found herself wide awake. During these moments, resting in her husband's arms, she would stare at the ceiling, or at his face, which sleep robbed of strength, with an uneasy expression, as though she saw or heard some intimation of the great years ahead.

She was not certain what she wanted from life, or what to expect from it, for she had seen so little of it, but she was sure that in some way – because she willed it to be so – her wants and her expectations were the same.

For a while after their marriage she was in such demand that it was not unpleasant when he fell asleep. Presently, however, he began sleeping all night, and it was then she awoke more frequently, and looked into the darkness, wondering about the nature of men, doubtful of the future, until at last there came a night when she shook her husband awake and spoke of her own desire. Affably he placed one of his long white arms around her waist; she turned to him then, contentedly, expectantly, and secure. However nothing else occurred, and in a few minutes he had gone back to sleep.

This was the night Mrs Bridge concluded that while marriage might be an equitable affair, love itself was not.

2 Children

Their first child, a girl, curiously dark, who seldom cried and who often seemed to want nothing more than to be left alone, was born when they had been married a little more than three years. They named her Ruth. After the delivery Mrs Bridge's first coherent words were, 'Is she normal?'

Two years later – Mrs Bridge was then thirty-one – Carolyn appeared, about a month ahead of time, as though she were quite able to take care of herself, and was nicknamed 'Corky'. She was a chubby blonde, blue-eyed like her mother, more ebullient than Ruth, and more demanding.

Then, two years after Carolyn, a stern little boy was born, thin and red-haired like his father, and they named him Douglas. They had not wanted more than two children, but because the first two had been girls they had decided to try once more. Even if the third had also been a girl they would have let it go at that; there would have been no sense in continuing what would soon become amusing to other people.

3 Preliminary training

She brought up her children very much as she herself had been brought up, and she hoped that when they were spoken of it would be in connection with their nice manners, their pleasant dispositions, and their cleanliness, for these were qualities she valued above all others.

With Ruth and later with Carolyn, because they were girls, she felt sure of her guidance; but with the boy she was at times obliged to guess and to hope, and as it turned out – not only with Douglas but with his two sisters – what she stressed was not at all what they remembered as they grew older.

What Ruth was to recall most vividly about childhood was an incident which Mrs Bridge had virtually forgotten an hour after it occurred. One summer afternoon the entire family, with the exception of Mr Bridge who was working, had gone to the neighborhood swimming pool; Douglas lay on a rubber sheet in the shade of an umbrella, kicking his thin bowed legs and gurgling, and Carolyn was splashing around in the wading pool. The day was exceptionally hot. Ruth took off her bathing suit and began walking across the terrace. This much she could hardly remember, but she was never to forget what happened next. Mrs Bridge, having suddenly discovered Ruth was naked, snatched up the bathing suit and hurried after her. Ruth began to run, and being wet and slippery she squirmed out of the arms that reached for her from every direction. She thought it was a new game. Then she noticed the expression on her mother's face. Ruth became bewildered and then alarmed, and when she was finally caught she was screaming hysterically.

4 Marmalade

Her husband was as astute as he was energetic, and because he wanted so much for his family he went to his office quite early in the morning while most men were still asleep and he often stayed there working until late at night. He worked all day Saturday and part of Sunday, and holidays were nothing but a nuisance. Before very long the word had gone around that Walter Bridge was the man to handle the case.

The family saw very little of him. It was not unusual for an entire week to pass without any of the children seeing him. On Sunday morning they would come downstairs and he might be at the breakfast table; he greeted them pleasantly and they responded deferentially, and a little wistfully because they missed him. Sensing this, he would redouble his efforts at the office in order to give them everything they wanted.

Consequently they were able to move to a large home just off Ward Parkway several years sooner than they had expected, and because the house was so large they employed a young coloured girl named Harriet to do the cooking and cleaning.

One morning at the breakfast table Carolyn said petulantly, 'I'm sick and tired of orange marmalade!'

Mrs Bridge, who was mashing an egg for her, replied patiently, 'Now, Corky, just remember there are lots and lots of little girls in the world who don't have any marmalade at all.'

5 Christmas basket

That there should be those who had marmalade, and those who did not, was a condition that appealed to Carolyn. She looked forward to Christmas, at which time the newspaper printed a list of the one hundred neediest families in Kansas City. Every year Mrs Bridge adopted one of these families, seeing to it that they had a nice holiday, and Carolyn now took a definite interest in this annual project. Each needy family was described in the paper – how many children, how old, what they needed particularly, and so forth – and Carolyn helped her mother decide which family they should adopt. Ruth and Douglas did not seem to care very much.

A bushel basket, or perhaps two, would be filled with canned goods, possibly some clothing, and whatever else the poor family could obviously use – a smoked ham, a bag of flour, a bag of salt – and the basket would then be topped with candy canes and a paper angel or a Santa Claus, and the edges trimmed with scallops of red and green crepe. Then on the day before Christmas Mrs Bridge and the children would deliver the basket to the address furnished by the newspaper.

During the preparations Mrs Bridge would sometimes ask the children if they could remember the family they had adopted last year. Ruth, being the oldest, usually could, but it was always Carolyn who could describe most sharply the details of poverty.

Douglas, possibly because he was so young – or so Mrs Bridge reasoned – did not enjoy these trips. Each Christmas when he saw the basket being filled and trimmed he grew restless and obstinate; she did not know why, nor could she get him to explain. He did not want to go, that was clear, but she wanted him to appreciate his own good fortune, and not to grow up thinking he was better than someone else, so she insisted he go along to visit the poor family; he would ride in the back seat of the Reo with one arm resting on top of the Christmas basket, and he never said a word from the moment the trip started until they were home again. But he, like Ruth, remembered. This was why he hated to go. He could remember the very first visit. He had been just three years old when he first joined his sisters on the annual expedition to the north end of the city – had it been to Strawberry Hill, where he had expected to see a bowl of strawberries on top of the hill? – no matter, he remembered how he had been sitting in the back of the Reo when the door was opened and a man leaned in and took the basket away. Then, while the door was still open and snowflakes were falling on his knees, someone else leaned in – he could not remember whether it was a man or a woman – and quickly, neatly touched the cushion of the Reo.

Although many years were to pass before Douglas could under-stand why someone had wanted to touch the cushion, or why the memory of that gesture should persist, each Christmas thereafter when he saw the basket being filled and trimmed he grew restless and obstinate.

6 Displaced dummy

On a winter morning not long after one of these excursions Mrs Bridge happened to come upon Douglas in the sewing room; he was standing quietly with his hands clasped behind his back and his head bent slightly to one side. So adult did he look in the depth of his meditation that she could not resist smiling. Then she saw that he was staring at the dummy of her figure. She had kept the dummy there near the sewing machine for a long time and had supposed that no one in the family paid any attention to it, but after this particular day – unless she was using it to make herself a dress – the dummy stood behind an up-ended trunk in the attic.

7 Alice Jones

That summer Carolyn began playing with Alice Jones, the daughter of the colored gardener who worked next door. Every Saturday morning he would appear from the direction of the streetcar line, his daughter Alice capering wildly around him. As soon as they came in sight of the Bridges' house she would rush ahead, pigtails flying. In a minute she would be at the back door, pressing the bell with both hands. Often Mrs Bridge would be in the kitchen polishing silver or planning the week-end menu while Harriet did the heavy cleaning somewhere else in the house, so Mrs Bridge would answer the door.

Alice Jones was always out of breath from the run and her eyes were shining with expectation as she inquired if Corky could come out and play.

'Why, I think she can,' Mrs Bridge would say, and smile. 'Providing you two behave yourselves.' About this time the gardener would come walking up the neighbor's driveway and she would say through the screen door, 'Good morning, Jones.'

'Mornin', Mrs Bridge,' he always answered. 'That child bothering you all?'

'Not a bit! We love having her.'

By this time Carolyn would appear and the two children would begin their day. In spite of Carolyn's excellence at school she was not very imaginative, and no matter what she suggested they do that day Alice Jones had a better idea. Carolyn was a little stunned by some of the suggestions, and for a few minutes would grow petulant and arrogant, but when she found that Alice could not be intimidated she gave way and enjoyed herself.

One morning they decided to take apart the radio-phonograph and talk to the little people inside the cabinet; another morning they made sandwiches and filled a Thermos jug with milk because they planned to leave on a trip to Cedar Rabbits, Iowa. Again, they composed a long cheerful letter to Sears, Roebuck & Co. in which Alice told how she murdered people. Some Saturdays they would stage extremely dramatic plays which went on for hours – with time out for other games – the leading part always being taken by Alice Jones because, at her grade school in the north end of the city, she was invariably the Snow Queen or the Good Fairy or some other personage of equal distinction. Carolyn, whose stage experience had been limited to a Thanksgiving skit in which she had been an onion, seldom objected and in fact had some difficulty keeping up with the plot.

Long before noon they were at the back door, wanting to know if it was not yet lunchtime, and when at last Harriet, or perhaps Mrs Bridge, set up the breakfast-room table for them they would turn on the radio so that during lunch they might listen to the livestock reports, which Alice Jones found hilarious.

One day a fire truck went by the house and Alice, wagging her head in amazement, exclaimed, 'There they go again! Who they going to burn down this time?' Dismayed by the wickedness of the firemen, she rolled her eyes and sighed and helped herself to more caramel pudding.

Mrs Bridge, who was making up a grocery list, paused and smiled affectionately at both children, pleased that Carolyn was not conscious of the difference between them.

Alice and her father appeared every Saturday, and the two

children, occasionally joined by Ruth – who more often spent the day lying on the porch swing – would play together as comfortably as on the first Saturday they met. The gardener never failed to ask Mrs Bridge if Alice was a nuisance; Mrs Bridge always smiled and assured him she was not.

For a month each summer the Bridges went to Colorado; they hired Jones for this month to water the grass after he had finished working for the neighbors, and so Alice amused herself on the familiar grounds and frequently asked her father how soon Corky would be back.

'Soon enough,' was his usual reply, but one day he paused, and as if considering the future, he told her, cryptically and a little sadly, 'She liable to not come back, child.'

But at last the vacation ended and Carolyn returned, full of sunshine and sophistication.

'The mountains are awfully big,' she said primly, and, echoing her mother, 'It was just grand.'

Then Alice Jones said, 'You know what I got in this here pocket?'

Carolyn, reluctant to become once more the planet instead of the star, affected disdain.

'Who cares?' she announced, coolly turning away.

'A human gizzard,' murmured Alice with a mysterious expression, and before much longer Carolyn was convinced a summer in Kansas City would have been much more exciting than the mountains. She said as much to her mother, who replied a trifle brusquely, being harried at the moment, 'Don't be silly, dear.' And Mrs Bridge was about to add that there must be other girls besides Alice to play with, but she did not say this; she hesitated, and said, 'Corky, you know perfectly well you enjoyed Colorado.' Soon, she knew, the girls would drift apart. Time would take care of the situation.

8 Who can find the Caspian Sea?

As time went on it became evident that Douglas was the most introspective of the three children, but aside from this – to his father's disappointment – he appeared to be totally unremarkable. Mr Bridge had hoped for a brilliant son, and though he had not yet given up that hope he was reluctantly adapting himself to the idea that his son was no prodigy. If Douglas amounted to anything in later life, he concluded, it would be less the result of brilliance than of conscientious effort.

Ruth, even more obviously, had no intention of relying on her brains; but Carolyn, as soon as she entered kindergarten, began to make a name for herself, and very shortly was known as the brightest child in the class. Furthermore she appeared to understand her own superiority and when, through some mischance, another child equaled or exceeded her for a moment, Carolyn would grow furiously vindictive, and was not above lying or cheating in order to regain her position at the head of the class, so that by the time she was in the third grade she was beginning to be envied and disliked by her classmates and carefully observed by her teachers. It was no surprise to anyone when she was allowed to skip the second half of the third grade.

The teacher of Carolyn's fourth-grade class was a young lame woman named Bloch, who wore eye shadow and mascara and had one rather strange habit: every day she would call one of the children to her desk, give the child a comb, and then, bowing her head and shutting her eyes, she would instruct the child to take the pins out of her hair. Her hair was thick and greasy and hung down to her waist.

'Who can find the Caspian Sea?' she would murmur, and the child behind her would begin combing.

'Who knows where to find the Caspian Sea?' she would ask again, and without opening her eyes she would say, 'Albert Crawford knows.'

Then the boy she had named would walk to the great green and blue map pulled down over the blackboard, and with the pointer he would locate the sea.

'Carefully, dear,' she would whisper if the comb snarled, but even then she seemed not displeased.

Although the children did not like this curious task they seldom thought of it once they were out of class. Carolyn, however, happened to mention at home that she had been chosen that morning. Mrs Bridge was aghast; she had never heard of Miss Bloch's habit. After questioning Carolyn and becoming convinced it was the truth, she resolved to telephone the school and report the incident to the principal, and yet, for some reason, she could not do it. Several times she picked up the telephone, shivering with disgust, but each time she put down the receiver with an expression of doubt and anxiety; she decided it would be better to visit the principal's office, and yet this, too, was beyond her. She did not know why. In the end she told Carolyn that if she was ever again called upon to comb the teacher's hair she was to refuse. Having done this, Mrs Bridge told herself the teacher was no longer a threat and the entire affair, therefore, was closed. And so it was. Carolyn was not called upon for the remainder of the term, and the following September she had a different teacher. There were times later on when Mrs Bridge wondered if she had done the right thing; she wondered if Miss Bloch was still calling children to comb her hair, and when Douglas entered fourth grade she waited anxiously to learn who his teacher would be. It was not Miss Bloch; if it had been she would have gone to the principal and demanded that something be done. But it was not, and Mrs Bridge, who disliked making trouble for anyone, was greatly relieved, and found that she was no longer obliged to think about the matter.

9 Of ladies and women

For semi-annual housecleaning Mrs Bridge hired additional help. Carolyn answered the back door and reported to her mother, 'The cleaning lady is here.'

'Oh, fine,' Mrs Bridge said, and put away her sewing basket and went to the back door, smiling and saying genially, 'How do you do? Come right in, won't you?'

That evening she instructed Carolyn. 'You should say the cleaning "woman". A lady is someone like Mrs Arlen or Mrs Montgomery.'

10 Table manners

Mrs Bridge said that she judged people by their shoes and by their manners at the table. If someone wore shoes with run-over heels, or shoes that had not been shined for a long time, or shoes with broken laces, you could be pretty sure this person would be slovenly in other things as well. And there was no better way to judge a person's background than by watching him or her at the table.

The children learned it was impolite to talk while eating, or to chew with the mouth open, and as they grew older they learned the more subtle manners – not to butter an entire slice of bread, not to take more than one biscuit at a time, unless, of course, the hostess should insist. They were taught to keep their elbows close to their sides while cutting meat, and to hold the utensils in the tips of their fingers. They resisted the temptation to sop up the gravy with a piece of bread, and they made sure to leave a little of everything – not enough to be called wasteful, but just a little to indicate the meal had been sufficient. And, naturally, they learned that a lady or a gentleman does not fold up a napkin after having eaten in a public place.

The girls absorbed these manners with greater facility than Douglas, who tended to ask the reason for everything, sometimes observing that he thought it was all pretty silly. He seemed parti-cularly unable to eat with his left hand lying in his lap; he wanted to leave it on the table, to prop himself up, as it were, and claimed he got a backache with one arm in his lap. Mrs Bridge told him this was absurd, and when he wanted to know why he could not put his elbow on the table she replied, 'Do you want to be different from everyone else?'

Douglas was doubtful, but after a long silence, and under the weight of his mother's tranquil gaze, he at last concluded he didn't.

The American habit of switching implements, however, continued to give him trouble and to make him rebellious. With elaborate care he would put down the knife, reach high across his plate and descend on the left side to pick up the fork, raising it high over the plate again as he returned to the starting position.

'Now stop acting ridiculous,' she told him one day at lunch.

'Well, I sure bet the Egyptians don't have to eat this way,' he muttered, giving 'Egyptians' a vengeful emphasis.

'I doubt if they do,' she replied calmly, expertly cutting a triangle of pineapple from her salad, 'but you're not an Egyptian. So you eat the way Americans eat, and that's final.'

11 Alice Jones again

It seemed to Mrs Bridge that Saturday came around quite often. She was selecting some sugar buns from the bakery man when Alice dashed up the driveway with a long piece of clothesline in her hand, and the first thing that came to Mrs Bridge's mind was that the girl had stolen it.

'Good morning, Alice,' she said. Alice dropped the clothesline on the back steps and ran directly into the house to find Carolyn. A few minutes later the gardener appeared and asked, as he always did, whether she was being a nuisance. Mrs Bridge smiled briefly and shook her head, not knowing how to be truthful without hurting his feelings.

The children were in Carolyn's room playing jacks. Mrs Bridge looked in on them after a while and asked why they didn't play out of doors, the day being so nice, and she thought – but could not be sure – that as she suggested this the little Negro girl gave her a rather strange look. In any event the suggestion appeared to take hold, because a few minutes later she heard them outside shouting with laughter about something.

Shortly before noon, while rearranging the handkerchiefs in her husband's bureau, Mrs Bridge heard Carolyn singing at the top of her voice: 'My mother, your mother, live across the way, eighteen-sixteen East Broadway! Every night they have a fight, and this is what they say—' Here Alice Jones took over the song: 'Goddamn you, goddamn you, goddamn you, goddamn you—'

Mrs Bridge rushed to the nearest window and looked down. One end of the clothesline was tied to the rose trellis. At the other end was Carolyn, churning the rope with both arms, and in the center was Alice leaping up and down.

Next week, when Alice came racing up the driveway and tried to open the screen door to the kitchen, she found it locked. Mrs Bridge was in the kitchen and said, 'Who is it, please?'

'It's me,' replied Alice, rattling the door.

'Just a minute, Alice. I'll see if Carolyn is at home.' She went into the living room and found her daughter looking at one of the movie magazines that Ruth had begun buying.

'Alice is here again. I'll tell her you're busy.'

But at the first word Carolyn had jumped up and started for the back door.

About ten o'clock both of them came into the kitchen for a bottle of soda pop and wanted to know what there would be for lunch.

'Corky is having creamed tuna on toast and spinach,' said Mrs Bridge pleasantly.

Alice observed that she herself didn't care for spinach because it was made of old tea bags.

'I believe you're supposed to have lunch with your Daddy, aren't you?'

Alice heard a note in her voice which Carolyn did not; she glanced up at Mrs Bridge with another of those queer, bright looks and after a moment of thought she said, 'Yes'm.'

12 Agreeable conversation

The Van Metres were no more Egyptian than Douglas was, but in a sense they were quite foreign to Mrs Bridge. She thought them very odd. The Van Metres, Wilhelm and Susan, were about fifteen years older than the Bridges; they were rather pompous – particularly Wilhelm – and they were given to reading literary magazines no one had ever heard of and attending such things as ballet or opera whenever a company stopped in Kansas City. Mrs Bridge could not quite recall how she and her husband became acquainted with the Van Metres, or how they got into the habit of exchanging dinners once in a while. Nevertheless this situation had developed and Mrs Bridge was sure it was as awkward for the Van Metres as it was for them – each couple felt obligated to return the other's hospitality.

On those occasions when the Van Metres were hosts they drove over to the east side of the city to a country club that had gone out of fashion ten years before. Wilhelm Van Metre never drove faster than about fifteen miles an hour, and he sat erect and tense with both hands firmly on the wheel as though expecting a fearful crash at any instant. He came to a dead stop at almost every intersection, ceased talking, and examined the street in both directions. Then, unless his wife had something to say, he would proceed, the result of all this being that they seldom reached the club before nine o'clock. Once there he would drive the old automobile cautiously around the circular gravel drive and switch off the engine at the front entrance.

'Ladies,' he would say, suggestively, in his rumbling and pontifical monotone, whereupon Mrs Bridge and Mrs Van Metre got out and walked up the steps to the club. He did not start the engine again until he had seen them pass safely into the clubhouse; then, driving in low gear, he went on around the gravel circle to the parking lot.

'I see there are no other autos this evening, Walter,' he said. 'I wonder where everyone can be.'

Mr Bridge, already bored and thinking of an important case at the office, made no attempt to answer.

The women were waiting for them in the deserted lobby.

'It seems,' Van Metre chuckled, 'we have the place to ourselves this evening.'

'I do get so sick of crowds sometimes,' Mrs Bridge answered brightly.

The four of them began to walk along the corridor toward the rear of the building, where the dining room was. There was a series of rugs along the length of the corridor so that they would be walking in silence, then on the hardwood floor, then in silence, and so on. Whenever their heels struck the floor the noise echoed ahead of them and behind them as though they were being preceded and followed.

When the silence became unbearable Mrs Bridge looked over her shoulder, smiling, and said, 'Everyone says the chef here is the best in the city.'

'We feel he's competent,' said Wilhelm Van Metre, who was walking directly behind her with his head slightly bowed.

On they went, two by two, down the long corridor. Small tables of various shapes had been set against the wall at intervals in a desperate attempt to conceal the length of the corridor. On one of the tables was a wreath, on another was an unlighted candle, on another was a silver bowl, another held a telephone book in a gray leather binding. There were half a dozen mirrors along the wall. Mrs Bridge did not dare look into any of the mirrors, and as the four of them marched along she wondered if she was about to lose control of herself. Where are we going? she thought. Why are we here?

'What lovely tables,' she said.

Van Metre cleared his throat. 'Tables are appropriate here.'

'We really should get together more often,' she said.

'Yes. Susan and I often say, "We really should stop by to visit Walter and India".'

Finally they came to the frosted glass doors of the dining room.

'Ladies,' Van Metre said, holding open the door.

There were two people in the dining room.

'Susan, I believe that's young Blackburn over there with his father.'

'He must be home from the university.'

'I believe I'll go speak to them. Walter and India, I'm certain you will excuse me.' He walked slowly across the dining room, said something to them, and they looked around at Mr and Mrs Bridge.

In a few minutes he returned, rubbing his hands. 'Now, let's have a look. Which table shall we sit at? Anyone feeling particular?'

'I don't think it makes a bit of difference,' said Mrs Bridge. All the tables had been set. There was a candle burning on each table as though a great crowd of people were expected.

'As you probably know, the club was designed by Crandall.'

Mrs Bridge had never heard of this architect, but she thought his tone implied she should have. 'Let me think,' she said, touching her cheek, 'is he the City Hall man? I really should know, of course.

His name is so familiar.'

Van Metre turned to stare at her. He smiled bleakly. 'I'm afraid Crandall is not the City Hall man, India. No, I'm afraid not.' After a pause he said, 'In what connection have you heard of him?'

'He was mixed up in that USHA mess,' said Mr Bridge unexpectedly.

'You're correct about that, Walter,' Van Metre said, 'although that was hardly what I had in mind. Crandall also designed the famous Penfield house.' He studied the empty tables, deliberated, and selected one, saying with a courtly gesture, 'And now, ladies, if you will.'

They seated themselves around an oval table in front of some French doors that opened onto the terrace. They could see a flood-lighted, empty swimming pool, a number of canvas-backed chairs, the flagpole, and a winding gravel path lined with white-washed rocks. In the distance above the dark wall formed by the trees, the sky was suffused with a chill pink color from the down-town lights of the city.

'What a lovely view,' Mrs Bridge exclaimed.

'I'm afraid you're too kind,' Van Metre said, unfolding his napkin. 'There isn't much to look at.' He began to frown in the direction of the kitchen.

'I do think the pool look awfully nice with the lights on it that way.'

'Those rocks are absurd,' said Susan Van Metre.

'Well, most places they would be a little too-too, but don't you think they look nice out here in the country? They seem to give such a homey touch.'

'The club isn't precisely in the country, India,' Van Metre said, and cleared his throat. Then he turned around in his chair and again frowned at the kitchen. 'I am commencing to wonder if we have a waiter this evening.'

'We're certainly in no hurry,' said Mrs Bridge.

Van Metre snapped his fingers, at which the father and son looked across the room.

'Don't we have any service?' Van Metre called with a note of joviality.

The father spoke to his son, who got up and walked to the swinging doors, pushed halfway through, and apparently spoke to someone in the kitchen. Presently a Filipino waiter came out with a napkin folded over one arm.

'What do you recommend this evening?' Van Metre asked him.

The waiter said the roast beef was especially nice.

'How does that sound? India? Walter? Susan? Roast beef, everyone?'

'Grand,' said Mrs Bridge.

'Four roast beeves,' said Van Metre, and chuckled. 'It sounds as though I'm ordering four beeves. Entire animals.' He took a sip of water, removed his glasses, and while examining them against the light he said, 'Possibly I have told you of my experience in Illinois last summer on the way home from my annual fishing trip.'

'Why, no, I don't believe you have,' Mrs Bridge said attentively. 'What happened?'

'I went fishing with Andrew Stoner,' he said, and lifted his bushy white eyebrows in what appeared to be an inquiring manner.

Mrs Bridge thought quickly. 'Stoner Dry Goods?'

'No, no,' he chuckled. 'I should say not! Stoner Dry Goods, my Lord, no!' He continued to chuckle while he put on his glasses, and Mrs Bridge noticed with a slight feeling of discomfort that the hair of his eyebrows actually touched his glasses.

'I've met that fellow,' he was saying. 'No, India, not Stoner Dry Goods, not by a damn sight, no sir. Andrew Stoner, not John Stoner. My man is in the winter-wheat business. In fact, I expect you've met him.'

'A rather short man with quite an attractive wife?'

'You're probably thinking of Dr Max Hamm. He wears gold-rimmed glasses and speaks with a German accent.'

'Oh – well, I don't believe I know the Stoners.'

'I'm sure you must have met him somewhere.'

'Oh, I'm sure of it. I'm terrible about names.'

'However, you may not have met him.' Van Metre thoughtfully rubbed his chin and took another sip of water. 'I believe, now that I think of it, Andrew's wife died before you moved into the neighborhood. Andrew went away for several years.' He turned the water pitcher around; apparently he was inspecting the design etched into it. 'At any rate, we were returning from our annual fishing expedition when we had occasion to put up for the night at a small hotel in Illinois. It was in the town of Gilman, as I recall. Not too far from Peoria.' His expression was inquiring again.

'I don't believe I've ever been there. It must be nice.'

Van Metre put the napkin to his mouth and coughed. Then he continued. 'Well, India, I shouldn't care to live there. However, Andrew and I did stop there overnight, although at this moment I am unable to recall our reasoning. It was a mistake, you may be sure of that.'

'Sounds dreadful.'

'Well, I wouldn't say it was quite that bad.'

'I didn't mean that exactly, it's just that those little farming towns can be awfully depressing.'

'I wouldn't call Gilman a farming town.'

'Oh, I didn't mean that it was.'

'It's quite a little city. Good bit of industry there. In fact, Gilman may have quite a future.'

'Is that so? I suppose it *is* altogether different than I imagine.'

Wilhelm Van Metre stared at the tablecloth for a while, as though something had annoyed him.

'We stopped there overnight. We got a room in the hotel, not a bad room, though small, and as we were walking downstairs for supper Andrew said, "Wilhelm, how about a drink?" Well, India and Walter, I said, "That sounds like a good idea, Andrew. Let's have a drink." We decided to have a martini. I've forgotten just why. We didn't know if the bartender in that little hotel even knew what a martini was, but we decided we would try him out.'

Mrs Bridge, thinking the story was about a terrible martini, said, 'That certainly was taking a chance.'

'Well sir,' Van Metre said, leaning back in his chair and all at once slapping the table, 'that martini was the finest I ever tasted.'

'What a surprise that must have been!'

The waiter was coming across the floor trundling a cart with the roast beef under a large silver bell. After he had served them and refilled their water glasses he returned to the kitchen. They began to eat.

'This beef isn't quite done,' Van Metre observed.

Mrs Bridge said it was just the way she liked it.

13 Guest towels

Boys, as everyone knew, were more trouble than girls, but to Mrs Bridge it began to seem that Douglas was more trouble than both the girls together. Ruth, silent Ruth, was no trouble at all; Mrs Bridge sometimes grew uneasy over this very fact, because it was slightly unnatural. Carolyn made up for Ruth, what with temper tantrums and fits of selfishness, but she was nothing compared to Douglas, who, strangely enough, never actually appeared to be attempting to make trouble; it was just that somehow he *was* trouble. Invariably there was something about him that needed to be corrected or attended to, though he himself was totally oblivious to this fact, or, if he was aware of it, was unconcerned. Whenever she encountered him he was either hungry, or dirty, or late, or needed a haircut, or had outgrown something, or had a nosebleed, or had just cut himself, or had lost something, or was just generally ragged and grimy looking. Mrs Bridge could not understand it. She could take him down to the Plaza for a new pair of corduroy knickers and a week later he had worn a hole through the knee. He was invariably surprised and a little pained by her dismay; he felt fine – what else mattered?

He was hostile to guest towels. She knew this, but, because guest towels were no concern of his, there had never been any direct conflict over them. She had a supply of Margab, which were the best, at least in the opinion of everyone she knew, and whenever guests were coming to the house she would put the ordinary towels in the laundry and place several of these little pastel towels in each of the bathrooms. They were quite small, not much larger than a handkerchief, and no one ever touched them. After the visitors had gone home she would carefully lift them from the rack and replace them in the box till next time. Nobody touched them because they looked too nice; guests always did as she herself did in their homes – she would dry her hands on a piece of Kleenex.

One afternoon after a luncheon she went around the house collecting the guest towels as usual, and was very much surprised to find that one of the towels in Douglas's bathroom had been used.

It was, in fact, filthy. There was no question about who had used this towel. She found Douglas sitting in a tree in the vacant lot. He was not doing anything as far as she could tell; he was just up in the tree. Mrs Bridge approached the tree and asked him about the towel. She held it up. He gazed down at it with a thoughtful expression. Yes, he had dried his hands on it.

'These towels are for guests,' said Mrs Bridge, and felt herself unaccountably on the verge of tears.

'Well, why don't they use them then?' asked Douglas. He began to gaze over the rooftops.

'Come down here where I can talk to you. I don't like shouting at the top of my lungs.'

'I can hear you okay,' said Douglas, climbing a little higher.

Mrs Bridge found herself getting furious with him, and was annoyed with herself because it was all really so trivial. Besides, she had begun to feel rather foolish standing under a tree waving a towel and addressing someone who was probably invisible to any of the neighbors who might be watching. All she could see of him were his tennis shoes and one leg. Then, too, she knew he was right, partly right in any event; even so, when you had guests you put guest towels in the bathroom. That was what everyone did, it was what she did, and it was most definitely what she intended to continue doing.

'They always just use their handkerchief or something,' said Douglas moodily from high above.

'Never mind,' said Mrs Bridge. 'From now on you leave those towels alone.'

There was no answer from the tree.

'Do you hear me?'

'I hear you,' said Douglas.

14 Late for dinner

Not long after the battle of the guest towels he came in late for dinner, and when asked for a suitable explanation he announced with no apparent concern, yet with a faint note of apology discernible in his tone as though he had let himself be tricked, 'I got depantsed.'

'You *what*?' Mrs Bridge exclaimed, clutching her napkin. She and the girls were halfway through dinner, having decided not to wait on him any longer. Mr Bridge was not yet home from the office.

Douglas stepped over the seat of his chair as if it were a hurdle and sat down astraddle. This was a habit that exasperated his mother; he knew it and she knew he knew it.

'Why must you do that?' she asked. She was relieved he had come home, but she could not help scolding now that she knew he was safe.

'Do what?'

'You know perfectly well what.'

Every time they argued about the way he got into his chair he proceeded to explain that he did it in order to save wear and tear on the carpet. It was his theory that if he pulled out the chair every time, it would soon wear a groove in the carpet, and he was only trying to save things from wearing out because she was always telling him not to be so hard on the furniture. This was the way the argument went; it was quite familiar to everyone.

'Now,' said Mrs Bridge, settling the napkin in her lap and beginning to butter a hot biscuit, 'let's start all over again.' As soon as she said this she regretted it.

'They depantsed me,' Douglas repeated cheerfully.

'What *are* you talking about?'

'They took my pants and threw them up on top of Goldfarb's garage.'

'Who did?' she said, putting down the biscuit.

Carolyn, who often imitated her mother, also stopped eating and assumed a severe expression. Ruth quietly went on with dinner.

'Oh,' said Douglas, 'the guys. You know. Tim and Louie and those guys.'

'But *why*?'

'I don't know.' He was not greatly interested in the conversation. He began to help himself to everything on the table, building a mound of food just high enough to exceed the limits of good manners but not quite high enough to draw fire from his mother. He was quite conscious, however, that she was observing the size of the helpings.

'Well, for heaven's sake, they must have had a reason. Hadn't you done something to provoke them?'

'Nope. We were just wrestling in the vacant lot – sort of gang piling, you know – and I was on the bottom and then just all of a sudden they decided to depants me, that's all.' He was ladling gravy onto his plate; he had built a semi-circular dam out of mashed potatoes and was making the lake with gravy.

'Now that's enough, do you hear?'

With a pained expression he put down the gravy and began looking around for something else.

'I simply can't understand why they would do a thing like that,' she went on, half to herself.

'They just felt like depantsing somebody, I guess,' Douglas went on obligingly, 'and I was on the bottom, that's all. We depantsed Eliot Hoff a couple of weeks ago and he yelled bloody murder and cried all over the place.'

'All right, all right, that'll do,' said Mrs Bridge. 'I think we've covered the situation.'

'How did you get them back?' asked Carolyn.

'Oh, I just climbed the telephone pole and there's a big cable that leads over to Shafer's garage, so after I got there I just took a run and jumped across to Goldfarb's garage.' He was becoming voluble now. 'Those garages look pretty close together from this side of the fence, but when you get up there, why, they're not, because I didn't think I was going to make it. I was just up there like the man on the flying trapeze without any pants and—'

'That will do!' Mrs Bridge interrupted, looking him firmly in the eye.

'Well, gee whiz—'

'The subject is closed.'

'Okay, okay,' he muttered, and reached suddenly for the gravy.

15 Holiday news

On the fifteenth of each month there appeared in the south side of Kansas City a magazine called *The Tattler*. It was very thin — sixteen pages of coated ivory stock – but the format was large: it was about half the size of a newspaper. The typography, for reasons known only to the publisher, was in the style of 1910. *The Tattler* was Kansas City's magazine of society; it consisted of photographs of significant brides, of visiting celebrities feted at the homes of wealthy Kansas Citians, and pictures of subscribers, together with long lists of names of those who had either given or attended social affairs during the month. These lists of names were so long that it was found advisable to break them up into paragraphs and from time to time to insert a description of something – anything – that was reasonably pertinent.

A typical entry:

Seen wolfing the delicious hors d'oeuvres at the charming Lane Terrace residence of the Bob Brewers (she, née Nancy Page of Santa Barbara, California) a week ago Tuesday-last were Humboldt Aupp, Jr., Buzz Duncan with his captivating guest from Dixie, Lola Anne Sharpe in a positively stunning cardinal gown with net bodice; Nathalie Blakely, Gordon A. Spencer III home with Yule tidings from Yale, Jo Power with her sister-in-law from Gotham, Mrs Andrew Koeppel and hubby (he the newly appointed chairman of the board of Koeppel, Koeppel & Ingle), the McKinney twins indistinguishable in saffron except for Wendy's rhinestone bracelet and Lt Hal Graves, and last but far from least in stunning shell pink taffeta aglow with sequins, Mrs Albert Tate fascinated by Mrs Russ Arlen on the topic of Bermuda.

There followed a list of about thirty names, a description of the rumpus room, and more names.

The Tattler mentioned Mr and Mrs Bridge whenever they were present at a major social function, and occasionally took their picture. The most memorable photograph of Mrs Bridge was taken during a family vacation in Colorado. She had always been rather fond of horses, and before her marriage she used to go riding. In recent years, however, she had not had much to do with horses, partly because she was growing stout and was apprehensive that from certain angles she might not cut so sleek a figure in jodhpurs as she used to. In fact, at the time this picture was taken, she had not been on a horse for about ten years. The horse, unfortunately, had just sneezed and its head was down between his knees; Mrs Bridge, her attention divided between the beast and the photographer, was leaning over its neck with a doubtful smile. The caption read, 'Mrs Walter G. Bridge, holidaying with spouse and young at Rocky Point Lodge, Estes Park, Colorado, likes nothing better than a canter on the bridle paths.'

16 A matter of taste

At Christmas time *The Tattler* customarily published photographs of the lights in the Plaza shopping center and of various homes in the country club district that were more than usually decorative. There was a great deal of interest in Christmas decorations; Mrs Bridge very much enjoyed them, but at the same time they presented her with a problem: if you did not put up any decorations you were being conspicuous, and if you put up too many you were being conspicuous. At the very least there should be a large holly wreath on the front door; at the most there might be half a dozen decorations visible, including the Christmas tree. In her annual attempt to strike the proper note she came to rely more and more on Carolyn, who possessed, she thought, better judgment than either Ruth or Douglas, although she was careful to keep this opinion to herself.

Every year, then, the Bridges' home was festive without being ostentatious. A strand of green lights was woven through the branches of a small spruce tree near the front porch, and there was a wreath in each of the first-floor windows and a large wreath with a red ribbon and a cluster of bells attached to the knocker of the front door. Inside, in a corner of the living room away from the heat of the fireplace, stood the tree, its topmost branches clipped or bent so as not to stain the ceiling, and a bed sheet draped around the bottom in order to conceal the odd-looking metal device that held the tree upright. Presents were arranged on the sheet and a few small presents tied to the limbs. There was tinsel on the tree, and there were peppermint-candy canes and popcorn balls and electric candles, and some new ornaments each year to replace the broken ones. On the mantel was a group of angels with painted mouths wide open and hymn books in their hands, and beside them a plastic crèche. Whatever pine boughs had been clipped from the top of the tree were laid along the mantel, with occasional tufts of cotton to simulate snow.

During the course of the holidays Mrs Bridge would drive the children around to see how other houses were decorated, and on one of these trips they came to a stucco bungalow with a life-size cutout of Santa Claus on the roof, six reindeer in the front yard, candles in every window, and by the front door an enormous cardboard birthday cake with one candle. On the cake was this message: HAPPY BIRTHDAY, DEAR JESUS.

'My word, how extreme,' said Mrs Bridge thoughtfully. 'Some Italians must live there.'

17 Good-by Alice

Alice Jones was now appearing every month or so, though her father came to work at the neighbors each Saturday as usual. On those occasions when she accompanied him she would spend the morning with Carolyn, but then, about noon, she would get on the streetcar and go home by herself. During the morning she and Carolyn would have a confidential talk, usually in Carolyn's room, that is, in the room that Carolyn and Ruth shared. Ruth was seldom at home on Saturday; nobody in the family knew where she went. So Alice Jones and Carolyn would shut the door to the room and converse in low tones or in whispers about school and clothes and friends and boys and how they intended to raise their children.

'How many are you going to have?' asked Carolyn.

'Eleven,' Alice said firmly.

'Heavens!' said Carolyn. 'That's certainly telling.'

'What kind of talk is that?' Alice wanted to know. 'How many are you going to have?'

'Two, I believe. That makes a nice family.'

One Saturday at lunch time, shortly after Alice had started to the streetcar line, Carolyn said that Alice had invited her to come to a party next Saturday afternoon.

'Well, that was nice of Alice, wasn't it?' Mrs Bridge replied, and with a tiny silver fork she ate a slice of banana from her fruit salad, and then a piece of lettuce.

'Where is the party to be?'

'At her house.'

'Where does Alice live?'

'Thirteenth and Prospect.'

Mrs Bridge took up a little silver knife and began to cut a slice of peach which was rather too large to be eaten in one bite. She knew where Thirteenth and Prospect was, although she had never stopped there. It was a mixed neighborhood.

'Can I go?'

Mrs Bridge smiled affectionately at Carolyn. 'I wouldn't if I were you.'

18 Never speak to strange men

It was necessary to be careful among people you did not know. Mrs Bridge did not wish to be rude, but, as her husband had more than once reminded her, and as anyone could see from the newspapers, there were all kinds of people in the world, and this, together with several other reasons, was why she did not want Carolyn running around in the north end of town.

Not long after Alice's invitation had been rejected Mrs Bridge was downtown shopping, paying very little attention to the people around her, when all at once she was conscious that a man was staring at her. She could not help glancing at him. She saw only that he was in his forties and that he was not badly dressed. She turned away and walked to another counter, but he followed her.

'How do you do?' he began, smiling and touching the brim of his hat.

Mrs Bridge grew a little frightened and began looking around for assistance.

The man's face became red and he laughed awkwardly. 'I'm

Henry Schmidt,' he said. There was a pause. He added nervously, 'Gladys Schmidt's husband.'

'Oh, for heaven's sake!' Mrs Bridge exclaimed. 'I didn't recognize you.'

They talked for a few minutes. He mentioned having seen Ruth coming out of a movie the previous week and commented that she was growing into quite a beauty, for which Mrs Bridge thanked him. Finally he tipped his hat and said good-by.

'It's so nice to see you,' she responded. 'Do say hello to Gladys for me. We really should get together some evening.'

19 Grace Barron

Grace Barron was a puzzle and she was disturbing. She belonged in the country-club district, for Virgil was a banker, and yet she seemed dissatisfied there. Mrs Bridge could not altogether grasp whatever it was Grace Barron was seeking, or criticizing, or saying.

Grace Barron had once said to her, 'India, I've never been anywhere or done anything or seen anything. I don't know how other people live, or think, even how they believe. Are we right? Do we believe the right things?'

And on another occasion, when Mrs Bridge had passed a nice compliment on her home, Grace replied, 'Virgil spent fifty thousand dollars on this place.' It had not been a boast; it had been an expression of dissatisfaction.

At luncheons, Auxiliary meetings, and cocktail parties Mrs Bridge always found herself talking about such matters as the by-laws of certain committees, antique silver, Royal Doulton, Wedgwood, the price of margarine as compared to butter, or what the hemline was expected to do, but since Grace Barron had entered the circle she found herself fumbling for answers because Grace talked of other things – art, politics, astronomy, literature. After such a conversation Mrs Bridge felt inadequate and confused, if a little flattered and refreshed, and on the way home she would think of what she would have said, and could have said, instead of only smiling and replying, 'It does seem too bad,' or,

'Well, yes, I expect that's true.'

Said Mr Bridge, glancing over the edge of his evening news-paper while she was talking about Grace Barron, 'Ask her if she wants one to marry her daughter.'

Mrs Bridge replied defensively, 'They just have a son.' She knew this was a silly remark and added hurriedly, 'I suppose you're right, but—'

'If you doubt me, ask her and see what she says.'

'Goodness,' Mrs Bridge said, picking up the latest *Tattler*, 'suppose we drop the subject. I certainly didn't mean to provoke you so.'

Yet she continued to think about many things Grace Barron had said and about Grace herself because she was different somehow. The first time she had ever seen Grace was one afternoon in October of the previous year, and she could remember it so clearly because it was the day of the first Italian air raid against Ethiopia. In Kansas City the sun was shining and the leaves of the trees were changing color. It was a beautiful day. The Barrons had just moved into the neighborhood and Madge Arlen, whose husband had attended high school with Virgil Barron, was going to stop by and get acquainted, and Mrs Bridge went along. The Barrons had moved into an enormous Colonial home near Meyer Circle, and that afternoon as Mrs Bridge and Madge Arlen drove up to the house they saw a gang of boys playing football in the street. Apparently Grace Barron was not at home because no one answered the bell; they were about to leave when one of the boys came running up from the street. He stopped and kicked the ball back to the other players, then jumped over a flower bed, and with a whoop and a wave came running straight across the lawn.

'That must be her son,' Madge Arlen observed.

'His name will be mud if she catches him leaping over her flowers,' said Mrs Bridge.

They waited, a trifle critically, for him to approach. He was wearing a baggy sweatshirt, faded blue jeans, dirty white tennis shoes, and a baseball cap. He was a thin, graceful boy, about the same height as Douglas, and as he came nearer they could see that he had freckles and a snub nose. He was laughing and panting for breath.

'Hello!' he called, and at that moment they realized he was not a boy at all. It was Grace Barron.

And Mrs Bridge recalled with equal clarity an evening when she and Grace attended an outdoor symphony. Music was one of the things Mrs Bridge had always wanted to know more about, and so she was pleased, if startled, when Grace, whom she scarcely knew, simply telephoned one evening and asked if she would like to go to the concert in the park. They sat on folding chairs and listened, and it was like nothing else Mrs Bridge had ever experienced. When the symphony ended, while the musicians were packing away their instruments and the conductor was autographing programs, Grace suggested they come to the next concert.

'I'd love to!' Mrs Bridge exclaimed. 'When is it?' And upon learning the date she said regretfully, 'Oh, dear, the Noel Johnsons are having a few people over for cocktails—'

'That's all right,' Grace interrupted. 'I know how it is.'

And there was an afternoon when they happened to run into each other downtown. Mrs Bridge was looking over some new ovenware she had heard advertised on the radio. She decided not to buy, and in the course of wandering around the store she suddenly came upon Grace Barron staring fixedly at a gift item – an arrangement of tiny silver bells that revolved around an elaborate candlestick.

'Oh, isn't this tricky!' Mrs Bridge said, having a look at the price tag. 'But I think they're asking too much.'

'I feel like those bells,' said Grace. 'Why are they turning around, India? Why? Because the candle has been lighted. What I want to say is – oh, I don't know. It's just that the orbit is so small.' She resumed staring at the contrivance, which went slowly around and around and gave out a faint, exquisite tinkling.

20 What's up, Señora Bridge?

Spanish was a subject she had long meant to study, and quite often she remarked to her friends that she wished she had studied it in school. The children had heard her say this, so for her birthday that year they gave her an album of phonograph records consisting of a lethargic dialogue between Señor Carreño of Madrid and an

American visitor named Señora Brown. Along with the records came an attractive booklet of instructions and suggestions. Mrs Bridge was delighted with the gift and made a joke about how she intended to begin her lessons the first thing 'mañana'.

As it turned out, however, she was busy the following day, and the day after because of a PTA meeting at the school, and the day after. Somehow or other more than a month passed before she found time to begin, but there came a morning when she resolved to get at it, and so, after helping Harriet with the breakfast dishes, she found her reading glasses and sat down in the living room with the instruction booklet. The course did not sound at all difficult, and the more pages she read the more engrossing it became. The instructions were clear enough: she was simply to listen to each line of dialogue and then, in the pause that followed, to repeat the part of Señora Brown.

She put the first record on the phonograph, turning it low enough so that the mailman or any delivery boys would not overhear and think she had gone out of her mind. Seated on the sofa directly opposite the machine she waited, holding onto the booklet in case there should be an emergency.

'Buenos días, Señora Brown,' the record began, appropriately enough. 'Cómo está usted?'

'Buenos días, Señor Carreño,' Señora Brown answered. 'Muy bien, gracias. Y usted?'

The record waited for Mrs Bridge who, however, was afraid it would begin before she had a chance to speak, and in consequence only leaned forward with her lips parted. She got up, walked across to the phonograph, and lifted the needle back to the beginning.

'Buenos días, Señora Brown. Cómo está usted?'

'Buenos días, Señor Carreño,' replied Señora Brown all over again. 'Muy bien, gracias. Y usted?'

'Buenos días, Señor Carreño,' said Mrs Bridge with increasing confidence. 'Muy bien, gracias. Y usted?'

'Muy bien,' said Señor Carreño.

Just then Harriet appeared to say that Mrs Arlen was on the telephone. Mrs Bridge put the booklet on the sofa and went into the breakfast room, where the telephone was.

'Hello, Madge. I've been meaning to phone you about the Auxiliary luncheon next Friday. They've changed the time from twelve-thirty to one. Honestly, I wish they'd make up their minds.'

'Charlotte told me yesterday. You knew Grace Barron was ill with flu, didn't you?'

'Oh, not really! She has the worst luck.'

'If it isn't one thing, it's another. She's been down since the day before yesterday. I'm running by with some lemonade and thought you might like to come along. I can only stay a split second. I'm due at the hairdresser at eleven.'

'Well, I'm in slacks. Are you going right away?'

'The instant the laundress gets here. That girl! She should have been here hours ago. Honestly, I'm at the end of my rope.'

'Don't tell me you're having that same trouble! I sometimes think they do it deliberately just to put people out. We're trying a new one and she does do nice work, but she's so independent.'

'Oh,' said Madge Arlen, as if her head were turned away from the phone, 'here she comes, Lord, what next?'

'Well, I'll dash right upstairs and change,' said Mrs Bridge. 'I suppose the garden can wait till tomorrow.' And after telling Harriet that she would be at Mrs Barron's if anyone called, she started toward the stairs.

'Qué tal, Señora Brown?' inquired the record.

Mrs Bridge hurried into the living room, snapped off the phonograph, and went upstairs.

21 The Leacocks

New people in the neighborhood never failed to provide a topic for discussion. As time went by and they became more familiar they became, naturally, less newsworthy; the Leacocks, however, seemed more remarkable with every passing day. The family consisted of Dr Gail Leacock, who was not a physician but an academic doctor – an associate professor of psychology – his wife Lucienne, who was reputedly quite wealthy, and Tarquin. Tarquin was about the same age as Douglas but here all similarity ended. For one thing, Tarquin was said to have an IQ of 185. Mrs Bridge had not the vaguest notion what Douglas's IQ might be, and she was not particularly anxious to have him tested; not that she thought he was dull, but it would be just like him deliberately to answer the questions wrong. The discrepancy between their intellects, whatever it might be, was only the focal point of the difference between them; Douglas and Tarquin were, to say the least, oil and water.

Dr Leacock, like the majority of husbands, was seldom seen in the daytime, but Mrs Leacock and Tarquin liked to visit about the neighborhood, and within a few weeks of their arrival it had become evident that for some reason they had chosen Mrs Bridge as a special friend. Mrs Bridge, somewhat disconcerted by Lucienne Leacock's progressive ideas and a little frightened by Tarquin's self-possession, nevertheless felt vaguely flattered at being the object of so much attention.

One afternoon, while the three of them were drinking iced tea on the back porch, Douglas came sauntering home from a baseball game. He was barefoot – his sneakers were tied together by the laces and were dangling around his neck so that the toes bumped against his chest – and he had an apple in his mouth, and as he approached it became obvious that he was trying to eat the apple without using his hands. He was twisting his head around and making agonized faces. He did not see the visitors until he had opened the screen door. Then he stopped dead, looked first at Tarquin, then at Mrs Leacock, then at his mother, and then back at Tarquin. Unmistakably – Mrs Bridge saw this – Tarquin's upper lip curled backward in a sneer. Slowly Douglas took the apple out of his mouth and said in a low voice, in which there was no ignoring the hostility, 'How'd you like a punch in the snoot?'

Mrs Bridge had trained her children to be courteous no matter what occurred, for she valued courtesy as highly as she valued cleanliness, honesty, thrift, consideration, and other such qualities. Douglas, though rebellious, had never failed her when, so to speak, the chips were down. She knew he disliked being polite to visitors, but he was, nonetheless; in fact, though he grumbled more than his sisters, Mrs Bridge had noticed with some surprise that he was actually less apt to be rude to guests than were the girls. He did try hard to be decent, and she knew it was difficult for him. He had been doing so well recently that she was flabbergasted by his remark to Tarquin, and by the absolute antagonism apparent in his stance – he was now standing just inside the screen with his fists balled and his head thrust truculently forward. Mrs Bridge was so amazed that for several seconds she was unable to speak. Upon recovering her wits she began to get to her feet but was restrained by Mrs Leacock who had been smiling rather earnestly at Douglas from the moment he first wandered into view.

'What else would you do, Doug?' said Mrs Leacock. 'We'd like to hear.'

Douglas then gave her a long, baleful stare. Mrs Bridge had not been so shocked in years. Without a word, as though there were no one on the porch, Douglas put the apple in his mouth and slowly backed out the door and around the corner of the house.

'Young man,' Mrs Bridge began, furiously shaking a finger at him when she found him sitting in the rafters of the garage a few minutes after the departure of the guests, 'I don't know what got into you and I honestly don't care, but you're most certainly going to hear from your father when he gets home.'

Douglas stepped across to another rafter and peered into the corner where some wasps had built a nest.

'What in the world made you behave like that?' demanded Mrs Bridge, who was as nonplused as she was humiliated.

Douglas mumbled; it was not clear what he said.

'Well, I don't care whether you like him or not,' she continued, assuming he had made some reference to Tarquin. 'When we have guests you'll treat them courteously. How would you like it if we visited them and Tarquin behaved as you did?'

'I'm not going to visit them,' he answered, still looking at the wasp nest.

'Well,' said Mrs Bridge after a pause, 'we're not going to have any more of that, and that's final. Now I mean business. I've never been so ashamed in my life.'

Douglas was sorry he had embarrassed his mother, but he could not say so. With his arms outstretched for balance he began to walk the length of the rafter.

'You're going to fall and break your neck,' said Mrs Bridge.

Douglas did not reply. He teetered a little and his mother gasped. He had only meant to frighten her but he had gotten a little farther off balance than he intended and had scared himself, so he sat down and began to swing his legs.

'The next time they're here you're going to behave yourself, is that clear?' She spoke as severely as possible, but by this time she knew that somehow he had defeated her.

A small, affirmative noise came from him and she decided that was the most she could hope for, at least for the time being. She returned to the house, puzzled by the violence of his reaction. Tarquin of course had been extremely rude to sneer, and, in truth, Mrs Bridge herself did not like Tarquin. Even so she was baffled by Douglas's extraordinary hostility, and she was quite apprehensive about the future.

The Leacocks continued to appear, unannounced, every few weeks – Tarquin always with a book – and Douglas was unquestionably able to divine their approach, because he vanished a few minutes before they arrived and nobody could find him until shortly after they had gone. Mrs Bridge, while disapproving of some of the things Tarquin did and said, was nevertheless impressed by his brilliance.

Progressive education was Lucienne Leacock's favorite topic of conversation; politics was second. Mrs Bridge did not know a great deal about either. Mrs Leacock was a Socialist who voted the straight Democratic ticket because, as she phrased it, 'We poor bloody Socialists never have a chance.' Mrs Bridge had never before known a Socialist, and only a very few Democrats, moderate Democrats at that, and she felt slightly guilty as she sat on the porch or in the living room listening to Mrs Leacock lambast the conservatives.

As for the public educational system, well, she could not speak of it without profanity, and at every word Mrs Bridge inwardly flinched. Superior children, the same as Socialists, did not have a chance. The system was geared to bourgeois mediocrity. Tarquin, as anyone could guess, attended a private school and he was as voluble a critic of public education as his mother, despite the fact he had never been inside a public school. He seemed unusually scornful of the school Douglas attended. Mrs Leacock listened with an intent, forceful expression to whatever he said, afterward suggesting how he might have expressed himself more vigorously.

Progressive education had certainly developed Tarquin's sense of being an individual, but some of the results were so startling that Mrs Bridge was reduced to a bewildered silence. One April afternoon while they were enjoying the rose garden Mrs Leacock suddenly threw back her head and gave a loud neighing laugh and then, fixing Mrs Bridge with a forcible look, she said, 'Priceless! I must tell you. About two years ago when we lived in – New Haven?' She looked at Tarquin to see if her memory was correct.

'New Haven,' said Tarquin, grinning.

'This young monster threw a temper tantrum, and what a tantrum! He set fire to the garage.'

'I used benzine,' said Tarquin indifferently as he began to pull the petals from a particularly fine rose. 'I should have used kerosene.'

Mrs Bridge often thought about that afternoon. She did not think the Leacocks had been joking; on the other hand it seemed impossible that Tarquin could be so irresponsible. She was puzzled and irked and could not finally decide how she felt toward the Leacocks: at times she was positive she disliked them, then a moment later she would feel ashamed of herself. If only Tarquin would not curse! Mrs Bridge had no use for profanity; she had always considered it not only vulgar but unnecessary, and was distressed by the fact that Lucienne Leacock encouraged the boy to swear. Furthermore, Tarquin smoked cigarettes and was allowed to stay up as late at night as he wanted to; yet he was not an adult, he was a boy, a large, shambling fleshy boy with a flushed, freckled complexion and moist red lips the color of liver. His eyes were alert and glassy, yellowish-brown and luminous like the eyes of a dog, and very knowing; it was all Mrs Bridge could do to look him straight in the eye, and, what was worse, she knew he was aware of this and relished it. He clearly enjoyed catching and holding her attention until she could hardly keep from shuddering.

'Why don't you tell India what you said to your science adviser yesterday?' his mother suggested. She was wearing moccasins and white wool athletic socks and a baggy skirt and sweater, so that she looked like a high-school girl, except for her face, which was creased and shriveled like the face of a very old woman.

'Lucienne, really!' said her son. 'How can I possibly express myself in regard to a man so jejune?' And he drew on his cigarette with a look of boredom. Mrs Bridge was fascinated and exasperated whenever he pulled out a cigarette; the whole thing was beyond her understanding.

Although Douglas was absent whenever Mrs Leacock and

Tarquin were around, he was evidently somewhere within earshot, because one evening during an argument with his father about the size of his allowance he blurted, 'Jeez, how am I supposed to express myself with nothing but a measly fifty cents a week?'

'What's that?' demanded Mr Bridge, lowering the newspaper through which the discussion had been carried on.

'Well, I gotta express my personality, don't I?'

'Express your personality?' asked Mr Bridge, and gazed at his son curiously.

'That's what Tarquin does. He gets to express it whenever he feels like it.'

Mr Bridge and Douglas studied each other for a while, one of them bemused and the other defiant, and Mrs Bridge waited uneasily to find out how it was going to end.

'You'll express yourself when I say you can,' Mr Bridge replied quietly. He shook up the newspaper and continued reading.

22 Victim of circumstances

There was another expressionist in the neighborhood, a boy several years older than Tarquin Leacock, whom Douglas avoided with equal assiduity, though for a different reason. His name was Peters and he was a bully.

One evening it was long after dark when Douglas finally came home. He was exhausted and covered with dirt, although this in itself was not remarkable.

'Where *have* you been?' Mrs Bridge cried, rushing toward him the moment he entered the house. 'We've been looking high and low for you. I was just about to phone the police.'

'It was that big Peters guy's fault,' Douglas said in a low voice. He wiped his nose on the sleeve of his sweatshirt and trudged upstairs to his room.

'Well, thank heavens you're safe, at least,' she resumed when he came down. He looked a little more respectable. 'Where on earth were you?'

He replied that he had been on top of Pfeiffer's garage.

'Until twenty minutes to nine?' she asked with as much sarcasm as she could muster, and this was not much.

'I figured it was probably later than that,' he muttered very glumly. 'It felt like it was about midnight.'

She followed him to the breakfast room, where Harriet was setting his place.

'What were you doing on Pfeiffer's garage? I'm sure they didn't want you up there.'

He started to answer, then sneezed, started to wipe his nose with his hand and then, thinking better of it, took out his handkerchief.

'I was hiding,' he said and sneezed again.

'Hiding! From whom, may I ask?'

'From that big Peters guy,' he replied with some annoyance, as though she should have known. 'What did you think I was going to do, stick my head up and get it blown off?'

'I think you'd better explain yourself, young man, or your father's going to hear about this.'

'That's okay with me,' he muttered.

'All right, now. Begin at the beginning.'

'Well,' he said, wearily buttering a slice of bread, 'he just chased me up there, that's all there is to it.'

'Who chased you? What *are* you talking about?'

He put down the bread and explained with elaborate emphasis. 'That big fat slob Peters. He trapped me on top of Pfeiffer's garage and wouldn't let me come down. Every time I'd stick my head up he took a shot at me. He almost hit me a couple of times.'

'Do you mean he had a gun?'

'Well, what did you think he was shooting at me with?' He glanced uncertainly at his mother, knowing he was not supposed to end a sentence with a preposition, but he saw that this time he would get away with both. She had the shocked look she sometimes got.

'What sort of a gun?'

'Oh, it was a beebee gun, one of those pump guns. He'd pumped it up about seventy-five times, I guess, because every time he took a shot at me it'd knock off a piece of cement. I guess,' he added thoughtfully, 'you could just about kill a horse with a good pump gun if you pumped long enough.'

Mrs Bridge did not know exactly what he was talking about, but she did know that he knew what he was talking about.

'Why on earth was he shooting at you?' she asked, rather weakly. She had never come up against a situation like this.

Douglas shrugged. 'He just wanted to. I don't know. I didn't ask him, you can bet on that. He'd of probably shot my block off.'

'But you must have provoked him.'

'Oh, sure! A guy about sixteen times as big as me that's got a pump gun. That's a big laugh. Hah!'

'I'm going to telephone the police,' she said resolutely, because it did seem like something the police would be interested in.

'Okay by me,' said Douglas. 'I guess they can find him easy enough if they just hang around Pfeiffer's garage. He's probably got somebody else up there by this time.'

'Well, who is he? Does he live around there?'

'I don't know. All I know is he just hangs around that garage.'

'But *why*?' There was something nightmarish about the whole affair.

Douglas, however, was not in the least mystified. 'Well, because it's a good garage for trapping littler kids so they can't get away. It's flat on top and it's got this kind of a little tiny wall around the top. So he just hangs around there and usually about the time school gets out he catches somebody on their way home and starts shooting, so naturally they go up the telephone pole and scrooch down behind the wall. He always runs them that way,' he added as a final explanation. After a pause he said moodily, 'I usually detour, but I guess today I was thinking about something else and forgot. Then all of a sudden *zing!* – and boy, I jumped about a thousand feet in the air, believe me! So anyway I went up the telephone pole like I said, because I figured he could probably outrun me even if he is a big slob, and then there wasn't any way to get down except the same way and he was there with that old pump gun. I didn't think he was ever going to leave.'

'Why didn't you call for help?'

'Well, because if I did he'd of probably got sore at me and then I'd really've got fixed.'

Mrs Bridge had become so confused that she could not even begin to understand this statement; she gazed at him in despair. 'Well, don't you know where this boy lives?'

Douglas shook his head.

'He must go to school somewhere, doesn't he?'

Douglas didn't know. 'He's one of those big high-school guys, except he's probably too dumb. They probably expelled him.'

'But you must know something about him.'

'He's a big fat slob!' Douglas said, flaring up. He was getting peeved with his mother for asking so many questions; he had been trapped on the garage, he had escaped, that was all there was to it. He hated Peters, but that was irrelevant. He wished his mother would drop the subject.

The case had begun to seem a little weaker to Mrs Bridge. She was on the point of telephoning the Sixty-third Street police station, for she was certain Douglas was telling the truth and she knew perfectly well that a beebee gun could put out someone's eye, and yet she could not very well call the police station to report a high-school boy with a beebee gun – just that and nothing more.

'But can't you tell me anything about him? Anything at all?'

Douglas shook his head. He could have found out more about Peters, but there was no need to. He would avoid Pfeiffer's from now on and that was all there was to it.

'I'm going to tell your father about that boy,' she said positively. 'Something ought to be done about him.'

'Okay by me,' Douglas assented. 'Can I have some more potatoes and gravy?'

'*May* I?'

'Okay, *may* I?'

23 Rock fight

Mr Bridge did hear about the next adventure.

On his way home from the public school one afternoon shortly before the start of summer vacation, Douglas came across Tarquin seated beneath a chestnut tree. There was a book in his lap and he seemed to be innocently reading. Douglas was carrying a weed he had pulled up, and was using it to whip the horse on which he was making an escape from some Indians.

'Whoa!' said Douglas softly, reining to a stop. Then, conscious that Tarquin knew about the fictitious horse and was snickering at him, he abandoned the game and dropped the weed.

'Hello,' Tarquin said without moving.

After a pause Douglas said, 'H'llo.' After another pause, during which he gazed up into the branches of the chestnut tree and industriously scratched first one ankle and then the other, he added, 'What're you doing here?'

'Haven't I a right to be here?'

Douglas was thinking this over when Tarquin suddenly threw a rock at him. He had kept the rock hidden under the book. Douglas saw it coming and ducked, but even so it scraped the side of his head.

'Okay,' he said. 'You asked for it,' and ran forward with his fists doubled up.

When he got home later that afternoon, after stopping by the high school to watch the track team at practice, and having searched the bleachers for valuables, he was disconcerted to find not only that his father was at home but that he had heard about the fight with Tarquin. Mrs Leacock had telephoned Mr Bridge at the office.

'Well, he started it,' said Douglas defensively, and when told to continue with his version of the fight he said, 'Well, he sort of jumped up and took out across the streetcar tracks toward Wornall Road, so I took after him – and boy, I just about didn't make it – and he kept yelling over his shoulder how I better not touch him because he knew how to fight with jiu-jitsu and—'

'What do you mean you just about didn't make it? Didn't make what?'

'Boy, that streetcar just about got me. But anyway, he—'

'Tell this to me again,' said Mr Bridge. He had been standing up; now he seated himself and listened to the story with extreme attention. 'Do you mean,' he asked, 'that Tarquin threw the rock at you and led you across the tracks in front of a streetcar?'

Douglas nodded enthusiastically. He had, in fact, come very close to being hit.

'I see,' Mr Bridge said. For a long time he was lost in thought, but finally he glanced up and said, 'I understand you caught him.'

'Oh, sure. He runs like a girl. That's because he's knock-kneed.'

'So then what transpired?'

Douglas gazed at his father doubtfully.

'What happened next?'

'Oh. Well, let's see. I sort of punched him in the nose once or twice, I think.'

'You think?'

'I guess I did.'

'Was that the end of the fight?'

'Pretty much. I suppose you could actually say it was because he started to bawl like a little kid, so – uh – that's about all.'

'Go on.'

Douglas groaned and made an agonized face. He was embarrassed about this next item because he knew he had not behaved very well. Unfortunately it was impossible to distract his father in the way he could usually distract his mother, so he did not even try to change the subject. Reluctantly he said, 'I can't stand crybabies.'

'Go on.'

Douglas heaved a deep sigh. 'Okay, okay. I hauled off and socked him one in the breadbasket.'

'While he was lying down?'

'He was up. I mean he was up when I let him have it in the bread-basket. Then he fell down again and wouldn't get up any more even when I dared him to. He only lay there and screamed about how he was going to stab me to death.' Scarcely had he finished saying this when he became aware of a change in his father's attitude; inquiringly he looked at his father, and next at his mother, who had been lingering in the hall.

With modest pride he concluded, 'I guess he won't bother anybody any more, not after what I did to him.' He was astonished when his father reached forward and grabbed his arm. 'I can fix his wagon any old day!' Douglas shouted. He was frightened at finding himself caught like this and he did not know what was going on.

'Listen, son,' his father said earnesly. 'If that boy starts another fight I want you to do something. Are you listening to me?'

'What do you want?'

'I want you to walk away. Don't take your eyes off him, just walk away, that's all.'

Douglas attempted to twist out of the grip on his arm. He was deeply surprised by his father's strength. His arm had begun to throb from the pain. He was confused and defiant, and all that

51

occurred to him was that he was being asked to run away from a fight, and not only that but from a boy he knew he could lick.

'Do you hear me?'

'Well, why?'

'Never mind why.'

'Okay,' he responded grudgingly, but added, as soon as his arm was released, 'only he better cut out throwing rocks at me.'

'Under no circumstances. I want this clearly understood.'

'All right,' he said. He was resentful and ashamed. More than anything else he was afraid of being thought a coward.

After he had gone upstairs his parents were silent for a few minutes. Mr Bridge was thoughtful and Mrs Bridge was waiting for what he would say.

'That Leacock boy is going to kill somebody one of these days,' he observed.

'I do think they let him run wild,' she agreed, 'but I'm certain he wouldn't do anything really wrong.'

'You just watch,' he said angrily.

'It *was* awfully strange about setting the garage on fire,' she admitted. 'And gracious, I certainly don't approve of fighting, but it does seem that Douglas can look out for himself.'

'Douglas is a boy and thinks like a boy. Tarquin Leacock has the mind of an adult.'

'Well,' said Mrs Bridge as she put on her reading glasses and opened the latest copy of *The Tattler*, 'if that's the case, I shouldn't think there'd be much to worry about.'

24 Advanced training

Appearances were an abiding concern of Mrs Bridge, which was the reason that one evening as she saw Ruth preparing to go out she inquired, 'Aren't you taking a purse, dear?'

Ruth answered in a husky voice that whatever she needed she could carry in her pockets.

Said Mrs Bridge, 'Carolyn always takes a purse.'

Ruth was standing in front of the hall mirror, standing in a way that disturbed Mrs Bridge, though she did not know precisely why, unless it could be that Ruth's feet were too far apart and her hips a little too forward. Mrs Bridge had been trying to cure her of this habit by making her walk around the house with a book balanced on her head, but as soon as the book was removed Ruth resumed sauntering and standing in that unseemly posture.

'And you're older than Corky,' Mrs Bridge went on with a frown; and yet, looking at her elder daughter, she could not continue frowning. Ruth really was quite lovely, just as Gladys Schmidt's husband had said; if only she were not so conscious of it, not so aware of people turning to look at her, for they did stop to look – men and women both – so deliberately sometimes that Mrs Bridge grew uneasy, and could not get over the idea that Ruth, by her posture and her challenging walk, was encouraging people to stare.

'Is somebody coming by for you?'

'I'm only going to the drugstore.'

'What on earth do you do in the drugstore?' asked Mrs Bridge after a pause. 'Madge Arlen told me she saw you there one evening sitting all by yourself in a booth. She said she supposed you were waiting for someone.'

At this Ruth stiffened noticeably, and Mrs Bridge wanted to ask, 'Were you?'

'I really don't approve of you sitting around in drugstores,' she went on, for she was afraid to ask directly if Ruth was going there to meet a boy – not afraid of asking the question, but of the answer. 'And I don't believe your father would approve of it either,' she continued, feeling helpless and querulous in the knowledge that her daughter was hardly listening. 'Goodness, I should think you could find something else to do. What about playing with Carolyn and her friends?'

Ruth didn't bother to answer.

'I'll lend you my blue suede purse, if you like,' said Mrs Bridge hopefully, but again there was no response. Ruth was still admiring herself in the mirror.

'I shouldn't think you could carry much in those pockets.'

Ruth stepped backward, narrowed her eyes, and unfastened the top button of her blouse.

'Really, you *need* some things,' Mrs Bridge remarked a trifle sharply. 'And button yourself up, for goodness sake. You look like a chorus girl.'

'Good night,' said Ruth flatly and started for the door.

'But, dear, a lady always carries a purse!' Mrs Bridge was saying when the door closed.

25 *Another world*

Ruth was not particularly extravagant, in contrast to Carolyn, who spent her allowance the day she received it – usually on a scarf or a baggy sweater, despite the fact that her dresser drawers were filled with scarves and sweaters – but Mrs Bridge did not approve of Ruth's taste. Her allowance was apt to go for a necklace, or a sheer blouse, or a pair of extreme earrings. The earrings were impossible. Mrs Bridge, whose preference in earrings tended towards the inconspicuous, such as a moderately set pearl, tried to restrain herself whenever she caught sight of Ruth wearing something unusually objectionable, but there was one morning when she appeared for breakfast in Mexican huaraches, Japanese silk pajamas with the sleeves rolled up – displaying a piece of adhesive tape where she had cut herself while shaving her forearms – blue horn-rimmed reading glasses, and for earrings a cluster of tiny golden bells that tinkled whenever she moved. She might have gotten by that morning except for the fact that as she ate she steadily relaxed and contracted her feet so that the huaraches creaked.

'Now see here, young lady,' Mrs Bridge said with more authority than she felt, as she dropped a slice of bread into the automatic toaster. 'In the morning one doesn't wear earrings that dangle. People will think you're something from another world.'

'So?' said Ruth without looking up from the newspaper.

'Just what do you mean by that?'

'So who cares?'

'*I* care, that's who!' Mrs Bridge cried, suddenly very close to hysteria. 'I care very much.'

26 Tower

Douglas did a peculiar thing.

Instead of building a cave, or a house in a tree, as most of his friends were doing, he chose to build a tower of rubbish.

'Sounds awfully exciting,' Mrs Bridge responded somewhat absently when he first told her of his project; then, because she knew children wanted their parents to be interested in what they were doing, she asked how big it was going to be. He was vague, saying only that it was going to be the biggest tower anybody ever saw. She smiled and patted him affectionately. He looked at her for a long moment, shrugged in a singular way, and returned to the vacant lot where he intended to build the tower.

In the lot he had found some two-by-fours and a number of old bricks and half a bag of cement. He did not know where these materials had come from; he waited several days to see if they belonged to anybody. Apparently they didn't, so he claimed them. He got a shovel and went to work.

Having dug a hole about four feet deep, he lined it with brick and cement, planted the two-by-fours solidly upright, and liberally sprinkled this foundation with water. He then waited for his friends, the trash collectors, and followed their truck around the neighborhood. There was a moment between the time a rubbish barrel was rolled to the curb and the time the truck stopped for it that Douglas made good use of; he grabbed anything he thought belonged on his tower. He collected a great quantity of useful objects, and, on the side, about forty or fifty cereal boxtops, which he mailed to such places as Battle Creek, where there was a cereal factory, getting in return all kinds of prizes.

Within a week he had accumulated enough junk to keep the construction going for a long while. Half-hidden in the tall grass and wild shrubbery of the vacant lot lay a bundle of brass curtain rods which the Arlens thought were now in the city dump, a roll of electrician's tape and a bent skillet from the Pfeiffers' trash barrel, a hatchet with a splintered handle, a cigar box full of rusty nails, a broken fishing rod, several lengths of clothesline and wire, coat hangers, bottles, two apple boxes, an old raincoat and a pair of worn galoshes, a punctured inner tube, some very old golf clubs with wooden shafts, the cylinder from a lawnmower, springs from an over-stuffed chair, and, among other articles, thanks again to the unconscious generosity of the Arlens, a mildewed leather suitcase.

'My!' said Mrs Bridge, when he told her he was working on the tower, 'I can see you're going to be an architect or an engineer when you grow up. Now we're having an early lunch because this is my day for bridge club, so don't run off somewhere.'

Douglas said he would be in the vacant lot.

During the next week he managed to steal a full bag of powdered cement from a house going up in the next block; he broke it open after the workmen left, shoveled the powder into a wheelbarrow, and eventually managed to push the wheelbarrow into the vacant lot, where he dumped the powder in the pit and gave it a thorough watering. Thereafter he stopped mentioning his tower, and if asked what he was doing in the lot he would reply laconically that he was just playing.

With the addition of jugs and stones, tin cans, tree limbs, broken bottles, and all the other trash he could find, tied or nailed or cemented to the uprights, the tower continued to grow, until there came a Sunday morning when a man named Ewing who lived on the far side of the lot saw the tower rising above his hedge. At this point it was nearly six feet high. Ewing went around for a better look, and, discovering Douglas watching him from behind a sycamore tree, said to him, 'What have you got here, my friend?'

'Nothing,' replied Douglas, coming out from behind the sycamore. 'It's just a tower, that's all. It isn't hurting anybody.'

Having inspected the tower from all sides, Ewing turned his attention to Douglas, because it was the builder, after all, and not the building which was remarkable; and Douglas, embarrassed by the speculative eyes, picked up a length of pipe and struck the tower a resounding blow to prove it was as substantial as it looked.

Shortly thereafter Mrs Bridge saw it too – it rose jaggedly above the fence that divided their grounds from the lot – and went out to investigate. She looked at it for a considerable period, tapping a fingernail against her teeth, and that same afternoon she said lightly to her son, 'My, but that certainly is a big old tower.'

Douglas thrust his hands in his pockets and gazed with a distant expression at his shoes.

'Think what would happen if it fell over ker-*plunk* and hit you square on the head,' she continued, ruffling his hair, and reflecting automatically that he needed another haircut.

Douglas knew his tower would stop a truck, so he only sighed and pursed his lips.

Mrs Bridge was not overly concerned, being under the impression he was going to become bored with the tower and would dismantle it. But about two weeks later she realized he was still working on it, because she could see a cider jug and a chicken coop wired to the top of a broken chair, and she recalled that on her last visit this chair had been on top of everything. She had assumed this chair was his throne; she remembered how he liked to play king-of-the-mountain, and possibly he only built the tower in order to have a throne. Now, wondering how much higher he meant to go, she walked out to the vacant lot for another look, and this time she remained somewhat longer. Tentatively she pushed at the tower and was troubled by its solidity. She pushed again, with her palm, and again, much harder. The tower did not sway an inch. She began to wonder whether or not he would be able to destroy his creation – assuming she could convince him it ought to be torn down.

She intended to speak to him that same afternoon, but she did not know precisely how to begin because, like the tower, he seemed to be growing out of her reach. He was becoming more than a small boy who could be coaxed this way or that; the hour was approaching when she must begin to reason with him as with an adult, and this idea disturbed her. She was not certain she was equal to it. And so a few days, a week, two weeks went by, and though she had not spoken neither had she forgotten.

'Well!' she finally exclaimed, as though she had just thought of it, 'I see that ugly tower keeps getting bigger and bigger.' It was, to tell the truth, quite a bit bigger. When he did not say a word, or even look at her, she wanted to grab him by the shoulders and shake loose whatever was growing inside him.

'It seems to me that a big boy like you wouldn't want to go on building a silly tower,' she said, hopefully, and then he glanced at her in a way that was somehow derisive, as if he were reading her mind.

'I'll tell you what let's do!' She stooped in order to look directly into his face. 'First thing after dinner we'll get some wire clippers and a hammer and a screwdriver and – well, just everything we need, and you and I together will tear it to bits. Won't that be fun?'

He turned his head away and said very softly, 'No.'

'No? Why not?'

After a while Douglas rubbed his nose and muttered that there was too much concrete.

'Oh, I'll bet we—' Mrs Bridge hesitated. Her insights usually arrived too late to illuminate the situation, but this one was in time.

'You're probably right,' she said, continuing with treacherous frankness, 'I doubt if you or anybody else could tear it down.'

She watched him almost fall into the trap. He was ready to defy her by saying he could if he wanted to, and if she could get him to say that she knew the battle would be half over. He was on the verge of it; she could see the defiance on his face and in the way he stood. But then, instead of answering, he paused to think, and Mrs Bridge was dismayed. All her life she had been accustomed to responding immediately when anyone spoke to her. If she had been complimented she promptly and graciously thanked the speaker; or if, by chance, her opinion was asked on something, anything – the cost of butter, the Italian situation – no matter what, if she was asked she answered readily. Now, seeing her son with his mouth clamped shut like a turtle with a seed and his face puckered in thought, she did not know what to do. She gazed down on him expectantly.

After a long silence Douglas said, 'Maybe.'

And here, for the time being, the matter rested.

27 *Sentimental moment*

Mrs Bridge stood alone at a front window thinking of how quickly the years were going by. The children were growing up so rapidly, and her husband— She stirred uneasily. Already there was a new group of 'young marrieds', people she hardly knew. Surely some time had gone by – she expected this; nevertheless she could not get over the feeling that something was drawing steadily away from her. She wondered if her husband felt the same; she thought she would ask him that evening when he got home. She recalled the dreams they used to share; she recalled with a smile how she used to listen to him speak of his plans and how she had never actually cared one way or another about his ambition, she had cared only for him. That was enough. In those days she used to think that the long hours he spent in his office were a temporary condition and that as soon as more people came to him with legal problems he would, somehow, begin spending more time at home. But this was not the way it turned out, and Mrs Bridge understood now that she would never see very much of him. They had started off together to explore something that promised to be wonderful, and, of course, there had been wonderful times. And yet, thought Mrs Bridge, why is it that we haven't – that nothing has – that whatever we—?

It was raining. Thunder rumbled through the lowering clouds with a constant, monotonous, trundling sound, like furniture being rolled back and forth in the attic. In the front yard the evergreen trees swayed in the wind and the shutters rattled in the sudden rainy gusts. She noticed that a branch had been torn from the soft maple tree; the branch lay on the driveway and the leaves fluttered.

Harriet came in to ask if she would like some hot chocolate.

'Oh, no thank you, Harriet,' said Mrs Bridge. 'You have some.'

Harriet was so nice. And she was a good worker. Mrs Bridge was very proud of having Harriet and knew that she would be next to impossible to replace, and yet there were times when Mrs Bridge half wished she would quit. Why she wished this, she did not know, unless it was that with Harriet around to do all the work she herself was so often dismally bored. When she was first married she used to do the cooking and house-cleaning and washing, and how she had looked forward to a few minutes of leisure! But now – how odd – there was too much leisure. Mrs Bridge did not admit this fact to anyone, for it embarrassed her; indeed she very often gave the impression of being distracted by all the things needed to be done – phone the laundry, the grocer, take Ruth to the dentist, Carolyn to tap-dancing class, Douglas to the barber shop, and so on. But the truth remained, and settled upon her with ever greater finality.

The light snapped on in the back hall. She heard his cough and the squeak of the closet door and the familiar flapping sound of his briefcase on the upper shelf. Suddenly overwhelmed by the need for reassurance, she turned swiftly from the window and hurried toward him with an intent, wistful expression, knowing what she wanted without knowing how to ask for it.

He heard the rustle of her dress and her quick footsteps on the carpet. He was hanging up his coat as she approached, and he said, without irritation, but a trifle wearily because this was not the first time it had happened. 'I see you forgot to have the car lubricated.'

28 Soft gift

She reflected that her difficulties with Ruth and Douglas might be inevitable; after all, years had passed since she was their age.

Each of her own birthdays she celebrated with joy, with a certain resignation and doubt; it came and went as it was supposed to, and a few months later she would find herself depressed and unaccountably perplexed by how old she was. Thirty, thirty-five, forty, all had come to visit her like admonitory relatives, and all had slipped away without a trace, without a sound, and now, once again, she was waiting.

Someone was at the front door; the chimes were jingling sweetly. It was the postman with a package. It was from Memphis. She cut the masking tape, lifted the cardboard flaps, and underneath the excelsior she found a pewter tray in the shape of a clover. She took hold of the stem to lift it out, but the tray, instead of remaining rigid like all the other trays she had ever seen, began to droop. The alloy was much too soft to support its own weight, so that in a few seconds the tray was dangling almost straight down from the handle. Mrs Bridge was not surprised. She pressed it back into shape, returned it to the box, carried the box to the attic, and that afternoon wrote her annual thank-you note to second-cousin Lulubelle Watts. In years past Mrs Bridge had received from Lulu such birthday gifts as a bile green kitchen alarm clock, a longhaired pillow, a framed photograph of the Great Smokies, and a pair of heavy bronze balls which apparently should have had an instruction booklet. In thinking over these gifts she often tried to decide whether Lulubelle disliked her and was deliberately insulting her, or whether it was simply that Lulu had the world's worst taste. She also thought of picking out something just as grotesque to send in return, but minding the Golden Rule she always shipped to Memphis on Lulu's birthday some very nice gift in the nature of a leather-covered engagement calendar, guest towels, a cake knife, or a bisque figurine.

29 Nothing spectacular

At his wife's suggestion Mr Bridge had walked around to the vacant lot to examine the eccentric and mystifying memorial Douglas had built and which he had not yet abandoned; Mr Bridge tried to topple it and then simply attempted to shake it. The tower did not move. Satisfied that it would not collapse while Douglas or his friends were clambering about, and that they had sense enough not to impale themselves on the outcroppings, he returned to his evening newspaper and thought no more about it.

Mrs Bridge, however, was uneasy. She sensed that people in the neighborhood were aware of the tower. Even so, she did not become actively alarmed until a man at a cocktail party, upon being introduced to her, mentioned that he had driven over to see the tower.

'Oh, horrors!' she exclaimed as a means of registering her attitude. 'Is it famous all over the city?' And though she was joking she was dead serious.

'A curious form of protest,' the man replied, tucking his pipe with tobacco; then, after a sharp glance directly into her eyes, he added, 'You *are* aware of the boy's motivation, are you not?'

To which she smiled politely, being somewhat confused, and made a mental note that the man had been drinking.

The next morning as soon as Douglas left for school she telephoned the fire department. Everyone called the fire department when there was a problem that defied classification. Shortly before noon a small red truck parked in front of the house and two firemen

– she had never spoken to a fireman before and found the experience rather strange – two of them entered the house as though it were the most natural thing in the world, and listened to what she told them about the tower. Then they went out to have a look. Mildly amused at first, presently they were startled. However they had been called upon by housewives for many unnatural labors, and so they unhooked their tools of destruction and set to work. It took them until almost dark to turn it into a mound of rubble, but at last an area of several square yards was covered with splintered wood, broken glass, wire, great gritty chunks of lumpy concrete, and whatever else had gone into the creation of it, and the air was filled with dust as though there had been a peculiar explosion. The firemen said they would make a report of the tower and its destruction and that the lot would be cleaned up within a day or two.

Douglas, having come home a few minutes before the firemen left, stood watching them in grieved silence. Mrs Bridge, seeing him from an upstairs window, went out to stand behind him with her hands resting on his shoulders, and occasionally rumpled his hair.

'It was just getting too big,' she confided to him gently. 'People were beginning to wonder.'

30 The search for love

It seemed to Mrs Bridge that she had done the necessary thing, and therefore the right thing, in regard to the monstrous tower. Again and again she thought about it, and the reason she thought about it so intensively was that she perceived a change in Douglas's attitude toward her. He was more withdrawn.

As time went on she felt an increasing need for reassurance. Her husband had never been a demonstrative man, not even when they were first married; consequently she did not expect too much from him. Yet there were moments when she was overwhelmed by a terrifying, inarticulate need. One evening as she and he were finishing supper together, alone, the children having gone out, she inquired rather sharply if he loved her. She was surprised by her own bluntness and by the almost shrewish tone of her voice, because that was not the way she actually felt. She saw him gazing at her in astonishment; his expression said very clearly: Why on earth do you think I'm here if I don't love you? Why aren't I somewhere else? What in the world has got into you?

Mrs Bridge smiled across the floral centerpiece – and it occurred to her that these flowers she had so carefully arranged on the table were what separated her from her husband – and said, a little wretchedly, 'I know it's silly, but it's been such a long time since you told me.'

Mr Bridge grunted and finished his coffee. She knew it was not that he was annoyed, only that he was incapable of the kind of declaration she needed. It was so little, and yet so much. While they sat across from each other, neither knowing quite what to do next, she became embarrassed; and in her embarrassment she moved her feet and she inadvertently stepped on the buzzer, concealed beneath the carpet, that connected with the kitchen, with the result that Harriet soon appeared in the doorway to see what it was that Mrs Bridge desired.

31 Treachery

Mrs Bridge often referred to Harriet as a 'gem', adding that she had been with the family for more than nine years and that she didn't know what she would do if Harriet ever decided to leave. Considering that cooks and chauffeurs in south-side Kansas City often stayed with a family for twenty or thirty years, Harriet's nine years was nothing to boast about. Even so there were a good many matrons who knew her by sight at the bus stop and had been elegantly served by her during luncheons or cocktail parties, with the result that Harriet, though a comparative newcomer, had the reputation of being a catch.

Indeed there were few things about her to which Mrs Bridge could object. The main thing was her smoking. She was an expert at smoking, expelling it through her nostrils and blowing rings like a man, and she had to be warned occasionally because she did not mind answering the door with a cigarette in her mouth. Otherwise Mrs Bridge very rarely had to speak to her. On certain humid summer days when she was alone in the house she would take off her uniform and put on a halter and an alpine dirndl skirt, and once or twice she had been caught wearing this outfit. But she was not lazy, and she did not drink at all, she was an excellent cook, and not only the children but Mr Bridge seemed to like her.

So it came as a blow to Mrs Bridge when, altogether by accident, she heard Harriet flirting with Mrs Ralph Porter. The Porters had never been close friends but were decidedly in the same circle as the Bridges. It was one cloudy afternoon in spring when Mrs Bridge, who had a headache, decided to telephone her husband at the office and ask him to bring home some Empirin. She was upstairs in the bedroom at the time, so she walked into the hall and picked up the receiver. The line was busy. She was about to replace the phone in its niche when she heard Harriet asking, 'How much do you all pay?' Some instinct warned Mrs Bridge what the conversation was about, and for a moment she had not the strength of character to stop eavesdropping. Mrs Porter's voice answered, 'Whatever you're receiving there, Harriet, I'll pay you ten dollars a month more.'

'Do tell,' murmured Harriet, her voice not giving away her thoughts, and Mrs Bridge, frozen to the upstairs phone, could almost see her seated on the pantry stool with her legs crossed, blowing smoke rings.

There was a crucial pause. Mrs Bridge was now afraid to replace the receiver because the click would be audible; all she could do was hold her head and wait.

'I feel,' Harriet murmured, 'Mr and Mrs Bridge could not precisely survive too well should I depart here.' With chilling poise she added, 'However, it was extremely nice of you to call.'

And that, as even such a bald soul as Mrs Porter could tell, was the end of the matter.

32 No scenes in church

The Porters were regular church-goers, and after the telephone incident Mrs Bridge felt a sense of exasperation whenever she saw Mrs Porter in church. It was difficult to imagine how a person could be so devout and so conniving, but that was Mrs Porter.

For better or worse Mrs Bridge did not often encounter her there, the reason being that she did not like attending church alone and it was quite difficult to get Mr Bridge to go. He had little enough use for dogma and would rather lie abed reading vacation brochures on those Sunday mornings when he did not go to the office, or, dressed in old clothes, he would spend the morning in the yard with a can of snail poison. Now and then she became worried about his apathetic attitude toward religion, especially after one of Dr Foster's sermons on the consequences of atheism, and she would then half-fearfully go after her husband.

'When I need to know anything,' he would reply with awful finality, 'I go to someone who knows more than I do.' This was quite a slam at Dr Foster.

'But don't you think he has some very good ideas?' she would counter. 'It certainly wouldn't hurt you to attend once in a while. And people do ask where you are.'

So it came about that once or twice a year he would silently drive to church. They would climb to the balcony, for what reason she could never understand, and there with heads almost touching the stained-oak rafters, surrounded by stifling, humid air, they sat through the sermon.

One Easter, an unusually warm day, just as Dr Foster began easing into the familiar narrative – the empty tomb, and so forth – the scent of lilies became overpowering. Or was it the sight of Mrs Porter looking altogether righteous? In any event Mrs Bridge felt herself swaying. She reached towards the balcony rail for support and whispered giddily that she was going to faint. Mr Bridge had been dozing, but he woke up immediately and turned his head and glared at her severely.

'Not here! Wait until we get outside,' he told her in a voice that was audible throughout the balcony.

'All right, I'll try,' she whispered. She thought he meant to escort her outside, but apparently not, because he did not get up, and in a few minutes she realized he meant for her to wait until church was over. There was nothing to do but to try not to faint, and so she did try, and succeeded.

33 Powerful vocabulary

Dr Foster had such an impressive vocabulary that Mrs Bridge was moved to amplify her own. She intended to, she had been intending to for quite a while, but the opportunity never presented itself until she received as second prize at bridge club a little book on how to build a more powerful vocabulary in thirty days. The dust jacket, an eye-catching red, guaranteed that if the reader spent only a few minutes a day, his ability to express himself would so noticeably improve that within two weeks friends would be commenting. Tests had proved, so said the dust jacket, that the great majority of employers had larger vocabularies than their employees, which, the jacket hinted, was the reason for the status quo.

Although Mrs Bridge had no more thought of becoming an employer than an employee, she was delighted with her prize; everyone else in Kansas City was reading it and she had, therefore, been planning on buying a copy if she could not get it from the rental library. She began to read it that same afternoon as soon as she got home. The next day she was busy, but the day after that she spent almost three hours studying, completing several lessons – filling in the blanks and doing the multiple-choice exercises at the back of the book. She spoke of it enthusiastically to her friends, most of whom had either read it or were definitely intending to, with the exception of Grace Barron, who always read books no one else ever heard of.

At the end of two weeks she was on her thirteenth lesson, very nearly on schedule, when the telephone interrupted; Madge Arlen was calling to say that a delivery truck had run over their next-door-neighbor's boxer. Dogs were always being run over by delivery trucks. The Bridges had lost a collie several years before, and some people named Ilgenfritz who lived in the next block had lost two dachshunds.

'Oh, not really!' Mrs Bridge began. 'What a shame!'

'I tell you I'm up in arms!' replied Madge. 'When Edith told me about it I was so put out I simply couldn't speak.'

Presently the conversation got around to the vocabulary book and Mrs Bridge praised it and recommended it quite strongly to Madge, who answered that she'd just finished reading it.

Mrs Bridge was very much surprised by this news. 'You did?' she asked uncertainly, for the book had obviously not affected Madge's vocabulary.

'Yes, and it was marvelous! Every last one of us ought to read it.'

Mrs Bridge felt rather subdued after this talk with Madge; however she continued with her lessons whenever there was time. She did want to complete the book because she was always meeting people who asked if she had read it, and within the month she had reached the twentieth lesson, where one turned adverbs into nouns. So far none of her friends had commented as the dust jacket promised; consequently Mrs Bridge was a little discouraged. The book began to wander around the house. It found its way from the coffee table in the living room to the window seat in the breakfast room; after that it lay in a dresser drawer in the upstairs bedroom for about a week, and briefly in the room shared by Carolyn and Ruth. From there it traveled again to the breakfast room, to the basement, and finally, its pages already turning a sulphur color and its jacket mended with Scotch Tape, it died on a shelf between T. E. Lawrence and *The Rubáiyát*.

34 *Tobacco Road*

Madge and Grace were so different; Mrs Bridge felt drawn to them both, and was distressed that the two of them did not care for each other. Now and then she felt they were competing for her friendship, though she could not be sure of this, but if it was true it was both exciting and alarming. She often thought about them. She felt more comfortable with Madge, who liked everything about Kansas City, more secure, more positive; with Grace Barron she felt obliged to consider everything she said, and to look all around, and she could never guess what Grace would say or do.

Tobacco Road, practically uncensored, had come to Kansas City, and Madge Arlen – possibly jealous of Grace Barron's attentions – called to ask if Mrs Bridge wanted to go to the Wednesday matinee. She had not thought about it, but there was no reason not to, particularly since almost everyone was going to see it in spite of its shady reputation, so she agreed.

The play had scarcely got under way when she received a brief but severe shock: one of the girls in the cast looked extremely like Ruth with her hair uncombed. For an instant she feared it truly was Ruth; it wasn't, of course, and as the play went on she could see that the actress was a few years older.

She did not enjoy the play, neither did Madge Arlen; they left after the second act. On the way out of the theater Mrs Bridge remarked, 'Frankly, I don't see why a play like *Tobacco Road* is necessary.'

'We expected it to be earthy,' Madge Arlen observed with some lenience, 'however, I do agree with you. It went much too far.'

35 *One summer morning*

It was very hot that summer.

For as long as she could remember, Mrs Bridge had known that unless she was wearing slacks – slacks were worn only for gardening – she must wear stockings. In summer this could be uncomfortable, but it was the way things were, it was the way things had always been, and so she complied. No matter where she was going, though it might be no farther than the shopping center at Sixty-third Street, or even if she was not going out of the house all day, she would put on her stockings.

But one morning – and an extraordinarily hot day it promised to be, because by ten o'clock the tar in the street was glistening – she decided not to wear stockings. It was Harriet's day off, Ruth and Carolyn had gone swimming at Lake Lotawana, and Douglas had gone to a model-airplane meet in Swope Park, so nobody would ever know the difference. Having selected the lightest dress she could find in her closet, she put on a pair of blue anklets and the clogs she wore at the country-club swimming pool. Thus dressed, she considered herself in the mirror and shook her head at the sight, but went downstairs all the same. The Beckerle sisters, two elderly widows who were seldom seen about the neighborhood, chose that morning to come visiting.

'Oh, goodness,' cried Mrs Bridge as she greeted them at the door, 'I look like something out of *Tobacco Road*!'

36 Growing pains

Having been repelled by *Tobacco Road* to the point where it obsessed her, she employed it as a pigeonhole; whatever she found unreal, bizarre, obnoxious, indecorous, malodorous, or generally unsavory, unexpected, and disagreeable henceforth belonged in *Tobacco Road*, was from there, or should have been there. So, finding her son in ragged tennis shoes, she let him know where he was from. He didn't mind. He had never cared about clothes one way or another, unless he had become attached to a particular garment, in which case he wore it until she threw it away. Whenever it became necessary to get him some new clothing there would be a quarrel, and after much wrangling the two of them would drive off to one of the young men's shops where he would be turned over to a clerk experienced in these situations, and finally, after all three of them were exhausted, the purchase was made. The argument in regard to the gray suit was typical:

'I've already got a suit.'

'But that's a summer suit,' she countered.

He looked in his closet and found another outfit. 'What's the matter with this, I'd sure like to know?'

'You've outgrown it, and besides, it's time you got another.'

'I never wore it anyway,' he said triumphantly, his voice changing pitch during the sentence.

'This is absolutely ridiculous. We're going down to the Plaza right now and get you something to wear, so you might as well get used to the idea.'

'This suit works all right. I don't want another one.'

'Can you imagine your father going to work in old clothes? Why, he'd be laughed out of court!'

Douglas said he didn't think it was so funny, and furthermore he couldn't understand what difference it made; for her part she could not understand why he objected to having new clothes. But, as always, they ended by going to the Plaza, where a very nice gray suit was purchased, although on the way home he said bitterly that he would not ever wear it. He did, of course, as they both knew he would; it was just that he could not admit he liked the suit. In fact he decided it was necessary to claim the suit was giving him a heart attack. Mrs Bridge was so startled by this announcement that she was temporarily unable to reply.

'Well, it is!' he said, and began to stagger and clutch his chest. 'It's too heavy. I can't breathe.'

'The only thing wrong with you, my young friend, is your big imagination.'

'Okay, then,' he retorted gloomily. And with his head lowered he walked slowly away, stopping every few steps to feel his heart. At the door he hesitated, and before going out he said truculently, 'But I'm just telling you, if I keel over dead, don't be surprised.'

'Very well,' she replied, 'I won't.'

37 Maid from Madras

Mr and Mrs Bridge were giving a party, not because they wanted to, but because it was time. Like dinner with the Van Metres, once you accepted an invitation you were obligated to reciprocate, or, as Mr Bridge had once expressed it, retaliate.

Altogether some eighty people showed up in the course of the evening. They stood around and wandered around, eating, drinking, talking, and smoking. Grace and Virgil Barron were there – Grace sunburned, freckled, and petite, and looking rather pensive; the Arlens arrived in a new Chrysler; the Heywood Duncans were there; and Wilhelm and Susan Van Metre, both seeming withered, sober, and at the wrong party; Lois and Stuart Montgomery; Noel Johnson, huge and alone, wearing a paper cap; Mabel Ong trying to begin serious discussions; and, among others, the Beckerle sisters in beaded gowns which must have been twenty years old, both sisters looking as though they had not for an instant forgotten the morning Mrs Bridge entertained them in anklets. Even Dr Foster, smiling tolerantly, with a red nose, stopped by for a cigarette and a whisky sour and chided a number of the men about Sunday golf.

There was also an automobile salesman named Beachy Marsh who had arrived very early in a double-breasted pin-stripe business suit, and, being ill at ease, sensing that he did not belong, did everything he could think of to be amusing. He was not a close friend but it had been necessary to invite him along with several others.

Mrs Bridge rustled about her large, elegant, and brilliantly lighted home, checking steadily to see that everything was as it should be. She glanced into the bathrooms every few minutes and found that the guest towels, like pastel handkerchiefs, were still immaculately overlapping one another – at evening's end only two had been disturbed, a fact which would have given Douglas, had he known, a morose satisfaction – and she entered the kitchen once to recommend that the extra servant girl, hired to assist Harriet, pin shut the gap in the breast of her starched uniform.

Around and around went Mrs Bridge, graciously smiling, pausing here and there to chat for a moment, but forever alert, checking the turkey sandwiches, the crackers, the barbecued sausages, quietly opening windows to let out the smoke, discreetly removing wet glasses from mahogany table tops, slipping away now and then to empty the solid Swedish crystal ashtrays.

And Beachy Marsh got drunk. He slapped people on the shoulder, told jokes, laughed uproariously, and also went around emptying the ashtrays of their cherry-colored stubs, all the while attempting to control the tips of his shirt collar, which had become damp from perspiration and were rolling up into the air like horns.

Following Mrs Bridge halfway up the carpeted stairs he said hopefully, 'There was a young maid from Madras, who had a magnificent ass; not round and pink, as you probably think – it was gray, had long ears, and ate grass.'

'Oh, my word!' replied Mrs Bridge, looking over her shoulder with a polite smile but continuing up the stairs, while the auto salesman plucked miserably at his collar.

38 Revolt of the masses

The evenings were growing cooler, September was here, autumn not far to the north, and the trees rustled uneasily.

Having ordered the groceries and having spent the remainder of the morning more or less listening to the radio, and being then unable to find anything else to do, she informed Harriet – who was in the kitchen furiously smoking one cigarette after another while cutting up dates for a pudding – that she had some shopping to take care of on the Plaza and would not be home until late that afternoon. She felt somewhat guilty as she said this because in reality there was no shopping to be done, but, with the children again in school and with Harriet to do the cooking and housekeeping and with the laundress coming once a week to do the washing Mrs Bridge found the days were very long. She was restless and unhappy and would spend hours thinking wistfully of the past, of those years just after her marriage when a day was all too brief.

After luncheon in her favorite tearoom she decided she might as well look at candlesticks. She had been thinking of getting some new ones; this seemed as good a time as any. On her way to Bancroft's, which carried the nicest things on the Plaza, she stopped at a drugstore for a box of aspirin, then paused in front of a bookstore where her eye was caught by the title of a book in the window display: *Theory of the Leisure Class*. She experienced a surge of resentment. For a number of seconds she eyed this book with definite hostility, as though it were alive and conscious of her. She went inside and asked to see the book. With her gloves on it was difficult to turn the pages, so she handed it back to the clerk, thanked him, and with a dissatisfied expression continued to Bancroft's.

39 Minister's book

If she bought a book it was almost always one of three things: a best-seller she had heard about or seen advertised, a self-improvement book, or a book by a Kansas City author no matter what it was about. These latter were infrequent, but now and again somebody would explode in the midst of Kansas City with a Civil War history or an account of old Westport Landing. Then, too, there were slender volumes of verse and essays usually printed by local publishing houses, and it was one of these that lay about the living room longer than any other book, with the exception of an extremely old two-volume set of *The Brothers Karamazov* in gold-painted leather which nobody in the family had ever read and which had belonged to Mr Bridge's grandfather. This set rested gravely on the mantelpiece between a pair of bronze Indian-chief heads – the only gift from cousin Lulubelle Watts that Mrs Bridge had ever been able to use – and was dusted once a week by Harriet with a peacock-feather duster.

The volume that ran second to *The Brothers Karamazov* was a collection of thoughts by the local minister, Dr Foster, an exceptionally short and congenial man with an enormous head which was always referred to as leonine, and which was crowned with golden white hair. He allowed his hair to grow very long and he brushed it toward the top of his head so as to appear taller. He had written these essays over a period of several years with the idea of putting them into book form, and from time to time he would allude to them, laughingly, as his memoirs. Then people would exclaim that he surely mustn't keep them to himself until he died, at which Dr Foster, touching the speaker's arm, and perhaps rising on tiptoe, would laugh heartily and reply, 'We'll see, we'll see,' and thereupon clear his throat.

At last, when he had been preaching in Kansas City for seventeen years and his name was recognized, and he was often mentioned in *The Tattler* and sometimes in the city paper, a small publishing firm took these essays, which he had quietly submitted to them several times before. The book came out in a black cover with a dignified gray and purple dust jacket that showed him gazing sedately from his study window at dusk, hands clasped behind his back and one foot slightly forward.

The first essay began: 'I am now seated at my desk, the desk that has been a source of comfort and inspiration to me these many years. I see that night is falling, the shadows creeping gently across my small but (to my eyes) lovely garden, and at such times as this I often reflect on the state of Mankind.'

Mrs Bridge read Dr Foster's book, which he had autographed for her, and she was amazed to find that he was such a reflective man, and so sensitive to the sunrise which she discovered he always got up to watch. She underlined several passages in the book that seemed to have particular meaning for her, and when it was done she was able to discuss it with her friends, all of whom were reading it.

This book came to her like an olive branch. It assured her of God's love for man, of man's love of God: in the ever-lengthening shadow of Hitler and Mussolini her faith was restored, and the comfortable meditations of her minister found lodging.

40 Lady poet

Quite a different sort of writer was Mabel Ong. There were persistent rumors that Mabel was a poet – supposedly quite good – and that one of her poems had been published in a magazine. Mrs Bridge, having made discreet inquiries which failed to elicit either the name of the magazine or the title of the poem, was therefore pleased to hear Lois Montgomery announce that as a special treat immediately following the next Auxiliary meeting Mabel would read from her works. She was a vigorous, muscular woman of about thirty-five, with a sprinkling of moles on her forehead, and close-cropped hair, who generally wore a tweed coat and stood with her hands thrust into the pockets like a man. She had a positive manner of speaking, now and then turning her head aside to cough or to laugh; she spoke bitterly about capitalism and would relate stories she had heard from unquestionable sources about women dying in childbirth because they could not afford the high cost of hospitalization, or even the cost of insurance programs.

'If I should bear a child—' she was fond of beginning, and would then tear into medical fees.

On the appointed day Mabel Ong walked briskly to the front of the room, carrying a briefcase as though it were a book, and having placed this briefcase on a card table she unzipped it, spent several minutes shuffling through some papers, frowning, but eventually located whatever she was after. She poured herself a drink of ice water from the pitcher, lighted a cigarette, and with one eye closed against the smoke she shuffled through the papers again. Mrs Bridge watched attentively, thinking that Mabel certainly looked capable of being a poet.

After another drink of water she crushed out her cigarette, ran her tongue over her teeth, and pensively frowned into space. All at once she began:

'Out of the wild womb weeping—'

Mabel was just a bit tongue-tied and Mrs Bridge, in the back row, was not certain whether she had said 'weeping' or 'leaping', but decided not to inquire. When the reading concluded she applauded along with everyone else, and she stood around for a while and listened as various members of the Auxiliary asked Mabel about the significance of one line or another. Mrs Bridge had not enjoyed the poems – they sounded quite free and not very poetic – and she hoped no one would ask for her opinion of them. No one did, though on a certain occasion she was rather surprised to hear herself volunteering the information that she had not cared for them; and being embarrassed by this critical observation, for she was conscious of her own limitations, she quickly added, 'However, I'm sure I couldn't do half as well.'

41 Voting

She had never gone into politics the way some women did, though she listened attentively whenever such topics as the farm surplus or public works programs were discussed at luncheons or at circle meetings; she felt her lack of knowledge and wanted to improve herself, and she often resolved to buckle down to some serious studying. But so many things kept popping up, always at the very moment she was about to begin, and then too she did not know exactly where to start. Once in a while she would be on the point of questioning her husband, but, after thinking it over, she realized she would be asking silly questions, and he was so over-burdened with business problems that she did not want to distract him. Besides, there was not much she herself could accomplish.

This was how she defended herself to Mabel Ong after having incautiously let slip the information that her husband always told her how to vote.

'Don't you have a mind of your own?' Mabel demanded, and looked quite grim. 'Great Scott, woman! Speak out! We've been emancipated!' She rocked back and forth, hands clasped behind her back, while she frowned at the carpet of the Auxiliary club-house.

'You're right, of course,' Mrs Bridge apologized, discreetly avoiding the stream of smoke from Mabel's cigarette. 'But don't you find it hard to know *what* to think? There's so much scandal and fraud everywhere you turn, and I suppose the papers only print what they want us to know.' She hesitated, and then spoke out boldly. 'How do you make up *your* mind?'

Mabel Ong, without removing the cigarette from her lips, considered the ceiling, the carpet, and squinted critically at a Degas print on the wall, as though debating how to answer such an ingenuous question, and finally she suggested that Mrs Bridge might begin to grasp the fundamentals by a deliberate reading of certain books, the titles of which she jotted down on the margin of a tally card. Mrs Bridge had not heard of any of these books except one, and this one because the author had committed suicide, but she decided to read it anyway.

The lady at her favorite rental library had never heard of the book, which was somehow gratifying; even so, having resolved to read it, Mrs Bridge set out for the public library. Here, at last, she got it, and settled down to the deliberate reading Mabel had advised. The author's name was Zokoloff, which certainly sounded threatening, and to be sure the first chapter dealt with bribery in the circuit courts.

When she had gotten far enough along to feel capable of discussing it she left it on the hall table; however Mr Bridge did not even notice it until it had lain there for three days. She watched him pick it up, saw his nostrils flatten as he read the title, and then she waited nervously and excitedly. He opened the book, read a few sentences, grunted, and dropped the book on the table. This was disappointing. In fact, now that there was no danger involved, she had trouble finishing the book; she thought it would be better in a magazine digest. But eventually she did finish it and returned it to the library, saying with a slight air of sophistication, 'I can't honestly say I agree with it all, but he's certainly well informed.'

Certain arguments of Zokoloff remained with her, and she found that the longer she thought about them the more penetrating and logical they became; surely it *was* time, as he insisted, for a change in government. She decided to vote liberal at the next election, and as time for it approached she became filled with such enthusiasm and with such great conviction and determination that she planned to discuss her new attitude with her husband. She became confident that she could persuade him to change his vote also. Politics were not mysterious after all. However, when she challenged him to discussion he did not seem especially interested; in fact he did not answer. He was studying a sheaf of legal papers and only glanced across at her with an annoyed expression. She let it go until the following evening when he was momentarily unoccupied, and this time he stared at her curiously, intently, as if probing her mind, and then all at once he snorted.

She really intended to force a discussion on election eve. She was going to quote from the book of Zokoloff. But he came home so late, so exhausted, that she had not the heart to upset him. She concluded it would be best to let him vote as he always had, and she would do as she herself wished; still, on getting to the polls, which were conveniently located in the country-club shopping district, she became doubtful and a little uneasy. And when the moment finally came she pulled the lever recording her wish for the world to remain as it was.

42 Oaths and pledges

At one of the Auxiliary meetings a discussion arose as to whether it might not be a good idea to amend the constitution of the Auxiliary so as to include the words 'under God'. Throughout this debate Grace Barron gazed out the window. Everyone else got up to say it was a good idea, except Mabel Ong – being particularly severe in a tailored suit and a string tie – who argued against it, and it was common knowledge that Mabel, being an intellectual, argued against the majority rather than against the question. So, late in the afternoon, the resolution was passed. Of fifty-six ladies present, fifty-four voted to include God. Mabel was against. Grace abstained; in fact when her name was called she jumped and said, 'What?'

Mrs Bridge wished it could have been unanimous; unanimity was so gratifying. Every time she heard or read about a unanimous vote she felt a surge of pride and was reminded, for some reason, of the Pilgrims. She enjoyed all kinds of oaths and pledges and took them regularly, remaining cautious only if her signature was required; signatures were binding, this she knew, and she was under the impression that they were often photographed, or forged, or whatever it was that unscrupulous persons did with signatures.

Oral resolutions, however, seemed quite safe and gave her a sense of participating, and she liked to discuss them. Often she could be heard urging ladies she scarcely knew to join with her and the others, saying, 'It might help and it certainly can't do any harm.'

43 Another victim of circumstances

Lois Montgomery was one of the most prominent members of the Auxiliary. Mrs Bridge had known her for a good many years without regarding her in any way special until one afternoon when,

78

not by accident, Mabel Ong let slip an allusion to the time when Lois had been raped. Mrs Bridge's pleasantly neutral expression did not change, just as though she knew all about the case, or at least had had a good deal of experience with that sort of thing, but afterward she found out more. Lois Montgomery was now a tall, stately eagle of a woman with a deep snowy breast and rather overwhelming perfume. She wore her black hair in a huge ballerina knot, lacquered, through tiny cracks of which could be seen a tight roll of false brown hair. Mrs Bridge would not have considered her the sort of person a sex maniac would attack, and yet the story, so far as she could ascertain, was true. It had taken place years ago when the Montgomerys were living in Butte, Montana, where Stuart had some kind of position with the railroad. How the story followed them from Butte to Kansas City so many years later there was no means of discovering.

Mrs Bridge visualized the scene: Lois in her Fifth Avenue suit and silver fox boa striding imperially down a dark Montana street with the Canadian wind howling, and then the man rising from behind a bush, or stepping quickly around a tree – he was dressed in a shabby suit with the collar turned up, and he had not shaved, or he could have been wearing a leather jacket and a mask, a stocking cap perhaps. She tried to imagine Lois struggling with him in the darkness, shrieking for help; she wondered if the man had choked Lois with the silver fox boa. Afterward there was the ruined woman collapsed on the sidewalk and the man running away. Later she was lying in a hospital bed, having been given a sedative, and there were police lieutenants in their ill-fitting serge suits asking her embarrassing questions. After that there were relatives and friends who entered with flowers. The scene always ended in the hospital when the room was full of flowers and Mrs Montgomery's perfume.

She also thought about Stuart Montgomery and how the affair must have affected him. She saw him in Kansas City as a tall, leathery man with a hard, bulbous face like those carved on bottle openers or on the knobs of canes. He did not have much to say if she chanced to meet him on the street with his odd yellow briefcase, and when he tipped his hat he seldom bothered to smile. She wondered if he had wept when he learned what had happened, and if he tried to apologize for having allowed her to go home alone that night, or whether he had been with her and had been frightened away by the man's gun. Or had he been struck over the head? Did he still respect her?

Mrs Bridge wanted to make some gesture to tell Lois Montgomery how she sympathized, but, after all, what could be done when no one ever mentioned it and when Lois simply stood there smiling and chatting and eating crabmeat sandwiches like everyone else?

44 Leda

During one of the luncheons she got to talking with Grace Barron about art, the result being that the two of them left the clubhouse and drove to the William Rockhill Nelson art gallery and stayed there till it closed. Mrs Bridge felt excited and guilty about the way they had gone off by themselves, but it was how Grace did everything.

Goya, Holbein, Dürer, Corot – these names, at once so familiar and so meaningless to Mrs Bridge, were old friends of Grace Barron. And before long Mrs Bridge knew this was a day to be remembered, like a day in February when, after months of lowering skies, the clouds roll back.

A little self-conscious still, not yet ready to let Grace know what she was intending to do, Mrs Bridge enrolled in a painting class for adults at an art school near the gallery. She bought a kit which contained some paints and brushes, a palette – she had thought all palettes were of that peculiar ornamental shape and was slightly disappointed to find the one in her kit was plainly rectangular – and a bottle of linseed oil and a bottle of turpentine, along with two metal cups which the clerk told her were to be used for the turpentine and the oil. She also bought a sugar sack for wiping the brushes, and a smock embroidered with bluebirds, and thus equipped she began her art lessons three evenings a week. She attended regularly for almost a month, skipped one night, got to several more, skipped three, attended spasmodically for another month, and finally dropped out altogether. But while she did paint she painted with a certain gusto and feeling, and with not a bad eye. The instructor once or twice gave her nice compliments and encouraged her to continue. He was a morose and rumpled little man of about forty with strong breath and bags under his eyes, who was in the habit of scratching his head and saying, 'Well, let's see, folks, tonight why don't we sort of let ourselves go?'

Occasionally there would be a model in costume, often an elderly immigrant in boots and a kerchief; sometimes they would paint an arrangement of driftwood and wine bottles. But one evening the instructor, whose name was Gadbury, told them to try a subject from mythology and work from imagination. He suggested Wotan as a subject, but added that they might do anything they wished. Mrs Bridge could not recall anything about Wotan, but she did remember with stark clarity the legend of Leda and the swan. She proceeded to paint a small, zinc-white swan and a Leda standing stiffly erect, with hands behind her back and ankle-deep in water because hands and feet always gave her trouble, and she clothed Leda in a flowered dressmaker bathing suit not unlike her own.

Mr Gadbury, making his rounds, stood for a while looking over her shoulder at this Leda and at last he said he thought the lake was too blue.

45 The clock

She spent a great deal of time staring into space, oppressed by the sense that she was waiting. But waiting for what? She did not know. Surely someone would call, someone must be needing her. Yet each day proceeded like the one before. Nothing intense, nothing desperate, ever happened. Time did not move. The home, the city, the nation, and life itself were eternal; still she had a foreboding that one day, without warning and without pity, all the dear, important things would be destroyed. So it was that her thoughts now and then turned deviously deeper, spiraling down and down in search of the final recess, of life more immutable than the life she had bequeathed in the birth of her children.

One fathomless instant occurred on a windy, rainy night when Harriet had gone to church, and the children were out, and only she and her husband remained at home. For some time, perhaps an hour or more, they had been reading, separately; he had the financial page of the newspaper and she had been idly reading of the weddings that day. The rain blew softly against the window-panes, shutters rattled, and above the front door the tin weather stripping began to moan. Mrs Bridge, with the newspaper in her lap, listened to the rumbling and booming of thunder over the house. Suddenly, in total quiet, the room was illuminated by lightning. Mr Bridge lifted his head, only that and nothing more, but within Mrs Bridge something stirred. She looked at her husband intently.

'Did the clock strike?' he asked.

'No, I don't believe so,' she answered, waiting.

He cleared his throat. He adjusted his glasses. He continued reading.

She never forgot this moment when she had almost appre-hended the very meaning of life, and of the stars and planets, yes, and the flight of the earth.

46 Countess Mariska

The one person she ever met who surely had experienced similar moments was a Russian-Italian-Hungarian countess who passed through Kansas City like a leaf in the wind.

'The Countess Mariska Mihailova Strozzi,' was how Lois Montgomery, who was the newly elected president of the Auxiliary, introduced her at luncheon.

'Ladies,' the countess began, and went on talking for an hour, but it was an hour that seemed like a minute. No one whispered, no one left the room. The countess was electrifying, and the women who missed hearing her were told about her for months afterward. She was born in Shanghai, the daughter of an elderly Russian diplomat who, until an intrigue at the court, had been a close friend of Czar Nicholas II. The family had been exiled, there had been murders, abductions, espionage, and no one knew what else. At fourteen she was married to an Italian millionaire who claimed direct descent from the great Renaissance family which opposed the Medici, but she had run away from him. Later she married a rich Greek. Now she was divorced and on her way to San Francisco at the invitation of a munitions maker. She talked of her experiences, but mostly of the Nazis, and there was a rumor that just before coming to America she had killed a Nazi colonel with his own revolver. Mrs Bridge, sitting in the front row, looking up into the glittering violet eyes, could easily believe it.

The countess was quite small and chic, and wore a black sheath dress. Her only jewelry was a large star sapphire that accentuated a strange bluish-white scar across the back of her hand. Mrs Bridge was certain everyone was dying to know what had caused the scar, but no one dared ask. It was only one of the mysteries of the countess. She was delicate and utterly feminine, but at the same she was as blunt as a man. It was clear she had been witness to many kinds of folly and wisdom and agony and joy. Once she paused and leisurely fitted a European cigarette into an ebony holder; several minutes must have gone by while she smoked and stared over the heads of her audience, but they were so transfixed that no one moved. Tamping out the cigarette, she continued in her perfect, heavy English, 'We must destroy the Fascist . . .'

Later Mrs Bridge introduced herself to the countess, for that was what everyone else was doing, and for a minute or so they chatted. Two things Mrs Bridge remembered about her: the first was a fresh red bruise on the tiny golden throat, a bruise such as a man's mouth would leave, and the second was that husky voice murmuring, 'To be afraid is, I tell you, Madame, the most terrible thing in the world.'

47 Tea leaves

Not long after the countess left for San Francisco and the hospitable munitions maker, Mrs Bridge was having lunch on the Plaza with Grace Barron. Grace seemed despondent, and Mrs Bridge, thinking to cheer her up, looked into her tea cup and pretended to be studying the leaves. Laying one finger alongside her nose she said, 'My gypsy blood tells me you—'

'My fortune?' asked Grace absently. 'I know my fortune.'

And then, while Mrs Bridge stared at her in frightened amazement, two large tears came rolling down her cheeks.

48 Liberal

Whether it was in the pattern of the leaves, or in Grace herself, Mrs Bridge could not be sure, but at a cocktail party honoring Mrs Albert Tate, who was packing for a voyage around the world, Grace became unreasonable. The affair was held in the Arlens' new yellow brick Colonial on Shoat Drive and there were over one hundred people present. According to the invitations the party was to be from six till nine-thirty, but at ten o'clock the crowd was as thick as ever, and about that time the word began spreading that Grace Barron was in the basement recreation room having an argument with the host.

'—ethnocentricism, that's what!' Grace was saying just as Mrs Bridge hurried anxiously down the basement steps.

Russ Arlen scowled and muttered. Grace took a long drink from a martini glass and smacked her lips.

'Furthermore,' she announced to the crowd, 'if we go to war again do you know who I accuse? The American press! Scare headlines sell copies. I accuse. Monsieur, j'accuse!'

Andrew Koeppel, who had been congratulated throughout the evening for having bought another hotel, suggested, 'Let me put in a word. A few minutes ago you mentioned some Semite friend of yours who thought a pogrom was as likely in this country as in Germany. Let me tell you: Nazi Germany is the most fascistic nation on the face of this earth, and if your friend doesn't like it here, let her go back. I've fought the Jews for whatever I own and I intend to keep it. My father, mind you, came to this country without a penny in his pocket and by the time he was thirty-six years old—' Here he began a long and rather uninteresting story having to do with pulling up cornstalks for eleven cents a day.

Attention gradually was reverting to Grace when there came shouts from upstairs of 'Fire! Fire!' and everyone crowded the stairway, cocktail glasses in hand. There was indeed a fire, but not in the house. Somehow the back seat of the Ralph Porters' Cadillac had begun to smoulder. An alarm was not turned in for quite a while because everyone assumed someone else had taken care of it, but eventually a fire engine came clanging up Ward Parkway and swerved into Shoat Drive, one of the ladders scratching the fenders of several automobiles, and the firemen broke the window of the Cadillac and began spraying the rear seat. Smoke billowed out while Mrs Porter wept and begged them to stop. The firemen believed a cigarette stub had caused it, but the Beckerle sisters, who had been riding in the back seat, denied this. A few minutes later almost everybody had returned to the house, and Grace was at it again, this time in the library under a full-length portrait of Madge. Mrs Bridge entered the library to hear Grace saying, '—and the Modocs and the Nez Percé! And the Mimbreno Apache, the Teton Sioux, and Custer's deliberate violation of the treaty of eighteen-sixty-eight and—'

'Shrimp, anybody?' It was Madge hurrying in to save the day, followed by her new maid, who was carrying an immense silver platter heaped with hors d'oeuvres.

'I want another drink,' Grace announced. 'And what about the Seminoles? They never harmed us but we invaded their swamps and cut them to ribbons.'

Mrs Bridge felt the discussion to be beyond her depth, but, in hopes of moderating what could turn into an unfortunate scene, she asked hopefully, 'It does sound as though we've done some dreadful things, Grace, but isn't it possible that when you investigate fully you'll discover the Seminoles attacked us?'

The conversation continued for some time, Grace Barron being the center of it all, arguing now against censoring books, now against opening the mail of suspected Fascists and Communists. Once or twice Mrs Bridge attempted to direct the conversation elsewhere, praising the somewhat regal portrait of Madge under which they were standing, and also trying the fire in the Cadillac, but at the very moment she was about to succeed, Grace herself would irritate someone all over again.

There were several echoes of this evening. The very next night someone unbuckled the windshield wipers from the Barrons' automobile, which had been parked on the street in front of their home. The wipers were found in the gutter a few yards away, twisted out of shape.

The scoutmaster of David Barron's troop received an anonymous letter telling him to watch young Barron. The scoutmaster, who had never before gotten such a letter, did not know what to do with it, and being very much agitated he gave it to Dr Foster, who telephoned the police and talked for a long time on various subjects before telling them why he had called. The letter had a postscript demanding to know how many years young Barron had been playing the violin and adding triumphantly that he had not been invited to join a high-school fraternity.

Days passed. It seemed the affair was being forgotten. Then Madge Arlen happened to remark that her husband had switched accounts from Virgil Barron's bank to the Security First.

'Oh, my word!' Mrs Bridge breathed. 'What did Virgil say?'

'Russ told me he didn't open his mouth.' Madge paused to light a cigarette and shake out the match. After inhaling deeply she said, 'We weren't the first to change.'

Mrs Bridge thought for an instant she was going to faint, and even as her head stopped whirling she heard herself remarking in a sympathetic tone, '—suppose it was the best thing.'

49 The private world of Wilhelm and Susan

Quite possibly the only persons unaware of Grace Barron's indiscretion were Wilhelm and Susan Van Metre.

'We chanced to be driving this way,' Wilhelm Van Metre said, having cleared his throat twice in the midst of the remark, 'and I said to Mrs Van Metre, "Susan, as long as we are in this neighborhood it might not be a bad idea to stop for a nice little visit with the Bridges." ' He cleared his throat again. 'I seem to be having some slight difficulty with my vocal apparatus. But at any rate, Susan agreed with me.' He turned to smile at her.

'What a nice surprise!' Mrs Bridge replied. 'Here, let me take your coats.' And going to the bottom of the stairs she called, 'Walter! Guess who's here?' This meant he was to put away his detective magazine or his vacation brochures or whatever he was looking at, and get out of bed and get dressed and come down.

'Now!' she resumed, having gotten them seated and having told

Harriet to fix some tea, 'Now, tell me what's new with you all?'

Wilhelm chuckled and slapped his knee. 'Susan, did you hear India? Now you tell me,' he continued, addressing his wife, 'does anything new or extraordinary ever happen to us? Not much, I'm afraid, not much.' He leaned back and touched his nostrils one after the other as though to prevent himself from sneezing. 'No, not very much, not much.'

It was quite a while before Mr Bridge came downstairs to join the conversation; he had recognized the voices and was in no hurry. Then, for about three hours, they sat in the living room with the pot of tea. Mrs Bridge, who was afraid her husband might walk out of the room and go back to bed, attempted to keep the conversation going; she also tried to get them to play a horse-racing game which was quite popular, and then she suggested cards. Wilhelm had a better idea; he thought he might tackle Mr Bridge for a round of dominoes. However there were no dominoes in the house. Wilhelm suggested chess; there was no chess set. For a moment it looked as though Wilhelm might drive home to get his own chess set. Finally Mrs Bridge got him off this subject. Presently he asked their opinion of the ballet troupe that had just completed an engagement in Kansas City.

'Oh, goodness,' she said quickly, 'now let me see – the ballet – yes, it *was* in town, wasn't it, because Grace Barron called—'

'I found the interpretation of the premier danseur rather too old-fashioned,' said Wilhelm, tapping his fingertips and frowning. 'Although Susan, if memory serves, thought not, especially the *Swan Lake*. We both enjoy *Swan Lake*.' He also inquired if Mrs Bridge agreed with the criticism of Kafka in the latest issue of a literary review.

'I'm afraid I missed that altogether,' she replied. She had never heard of the magazine.

And eventually, inevitably, the conversation turned upon engineering because Wilhelm had been an engineer for thirty years. In spite of his experience, he said, 'I have found it inexpedient to rely on memory. I place my faith in instruments. You may or may not, India, be familiar with the log-log duplex decitrix.' He paused, lifting his bushy white eyebrows.

'I'm afraid I'm not,' she said.

'Well, since you are not an engineer that is excusable,' he said, chuckling. 'But I can tell you that in a tight spot there is nothing to help a man out like the duplex decitrix.'

Mrs Bridge replied that it sounded dreadfully complicated, and later, as they were leaving, said she hoped they would stop by again before long.

50 Sir William and Sir Thomas

The Van Metres had a disconcerting habit of believing what people said. Mrs Bridge, having expressed the hope they would stop by again, forgot about them. Yet two weeks had not passed before they came for another nice little visit. She pretended to be glad to see them. They drank several pots of tea and seemed not to be aware of the long periods of silence. Mrs Bridge desperately tried to prevent silences, and ordinarily she succeeded, but with the Van Metres it was an awful job. She was grateful when either of them began to speak because it gave her a moment to rest and to think of another topic. Susan very seldom had a word to offer; Wilhelm would be lost in thought for half an hour, after which he might take the next half hour to tell an anecdote. On this occasion he took very nearly that long to relate a tale about two sixteenth-century gentlemen: Sir William Roper and the lord chancellor of England whose name was Sir Thomas More. It seems that Sir William came calling on Sir Thomas with a proposal to marry one of his daughters. Sir Thomas, being agreeable to this idea, led Sir William to the bedside of his daughters and whipped off the covers. The two girls were lying on their backs with their smocks up as high as their armpits. They at once rolled over on their bellies. Sir William said, 'I have seen both sides.' He then patted one of the girls on the buttocks, and said, 'Thou art mine.'

'Well,' observed Mrs Bridge the moment the story ended, 'I'm certainly thankful times have changed.'

51 The low-pressure salesman

A few days after this visit with the Van Metres another old acquaintance turned up. Mrs Bridge was in the breakfast room wondering what to do – how to occupy herself till noon – when Harriet entered to say there was a man at the back door.

'What does he want?'

'That's what I asked him, and he wouldn't say.'

'Didn't he give his name?'

'No name,' said Harriet, 'and he looks suspicious.'

Everyone looked suspicious to Harriet. Mrs Bridge, after a moment of thought, got up and walked through the kitchen to the back door. It was snowing outside, and on the back step was a stoop-shouldered little man with a woeful expression who was shivering uncontrollably and stamping his feet. On seeing her he attempted a smile and his mouth formed the word 'Hello'. Mrs Bridge could not think where she had seen him; then she remembered the art instructor in whose evening class she had done some painting. Opening the door, but leaving the glass storm door locked, she said, 'Why, it's Mr Gadbury!' For some reason he did look suspicious, and more lost and defeated than in his studio. He was attempting to speak; his words were inaudible through the storm door. Mrs Bridge, conscious of Harriet's premonition, despite the familiarity of it, was therefore reluctant to let him in.

'Is there anything I can do for you?' she inquired.

A flurry of snow swept over him. He tried once more to smile. He was not a stranger, but on the other hand he was not exactly a friend who had come calling. He did not appear to have been drinking, in spite of his red nose, nor did he look violent; so she disregarded Harriet – who was standing with her arms crossed, emphatically shaking her head – and unlocked the door.

'Won't you step in, Mr Gadbury? It must be cold out there.'

Gadbury stepped in. His teeth were clattering and he walked with difficulty. He looked as though he had been out in the snow for hours. He followed her into the living room with his hat in his hands, glancing behind to see if he was leaving tracks on the carpet, and he was. She invited him to sit down. He did so, and finding no place to put his wet hat he hung it on his knee. He shivered constantly. He had turned a mottled yellow and grayish-blue color like a piece of sausage that had been in the refrigerator for several weeks, with the exception of his moist red nose. He twitched and jerked and did not seem to be breathing. He made no attempt to speak. His chin was tucked into his collar, his knees knocked together, and his feet occasionally sprang off the floor of their own accord.

Mrs Bridge, having observed him, said, 'I'm going to have Harriet fix you some hot tea.' She got up and walked across the room to the bell pull. The bell pull was a strip of material about eight feet long, resembling a sample of Persian rug, which was suspended from a lever near the ceiling. It hung down against the wall alongside the highboy. It was actually simpler to step into the kitchen and speak directly to Harriet, but whenever there were guests Mrs Bridge used the bell pull. She took hold of it about two feet from the bottom and gave a slow, gentle tug; she could never quite get over the feeling that someday when the room was full of people she would pull it and it would fall down around her neck like a Catholic chasuble. Presently Harriet appeared, looking overly insouciant, as though she suspected an intrigue.

'I believe we would like some tea,' said Mrs Bridge.

She then returned to her chair and waited for Mr Gadbury to speak, but he made no effort to do so. He continued to twitch and shiver. She heartily wished he would think of some way to stop his teeth from chattering.

Finding that she was observing him, Gadbury drew a handker-chief from the pocket of his coat and weakly blew his nose, and said, 'I'm pretty cold.'

'I'm sure you must be,' replied Mrs Bridge. 'The paper says it got down to zero at six o'clock this morning.'

Harriet appeared wheeling the cart. She rolled it to a stop in front of Mrs Bridge, who then poured out the tea. Harriet delivered a cup to Gadbury, who drank it at once and who then looked very hopefully and earnestly at the cart where the silver tea pot stood.

'Would you care for another cup, Mr Gadbury?'

He said that would be nice, so he had another, and before long he had another.

'How's the painting coming along?' he asked.

'I haven't had a spare moment in weeks, Mr Gadbury.'

'I sure remember that malachite sherry bottle,' he said. There was a pause. 'You really let yourself go on that one.'

Mrs Bridge smiled courteously. She waited for him to state his business. Gadbury stared around the room. He began to squint at an etching of a cathedral that occupied the space above the sofa. No one in the family had looked at it for years.

'I don't know about that,' Gadbury said, studying it intently. 'Maybe, but then again maybe not. There's a quality, all right.' He discovered the water which had been dripping on the carpet from his hat and his coat, and nervously placed his foot on a soggy spot. At length he became aware that she was waiting for him to explain the visit, so he worked out of his pocket a crumpled little magazine which was titled *The Doberman*, and he held this up for her to see.

'Oh?' said Mrs Bridge.

'I don't guess you or Mr Bridge'd be much interested in subscribing to this, would you?'

She had suspected he was selling something, and she knew that whatever it might be she would have no use for it.

'I really hadn't planned on subscribing to any more magazines, Mr Gadbury.'

He nodded in complete understanding. 'You wouldn't want it unless you had a Doberman.' Then an idea came to him and he sat erect and asked, 'You don't have one, do you?'

'No, we don't.'

'Nobody does,' he said despondently. 'They eat an awful lot, I think.'

'Oh? Don't you have one?'

'No. But when I was a boy I used to have a dog.' He looked to see if this fact would arouse her interest. Finding it did not, after wiping his nose on his sleeve, he considered his magazine and launched into a sales talk. 'This issue tells about one who wouldn't eat anything except sirloin steak and worked for the police department in Toledo.' He mulled over this information and added pertinently, 'Its name was Lieutenant.' Suddenly he opened the magazine to the center spread, which had snapshots of nine Dobermans, and he held this up for her to see.

'My, they're ferocious looking, aren't they?'

Gadbury then had another look at the photographs. 'I guess so. I hadn't thought about it.'

Mrs Bridge tipped her head slightly to indicate she was considering the pictures further. Gadbury became enthusiastic.

'This magazine comes out every month,' he said. He was overtaken by a chill; he shivered, sniffled, stamped his feet, and looked around wildly. 'It tells how you train these dogs,' he said, speaking with great rapidity, 'and, ah, eeehe-he-ahha-*sha*!' sneezed Mr Gadbury. 'I've got a cold,' he said feebly, and then the life went out of him and he sat with his head bowed, silent, while a few more drops of water sank into the carpet. 'It isn't that the school doesn't pay a living wage,' he went on without lifting his head. 'It's just that my daughter got in trouble and now she's in the hospital. I didn't know hospital bills were so high.' He rolled the magazine into a tube and began striking it against his palm.

'Do you sell many subscriptions?'

Gadbury made no attempt to answer.

'How long have you been at it?' she asked.

'About two months,' he said quietly.

Mrs Bridge took a deep breath and clasped her hands. 'Tell me, Mr Gadbury, tell me the truth. Have you sold any at all?'

'No. But there was a lady the week before last who said she'd ask her husband.'

'All right,' said Mrs Bridge. 'You may put me down for a subscription.'

Gadbury raised his head and looked at her in grave astonishment.

52 Second lesson in Spanish

While cleaning out the back-hall closet she came upon the phonograph records and the booklet on how to speak Spanish. The records were covered with dust and one of them was broken. On an impulse she let the closet remain as it was; she carried the records into the living room and placed the unbroken ones on the phonograph. Then she seated herself with the booklet to refresh her memory, and finding that she could recall the procedure with no difficulty she set the needle on the first record.

'Buenos días, Señora Brown. Cómo está usted?'

'Buenos días, Señor Carreño. Muy bien, gracias. Y usted?'

At the pause she was ready. 'Buenos días, Señor Carreño,' she said pleasantly. 'Muy bien, gracias. Y usted?'

'Muy bien.'

The record squeaked and clicked, clicked again, and continued. Señor Carreño remarked that Señora Brown was in Madrid. Señora Brown evidently realized this.

'Estoy en Madrid.'

'Estoy en Madrid,' Mrs Bridge repeated.

From upstairs Carolyn called, 'Mother!'

'What is it, dear?' Mrs Bridge called.

'La gusta Madrid?'

'Sí, mucho.'

'*Mother*!'

With a sigh Mrs Bridge got up and walked to the bottom of the stairs. 'What is it, Corky? I'm busy right now.'

'I can't find my saddle shoes.'

Mrs Bridge returned to the living room, turned off the phonograph, and came back to stand with one hand on the newel post. 'I couldn't hear you, dear. What did you say?'

'What happened to my saddle shoes? I left them out for Harriet to clean but they aren't here.'

Mrs Bridge began climbing the stairs, because there was bound to be an argument and she did not like shouting back and forth. 'I gave them to the laundress. They were simply too filthy to be worn.'

Carolyn moaned and rocked on her heels, this being the current method of expressing agony. 'What am I going to wear to the mixer?'

Mrs Bridge had stopped to catch her breath on the landing. Now she continued around the turn and up the remaining steps.

'Well, dear, you certainly can't wear saddle shoes to a dance.'

Carolyn spoke slowly and distinctly. 'It isn't a dance, Mother, it's a mixer. It's in the gymnasium after school.'

'I thought you danced at a mixer.'

'You do, but it's different. Totally.' Carolyn was rocking on her heels again. 'I mean, it's already practically the end of my free period and I've got to get back for Latin and obviously you don't expect a person to wear these Indian skins even if it is a mixer. Fortunately.' She held out one small moccasined foot and wiggled the toe.

'I should think you'd want to wear your new brown oxfords. They certainly cost enough.'

'Oh, ugh! I mean, you're so behind.'

'I suppose so,' Mrs Bridge responded drily. 'But I'll thank you not to be impertinent.'

'Oh, I'm sorry, Mother, but after all this is utterly tragic. I mean, let's not be bland.'

'Well, let's see, I suppose the only solution is to drive to the Plaza and get you a new pair of saddle shoes.'

'There isn't time! I mean I have this pathetic Latin!'

'Oh, dear,' said Mrs Bridge wearily, for it seemed such problems were always rising. 'I'm supposed to pick up Madge Arlen at two o'clock, but I suppose if you must have them I can run down to the Plaza right now and deliver them to you at school. I honestly believe half my life has been spent arranging the family schedule.'

Carolyn, who did not want anyone to see her mother delivering a pair of shoes, said, 'Just leave them in the principal's office.'

53 Servant's entrance

Everyone made use of the back door whenever it was convenient, but Douglas seemed to prefer it – she had noticed that when he came home from school, although approaching the house from the front, he was apt to go all the way around and come in through the back. From the window of her sewing room upstairs she had seen him do this. She was distressed by his habit because it was customary for members of the family and guests to enter and leave by the front, the back door being used principally by the laundress and the various delivery boys, and by Harriet.

One day at lunch, unable to stand it any longer, she abruptly asked, 'Do you have back-door-itis?'

Douglas had just started eating chipped beef; he lowered his knife and fork and gazed at her in stupefaction.

'You need another haircut,' she said automatically, noticing how shaggy he looked. 'And take that pencil from behind your ear. People will think you're a grocery clerk.'

'What?' said Douglas, blinking.

'What on earth possesses you to always use the back door?'

'I don't know,' said Douglas.

'Well, then,' said Mrs Bridge, 'why don't you do like everyone else?'

Douglas appeared to be thinking this over. Finally he said in the same vacuous tone, 'I don't know.'

'Well,' said Mrs Bridge, 'as long as we have a front door we might as well use it.'

Douglas said he guessed that was right, but he did not sound convinced.

54 Rumpy

There was no end to the problems of adolescence. Carolyn was beginning to blossom, not only in front but in back, and as she had gotten into the habit of walking with her spine unnecessarily arched she soon became known among the high school boys as 'Rumpy'. One of these boys, calling for the first time at her home, absently referred to her by that name. The next day Mrs Bridge, who was crocheting a nice muffler in case anybody wanted one, asked her about the name.

'That's nothing. You should hear what they call Ruth,' said Carolyn.

Mrs Bridge resumed crocheting with a displeased expression.

55 The Chrysler and the comb

Mrs Bridge, emptying wastebaskets, discovered a dirty comb in Ruth's basket.

'What's this doing here?' Ruth inquired late that afternoon when she got home and found the comb on her dresser.

'I found it in the wastebasket. What was it doing *there*?'

Ruth said she had thrown it away.

'Do you think we're made of money?' Mrs Bridge demanded. 'When a comb gets dirty you don't throw it away, you wash it, young lady.'

'It cost a nickel,' Ruth said angrily. She flung her books onto the bed and stripped off her sweater.

'Nickels don't grow on trees,' replied Mrs Bridge, irritated by her manner.

'Nickels don't grow on trees,' Ruth echoed. She was standing by the window with her hands on her hips; now, exasperated, she pointed to her father's new Chrysler, which was just then turning into the driveway.

'Put the comb in a basin of warm water with a little ammonia and let it soak,' Mrs Bridge went on. 'In a few minutes you can rinse the—'

'I know, I know, I know!' Ruth unzipped her skirt, stepped out of it, and threw it at the closet. She sat down on her bed and began to file her nails.

'So is a nickel going to break us up?' she asked, scowling.

'I wash my comb and I expect you to do the same. It won't hurt either of us,' replied Mrs Bridge. 'Taking out without putting in will soon reach bottom,' she added and left the room, shutting the door behind her.

For a few minutes Ruth sat on the bed quietly filing her nails and chewing her lower lip; then she snatched the comb and broke it in half.

56 No Evangelism

Christianity meant nothing to Ruth, at least so far as Mrs Bridge could determine. Ruth went to church reluctantly, sullen and uncommunicative, until she was old enough to defy her mother, knowing her father did not care if she went or not; and when Mrs Bridge pleaded with her, saying, 'Goodness, anyone would think you were a South Sea Islander!' Ruth only sighed and murmured, 'Mother, let me be.'

Douglas reacted quite differently; he objected strenuously when he was a small boy, but later, discovering the church had a basketball team in which he might play if he attended with reasonable regularity, he became more manageable.

Carolyn was no trouble at all. As a child she seemed to enjoy Sunday school, and when she was fourteen she joined the choir. Before long she was reading her Bible at home during the week and, on Sundays, listening quite attentively to the mellow sermons of Dr Foster. She also joined the Wednesday evening group of teenagers who met in the church basement.

Mrs Bridge customarily drove Carolyn to these Wednesday evening meetings and allowed one of the older boys or girls to bring her home. She felt a deep sense of pleasure, a pleasure that bordered on real happiness, whenever she thought of Carolyn's participation. She herself had never grown as close to the church as she would have liked, though she did not know quite why, and in consequence she blamed herself for Ruth's failure, and, to a lesser extent, for the fact that if it were not for the basketball team Douglas would drop out. Mrs Bridge felt proud and reassured each Wednesday evening. There, on the church steps, she beheld a group of nicely dressed, clean, smiling, courteous young people. Invariably they appeared cheerful and confident. Surely, these faces told her, no evil can befall us. Surely, she thought, none would.

The choir, the Sunday sermons, the Wednesday evening group – all this failed to satisfy Carolyn's appetite for religious experience. She became insatiable. She spent hours reading the Bible; she read the Apocrypha; she had long talks with Dr Foster. It was not enough. One evening she told her mother she intended to join a group of evangelists.

Mrs Bridge immediately saw eight or ten lower-middle-class people on a downtown street corner, the women in bonnets and dark shapeless gowns and the men somehow reminding her of Mr Schumann, who led the high-school band. Tubas in the rain, a tambourine being passed around – she had always looked upon these people with a mixture of pity and respect, and, if she could not avoid the tambourine, she put a quarter in it.

'Well,' she said, 'it's an awfully nice idea, of course. I just wonder if you'd be happy doing it. Let's see what your father says.'

97

Mr Bridge came home about nine o'clock. His briefcase was packed and he was harassed and short-tempered; he told Harriet to fix him a sandwich and some coffee and bring it into his study. Carolyn knew it was a poor moment to announce her decision, but she was too thrilled to wait.

'Nonsense,' he told her when she stopped him on the stairs. 'You'll continue with your schooling. I've already put in your application at the university.'

That ended the matter. Carolyn was enraged, but, like every other member of the family, with the possible exception of Ruth, who seemed unafraid of him, she did not dare argue.

Mrs Bridge sympathized with Carolyn, putting an arm around her waist and saying gently, 'I expect Dad knows best. But you're an awfully sweet person, Corky, to think of an idea like that.'

57 Chaperon

The telephone rang and it was Naomi Gattenberger, the fattest girl in the high school. She always wore a briliant red coat that hung down to her ankles and a pair of shell-rimmed glasses studded with rhinestones. Her father had recently made a fortune in the used-car business.

'How are you, Naomi?' Mrs Bridge asked.

'Just fine,' said Naomi.

'I saw your mother the other day.'

'That's what she said.'

As this exhausted their common interests, Mrs Bridge said, 'I'll see if Corky's home yet.' She put down the receiver and went to look, but Carolyn had not returned from having her hair set.

'I didn't want to talk to her anyway,' said Naomi. 'I'm chairman of the Activities Committee for the sorority dance and we decided on you for one of the chaperons.'

'Why, how nice! This is quite a surprise.'

Naomi guessed maybe it was a surprise.

'Well – when is the dance to be?' Mrs Bridge stalled.

'Two weeks from Friday from eight o'clock to twelve-thirty in the Elbow Room.'

Still fighting for time to set up her defenses Mrs Bridge asked about the Elbow Room.

'It's downtown. It used to be a pool hall, I think, only they took out the pool tables.' There was a pause. Naomi added hopefully, 'Lots of fraternities have parties there, I think.'

'It's very nice, I'm sure.'

Naomi guessed probably it was.

Another pause ensued, a longer one, during which Mrs Bridge could hear Naomi breathing. Obviously the question had already been put and some kind of an answer was expected.

'Well, just a minute, Naomi, I'll see if we're busy that evening.' She slid the tabulator of her plastic engagement book to the proper date and pressed: up popped the cover and Mrs Bridge found, to her dismay, that nothing was planned.

'I sure do hope you can do it,' Naomi said miserably. 'I already called up almost all the mothers.'

Mrs Bridge was a bit disconcerted by this confession, but she was touched by Naomi's despair. Then, too, Carolyn had been a sorority member for more than a year and during this time Mrs Bridge had not been called upon to serve as a chaperon at any of the parties, so she said, 'That'll be grand, Naomi. I'll make a note of it right now.' And while jotting it down she asked, 'What sort of decorations are you planning?'

Naomi said they hadn't gotten a majority vote on anything, but probably it would be a Hawaiian party.

'Well, you have lots of time. I'm sure it will be exciting.'

Naomi sounded despondent. 'I sure do hope so.'

This seemed to conclude their business, so, after a pause, Mrs Bridge said, 'I'll tell Carolyn you called.'

'She knows.'

'Oh! Well, thank you for asking me, Naomi. I'm flattered.'

'You're welcome,' said Naomi phlegmatically. 'Well, good-by.'

Mrs Bridge replaced the receiver and murmured, 'Oh, dear!' for it sounded like a dull evening.

The Elbow Room was decorated with Chinese lanterns hung from the ceiling and with hundreds of yards of crepe paper lividly criss-crossing the windows, framing the doors, and connecting the lanterns. Mrs Bridge, who was quite sensitive to odors, was certain the moment she entered that it had indeed been used as a pool hall, if not worse. The orchestra consisted of a piano, a complicated arrangement of drums, a bass viol, and five saxophones, all played by high-school boys. There was a girl about thirteen years old on the stage; she was wrapped as tight as a mummy in a piece of flowered silk and it was evident she intended to sing. Mrs Bridge, surveying this scene, found there were three other chaperons, two of them high-school teachers of whom she had heard a great deal and whose photographs Carolyn had pointed out to her in the school yearbook, and a swarthy young man named De Falla who was the father of one of the sorority girls.

The first half of the evening moved along smoothly enough; Mrs Bridge thought the orchestra played remarkably well, considering, and the dancers – some of them at least – looked as though they had been accustomed to this sort of thing for years. The boys in the stag line stood around with their hands in their pockets and did a great deal of staring and whispering. Later in the evening a fight broke out near the punch bowl, and shortly after this two boys in tuxedos began burning holes in a lantern with their cigarettes and had to be warned by Mr De Falla that if they did it again they would have to leave. Naomi was there in white taffeta, enormous, alone, and wretched; Mrs Bridge smiled to her and talked with her occasionally and wondered if, as a chaperon, she could flatly order one of the stags to dance with Naomi. She had a feeling there would be trouble if she attempted this.

Carolyn danced by every few minutes; Mrs Bridge waved and smiled and during the evening was introduced to a number of boys. Mr De Falla asked her to dance, and though she did not want to she felt it might look rude if she refused. He danced with a rather wild, swooping motion, but otherwise proved to be more cultured than she had expected and she found herself half-hoping he would ask for another dance. But he did not; when the music ended he escorted her back to her chair and resumed talking to the female mathematics teacher, who was wearing a low-cut gray satin gown, with a gardenia looking quite mashed in the crevice.

About eleven o'clock a game of dice was discovered in the cloakroom by Mr De Falla, because the sentinel was at the punch bowl, and the gamblers were dismissed from the party. Beyond this there were no incidents until shortly after midnight. This last affair was witnessed by Mrs Bridge alone. She never mentioned it to anyone.

She had been sitting quietly, partly concealed by the piano, for quite a while when she noticed a couple dancing in the corner where the lantern had burned out. Their motions were definitely erotic, though in time to the music. In a lesser degree such dancing had been evident throughout the evening, modern dancing being more suggestive than the dancing of Mrs Bridge's youth; but, because the other chaperons had taken it all without comment, she had not objected. This couple, however, thinking themselves un-observed in the darkened corner, were consciously beyond the limit: Mrs Bridge knew it immediately from the girl's apprehensive eyes. The boy was dancing, shuffling, insinuating himself, with his eyes closed and his nose thrust into the flower she wore in her hair, and on his pimpled face lay a sleepy smile. The girl, too, was dreamily smiling, though she remained alert. Mrs Bridge leaned forward in her chair and attracted the girl's attention; instantly the couple broke apart and went dancing rapidly to the other end of the room and on out the door. She saw them both look back to see if she had gotten up and was coming after them. She never saw them again and never learned who they were. She did not ask. This was the thing she remembered longest and most vividly about the sorority party, and the thing that caused her to look more carefully at the boys who came by the house for Carolyn. The horrifying part of it had been that the girl's back was turned to her partner.

58 Good night

Carolyn was dating a clumsy, bumptious boy with crew-cut hair and an idiotic laugh whose name was Jay Duchesne, and about whom Mrs Bridge had her doubts. Duchesne chewed gum with awful assurance and reputedly drove too fast, but because she wanted Carolyn to learn to judge people she said nothing, always greeting Duchesne with a neutral smile and saying, 'Good evening, Jay. Won't you have a chair? Carolyn will be down in a few minutes.'

'Why not?' Duchesne would answer, and after shaking his own

hand in congratulation he would sit and twirl his hat on his index finger and chew gum with a loud snapping noise.

Until Carolyn got in at night Mrs Bridge would lie awake or would sit up reading. Carolyn knew this and consequently talked to Duchesne in very low tones at the front door; Mrs Bridge could hear them murmuring because their voices carried much farther in the still night air than they realized. One evening, after they had been saying good night at the door for about an hour, she heard the next-door neighbor's fox terrier – which was often left out over-night – begin to growl, and she concluded that Duchesne must be molesting Carolyn. Throwing back the covers she hurriedly pulled on her robe and went to the banister, prepared to call out, but at that moment a cat hissed; with a sigh of relief Mrs Bridge prepared to go back to bed. Then, however, she heard Duchesne ask Carolyn for a kiss.

'You're frequently mad,' Carolyn responded.

'Nobody'll find out,' Duchesne answered.

'You're an ogre,' said Carolyn.

Duchesne didn't think that was a good reason.

'Then, because,' said Carolyn.

'Why, because?' inquired Duchesne.

'Because, that's why.'

'Because why?'

After this had gone on for several minutes Carolyn said her mother wouldn't approve. Duchesne apparently was thinking this over because his chewing gum snapped incessantly; then he muttered something Mrs Bridge could not hear.

'But of course not!' Carolyn sounded shocked. 'Are you mad?'

'Aw, why not?' Duchesne bleated. 'Don't be a duchess.'

In a very superior tone, then, Carolyn said distinctly, 'Because, that's all. We won't discuss it any further. And besides, don't be excruciating.'

Duchesne, sounding uncommonly like a musical saw, was heard to say, 'Awwwww, awwwww, jeez!'

'I feel terribly sorry for you,' Carolyn said with unnatural compassion. 'I'd like to, you know. Really, *really* I would, don't you know? So terribly, terribly much, you mad child. Because you're good,' she said earnestly, '*Good*!' And Mrs Bridge, puzzled, tried to recall that particular inflection because it did sound familiar. She wondered if Carolyn was running her fingers through Duchesne's hair, or, considering how short it was, over the top. He was working on the chewing gum again. Mrs Bridge sensed that Carolyn had him on the defensive.

'I am fond of you, Jay. Dreadfully so. I ache, actually. But – but—'

'Listen, Cork,' growled Duchesne, man of action, and his big feet scraped on the doorsill. 'You want to be a virgin forever?'

'Silly!' said Carolyn.

Mrs Bridge, clutching the banister in horror, was gathering strength to speak out when the door bumped shut and Carolyn sighed, clearly alone. A moment later the engine roared and the tires squealed out of the driveway. Carolyn went into the kitchen. Mrs Bridge, folding her robe more tightly, stood in the upper hall trying to regain her composure. If anyone had asked her such a question she was positive she would have slapped the boy with all her strength, but a moment afterward she thought of the night some twenty years ago when she had barely resisted the pleas of a boy whose very name she had long since forgotten. It was the moonlight that had weakened her, the moonlight and her own desire.

'Carolyn?' she called very softly through the silent house.

The refrigerator door closed. Carolyn walked into the downstairs hall and gazed upward.

'Are you all right, dear?'

'Natch.'

'Did you have a good time?'

'So-so.'

'That's nice,' Mrs Bridge said absently, drew the robe more tightly around herself, and started back to bed.

'Mother?'

'Yes, dear?'

'We're all out of peanut butter.'

'Oh, thank God!' whispered Mrs Bridge. Aloud, softly so as not to waken her husband, she called, 'I'll tell Harriet to order some in the morning. Don't stay up too late.'

59 Suitor

When Harriet, who was at times inclined to insubordination, brought in the breakfast tray Mrs Bridge exclaimed, 'For Heaven's sake! What on earth happened to you?'

'Couperin,' said Harriet, grinning.

'Oh, goodness! Is he the one with the motorcycle?'

'No, ma'am,' said Harriet vehemently. 'I took my last ride on a motorcycle, believe me. Approximately eight or ten weeks back.' She began to feel tenderly about her jaw, on which there was a large purple bruise.

'I certainly hope this was an accident,' said Mrs Bridge.

'It came about,' Harriet replied with regal poise, 'because only last evening it so happened that I and that Couperin had a grave dispute. Couperin, he got the worst.'

The evidence seemed to indicate Couperin had spoken the final word, but Mrs Bridge decided not to get involved.

'What does he do?' she inquired, to change the subject.

'He is associated with the collection bureau of this city.'

'Tax collectors, or—'

'Bureau of rubbish and trash. Then, too, he plumbs a bit. When he is inclined.'

Mrs Bridge, beginning to sense this would be one of Harriet's insolent days, sipped at the orange juice and then started to butter a slice of toast.

'Last evening,' Harriet continued, wetting a finger and touching up her eyebrows, 'I received this proposition.'

This obviously demanded some sort of acknowledgment, even though Couperin or one of the other suitors proposed every Thursday night. What jarred Mrs Bridge as much as anything was Harriet's referring to it as a proposition instead of a proposal, and every Friday when the subject was mentioned she was about to point out the difference.

'I hope you didn't accept,' she said, pouring some cream in the coffee.

'Frankly, I was tempted,' said Harriet. 'However I declined, as you say. The reason being he chooses to get disgustingly drunk following on the heels of his pay check. I disapprove of that, don't you?'

'I most certainly do,' agreed Mrs Bridge, busying herself at the table somewhat more than necessary. Then, as Harriet appeared to be reflecting on the previous evening, she said, 'Isn't that a new hair-do?'

'Well, it is, yes.' Harriet pushed it lightly with her fingertips. 'I believe it will prove suitable.'

'You look very chic.'

'Well, I find it pays to keep up appearances.'

Mrs Bridge had the feeling she was about to pull out a cigarette. 'Perhaps you'd better look in the refrigerator and see if we're going to have enough whipping cream for the week end.'

Harriet, holding her bruised jaw, turned to go into the kitchen.

Mrs Bridge, who was very thankful that Carolyn had no Couperin to contend with, said, 'I hope you won't be seeing him any more.'

'I believe not until next week on the customary evening,' replied Harriet.

60 Ingrid

Every Wednesday the laundress arrived, and as the bus line was quite a few blocks distant from the Bridge home someone would usually meet her bus in the morning. For years the laundress had been a withered old colored woman named Beulah Mae, who wore a red bandanna, a ragged velvet dress split at the seams, and a pair of tennis shoes with the toes cut out because her feet hurt. Mrs Bridge was very fond of Beulah Mae, speaking of her as 'a nice old soul' and frequently giving her extra money or an evening dress that had begun to look dated, or perhaps the cookies that she was obliged to buy from the Girl Scouts. But there came a day when Beulah Mae had had enough of laundering, extra gifts or no, and without a word to any of her clients she boarded a bus for California to live out her time on the seashore. Mrs Bridge was therefore without a laundress for an interval of several weeks, during which the work was taken to an establishment, but at last she got someone else, an extremely large, doleful Swedish woman named Ingrid, who said while being interviewed in the kitchen that for eighteen years she had been a masseuse on the island of Gotland and wished she had stayed there.

When Mrs Bridge arrived at the bus line the first morning Ingrid saluted her mournfully and got laboriously into the front seat. This was not the custom, but such a thing was difficult to explain because Mrs Bridge did not like to hurt anyone's feelings, so she said nothing about it and hoped that by next week some other laundress in the neighborhood would have told Ingrid.

But the next week she again climbed in front, and again Mrs Bridge pretended everything was satisfactory. However, on the third morning while they were riding up Ward Parkway toward the house Mrs Bridge said, 'I was so attached to Beulah Mae. She used to have the biggest old time riding in the back seat.'

Ingrid turned a massive yellow head to look stonily down on Mrs Bridge. As they were easing into the driveway she spoke. 'So you want I should sit in the back.'

'Oh, gracious! I didn't mean that,' Mrs Bridge answered, smiling up at her. 'You're perfectly welcome to sit right here if you like.'

Ingrid said no more about the matter and next week with the same majestic melancholy rode in the rear.

61 Parking

The elegant Lincoln her husband had given her for her birthday was altogether too long, and she drove it as prudently as she might have driven a locomotive. People were always sounding their horns at her, or turning their heads to stare when she coasted by. Because the Lincoln had been set to idle too slowly, the engine frequently died when she pulled up at an intersection, but as her husband never used the Lincoln and she herself assumed it was just one of those things about automobiles, the idling speed was never adjusted. Often she would delay a line of cars while she pressed the starter button either too long or not long enough.

Knowing she was not expert she was always quite apologetic when something unfortunate happened, and did her best to keep out of everyone's way. She shifted into second gear at the beginning of every hill and let herself down the far side much more slowly than necessary.

Usually she parked in a downtown garage where Mr Bridge rented a stall for her. She had only to honk at the doors, which would soon trundle open, after which she coasted inside, where an attendant would greet her by name, help her out, and then park the formidable machine. But in the country-club district she parked on the street, and if there were diagonal stripes she did very well, but if parking was parallel she had trouble judging her distance from the curb and would have to get out and walk around to look, then get back in and try again. The Lincoln's cushions were so soft and Mrs Bridge so short that she was obliged to sit erect in order to see whatever was going on ahead of her. She drove with arms thrust forward and gloved hands firmly on the wheel, her feet just able to depress the pedals. She never had serious accidents, but was often seen here and there being talked to by patrolmen. These patrolmen never did anything, partly because they saw immediately that it would not do to arrest her, and partly because they could tell she was trying to do everything the way it should be done.

When parking on the street it embarrassed her to have people watch, yet there always seemed to be someone at the bus stop or lounging in a doorway with nothing to do but stare while she struggled with the wheel and started jerkily backward. Sometimes, however, there would be a nice man who, seeing her difficulty, would come around and tip his hat and ask if he might help.

'Would you, please?' she would ask in relief, and after he opened the door she would get out and wait on the curb with an attentive expression while he parked the car. It was then a problem to know whether he expected a tip or not. She knew that people who stood around on street corners did not have much money; still she did not want to offend anyone. Sometimes she would hesitantly ask, sometimes not, and whether the man would accept a quarter or not she would smile brightly up at him, saying, 'Thank you so much,' and having locked the Lincoln's doors she would be off to the shops.

62 News of the Leacocks

She gasped when she saw the evening paper. On the front page was a picture of Tarquin Leacock taken a few minutes after he had been captured. The Leacocks had moved away from Kansas City about two years ago and no one had heard anything from them since that time. Every once in a while someone would ask what had become of them, for they had been such a remarkable family that it seemed they must be making news wherever they were. Now indeed they were.

'I saw it,' Mr Bridge said when he got home that night. He had been working late again; it was nearly midnight when his Chrysler turned in the driveway, but she had waited up.

'I simply can't believe it,' she said.

'I can,' said Mr Bridge as he took off his overcoat. 'You remember I warned you about that kid.'

'Oh, yes, I know,' she said faintly, 'but this!'

He hung his coat in the closet, placed his Homburg atop the briefcase and returned to the living room, where he glanced with no particular interest at the picture of Tarquin, who had developed into a surly, hulking youth.

'Well,' said Mr Bridge quietly, and tapped the newspaper with his index finger, 'I am sorry about this, but on the other hand those people had no one to blame but themselves. This doesn't surprise me in the least. They should have taught that youngster there are other people in the world besides himself.' He shook his head and took off his glasses, as he did whenever he was exhausted. 'It gets worse every day. These psychologists have bluffed parents into thinking nothing is more important than a child's right to assert himself. Lord knows where it will end. But I'll tell you this: Douglas is going to learn he's not the supreme authority. His personality can go to pot, so far as that's concerned, but my son is not going to run around pulling stunts like this!'

With which Mr Bridge again tapped the paper, significantly, and headed for the kitchen. Mrs Bridge followed him and began to warm the supper that Harriet had prepared and covered with oil paper and left on the drainboard, for it was Thursday night and she had stepped out with Couperin.

'Really, it just makes me ill to think about it,' Mrs Bridge said, and she lighted the oven and placed his supper in to warm.

'Society gets the crime it deserves,' Mr Bridge remarked with indifference. 'I'll never forget that kid calling his parents by their first names.'

'No, I don't approve of that either,' she said.

Tarquin, having had a bellyful of psychology, or, perhaps, only feeling unusually progressive, had entered the bedroom of his parents while they were asleep and had shot them dead.

63 The hat

Tarquin Leacock preyed on her mind and she therefore took to observing her son more closely, wondering if he, too, might unexpectedly go berserk. He was now in high school, and so far as she could tell he was less of an Apache than most of his companions, for which she was grateful, but he did become unpredictable, given to fits of introspection during which he dressed quite formally and stalked about with hands behind his back, followed by a grandiose kind of good-fellowship, and it was in this latter mood that the battle of the hat took place.

She was of the opinion that at certain ages one wore certain articles of clothing – each of the girls had received a girdle on their fourteenth birthday – and she now suggested to Douglas that he was old enough to begin wearing a hat.

'I don't need a hat,' he said.

'It's time you started wearing one,' she replied.

'They don't feel good on my head,' said Douglas.

'Your father would look awfully silly without a hat,' she argued.

'Who knows?' he countered, flinging up his hands.

So it went for a period of several weeks until finally they drove downtown and picked out a hat, a very nice conservative hat. She never expected to see it on his head, but strangely enough he began to wear it everywhere. He wore it to school and while playing ball after school, and he wore it around the house and in his room at night while doing homework. Very shortly she was sick of seeing the hat, but now he would not think of going anywhere without it. Furthermore there developed, somewhere between high school and the drug-store where he played the pinball games, the habit of wearing it on the back of his head; not only this but on the crown he pinned a glazed yellow button saying: LET'S GET ACQUAINTED!

64 First babies

That summer the family was invited to the wedding of a relative named Maxwell who was a postal clerk in the nearby town of Olathe. Carolyn was the only one who wanted to attend the wedding, but because it was an obligation of sorts the entire family – except Mr Bridge – drove to Olathe. When the bride came down the aisle they discovered the reason for the wedding.

After the ceremony they put in an appearance at the reception and then, in silence, drove home.

About three months later they received the traditional announcement concerning the birth of a child. It happened that Ruth, Carolyn, and Douglas were at home when this announcement arrived, and Mrs Bridge, having exclaimed, in spite of her disgust, 'Isn't that nice!' felt it necessary to add, 'First babies are so often premature.'

At this time Ruth was eighteen years old, Carolyn was sixteen, and Douglas, nobody's fool, a shrewd fourteen. A profound silence, a massive, annihilating silence, greeted her remark. Carolyn gazed out the window. Douglas became greatly interested in his fingernails. Ruth looked at Carolyn, then at Douglas, and she seemed to be considering. Finally she said quietly, 'Oh, Mother, don't.'

None of them said anything further. The Maxwells were not mentioned again.

65 Who's calling?

She was kneeling in the garden with a trowel in her hand when Harriet lifted the kitchen window to announce that some man who would not give his name was on the telephone asking for Ruth.

'I'll take it,' Mrs Bridge said, getting to her feet. She entered the house and approached the telephone with a feeling of hostility, and taking up the receiver more firmly than usual she said, 'Hello, Ruth is not in Kansas City at the moment. Who's calling, please?'

'Where's she at?' a deep voice asked.

Mrs Bridge signaled Harriet to stop running the vacuum cleaner.

'Ruth is visiting friends at Lake Lotawana. Who is calling, please?'

'What's the number out there?' the man demanded.

Despite his rudeness and obvious coarseness, if he had been inquiring about Carolyn she would have given him the number at the lake, but she had never liked or trusted the men who came after Ruth.

'I'm certain she would like to know who called.'

There was a pause. Mrs Bridge thought he was going to hang up, but he finally answered, 'Tell her Al called.' Then he added, 'Al Luchek.' And faintly, from wherever he was, came the clink of glasses.

For some reason Ruth's friends always had foreign names. Carolyn's companions were named Bob or Janet or Trudy or Buzz, but there was a malignant sound to Al Luchek, and to the others – the Louie Minillos and the Nick Gajadas. They sounded like gangsters from the north end. Mrs Bridge had once or twice asked Ruth who they were, and how she met them, but Ruth replied evasively that she had simply met them at So-and-so's house or at a New Year's Eve party.

'But what do they *do*?' she asked, and Ruth would shrug.

'Tom Duncan was asking about you the other day,' she would say, but Ruth would not be interested.

Now she said in cool and civil tones to the man on the telephone,

111

'Thank you for calling, Mr Luchek.'

Immediately the vacuum roared.

Mrs Bridge was disturbed. Ruth was incomprehensible to her and with every year she became more so, more secretive and turbulent, more cunning and inaccessible, more foreign. Where had she come from? How could she be Carolyn's sister? Mrs Bridge was deeply worried and found it more and more difficult to call her by the pet names of childhood, and before long she was unable to call her by any name except Ruth, though it sounded formal and distant and tended to magnify their separation. Are you mine? she sometimes thought. Is my daughter mine?

66 *Mademoiselle from Kansas City*

It was to Carolyn, though she was younger, that Mrs Bridge was in the habit of confiding her hopes for them all. The two were apt to sit on the edge of Carolyn's bed until quite late at night, their arms half-entwined, talking and giggling, while across the room Ruth slept her strangely restless sleep – mumbling and rolling and burying her face in her wild black hair.

Mrs Bridge could never learn what Ruth did in the evenings, or where she went; she entered the house quietly, sometimes not long before dawn. Mrs Bridge had always lain awake until both girls were home, and one evening during the Christmas holidays she was still downstairs reading when Carolyn returned, bringing Jay Duchesne, who was now considerably over six feet tall and was doing his best to grow a mustache. In certain lights the mustache was visible, and he was quite proud of it and stroked it constantly and feverishly, as if all it needed in order to flourish was a little affection. Mrs Bridge liked Jay. She trusted him. There were moments when she thought she knew him better than she knew Douglas.

'What's new, Mrs B?' he inquired, twirling his hat on one finger. And to Carolyn, 'How's for chow, kid?' So they went out to the kitchen to cook bacon and eggs while Mrs Bridge remained in the front room with the book turned over in her lap and her eyes closed, dozing and dreaming happily, because it seemed to her that despite the difficulties of adolescence she had gotten her children through it in reasonably good condition. Later, when Duchesne roared out of the driveway – he still drove as recklessly as ever and she was still not resigned to it – she climbed the stairs, arm in arm, with Carolyn.

'Jay's voice has certainly changed,' she smiled.

'He's a man now, Mother,' Carolyn explained a bit impatiently.

Mrs Bridge smiled again. She sat on the bed and watched as Carolyn pulled off the baggy sweater and skirt and seated herself at the dressing table with a box of bobby pins.

'Funny – it's so quiet,' said Carolyn.

Mrs Bridge looked out the window. 'Why, it's snowing again. Isn't that nice! I just love snowy winter nights.'

Large wet flakes were floating down and clasping the outside of the window, and the street light shone on the evergreen tree in the back yard.

'There goes a rabbit!' she cried, but by the time Carolyn reached the window only the tracks were visible.

'Is Daddy asleep?' Carolyn asked.

'Yes, poor man. He didn't get away from the office until after seven and insists he has to get up at five-thirty tomorrow morning.'

'That's silly.'

'I know, but you can't tell him anything. I've tried, goodness knows, but it never does any good.'

'Why does he do it?'

'Oh,' said Mrs Bridge irritably, for the thought of it never failed to irritate her, 'he insists we'll all starve to death if he doesn't.'

'That'll be the day!'

Both of them were silent for a while, watching the snow descend.

'I do hope Ruth gets home soon.'

'She can drop dead for all I care.'

'You know I don't like you to use that expression.'

Carolyn split a bobby pin on her teeth and jammed it into her curly blond hair. 'Well, what's the matter with her then? Who does she think she is, anyway?' She leaned to one side and opened the cupboard that belonged to Ruth. 'Look at that! Black lace bras. Mademoiselle from Kansas City.'

Presently the grandfather clock in the hall chimed twice, and Mrs Bridge, after brushing Carolyn's cheek with her lips, went

113

downstairs and into the kitchen, where she made herself some cocoa and moodily watched the snow building up on the sill. After a while she went upstairs again, changed into her nightgown, and got into bed beside her husband. There she lay with her hands folded on the blanket while she waited for the faint noise of the front door opening and closing.

She believed she was awake but all at once, without having heard a sound, she realized someone was downstairs. She heard a gasp and then what sounded like a man groaning. The luminous hands of the bedside clock showed four-fifteen. Mrs Bridge got out of bed, pulled on her robe, and hurried along the hall to the top of the stairs, where she took hold of the banister and leaned over, calling just loud enough to be heard by anyone in the living room, 'Ruth?'

No one answered.

'Ruth, is that you?' she asked, more loudly, and there was authority in her tone. She listened and she thought some delicate noise had stopped. The dark house was silent.

'I'm coming down,' said Mrs Bridge.

'It's me,' said Ruth.

'Is there anyone with you?'

'He's leaving.'

And then Ruth coughed in a prolonged, unnatural way, and Mrs Bridge knew she was coughing to conceal another noise.

'Who's there?' she demanded, unaware that she was trembling from anger and fright, but there was only the sound of the great front door opening and shutting and seconds later the crunch of auto tires on the crust of yesterday's frozen snow as whoever it was released the brake and coasted away.

A cold draft swept up the spiral staircase. Mrs Bridge, peering down into the gloom, saw her daughter ascending. She snapped on the hall light and they met at the top step. Ruth was taking the last of the pins out of her hair. She reeked of whisky and her dress was unbuttoned. Idly she pushed by her mother and wandered along the hall. Mrs Bridge was too shocked to do anything until Ruth was at the door of her room; there they confronted each other again, for Ruth had felt herself pursued and turned swiftly with a sibilant ominous cry. Her green eyes were glittering and she lifted one hand to strike. Mrs Bridge, untouched by her daughter's hand, staggered backward.

67 *Ruth goes to New York*

That was the year Ruth finally managed to graduate from high school. She was there five years and for a while they were afraid it would be six, though she had taken the easiest courses possible. Her electives were music, drawing, athletics, and whatever else sounded easy. She seldom studied, and even when she did study she did poorly. She had been a member of the swimming team and this was the only activity listed after her name in the yearbook: 'member of girls' swimming team' – that and the desperate phrase, 'interested in dramatics'. She had once tried out for a play, but gave a rather hysterical reading and failed to get the part. When she finished high school Carolyn was only one semester behind her, although they had started two years apart.

A few days after the graduation she said she was going to New York to get a job. She did not like Kansas City; she never had. She had not made many friends. She had never seemed happy or even much at ease in Kansas City.

Mrs Bridge tried to become indignant when Ruth announced she was going to New York, but after all it was useless to argue.

'What on earth would you do in New York?' she asked, because Ruth had been unable to learn shorthand, nor could she operate a typewriter as efficiently as Douglas, who tapped out his English themes with one finger.

'Don't worry about me,' Ruth said. She had grown tall and beautiful, and somehow – in the powerful arch of her nose and in her somber, barbaric eyes – she looked biblical, swarthy and violent.

'I'm putting a thousand dollars in the bank for you,' said Mr Bridge, 'on one condition.' This condition was that if she could not support herself by the time the money ran out she would agree to return to Kansas City. She laughed and put her arms around him, and no one in the family had seen her do this since she was a child.

Mrs Bridge was disturbed that she did not want to go to college, being of the opinion that although one might never actually need a college degree it was always nice to have; and yet, thinking the matter over, she realized Ruth would only be wasting four years – obviously she was no student. But why New York? Why not some place closer to home?

Soon she was ready to leave. The entire family went to the station.

'You didn't forget your ticket, did you?' asked Mrs Bridge.

'Not quite,' said Ruth drily.

'Be sure to look up the Wenzells when you get there. I've already written them you're coming to New York, but of course they won't know where to find you.' The Wenzells were people they had met one summer in Colorado and with whom they exchanged Christmas greetings.

'I will,' said Ruth, who had no intention of getting in touch with them.

'Have a good trip,' her mother said as they were embracing at the gate. 'Don't forget to write. Let us know as soon as you arrive.'

'Here are your traveling expenses,' her father said, handing her some folded bills. 'For God's sake, don't lose it. And behave yourself. If you don't, I'm coming after you.'

'I can look out for myself,' said Ruth.

He laughed, and his laughter rang out odd and bold, the laughter of a different man, a free and happy man, who was not so old after all. 'That isn't what I said,' he told her lightly, and Mrs Bridge, glancing from one to the other, was struck by their easy companionship, as though they had gotten to know each other quite well when she was not around.

Once on the train Ruth kicked off her shoes and curled up in the seat. She unsnapped the catch of her travelling bag and reached in for a copy of *Theatre Arts* but felt a strange envelope. She knew immediately what it was – it was called a 'train letter', and a generation or so ago they were given to young people who were leaving home for the first time. She withdrew her hand and sat motionless for quite a while. Tears gathered in her eyes and presently she was shaken with dry sobs, although she did not know whether she was laughing or weeping. Before long she dried her face and lighted a cigarette.

Much later Ruth took out the envelope, read the letter of advice, and seemed to see her mother seated at the Chippendale highboy with some stationery and a fountain pen, seeking to recall the guidance of another era.

68 Tornado at the club

Not long after Ruth's departure a very familiar day rolled around for Mrs Bridge.

Each year on her birthday she was distressed by the extravagance of her husband's gift. Invariably she protested to him, and meant it, but he was determined to give her costly presents and she could not dissuade him. Once he set his mind he was immovable. One year it had been the Lincoln, another year it was an ermine coat, another year it was a diamond necklace. She loved these things, to be sure, but she did not need them, and knew this quite well, and in spite of loving them she could not help being a little embarrassed by the opulence of her possessions. She was conscious of people on the street staring at her when, wrapped in ermine and driving the Lincoln, she started off to a party at the country club; she wanted to stop the car and explain to them that her husband was still at work in the office though it was nine in the evening, and that she had not asked for these expensive things but that he had given them to her for her birthday. But, of course, she could not stop to explain any more than she could stop people from staring.

This year, therefore, she was mildly surprised when her birthday arrived and all he said was that they were going to have dinner at the club. She supposed this was to be her gift. It was odd, considering the past, but she was not displeased; she was even a bit relieved.

And it came as an unforgettable shock when he remarked, slyly, pleased with himself, soon after they had been seated in the country-club dining room, that the two of them were leaving for Europe three weeks from Sunday. Mrs Bridge at first thought he was joking. He was not. And she learned that all her friends had known about the trip for the past month, but not one of them had so much as hinted about the surprise in store for her. The tickets were already bought and he had reserved hotel accommodations in the countries they were to visit. They would be gone, he told her, for about six weeks.

'I feel giddy,' said Mrs Bridge. 'I never dreamed of anything like this.'

And when the waiter had taken their order Mr Bridge proceeded to tell her of the cities they would visit, and as he talked she stopped listening, because she could not help thinking of another evening when he had told her of all he planned to do. He had said he would take her to Europe one day; she remembered having smiled at him fondly, not really believing, not caring, happy enough to be with him anywhere. How long ago, she thought, how very long ago that was! It seemed like eight or ten years ago, but it was more than twenty, and on this day she was forty-eight years old. She grew a little sad at this, and while he talked on and on – he was more excited than she – she gazed out the window at the gathering clouds. And the distant thunder seemed to be warning her that one day this world she knew and loved would be annihilated.

The clouds descended and the wind began to increase while they were eating. A few drops of rain spattered against the window. It was the season for tornados, and before much longer it had become evident that one was approaching. The club steward turned on the radio and listened to reports of the tornado's course; it was, he learned, bearing directly toward the country club at a speed of seventy miles an hour. The steward went from table to table explaining the situation and adding that if the storm continued to approach it would be necessary to take shelter in the basement.

'Thank you,' said Mrs Bridge. 'Do you suppose there's much chance of it hitting us?'

The steward didn't know. The tornado was still quite a few miles west; the course of it might alter, or the funnel might degenerate before reaching Kansas City.

'Well, you'll let us know,' said Mrs Bridge.

The steward said he would keep them informed.

Soon the trees on the terrace were bending from the wind, and the rain poured down. She saw a metal chair go skidding off the porch as though someone were pulling it away with a rope. A few of the diners had begun to leave the room, and the steward was coming around again.

'Goodness, this *is* a storm,' said Mrs Bridge. 'Do you think we should go to the basement?'

Mr Bridge replied that the storm was not going to strike the clubhouse and that he, for one, intended to finish his dinner.

'There goes the mayor,' she said, looking around. The mayor and his wife often ate at the club and the Bridges were acquainted with them.

'Good evening,' said the mayor as he passed by, preceded by his wife.

'Good evening,' said Mrs Bridge.

The rain was coming down so heavily it was no longer possible to see through the window. There was no lightning and very little thunder, only the rain and a sense of terrible oppression as though something were lurking nearby.

Mrs Bridge placed her napkin on the table and said, 'Well, it look like we're in for it.'

Her husband continued eating.

'Steward, have you any further information?' she asked as soon as he had finished speaking to a couple at the next table.

The steward said the tornado was still approaching and he thought it would be a good idea to go to the basement.

'Thank you,' said Mrs Bridge, and looked expectantly at her husband.

'I'm going to finish this steak,' said he.

The steward did not know quite how to proceed; he knew it was his responsibility to get everyone to the basement, and if Mr and Mrs Bridge should be swept up and carried away he would be called upon by the club directors for an explanation. On the other hand he did not care to begin giving orders to Mr Bridge who, he knew, was not only short-tempered but very much aware of having been warned. He gazed earnestly at Mr Bridge, who paid no attention to him, and at last, unable to decide whether he was more afraid of him or of the club directors, the steward hurried off to the radio in hopes that the decision would be taken out of his hands by the course of the storm.

The lights of the dining room looked extraordinarily bright because of the unnatural darkness outside. There was a curious stillness and the rain fell in waves. Mrs Bridge, looking about, saw that except for her husband and herself everyone had left the dining room.

'Don't you think we should go?' she asked.

He was chewing and unable to answer at the moment. He swallowed, wiped his lips with his napkin, took a drink of water, and began to butter a piece of cornbread. Finding that he did not have enough butter he began to frown. He liked butter very much and at home he got all he wanted, but whenever they ate out he kept asking for more. Mrs Bridge, who was on a diet, had already given him the butter from her plate, but this was not enough. Both of them looked around. There was not a waiter in sight.

'Well, I'll steal some from the next table,' said Mrs Bridge. 'I don't suppose anyone will mind.' And she got up and walked over to get a piece of butter for her husband. Fortunately there was an untouched square of it on the table and so she leaned across, holding her beads with one hand so they would not dip into the abandoned dishes, and picked up the butter plate. It was a small china plate with the crest of the country club stamped in gold and she thought as she picked it up how attractive it was. Just then the lights flickered. Apparently the tornado had struck a power line somewhere. Mrs Bridge turned to go back to the table. She noticed the club steward standing in the doorway. He was watching them. He was wringing his hands and standing on one foot. She smiled politely, feeling a little foolish because of the butter plate in her hand. He smiled briefly and resumed staring at Mr Bridge.

From the distance came a hooting, coughing sound, like a railroad locomotive in a tunnel; a very weird and frightening sound it was.

'Well, that must be the tornado,' she said, listening attentively, but Mr Bridge, who was eating the cornbread with great gusto, did not reply. She spread her napkin in her lap again although she had finished eating; she spread it because when she was a child her parents had taught her it was impolite to place her napkin on the table until everyone had finished, and the manners she had been taught she had, in her turn, passed on to her own children.

As the tornado approached the country club Mrs Bridge remained seated across the table from her husband. She listened to the curious grunting and snuffling of the storm; although she had never been in the path of a tornado before, she knew this must be it, this must be the sound it made – the hooting, sucking roar of the vacuum. Now that it was so close it reminded her of a pig rooting on the terrace.

It did not occur to Mrs Bridge to leave her husband and run to the basement. She had been brought up to believe without question that when a woman married she was married for the rest of her life and was meant to remain with her husband wherever he was, and under all circumstances, unless he directed her otherwise. She wished he would not be so obstinate; she wished he would behave like everyone else, but she was not particularly frightened. For nearly a quarter of a century she had done as he told her, and what he had said would happen had indeed come to pass, and what he had said would not occur had not occurred. Why, then, should she not believe him now?

The lights of the country club went out and she thought the breath was being drawn from her lungs. Short streaks of lightning flickered intermittently, illuminating a terrible cloud just outside — rushing toward them like a kettle of black water — and she caught the unmistakable odor of electricity. In darkness and silence she waited, uncertain whether the munching noise was made by her husband or the storm.

In a little while the lights came on again and the diners, led by the mayor, came up from the basement.

'There!' said Mr Bridge, looking about for something else to eat. 'I told you, didn't I?'

The tornado, whether impressed by his intransigence or touched by her devotion, had drawn itself up into the sky and was never seen or heard of again.

69 Non capisco

They left for Europe, as he said they would, three weeks later.

In New York they saw Ruth, who had gotten a job as an assistant to one of the editors of a women's magazine, and who was living alone in a Greenwich Village garret. They went up four flights of steps to have a look at her apartment, though she seemed not overly anxious to show it, and Mrs Bridge was relieved to find it was not quite so forbidding as it sounded. She was, however, surprised by the pictures on the walls — original oil paintings by one of Ruth's new friends — and by the other furnishings. The

121

apartment was so unlike her room in Kansas City. It was neither so tidy nor so comfortable. There was not even a rug; the black wood floor was partly covered by a pattern of Oriental mats. And there were so many phonograph records! Mrs Bridge had forgotten that she was so fond of music. The apartment, though slightly bizarre, was neatly balanced, she thought, except for one area where something was disturbing. She finally realized that a nail had been driven into the wall above the bed but no picture hung from it. She could not help staring at the nail, knowing Ruth had hidden whatever belonged there. How strange! she thought. What was Ruth concealing? A moment later Mrs Bridge became conscious that she herself was being studied. Turning, then, to her daughter, she was greeted with a look of implacable defiance.

The Atlantic voyage did not agree very well with Mrs Bridge, though she tried not to show that the motion of the sea was nauseating. She took some tablets and felt better, but could not truly enjoy the meals, and she looked forward to landing in England.

'I guess I'm just not cut out to be a sailor,' she remarked more than once, not only to her husband but to some very nice people they had met aboard ship, and those who were feeling a bit queasy themselves were the first to sympathize.

She often noticed an old Italian woman from the tourist deck who, somehow or other, managed to get up to the first-class deck in the afternoons. The old woman would drag a chair into a secluded, sunny corner and would sit motionless for hours. No one ever spoke to her or came to see if she wanted anything. She did not look well. She was raggedly dressed, all in black, with shoes broken open at the seams, and a black scarf bound over her head. Mrs Bridge, feeling better as the voyage progressed, thought that never in her life had she seen anyone so alone and wretched as this elderly woman, and so, resolving to help her, went one afternoon to the corner and bent over and gently touched her on the shoulder.

'Is there anything I can do for you?'

'Lei parla Italiano?'

'Oh, don't you speak English?'

'Non capisco,' the old woman replied, gazing up at her in vast despair.

'I'm awfully sorry,' Mrs Bridge said helplessly. 'I wish I knew what to do, but I just don't understand.'

70 England

They landed at Southampton long before dawn and took the train to London. It was a rainy morning and most of the passengers dozed, but Mrs Bridge stayed awake and stared out the train window, a trifle groggily, at the silent, stately, fogbound farmland. And as this train carried her across the English countryside, past cottages she had never seen and would never see again, where great birds nested in the chimney crook, and from the hedgerows smaller birds came fluttering in shrill desperation to circle twice, and then, finding nothing, to settle as before, and where the cattle in the mist grazed unperturbed by the train which rolled on and on beneath the somnolent English sky, as though there were no destination, past the rain-drenched, redolent fields, and the trees which cast no shadow, she thought to herself how familiar it was and that once this must have been her home. Yes, she said to herself slowly, yes, I was here before.

In London the hotel was just off Piccadilly Circus; they had some difficulty understanding the hall porter and the maid, and, in fact, at the desk or on the telephone they found it necessary to listen closely. Mrs Bridge, unpinning her hat as she stood before the mirror in their room – a black straw hat it was, with a shiny cluster of plastic cherries on the brim – replied to her husband's comment, 'I agree with you, but don't you suppose we sound funny to them, too?'

Next morning they hired a cab to the Tower of London, where Mrs Bridge enjoyed the ravens and the colorful costumes of the Beefeaters. Mr Bridge spent a good deal of time investigating the instruments of torture and the chopping block, after which they got into the cab again and reached Buckingham Palace just in time for the changing of the guard. Mrs Bridge used three rolls of color film on this but insisted it was worth every bit of it. After a very pleasant lunch they drove to Eton.

They also hired a car to Stratford-on-Avon, and to the Dover cliffs, to many historic spots throughout the city and around it, and yet, as they were leaving for Paris, it seemed to them both, and particularly to Mrs Bridge, that they had hardly begun to get acquainted with England. While they were settling themselves on the train she told him she thought England was the nicest birthday present she had ever received.

71 French restaurant

To Mr and Mrs Bridge it seemed that no matter where they went in Paris they ran into Americans; consequently it was no surprise when a young man named Morgan Hager, who was from Kansas City and whose father had written that the Bridges would be visiting, told them that in addition to tourists there were several thousand Americans who had taken up permanent residence in the city, mostly on the Left Bank. No, he did not know what all these expatriates did for a living; yes, he thought they were happy in France; he had no idea whether they intended to remain in a foreign country for the rest of their lives. Mrs Bridge could not imagine anyone wanting to live outside the United States. To visit, yes. To take up residence, no.

'I should think they would get awfully lonely,' she said.

'I guess so,' said Hager. 'I know I do.'

'But then why do you stay?'

'Because I'm happier here.'

This was puzzling and she wanted to understand. She observed him frankly and saw that he did not look happy; at least he seldom smiled. She did not think he was truly happy.

'If you have the time, Morgan,' said Mr Bridge, 'I'd like to see some of this Bohemian life we hear so much about.'

Hager looked at him doubtfully, for the request posed a problem. There were many things he could have shown them, but, even as certain murals in Pompeii are not open to casual tourists, so there were various Parisian experiences not listed in the guide-book.

'Well,' said Hager modestly, 'I really don't know of anything very Bohemian, but you might like to have dinner at a place on Montparnasse where a lot of art students eat. It's sort of dirty,' he added thoughtfully.

Mrs Bridge thought this sounded exciting. 'Perhaps we should

124

go back to the hotel and change,' she said.

Hager did not know whether she meant to get more dressed up or less dressed up, so finally he said, 'I don't think anybody will notice you.' This had a peculiar ring, so he added, 'You look all right.' Somehow this was not what he had in mind either, so he cleared his throat, scratched his nose, and said, 'The place is actually a real dump.' He tried again. 'I mean, you can get in with no trouble.' Having run himself into a cul-de-sac he stopped to meditate. 'Oh, well,' he said at last, 'let's go. I'm hungry as a sonofabitch.'

It was the smallest restaurant Mrs Bridge had ever seen. It was not much larger than her kitchen at home, but somehow or other there were a dozen oilcloth-covered tables jammed into it and every table was crowded. It reeked of cheese and wine and smoke and perspiration. Wedged between the door and a coatrack they stood and waited for three vacancies, and finally the waiter, who was a fat boy with crew-cut hair and a dirty apron, called through the smoke and the gabble, 'Alors, vite! J'ai trois! Vite!'

'Okay, step on it,' Hager muttered. 'He's got three but they won't last,' and he began pushing Mrs Bridge into the confusion.

Finding no room on the table for her purse, and no other place to put it, she was obliged to hold it in her lap. The menu was scrawled on a blackboard on the wall and Hager translated and made recommendations and both Mr and Mrs Bridge accepted his suggestions. Seated next to her was an unusually ragged person wearing a short-sleeved shirt and a filthy blue beret.

'Bonjour, Claude,' said Morgan Hager.

'Ah, mon ami!' said the dirty one. 'Comment ça va?'

'Oh, ça va,' replied Hager. 'Claude, je vous présente Monsieur et Madame Bridge.

'Enchanté!' said Claude, with his mouth full of bread. He looked at her speculatively. He plucked at his shirt and said, 'C'est un cadeau.'

'I gave him the shirt,' said Hager.

'Oh. How nice.'

'Oui,' said Claude, still chewing and eyeing her. He saw that her wine glass had not been filled, so he reached across the table for the community bottle and filled the glass for her, saying, 'C'est bon, alors.'

'Thank you,' said Mrs Bridge. The wine was bright red and had a few specks floating on the surface.

'It tastes like vinegar,' said Hager as he saw her looking at it doubtfully. 'We can get some better stuff. Claude's dead broke, that's why he drinks it. I mean, it's only about one cent a glass.'

'Oh, I'm sure it's quite good,' she replied, though she was sure it wasn't. She tasted it and smiled because Claude was watching.

'C'est bon, n'est-ce pas?' he demanded.

'Oh, yes, it's really awfully good,' she replied, and took another sip to prove she meant it. Claude nodded approvingly. He was eating salad now. He paused, leaned forward, and pulled a limp, black, stringy object out of the bowl. Mrs Bridge saw it was a spider. Evidently it had climbed into the salad, or had fallen in, and drowned. Claude indifferently dropped it into a shell half filled with ashes and cigarette stubs and continued eating. In a little while the spider recovered and crawled unsteadily out of the ash tray, across the table, and disappeared on the other side.

Presently the waiter arrived with the first course and stood around for a few moments to see if they would enjoy it. The spider had taken the edge from Mrs Bridge's appetite, and as for salad, though she tried valiantly she could eat nothing more than a bit of tomato.

Back at the hotel that night Mr Bridge observed that he had always heard so much about French cooking but if that was a fair sample he would rather eat in Kansas City.

'I thought it was very good,' she said loyally.

'You didn't eat much,' he said.

'Well, good heavens,' she replied, 'we didn't go there for the food.'

72 Winged victory

To the Louvre they went as soon as they got down from the Eiffel Tower. The Louvre was a symbol to Mrs Bridge. As Texas meant size, as Timbuktu meant the ends of the earth, so did the Louvre have meaning. To be sure, there were nice galleries in the United States; in Kansas City, for example, there was the William Rockhill Nelson gallery and although she had not been in it more than four or five times in the last twenty years she was very proud that it was in Kansas City. It had a national reputation, she knew, and once in a while she thought of visiting it, for she remembered that on the few occasions she had been there she had enjoyed herself. Once inside it was very nice and of course remarkably interesting; it was just that getting there was so difficult, not that it was out of the way, it was not far from the Plaza, and there was plenty of parking space, but somehow she could not bring herself to go there. Each time the idea came to her she began to feel uncomfortably cool and depressed, and would hear once again her footsteps echoing from the marble. The few visitors she had encountered had ignored her, or at best seemed distantly courteous. It was all so impersonal, a trifle ghostly. Now if there were music and if the windows were open – yes, that was the trouble. And if it could be nicely carpeted! – instead of spending all that money on marble pillars. And if there were a nice tea shop and a gift shop – perhaps Bancroft's could show the gallery directors how to make things more attractive . . .

And so she meditated in the taxicab as they were on their way to the Louvre. It was a lovely afternoon. Men were fishing from the banks of the Seine, couples browsing along the bookstalls – what oddly shaped green boxes! she thought, with the lids propped up and so many maps and pictures on display. And in the Tuileries, with the Louvre in the background, ladies were knitting and children were rolling hoops across the grass. Balloons waved at the end of sticks, or clustered together, bumping against one another in the afternoon breeze, and she noticed, as the taxicab stopped in front of the famous French museum, how many people were going in and out; Paris was really altogether different from Kansas City.

In the Louvre she immediately recognized the Venus de Milo, even though they happened to approach from the rear, and of course the Mona Lisa was unmistakable; it looked exactly like the reproductions. The tapestries seemed familiar somehow; perhaps it was just that most tapestries looked alike, and most Greek vases, and all mummies.

At the end of an hour Mr Bridge said he thought he would go outside and wait, with the result that she continued through the Louvre alone. It was tiring, but it was exciting, and she knew she would never forget this day; it was with a feeling of regret – despite the fact that she was so exhausted she could hardly walk – that at last she concluded it was time to leave. Her husband was probably bored to death waiting for her; she felt a little guilty about letting him wait, but knew he would understand. He knew how she had looked forward to visiting the Louvre.

She had not managed to see everything but she reflected as she walked toward the exit that she had seen all the most famous paintings and statuary – except the Winged Victory of Samothrace, she thought, and promptly stopped. It had been familiar to her as long as she could remember. There must have been a picture of it in one of her earliest school-books. Even now she could imagine it so clearly: that imperial figure advancing and the drapery streaming backward. How impressive it must be!

'Well,' she said, half aloud, 'it may be ages before I'm in the Louvre again, so if I'm going to see it I'd better see it now.'

She looked around, intending to inquire where it was, but for the moment there seemed to be no English-speaking people in the corridor, so she decided to continue to the exit where there should be an information desk, or at least a guard who would understand. She turned the corner and there, all of a sudden, was the Winged Victory. Mrs Bridge gasped and took a step backward, for the great statue seemed to be bearing down on her and it was the very image of Lois Montgomery in a nightgown.

73 Strangers in paradise

Next day they went window-shopping along the boulevards near the Opéra, and in the course of this stroll Mrs Bridge became slightly separated from her husband. They were walking slowly up the rue Auber, stopping at whatever interested them, and she had drifted ahead, musing on the difference between Paris and Kansas City, observing the French businessmen who seemed content to loiter for hours in sidewalk cafés, and whose attitude, she reflected, was certainly pleasure before business.

Finding herself alone, she looked back and saw him standing with his arms folded, staring into one of the shop windows. She waited a while, thinking he would be coming along, but whatever he saw had hypnotized him. Her curiosity aroused, she retraced her steps. He sensed her approach and looked around with a start. They wandered along as before, but she had seen the object of his attention: a black lace brassière with the tips cut off.

The more she mulled over this incident the more concerned she became. The French, after all, might do as they pleased; she need have nothing to do with the French, but she must live with her husband. She had lived with him for a long time now, and assumed she knew whatever was worth knowing about him. True, there were occasional surprises – once he had told her, and afterward seemed to regret having divulged the secret, that when he was a boy he used to dream of becoming a great composer – but the revelations of his nature had seemed meaningless, no matter how fascinating, and she was not apt to dwell on them, but now she did.

Why had he stood there looking? What had he been thinking? His expression had been so serious. Were there things he had never told her about himself? Who was he, really? From all the recesses of her being came the questions, questions which had never before occurred to her, and there on the foreign street she felt lost and forsaken, and with great longing she began to think of Kansas City.

74 Intellectual café

The guidebook spoke of a café called Le Dôme as having been the haunt of famous intellectuals at the beginning of the century, so there they went to spend an hour or two.

'Picasso used to linger here,' Mrs Bridge read from the book, and she went on to read the names of other celebrated individuals who had taken their leisure on this very terrace.

'Here comes Picasso now,' said Mr Bridge.

'Oh, I don't believe it,' she said, looking up nevertheless. In a moment she saw to whom he was referring; it was Morgan Hager, whom they had not seen for several days. Hager was carrying a portfolio under his arm and he was wearing a beret that for some reason made him resemble a fox. He looked startled when he saw them in the café, and for an instant seemed ready to flee, but then he smiled and nodded and came over to join them, placing his portfolio in a corner. Mrs Bridge thought about asking to see his drawings, and after some hesitation she did so. He said the drawings were not much good and she did not press the matter.

'Well,' he said, 'I see you're still here.' This was not what he meant to say, so he amended, 'I figured you'd probably left.' Since this was not right either he said, 'I never did know what you were doing here.' He saw Mrs Bridge smiling courteously and steadily, and Mr Bridge observing him with frank curiosity, so he took off his beret and scratched his head, gazed around Le Dôme in search of something whereby he might distract them from his inability to make conversation, and he exclaimed, 'Oh! Look at that!'

Mr and Mrs Bridge turned and looked and they saw a shaggy girl, rather pretty in a gypsy sort of way – so Mrs Bridge thought – who was wearing a silk blouse that was not tucked into her skirt but was simply tied in a loose knot so that a good deal of midriff was showing. She was laughing and shaking her head in response to the comments of two Frenchmen who were sitting on the next table. One of the Frenchmen took out his wallet and slipped a bill under the saucer of her coffee cup, and at this she promptly untied the knot in her blouse and straightened up, revealing her breast to her neighbors as well as to anyone else who cared to look, whereupon there was a burst of clapping from everyone else in the café, with the exception of Mr and Mrs Bridge.

'Well,' said Morgan Hager suddenly, 'I guess I'd better be running along.'

'Oh, must you go?' inquired Mrs Bridge.

'Yes, there's a girl at the ho— ah, I mean, I've got some plans for the next few hours.' He paused. 'It's just that I'd forgotten about Kansas City – what the people were like, if you know what I mean.' He stopped again. 'Well,' he said, picking up his portfolio, 'it's sure been an experience!'

Mrs Bridge was not certain what he meant, but replied courteously, 'Good-by, Morgan. We'll tell your parents we saw you.' To which Hager responded with an uneasy grin and vanished swiftly into the crowd on the street.

75 Sidewalk artist

'I never knew there were so many artists,' she observed as they wandered along the quay. 'How do you suppose they keep from starving to death?'

Mr Bridge had never been greatly interested in art, but if this was how she wanted to spend their final day in Paris it was all right with him. Some of the pictures in the book stalls he did rather like; then, too, it was a warm sunny afternoon near the end of August and he was pleased, and he made up his mind to buy her a painting. He said nothing, but he began to pay more attention, and near the cathedral of Notre Dame she paused to admire a water-color of the city.

'Parlez-vous anglais?' Mrs Bridge politely inquired of the old gentleman who sat beside the stall in a canvas chair. He shook his head and went on smoking his pipe.

'Well, combien?' she asked, pointing to the one that struck her fancy.

'Vingt mille,' he answered without looking around, and continued smoking.

'Vingt mille,' she repeated, for she had been listening closely, knowing he would speak in French. 'Now, let's see. Vingt is twenty, I believe. And mille is thousand. Well, that sounds like a lot.' Whereupon she opened her handbag and took out a little booklet which equated American money with virtually everything on earth. Having learned how much it would cost in dollars, she exclaimed, 'Oh, I'm afraid that's much too much,' and shook her head and regretfully moved along, remarking to her husband, 'I'm sure he's spotted us as tourists.'

Mr Bridge took a long, shrewd look at the picture so as not to forget it. He did not think it was very good – in fact he was of the opinion that Ruth had done better paintings when she was in high school – but he seldom offered an opinion on a subject with which he was not familiar. Later that afternoon, back at their hotel on the Champs Elysées, while she was packing the suitcases, he went out, hired a taxi, and drove to the quay, where he bought the painting and arranged to have it shipped to Kansas City. The next day as they were getting settled on the train for the trip to the Riviera he observed rather dryly that he thought he knew how the Parisian artists kept from starving, but since she had no idea he had bought the painting for her this remark meant nothing, and she replied as she took off her hat that she supposed they must manage some way.

76 Telegram

A telegram was waiting for them in Monte Carlo. Douglas, knowing the date of his parents' wedding anniversary, sent this message: MAY I TAKE THE OPPORTUNITY EXTEND FELICITATIONS UPON MEMORABLE OCCASION AND IN BEHALF ENTIRE COMPANY EXPRESS HOPE YOUR CONTINUED SUCCESS.

Mrs Bridge was touched by this thoughtfulness and wrote to him, 'It was awfully sweet to hear from you on our anniversary, but I do think the American Express company must have gotten their messages mixed up . . .'

77 Beautiful luggage

Before leaving on the trip she had checked over the luggage in the attic and concluded they did not have enough, so she had gone downtown and bought three elegant, darkly burnished leather suitcases. They were so beautiful that she was easily persuaded by the salesman to buy a set of canvas covers to protect the leather. These covers, to be sure, were ugly – as coarse as Boy Scout pup tents – but she bought them and had them fitted onto the suitcases. The covers remained on the suitcases while they were aboard ship, and as they had been in each city only a few days she had not bothered to remove them, but now she decided to see if the leather was being protected. She unfastened one of the canvas jackets, peeled it halfway off, and there – as beautiful as though still on display – the leather gleamed. Well pleased, she buttoned on the cover.

78 Mirror, mirror

Mrs Bridge slept later than she intended to the second morning in Monte Carlo; they had visited the casino the previous night, and while she had not gambled she had found it nonetheless a rather strenuous experience. Her husband was gone when she finally awoke, but this was not surprising because he had gotten so accustomed to rising early in order to put in a full day at the office that he was no longer able to lie in bed past seven o'clock. Probably he was walking briskly around town, and no doubt he would be waiting to check on the Italian reservations as soon as the travel agency opened its doors for the day. She often wondered where he found so much energy.

The clock on the night table told her it was almost noon. She felt a trifle guilty. And yet it was delicious to lie in bed and to feel on her cheek and on her arms the mild breezes drifting up the hillside from the Mediterranean. A few minutes more, she thought, then she really must get up. And so, with eyes half open, she lay motionless and knew how fortunate she was. And she inquired of herself what she had done to deserve all this. There was no answer. All at once she perceived something so obvious and vulgar that she could not imagine why it had failed to escape her attention. She could see herself in the mirror on the wall, the mirror faced the bed, and she had suddenly realized that in every one of their European hotel rooms a large mirror had faced the bed. At the significance of this her blue eyes opened wide and she quickly turned her head on the pillow. In Paris a beautiful ornate Louis Quatorze mirror had frankly revealed her intimacy with her husband, and in London, too, now that she thought about it, they had been mirrored.

Deeply troubled, puzzled, no longer thankful, Mrs Bridge lay in bed with an expression of listless despair and gazed through the opened doors of the balcony, through the iron grillwork to the distant sea, to the purple clarity and the white sails.

79 Psst!

Wherever they went they were promptly identified as American tourists. From every side street some young man would come gliding, a hand in his coat pocket, murmuring in broken English that he had a diamond ring for sale, a fountain pen, a Swiss watch.

'Psst! Hey, mister,' he would begin.

'How on earth do they always know we're Americans?' Mrs Bridge inquired.

It was not mysterious to Mr Bridge, who, however, chose to reply bitterly, for the trip was costing twice what he had estimated, 'Europeans can smell a dollar a mile away.'

80 Peculiar Roman

In Rome their hotel was situated near the Via Veneto, which the desk clerk, who had never been to America but who had a second cousin in Manhattan, insisted was the Broadway of Europe. Neither Mr nor Mrs Bridge was inclined to dispute him, the principal reason being that the day was overcast and the humidity so high it was difficult to breathe.

'Goodness, this is certainly different from the Riviera,' Mrs Bridge remarked as they were unpacking in their room. It had been hot in Monte Carlo – at least the temperature had been high – but in the shadows of the stone buildings it was usually cool, and even in the direct sunlight they had not been uncomfortable.

'This really is awfully muggy,' she said, looking through the blinds at the dank, motionless clouds. 'I certainly miss that breeze from the Mediterranean.'

They showered, changed into their lightest clothing, and decided to sit at a café on the Via Veneto. A weak, hot rain had begun to fall and they selected a table with an umbrealla. At the next table sat an Italian man in a white suit and white perforated shoes who soon addressed them in perfect English.

'You are Americans, are you not?'

Mrs Bridge said they were, again amazed at such prompt identification.

'And how do you find Italy? Do you enjoy yourselves?'

'Well, it's awfully warm,' she said hesitantly, not wanting to be ungracious, and was relieved when he was not offended. So many Europeans were excitable.

He asked how long they had been in Europe and how much longer they intended to stay, and when she replied that after visiting Florence and Milan and Geneva they would be returning to Paris and from there to the United States he offered a curious little gesture which somehow expressed sympathy.

'Unfortunate,' he added.

'Have you ever visited America?' she inquired pleasantly.

'No, Madame, I have not.'

'I suppose you must be dying to go.'

The Italian laughed. Lifting both arms in the gesture they had come to know so well, he said, 'My dear lady, why go to America?'

Later, when the rain had stopped, he bowed, told them what a pleasure it had been to make their acquaintance, and strolled along the boulevard.

'Don't let them fool you,' said Mr Bridge. 'These people would sell their souls to get to the United States.'

81 Change of itinerary

They came to enjoy sitting on the Via Veneto – so much so that Mrs Bridge said half jokingly, referring to the peculiar Italian who had no desire to go anywhere else, 'I really think he had a point.'

They were in front of a different café farther up the boulevard, one they had not tried before. The weather being muggy and cloudy as it had been ever since their arrival in Rome, they decided to have some iced coffee. In a few minutes a waiter approached, a very Italian-looking waiter.

'Let's hope this one understands English,' she murmured. 'Try him and see.'

'What else did you think I was going to speak?' Mr Bridge

replied. He had just finished changing the film in the camera and now placed it on an empty chair and gave the waiter their order.

'Very good, sir. Will there be anything else?'

'No,' he said. 'Just coffee with plenty of ice.' The waiter bowed and went inside the café. Mr Bridge wiped his forehead with his handkerchief and shook the sleeves of his linen coat. Mrs Bridge was fanning herself with a sightseeing folder.

'It certainly does make things simpler when they speak English,' she said, 'but my! – doesn't this one have an accent!'

They waited and waited. The iced coffee did not arrive. They looked around. It seemed that people were gathering inside the café and that an argument or a discussion of some kind was going on.

'They're usually so good about the service,' said Mrs Bridge, still fanning herself with the sightseeing folder.

They waited a while longer. Finally Mr Bridge got up, saying he would go into the café and find out what the trouble was.

'For heaven's sake, don't let yourself get involved,' she said, for it was obvious the Italians were excited about something. Several of them were waving their arms and denouncing one another; however this went on all the time in Italy and Mrs Bridge was growing accustomed to it. While her husband went inside she studied the folder. They were planning to visit the Vatican later that afternoon and she was hoping their schedule would permit a drive through the countryside. She looked up with a smile when her husband returned.

'We're getting out,' he said as he picked up the camera.

Her smile faded. She knew from his expression that he was not angry.

'What is it?' she said. 'What's happened?'

'The Nazis are in Poland.'

'Oh, my word!'

Two days later Mr and Mrs Bridge were on their way home.

82 Inside Europe

At luncheon the day after her return to Kansas City she was questioned about the situation in Europe and she replied that it had been frightening and that she really had no idea what was going on. They had not met any Nazis – at least she did not think so – and she could not honestly give an opinion. She felt more sure of herself when asked about the sights they had seen. Inevitably someone asked if they had gone to a bullfight.

'No, thank heavens,' she replied. 'We wanted to go to Spain, but Walter felt it would be dangerous so soon after the Civil War. But we did hear a great deal about it. Europe seems to be jam-packed with people who fought on the losing side.'

'It's hard to understand how the Spaniards can be so blood-thirsty,' Madge Arlen remarked.

'It certainly is,' said Mrs Bridge promptly.

'The poverty of the Europeans must be simply appalling.'

'Yes, it's simply unbelievable.'

'They say there's no middle class at all, just the rich and the poor.'

'Yes, it seems so unfair.'

'I suppose they're all dying to emigrate to this country.'

'Yes, though of course you can't blame them,' she replied. 'Grace, would you pass the cream?'

Luncheon being over with they moved into the living room, where the hostess, Lois Montgomery, had set up card tables. On each table there was a fluted yellow paper basket filled with salted chashews and peppermints, and there were four tasseled tally cards and four tiny pencils.

Being asked what she thought about England, she answered that it was lovely and that the people were quite nice, though rather reserved. The cooking was not as good as French cooking because the English boiled everything. The roast beef, however, was delicious, and the plum pudding. London was foggy and the English accent sounded strange until one got used to it.

'Aren't we lucky to be living in America!' someone said.

137

'Isn't that the truth!'

'Oh, by the way,' said Mrs Bridge, 'all the time we were abroad I kept wondering if that awful hole in the pavement just off Ward Parkway had been fixed.'

'They finally got to it last week. We were just about to give it up as a lost cause.'

'That was so maddening. I was so provoked with Douglas one day that I forgot to watch for it and ran right over it.'

'Well,' said Madge Arlen, who was shuffling the cards with a cigarette in her mouth and one eye closed against the smoke, 'you can thank Grace. She sent the mayor a telegram.'

'You'd think with taxes as high as they are the city could do something about those holes without waiting till kingdom come.'

'Well, you know these politicians. Who's ready for more coffee?'

'Buy any art treasures while you were there?'

'Oh, no. I'm afraid I wouldn't know one if it hit me. Three no trump.'

'I've been trying to talk Ralph into a trip somewhere, but now with this Polish thing I suppose it'll have to be postponed.'

'Yes, I don't suppose it's safe anywhere any more. Honestly, you can't imagine why we have so many wars.'

'I'm simply parched!' said Madge. 'Lois, do you mind if I scare up some ice water?'

'Oh, sit still. I'll ring for Belinda.'

'Is it true the Italian women get awfully heavy?'

'Yes, we saw some who were positively enormous. I suppose it's from eating so much starch.'

Late that afternoon as the party was breaking up someone said to her, 'I certainly envy you and Walter. It must have been a marvellous trip even if it did end that way.'

'I wouldn't have missed it for the world,' said Mrs Bridge, smiling all around, 'and I feel awfully lucky. Even so we were certainly glad to see the Union Station. I suppose no matter how far you go there's no place like home.' She could see they agreed with her, and surely what she had said was true, yet she was troubled and for a moment she was almost engulfed by a nameless panic.

83 Progress, madness, defeat

The only one of her friends who might understand how she felt was
Grace Barron, and so it was that a few days after the luncheon she
telephoned her. The maid answered and said Mrs Barron was in
bed. Mrs Bridge asked if she was ill. The maid didn't seem to
know, saying only that she had gone to bed about noon. This was
so strange that Mrs Bridge decided to drive over and find out what
was the matter.

She was sitting up in bed wearing her favorite sweatshirt and a
baseball cap and she was reading a monstrous Russian novel.
Closing the book on a hairpin she said, 'I'm losing my mind.'

'This is the first I've heard of it,' said Mrs Bridge with a smile.

'Do stop,' Grace said unhappily. 'Don't be gay, India. Please,
for once, don't.'

'Well, it *is* rather a shocking remark.'

'Life can be shocking.' She took off the ball player's cap and
began turning it around in her hands and frowning. 'It's just that I
do want to be a person. I do, I do!' Mrs Bridge did not know what
to say and presently Grace continued. 'Virgil says there's something wrong with me. He says he's never known another woman in
all his life who would wear a sweatshirt on the Plaza.'

'Well, you do attract attention. Not that I mind, and I can't see
where it's anyone else's business, and there certainly isn't any law
against it.'

'But I do attract attention.'

'Well,' Mrs Bridge answered uneasily, 'as Virgil says, you're the
only one from this neighborhood who dresses as though you were
going to work in the north end.'

Grace nodded. 'It's true. Yes, it's true.'

Both of them fell silent.

'Do you think we'll get in the war?' said Grace after a while.

'I don't know,' Mrs Bridge replied. 'I can't understand what's
going on. I hate to think about it. It's so senseless.'

Again they fell silent.

'Can you tell me what happened, Grace? Being in bed is so unlike you.'

'It was the washing machine's fault,' she answered without a smile, and went on to explain that she and the machine had never gotten along very well – 'We've always despised each other,' she said – and on this day it had defied her, it had knocked and trembled, and begun tearing the clothing, and so infuriated her that she had grabbed it by one leg and tipped it over, and the water ran all over the basement. The maid, who was upstairs in the kitchen preparing lunch, heard her screaming and summoned a doctor.

Mrs Bridge remained silent and was thoughtful, for here was someone less confident of the future than herself. An evil, a malignancy, was at work. Its nature she could not discern, though she had known of its carbuncular presence for many years. Until now, until this revelation of its existence, she had not imagined it could be more than a fanciful illness, nor that there could be other victims than herself. But her friend was ill and suffering and Mrs Bridge, too, was afflicted. Thinking back she was able to remember moments when this anonymous evil had erupted and left as its only cicatrice a sour taste in the mouth and a wild, wild desire.

One morning she had chanced to meet Grace downtown and Grace had wanted to look around in a toy store, and so, together, Mrs Bridge amused and puzzled by this whim, they stopped here and there. So much had changed from the years when she used to buy toys for Ruth and Carolyn and Douglas. Everything was more intricate now, more automatic. It seemed you no longer played with a toy, you operated it. Douglas used to spend hours on his knees – ruining his corduroy knickers – pushing a fire engine or a dump truck and making appropriate noises. Now, however, you simply pushed a lever and the toy ran around by itself and the sirens wailed and the lights flashed until you were able to catch the machine and stop it. And Grace had caught it and was trembling so she could hardly reverse the lever.

There was a doll, too, with its little frock tied up around its head in order to display the electronics in the abdomen. There was a booklet tied to the wrist of the doll and they had read the booklet and then Mrs Bridge turned the doll on. The eyes began to roll, the jaw drooped, and from the loud-speaker in the stomach came a nursery rhyme, and when this ended the doll sat down and a thin, colorless liquid appeared from beneath it and trickled over the counter.

'Can you help me?' Grace was asking, but Mrs Bridge was too depressed to speak.

84 Robbery at the Heywood Duncans'

The next time she met Grace was at a party given by the Heywood Duncans. Shortly after ten o'clock, while the two of them were chatting, just as Mrs Bridge was reaching for another anchovy cracker, four men appeared in the doorway and they did not look like guests. They were wearing plastic noses attached to horn-rimmed glasses and were carrying pistols. One of them said, 'All right, everybody, this is a stick-up!' Another of the men sprang to the top of the piano and pointed his gun at several different people. At first everyone thought it was a joke – it was so typical of a stunt Noel Johnson might dream up. But it wasn't a joke because the robbers made all the guests line up facing the wall with their hands above their heads. Then two of them walked around pulling bill-folds out of the men's pockets and taking bracelets and necklaces and rings from the ladies. Another of the men went upstairs and came down with his arms full of purses and fur coats. Just before the robbers reached Mrs Bridge, who was standing obediently with her hands as high as possible, something frightened them and the one standing on the piano – she afterward described him to the police as not having worn a necktie – called out in an ugly voice, 'Who's got the keys to that blue Cadillac out front?'

At this Mrs Ralph Porter screamed, 'Don't you tell him, Ralph!'

But the bandits took Mr Porter's keys, and after telling everyone not to move for thirty minutes they ran out the side door. Heywood Duncan immediately phoned the police while Dr Foster, who had dropped in unexpectedly and who had been robbed the same as the others, feebly seated himself in a corner and urged everyone to be calm, saying the bandits would not get away with it.

The bandits did get away, though, and it was written up on the front page of the newspaper with pictures on page eight, including a close-up of the scratched piano. Mrs Bridge, reading the account in the breakfast room next morning after her husband had gone to work, was surprised to learn that Stuart Montgomery had been carrying just $2.14 and that Mrs Noel Johnson's ring had been zircon.

85 No questions

As if one robbery were not enough, Mrs Bridge became involved in another – not much of a robbery, and she was detained less than ten minutes; still it was frightening. She was in a department store examining some brocade with the idea of altering the scheme in the dining room when, quite unknown to her, someone looted the cash register not six feet away. The theft was discovered a few minutes later and she, along with several other women, was herded into the manager's office. When it came her time to be interviewed she sat down in front of the desk, adjusted her fur neckpiece, and said, 'I surely hope you don't think I'm the guilty one.'

The manager raised both hands in a faint gesture of dismay at such a thought. He asked if he might see her driver's license, and when she produced it from her purse he handed it to the police lieutenant who was lounging on the edge of the desk with a felt hat pushed back off his forehead. Mrs Bridge knew he was a policeman the instant she saw him. She expected him to study the license and ask a great many questions; consequently she was both relieved and slightly ruffled when he barely glanced at her license before handing it back and asked her nothing at all.

'I certainly hope you catch whoever it was,' she said.

The lieutenant, who knew a bona-fide country-club matron when he saw one, responded by nodding politely.

The manager opened the door for her.

86 Follow me home

Kansas City was apparently headed for an epidemic of crime such as no one could remember since the days of the hoodlums and political bosses. How the latest scare actually started no one knew, although several women, one of whom was a fairly close friend of Madge Arlen, claimed to know the name of someone who had been assaulted not far from Ward Parkway. Some insisted it had happened near the Plaza, others thought farther south, but they were generally agreed it occurred late at night. The story was that a certain matron had been driving home alone and when she had slowed down for an intersection a man had leaped from behind some shrubbery – a clump of spirea, according to Madge – and had wrenched open the door. Whether or not the attack had been consummated the story did not say; the important part was that there had been a man and he had leaped up and wrenched open the door. There was nothing about it in the paper, nor in *The Tattler*, which did not print unpleasant material, and the exact date of the assault could not be determined, only that it had been one dark night not long ago.

As this story began to circulate through the country-club district none of the ladies cared to drive anywhere alone after sundown; if they did they locked themselves in the car and drove with great anxiety. And it became customary at the conclusion of parties where there were 'office widows' for the host to get his automobile out of the garage in order to follow the unescorted matrons home, which was the reason there could be seen processions of cars winding through the country-club district late at night.

So Mrs Bridge came home on those evenings when her husband did not get away from the office in time to attend the party, or when he was too tired to go. At her driveway the procession would halt, engines idling, everyone watching, while she drove into the garage and returned along the driveway so as to be constantly visible until she reached the front door. Having unlocked it she would step inside, switch on the hall lights, and call to him, 'I'm home!' if she had seen his car in the garage. If he failed to answer she necessarily assumed he was asleep or otherwise occupied. In any event, she would then flicker the lights a few times to show the friends waiting outside that she was safe, after which the caravan would move along.

87 Jules, Niki, et al

The idea of a chauffeur had begun to appeal to Mr Bridge. Traffic was getting more congested all the time, and as he did not enjoy driving anyway he thought it would be well worth the expense, so, after they had considered the matter, Mrs Bridge telephoned an employment agency and the following evening a tall, affable colored man came out for an interview. Both of them were impressed by his manners. He was from New Orleans, he told them, and this somehow added to his stature. He was dignified and courteous. The longer they talked to him the better they liked him, so he was employed.

In the rear seat of the Chrysler, his briefcase in his lap, Mr Bridge sat erect and tense, expecting an accident at every corner while being driven to the office. It was less exhausting to battle the traffic himself, but now that he had the chauffeur he could not dismiss him without a reason. Then, too, having set his mind to the proposition, he was determined to make a success of it. At the office he got out, very much relieved, and told the chauffeur what time to pick him up. The chauffeur spent the remainder of the day driving Mrs Bridge around in her Lincoln, or, when she had no use for him, he would loiter in the basement.

During the third week they began to receive mysterious telephone calls asking for Jules, which was his name. Drawling Negro voices would inquire, 'Well, whereabout you figure he at?' if it was his day off. Or, 'Yes, ma'am, it sho'ly am mighty impo'tant.' If, reluctantly, she went to the top of the basement steps and called, 'Jules? Jules? Someone wishes to speak to you on the phone,' he would not respond, and her patience was severely tested. Eventually they learned that Jules had bought a yellow satin easy chair for his apartment in the north end of the city, but so far he had been unwilling to pay for the chair and these were the creditors who were calling. When a few more weeks had passed an attempt was made to link Mr Bridge with the payment; a serious talk with Jules having produced no effect, he was dismissed.

Next day they interviewed and employed a Japanese called Niki who, with clasped hands, assured them he paid cash for whatever he bought. Mr Bridge felt more at ease with Niki than he had with Jules, but Mrs Bridge felt quite the opposite. She was terrified of the way he backed out of the driveway. She asked him to go slower and to pay some attention to where he was backing, and he grinned and agreed to do so, but there was no change. When she became severe about this he looked so grieved by the reprimand that she became ashamed of herself. Still he would not slow down. He never actually struck anything but there were some near misses, the worst when he roared over a pile of burning leaves and almost killed a boy with a canvas bag around his neck who was throwing circulars onto the front porches. It was such a close call that Mrs Bridge refused to ride with him any more, so there was nothing to do but dismiss him.

After Niki came another Negro man, but there was always a faint odor of whisky around him, and Harriet, when asked for an opinion, compressed her lips significantly and shook her head. After this man came another Oriental, who, within the first month, failed to show up five times. And so at last they were obliged to abandon the idea, and Mrs Bridge, when discussing the matter with her friends, some of whom had chauffeurs and some of whom were considering it, was apt to say, 'Well, it does have advantages, but of course there are drawbacks.'

88 The rich and the poor

The principal advantage, of course, so far as she was concerned, was that in case of difficulty there was a man around to take charge. Occasionally something unfortunate would occur while she was out driving and she then found herself in a quandary, not knowing whether to telephone her husband and run the risk of interrupting him at work or to try to handle the situation alone. One day, for instance, the Lincoln simply stopped in the middle of the Ward Parkway. Luck was with her on this occasion, because a tow truck came by and when she had explained what happened the man looked under the hood. He asked how long it had been since the Lincoln was overhauled. She did not know, but thought it had been quite a while. She knew mechanics often tried to take advantage of people who knew very little about automobiles and so she bent over to peer into the engine, holding her fur coat tightly to her breast so it would not touch anything greasy, and after looking at different things for a few seconds she withdrew and said, 'Well, do the best you can. About how long do you think it will take? I have a luncheon appointment on the Plaza.'

Aside from mechanical difficulties there was always the parking problem; she had been amazed and impressed with the way the chauffeurs could park the Lincoln, and now that she was again on her own she was more than ever conscious of her inadequacy. Douglas, inadvertently, made the situation worse. A few days after taking up the study of geometry he began to measure everything. In his pocket he carried a carpenter's flexible steel tape, a compass, and a scratch pad, and he was obsessed by a desire to calculate all such things as the number of cubic feet in the attic, the radius of the mahogany dining-room table if it had been circular instead of elliptical, and the angle formed by the radio and the sofa and the fireplace. Among other things he measured the chimney, the back porch, the stove, and the wicker laundry basket, and one evening he pedantically announced that the pantry was almost exactly two cubic feet smaller than the Lincoln. The next time she tried to park the car she was reminded of his calculations. She pulled on one side of the steering wheel with both hands, backed up a few feet, pulled on the opposite side of the wheel, moved forward, backed up, and so on, gasping for breath in her efforts to maneuver the formidable machine, and she was not assisted by the knowledge that it would have been easier to park the pantry.

89 Paquita de las Torres

Douglas liked it, though, and he had no more than gotten his first driver's license when he began asking to borrow the car. She was glad enough to let him have it, only cautioning him to drive carefully; if she had to run an errand while he was using the Lincoln she did not mind catching a bus, and if the weather was bad she could telephone one of her friends. She often wondered where he went and what he was doing, but she did not worry much about him because he was growing to be rather conservative, which gratified her, and furthermore he seemed to be using his head more effectively than he did as a child. He was even taking a reasonable amount of interest in schoolwork. In short he was becoming a sober, self-reliant young man, a bit too mysterious, perhaps, but otherwise agreeably normal.

She was, therefore, almost started out of her wits to encounter him on the Plaza with the wildest-looking girl in the world. He had borrowed the car to go bowling and Mrs Bridge had later decided to go shopping for some cocktail napkins and so, quite unexpectedly, they met. The girl was a gypsy-looking business with stringy black uncombed hair, hairy brown arms jingling with bracelets, and glittering mascaraed eyes in which there was a look of deadly experience. She was wearing a sheer blouse of burnt orange silk and a tight white skirt, and Mrs Bridge did not need a second glance to realize that was practically all.

'How do you do, Paquita?' she said, smiling neutrally, after Douglas had sullenly mumbled an introduction. The girl did not speak and Mrs Bridge wondered if she understood English. The hairy arms and the rancid odor were almost too much for Mrs Bridge to bear. 'I hope you two are having a nice time,' she said, and heard a bracelet jingle and saw Douglas and Paquita exchange a deep, knowing look.

'Dad will be home early this evening for a change, so Harriet is planning on dinner at six sharp. I hope you won't be late. It's nice to have met you, Paquita.' And she could not be sure, but it seemed to her that a moment after she turned away the girl spat on the sidewalk.

On the bus going home with the cocktail napkins she tried to make sense of it. She tried to be fair. Why would he want to go bowling with someone obviously from a different high school when there were so many nice girls at Southwest? Why would he want to see this girl at all? What could they possibly have in common? Where could he have met her?

'You'd think I was poison,' she said to him that evening, jokingly and very seriously, as they entered the dining room. 'Why not tell us when you're beau-ing someone new? Your Dad and I are interested in knowing your friends.'

Douglas, having pushed her chair in as usual, went around the table and seated himself without a word.

'Paquita certainly jingles.'

'She likes bracelets,' he said trenchantly.

Mr Bridge entered, and in passing behind Douglas's chair gave him a solid, affectionate rap on the skull with his knuckles.

'Well,' said Douglas, grinning, 'you must have had a good day today. You make another million bucks or something?'

Mr Bridge laughed and picked up the carving knife, and while examining the roast he said, 'I hear you're turning into quite a basketball player.'

'Who told you that?'

'Never mind who told me.'

'Oh, I don't know,' Douglas said, blushing. He played forward on the church team and was trying to make the high-school squad but so far had been unsuccessful.

'Maybe you should butter up the coach's daughter,' said Mr Bridge, busying himself with the roast.

Douglas groaned in elaborate agony. 'Anyway, I don't even know if he's got a daughter. And besides, that's no way to make the team.'

'Well, how else are you going to do it?'

'Oh, you have to play just the way the coach likes. I mean he likes real smooth dribbling and things like that that really aren't important. I guess I told you about our church team skunking the Southwest second team, didn't I?'

'Yes you did. Pass your mother's plate.'

'Well, doesn't it stand to reason that if we can beat the second team we ought to be at least as good as the first team? I mean, this coach has got his favorites, see? And if you aren't one of his favorites, well, you just don't have a chance.'

Mr Bridge glanced at him and said calmly, 'You're joking about that, so I don't mind. But don't let me catch you whining seriously. This million dollars you referred to – if I had earned it I wouldn't have earned it from being the judge's favorite. This country operates on the principle that the more industry and intelligence a man applies to his job the more he is entitled to profit. I hope it never changes.'

'Yuh, okay,' Douglas muttered, trying to end the conversation before it turned into a lecture.

'Remember that.'

'I will. Okay. Okay.'

The telephone rang at that moment and Harriet came into the dining room to say it was for Mr Bridge. No sooner was he out of the room when Mrs Bridge remarked, 'I saw Patty Duncan the other day. She asked how you were.'

'Tell her I'm still alive and kicking.'

'She's such a lovely girl. And they say she's becoming quite the pianist.'

'Okay,' said Douglas, who had found himself assaulted from both ends of the dinner table. 'For the love of Mike, I mean can't I live my own life?'

For the remainder of the meal she said no more about the encounter on the Plaza, but it had so disturbed her that she waited up until he got in late that night.

'Were you out with Paquita?' she asked, gazing at him earnestly.

In silence, face averted, Douglas took off his leather jacket.

'Does she live around here?' Mrs Bridge asked, following him to the closet and picking a bit of lint from his sweater.

He hung up the jacket and walked into the living room, where he took a comb from his hip pocket, stooped a little in order to see himself in the mirror, for he was now almost six feet tall and still growing – soon he would be taller than his father – and began combing his long red hair straight back in the style he had recently adopted. His hair would not lie down, it grew stubbornly in various directions, and the more he combed it the more rebellious it looked, but he would not give in and the hair would not lie down.

'You're just like your Dad,' she said, observing him, and there was not only love but vexation in her tone. Douglas, scowling, combed his hair and mashed it with his palms. As soon as he lifted his hands the hairs began to rise.

'Dear,' she said, having followed him from the closet. She now stood a little way in back of him, looking at his face in the mirror. He slipped the comb in his pocket and bent a look of deep hatred against the mirror.

'What is it?' he asked brutally.

'Oh, I don't know.'

'Well, good night,' he said and turned to go upstairs, but she reached out and caught his arm.

'Douglas, why do you want to go around with that sort of person?'

At this he jerked his arm free and went to the closet, where he got his jacket and left the house again. She remained with one hand resting on the banister and was sick with anxiety, not so much because of the girl, for she knew he would outgrow her, but because she did not want to lose his friendship. She had lost his love, she knew not why, as she had forfeited that of Ruth, and the thought of losing her son entirely was more than she could endure.

90 Extra-sensory perception

The next night he borrowed the Lincoln to escort Paquita to a basketball tournament in the municipal auditorium. While driving down Troost toward the north end of town, where she lived with her sister, who was a burlesque dancer, he passed a drive-in restaurant. He neither stopped nor slowed down, but as he went by his attention was caught by a singularly voluptuous carhop, with the result that when the traffic light changed he did not see it because he was looking backward. He drove into the rear of the car ahead of him. No one was injured, but all parties were somewhat dazed and Douglas got himself a lump on the forehead. The grille of the Lincoln was dented and a wheel knocked out of alignment.

At home, when asked how the accident occurred, he replied without hesitation that it was because of a woman.

'Oh-ho!' said Mr Bridge, who was of the opinion that traffic problems would disappear on the day women were no longer licensed to drive. 'What have I been saying all these years?' He asked his son no more questions, only took the paper on which Douglas had written the license number of the other car, and said he would notify the insurance company.

Douglas wisely volunteered no further information and believed he had gotten out of the embarrrassing accident rather cleverly until he chanced to look at his mother. Although she had not said a word, he perceived that in some fantastic manner she sensed the

150

complete truth, and he reflected that in matters however distantly related to sex she possessed supernatural powers of divination.

91 Frayed cuffs

Ordinarily Mrs Bridge examined the laundry that Ingrid carried up from the basement every Tuesday afternoon in a creaking wicker basket, but when she was out shopping, or at a luncheon, the job fell to Harriet, who never paid much attention to such things as missing buttons or loose elastic. Thus it was that Mrs Bridge discovered Douglas wearing a shirt with cuffs that were noticeably frayed.

'For heaven's sake!' she exclaimed, taking hold of his sleeve. 'Has a dog been chewing on this?'

He looked down at the threads as though he had never before seen them; in fact he hadn't.

'Surely you don't intend to *wear* this shirt?'

Since he was already wearing the shirt this struck him as a foolish question, but he said, 'It looks perfectly okay to me.'

'Why, just look at those cuffs! Anyone would think we were on our way to the poorhouse.'

'So is it a disgrace to be poor?'

'No!' she cried. 'But we're *not* poor!'

92 Sex education

Thereafter she kept a sharp eye on the laundry, going through it piece by piece to see what needed mending, after which she separated it into three stacks: one for the master bedroom, one for the room which Ruth and Carolyn had shared and which now was Carolyn's alone, and a third for Douglas's room. One by one she carried these piles of clothing into the proper room and there divided them further, handkerchiefs, underwear, blouses, and so forth, and arranged them neatly in the proper drawers.

One afternoon she carried Douglas's laundry into his room as usual and placed it on his bed as she always did in order to sort it. She put the newly laundered shirts on top of the others in his dresser and was about to go on with her work when it occurred to her that in all likelihood he was wearing the same shirts again and again; probably the ones in the bottom of the drawer were never being worn, and with the idea of reversing the order she took them all out and beneath the final shirt she found a magazine. Although she had never before seen one like it she knew instinctively what it was.

Mrs Bridge sank to the edge of the bed and gazed dismally at the wall, the unopened magazine in her hands. She could hear Harriet singing hymns in the kitchen while peeling green apples for a pie, and the fervency of those good shrill Christian notes caused Mrs Bridge to feel more desolate and abandoned than ever. She closed her eyes and shook her head in disbelief. The last thing on earth she wanted was to look into this magazine, but it had to be done. She looked at one page. There was a naked woman. That was enough. She looked no more. Never in her life had she been confronted with a situation like this and she did not know what to do. She was under the impression that these magazines had been legislated against and were not available. She asked herself where she had failed. With him, as with Ruth and Carolyn, she had adroitly steered around threatening subjects; in no way had she stimulated his curiosity – quite the contrary. Where, then, had she failed? She had let him realize, without her having to say so, that there were two kinds of people in the world, and this was true, she knew, for it was what she had been taught by her father and mother.

She kept expecting Douglas to say something about the magazine – which she burned in the incinerator – but if he noticed it was gone he gave no indication. Weeks passed. She did not want to rush him. She wanted him to come to her and confess of his own free will. Carolyn was now a freshman at the university, which was located in the town of Lawrence, about forty miles distant; she often came home on week ends, but during the week she was gone, with the result that Mrs Bridge and Douglas were sometimes the only members of the family at the dinner table. These dinners were silent and unpleasant for them both; they tended to avoid looking at each other. She waited patiently for the moment when he would

152

give a sign – a single deep look would be enough – and she would know then that he wanted to have a talk. Still time went by and, since he made no move, she began to fasten her eyes on him. These mute invitations had a singular effect on Douglas; whenever he became conscious of her mournful, wretched gaze he would leave the house. She thought he was touched and full of remorse at the unhappiness he was causing and so she continued to gaze deeply at him whenever they were alone. However, more time went by and for some reason he failed to come to her.

One evening, therefore, she walked upstairs to his room and tapped on the door with her fingernail. The door was closed but she knew he was at his desk and that he was staring at the door. She was right, because after she had waited a few minutes she heard the chair creak and then his footsteps on the carpet. He jerked the door open and found her there smiling miserably. She glided past him into the room and to his desk where, without a word, she placed on the blotter a slim, musty pamphlet with a gray cover and sepia pages which she had gotten from a trunk in the attic. The pamphlet had a faint dried odor, like the crumbled wings of moths, and the elaborate typography related a little story about the marriage of a sperm and an ovum. On the frontispiece, beneath an attached sheet of tissue, were two circular photographs taken from laboratory slides.

He had followed her across the room and was now standing on the opposite side of the desk with his fists clenched behind his back. Seeing him so tense she thought that if she could only manage to rumple his hair as she used to do when he was a small boy everything would be all right. Calmly, and a little shyly, she began easing toward him.

Seeing that she was after him he also moved to keep the desk between them.

93 Words of wisdom

A few days later on his return from high school Douglas saw, beneath the hairbrush on his dresser, a page torn from a magazine. On one side of the page was an automobile advertisement, and on the other side was a picture of an elderly Chinese gentleman called the Old Sage, together with a list of maxims:

It is as easy to grin as to growl.
Hatred is self-punishment.
Rotten or decayed wood cannot be carved.
Have no care for the future and you will sorrow for the present.
Life is a mirror that gives back as much as it receives.
A record is often broken when competition gets keen.
A good cure for drunkenness is while sober to see a drunken man.
Courage at the critical moment is half the victory.
Words show the wit of a man, actions his meanings.
The anvil lasts longer than the hammer.
The pleasure of doing good is never tiresome.
Contentment is an inexhaustible treasure.
A handful of common sense is worth a bushel of learning.

Douglas went through these more and more rapidly. Having finished, and not knowing exactly what to do with the list, thinking she might want it back, he put it in a desk drawer and paid no further attention to it. In the days that followed their eyes occasionally met and locked, inexpressively.

He knew she was waiting for him to comment; she knew he had read the maxims.

94 Very gay indeed

Ruth did not write home as often as Mrs Bridge had expected, nor was it possible to guess from her letters what sort of a life she was leading in New York; however she seemed to be getting along all right and did not sound unhappy. She wrote that she had moved into an apartment near the Hudson, that she was now working for a fashion magazine, and that she hoped for a promotion before long. In April she was promoted; she became an 'assistant editor', whatever that meant, but it did sound important and Mrs Bridge was very proud and let her friends know about Ruth's success. That same month they were surprised and delighted when she flew home for a visit. She had changed a great deal; she had become very sophisticated.

Carolyn came home from the university that week end, and Mrs Bridge was struck by the difference in the girls. It was hard to believe they were sisters – Ruth so dark and sleek, and really too thin, angular, sauntering about and smoking one cigarette after another and having cocktails with her father as though she had been drinking for years; Carolyn so active and blond and determined, and rather sturdy-looking in low-heeled golfing shoes, for she had begun playing golf in high school and was now getting exceptionally good.

Ruth was undeniably more mature and Mrs Bridge noticed an odd fact: Ruth and Douglas liked each other very much. There was no reason they should not – in fact they certainly should like each other – but she could not get over a sense of astonishment when she heard them laughing together, or saw them earnestly talking in the breakfast room, drinking pots of coffee and discussing she did not know what. They appeared to have developed a new relationship. They were no longer just brother and sister, and Mrs Bridge felt a little thrilled and more than a little sad.

She and Ruth did not have much time alone, and all at once, so it seemed, Ruth was on the telephone checking her plane reservation to New York. On her last evening in Kansas City the two of them remained in the dining room after Douglas and Mr Bridge had left the table. They had only a few minutes because a young man named Callaway Rugg was coming to take Ruth to a Little Theatre production of *Cyrano,* but while they were talking at the dinner table she mentioned that one of the men who worked in her office in New York was a homosexual.

'Just what do you mean, Ruth?' asked Mrs Bridge soberly. She had picked up a spoon and was slowly stirring her coffee.

'Why, he's gay, Mother. Queer. You know.'

'I'm afraid I don't know,' said Mrs Bridge.

Ruth could not tell whether her mother was serious or not. The idea of her mother not knowing was too incredible, and yet, thinking back, and having talked with Douglas about things that had happened recently, and after a long, probing look into her mother's eyes, Ruth knew her mother was speaking the truth. This realization so shocked her that she said coldly, 'Then it's time you found out.' Feeling cruel and nervous and frightened she continued, in the same tone, 'I'm very fond of him, Mother. One

155

morning he brought me a dozen long-stemmed roses.'

From the hall came the sound of the front door chimes. Immediately Ruth jumped up and hurried to open the door, leaving Mrs Bridge as isolated as she had ever been in her life, as she had been isolated by her husband that day on the rue Auber.

95 *Local talent*

Seldom had anyone from the country-club district attracted national attention, but there had been a few. A girl named Catlett, whose mother Mrs Bridge knew slightly, went off to the Bahamas for a summer vacation and came back triumphantly engaged to a senator. Then there were the twins who were featured in a toothpaste advertisement, and occasionally one of the older men would be mentioned. But of the younger people the most celebrated was Callaway Rugg. He was a few years older than Ruth, but he had known her in high school and used to take her on long drives through the country; he would speak of the brevity of human affairs and of how vital it was to live as one wanted to live. He himself did not know how he wanted to live, but after playing in some dramatic productions staged in a barn on the outskirts of the city he was picked up by a talent scout and sent to Hollywood, where for the first two weeks they were under the impression he was a lion tamer. After this was straightened out he was put into a movie. *The Tattler* spoke of 'Kansas City's own Carleton Reynolds,' which was what Hollywood named him. Surprisingly, or so Mrs Bridge had thought, the fact that he was a Kansas Citian did not noticeably increase the run of the picture. She had gone to see it. Rugg had appeared in only one scene: on the stroke of midnight, arms bound behind his back and a sack over his head, he fell out of a grandfather clock.

'Of course his part was small,' she had remarked while discussing it with Madge Arlen, 'but I do think he's quite talented.'

However Hollywood must not have thought so, for Rugg was next heard from selling encyclopedias on the Plaza.

96 Exchange of letters

The new *Tattler* came out a few days after Ruth returned to New York and Mrs Bridge mailed a clipping to her: 'Found holidaying at the charming home of her parents, Mr and Mrs Bridge of Crescent Heights Drive, was the lovely eldest, Ruth, now setting Gotham aflame. Scores of admirers hope the fascinating and exotic editoress-to-be won't become a permanent Manhattanite.' On the back of the clipping was the conclusion of an article of advice to hostesses: '. . . jungle the natives simply peel and eat, and so should we! No more worry about knives and forks, lefthand or righthand.' And below this was the first line of a quotation from Thoreau.

Mrs Bridge wrote that Carolyn was playing golf every afternoon and had beaten one of the boys who was on the university team, that the weather in Kansas City was awfully pleasant this time of year, that some man named Genaro had telephoned just after she returned to New York but hadn't left a message, that the city was finally widening the street in front of the Junior League clubhouse, and that her visit to Kansas City had seemed awfully brief. Ruth had remarked on the graft in New York, so Mrs Bridge wrote, 'Isn't it awful there's so much graft? We have it here, too. It just makes you wonder about people.'

She also mentioned what had been going on socially and what events were on the calendar. 'Wednesday evening the Arlens are staging a cocktail party for Anne who's off to Europe and it sounds quite intriguing. Thursday, Madge and I are off to a recital given by some folk singer who plays the dulcimer, and then on Friday there's to be a church doing (at which a Moslem will talk!) but I'm not sure I'll be able to make it. I've been having a siege of headaches and they just don't seem to be able to make heads or tails of them. Dr Stapp told me it's all mental but that doesn't make sense. Dr McIntyre (he's so nice!) thinks it may be an allergy but if so I wish they'd hurry up and get together, whatever it is. Then next Monday there's a reception at Crestwood for the McKinney

157

girls who're just back from a month at the Royal Hawaiian. That must have been grand . . .'

Ruth chose to answer this letter one night while she was in bed with a man named Dowdey, whom she had met the previous week. She wrestled the pillow away from him and put it behind her back in order to sit up more comfortably, and with an airmail pad on her knees she began:

'The weather in New York has been lovely, but otherwise there isn't very much news. I can't stand my boss because he's an absolute tyrant, but everybody else is nice, and we're trying a new format that I like better. A man who works in the next office' – and she dropped one hand to give Dowdey a pinch on the buttocks – 'has been awfully sweet although I don't know him very well yet. I haven't been going out much lately. I usually come home after work and go to bed early. It was marvelous seeing everybody in Kansas City.' Here she paused and tapped the pen against her teeth, and finally added that she hoped to visit Kansas City again before long.

Dowdey, having rolled over and raised himself to one elbow, was reading the letter with his chin propped on Ruth's shoulder.

'Jus' like I aim to get back to San Antone,' he said, and began kissing her throat.

'Hush,' she said. 'And stop. You're bothering me!'

'Come on down here and le's bother all over,' said Dowdey, 'on account of you can write yo' little mama in the mornin'.'

'Cut that out,' said Ruth. 'Now cut that out!'

'Yo' mama look like you?' he asked, sliding his arms around her waist.

'She's my sister's mother!'

And as if by hearing these words she realized what she had said, Ruth touched her lover gently and looked down into his unblinking hazel eyes. She caressed the wind wrinkles of his leathery face; he became solemn and expectant.

'I'll only be a little while,' she said. For a few minutes she sat with her knees drawn up to her chin and gazed across the river and the buildings on the western shore, and she was able to see her home, not as it was now, but ten years before, at a time in her life when she would never have thought to say her mother was not her own: when she had been as tall as the new evergreen trees in the yard, when her brother was a baby. Now this was gone, and it was gone forever. She wondered why she was in New York, why she would soon give herself to this man for whom she had no feeling.

'I don't think it's her fault,' Ruth whispered, with her head on her knees, and when Dowdey asked what she had said she did not answer. Presently she sighed and continued with the letter, thanking her mother for sending a box of oatmeal cookies Harriet had baked, and said they were wonderful, though in truth they had arrived broken and crushed, and she had sprinkled them on the window sill for the pigeons. Having signed the letter with love, as she always did, she ordered Dowdey to open his mouth and hold out his tongue to lick the envelope.

'That all?' he asked, grinning, as she leaned across him to place the letter on the night table.

'It depends on what you mean,' Ruth said. She turned out the light. When he covered her she was looking across the dark river, gravely thinking of home.

97 *Frozen fruit*

With Ruth gone and with Carolyn at home only an occasional week end, with Mr Bridge continuing to spend long hours at the office, and with Douglas appearing only for meals, Mrs Bridge found the days growing interminable; she could not remember when a day had seemed so long since the infinite hours of childhood, and so she began casting about rueful and disconsolate for some way to occupy the time. There were mornings when she lay in bed wide awake until noon, afraid to get up because there was nothing to do. She knew Harriet would take care of ordering the groceries, Harriet would take care of everything, Harriet somehow was running the house and Mrs Bridge had the dismal sensation of knowing that she, herself, could leave town for a week and perhaps no one would get overly excited. At breakfast – lunch if she chose to call it so – she would consider the newspaper with sober apathy, sighing at the events in Europe, lethargically eating whatever Harriet prepared – toast and orange juice, chipped beef and cinnamon rolls, fruit salad, bacon and tomato sandwich, a dish of sherbert; whatever it happened to be Mrs Bridge would eat some of it though it seemed tasteless. Summer had come again, another summer, another year.

One warm windy morning in June she could hardly open her eyes; she lay in the stuffy bedroom and listened to the wind in the trees, to the scratching of the evergreen branches against the house, and wondered if she was about to die. She did not feel ill, but she had no confidence in her life. Why should her heart keep beating? What was there to live for? Then she grew cheerful because she recalled her husband had told her to get the Lincoln waxed and polished. In fact he had told her that three weeks ago but she had not yet gotten around to it. Now, in any event, there was something to do; she would do the work herself. She would drive to the Plaza to an auto-supply store and buy a can of wax and some polish and a chamois, or whatever the salesman recommended, and she would spend the day working on the Lincoln. It had been years since she had done any work, with the exception of puttering in the garden, and it would be refreshing. But then, still in bed, she became doubtful and more reasonable. She had never attempted to polish an automobile, she knew nothing about it, nothing whatsoever, and if she should ruin the finish of the Lincoln what on earth could she say to her husband? He would be amazed and furious because it was so nonsensical; he would manage to control his temper but he would be infuriated all the same and want to know why she had done it. Could she explain how the leisure of her life – that exquisite idleness he had created by giving her everything – was driving her insane?

However, she reflected, as she got out of bed holding a hand to her brow to prevent herself from collapsing, she could at least drive to the Plaza and wander around while the Lincoln was being polished. She could look into Bancroft's; perhaps they had some new imports. She could have a late luncheon in the tea shoppe. Surely something else would come to mind by then and soon the day would be over.

Once out of bed she felt more alive, and while getting dressed she thought of telephoning Grace Barron. Perhaps they could spend the day together. No one answered the Barrons' phone. After a few minutes she tried again with no success and then dialed Madge Arlen. The line was busy. She knew from past experience that

Madge stayed on the telephone for hours, but now the Plaza idea had begun to sound exciting with or without company and she began to hurry around getting ready to go, and was annoyed with herself for having wasted the entire morning. It was fifteen minutes to one when Mrs Bridge came downstairs. Harriet was vacuuming the hall. Mrs Bridge signaled her to stop the machine, and when the roaring died away she said, looking quickly into her purse to see she had not forgotten anything, 'I've got to run to the Plaza to have the car taken care of. It needs waxing. If anybody calls, tell them I'll be home about five.'

Harriet replied that Mr Bridge had had the car waxed and polished the previous Saturday.

Mrs Bridge stopped and looked at her in stupefaction. 'He did? I wonder why he didn't mention it.'

Harriet did not say anything.

'Are you sure?' asked Mrs Bridge.

Harriet nodded.

'Oh. Well, then,' she said doubtfully, 'I suppose it doesn't need to be done again. Isn't that strange? He must have forgotten to tell me.' She noticed Harriet looking at her without expression, but intently, and she became embarrassed. She dropped the car keys back in her purse and slowly took off her hat. She had driven the Lincoln several times since Saturday and it was odd she had not noticed the difference.

Harriet turned on the vacuum.

After changing into more comfortable clothes Mrs Bridge wandered to the kitchen, fixed a sandwich for herself, and sat in the breakfast room for about an hour watching the sparrows in the garden. Finally she managed to get Madge Arlen on the telephone.

'Lord, I'm glad you called!' her friend exclaimed. 'I'm out of my wits for something to do.'

'Come on over this minute,' said Mrs Bridge.

'Are you in the same fix?'

'I should say I am!'

And now the day took shape and Mrs Bridge was no longer embarrassed. She had found she was not alone, and if others felt as she felt there was no reason to be depressed. The hours no longer loomed ahead; it was just another warm June day. A few minutes later Madge Arlen was coming in the front door, wearing a loose lavender gaucho blouse, chartreuse slacks, and cork wedgies that made her nearly six feet tall. She was smoking one of the English cigarettes she liked but which were now so hard to obtain. Harriet made some coffee, for Madge Arlen drank coffee all day, and they sat on the porch and talked. The British were concluding the evacuation of Dunkirk, and for a while Mrs Bridge and Madge Arlen discussed the war.

'So many of the boys are joining up,' Mrs Bridge remarked. 'It certainly changes things. I notice the difference everywhere. Piggly Wiggly still delivers, thank heavens, but the service is so much slower than it used to be and I was so surprised the other morning to see they have a girl driving the truck.'

'Just wait till Congress passes a draft law. Lord, we'll see the difference then!'

'Oh, I hope not! I'm sure the war will be over soon, and of course we're doing everything humanly possible to stay out of it.'

And they talked about people they knew. Grace Barron's son, David, had been taking violin lessons for a number of years and wanted to make a career of music. His father disapproved of this and, as everyone knew, the Barrons were not getting along well. Madge Arlen mentioned that the situation was worse.

'Being a professional musician does sound exciting,' Mrs Bridge observed. 'But I just wonder how practical it would be. Oh, my word, it's four o'clock already! I don't know about you, Madge, but I'm simply famished.'

They went to the kitchen and Mrs Bridge looked into the refrigerator.

'Strawberries and whipped cream?' she suggested. 'These are frozen, of course. They don't really taste the same as the fresh, but they certainly are a time-saver.'

98 Reflections on Montaigne

The Tattler killed many an interminable hour. She read it, not avidly, but thoroughly, from Bancroft's full-page ad inside the front cover to Mr Alexander's striking floral ad on the back.

Of all the things in *The Tattler* she was most impressed with the philosophy. Between snapshots of country-club residents enjoying themselves at their favorite swimming pool, or on the golf links, and items of gossip regarding prominent Kansas Citians, the editors of *The Tattler* customarily sandwiched a thought or two – preferably cheerful, affirmative at the very least. Emerson and Saint Francis were frequent contributors; Oliver Wendell Holmes was a great favorite. The observations of such eminent men were set in italics and were apt to be followed by, 'I wonder if the scion of a certain well-known *famille* doesn't realize his many conquests are causing talk among the younger set.'

Mrs Bridge, being considerably interested in these maxims, had at one point thought of beginning a nice scrapbook with the idea of handing it on to the children. Though she had not found time for this she continued to try to memorize certain quotations, despite the fact that there never seemed to be an appropriate occasion to re-quote them. A line from Montaigne set her to thinking.

I have always observed a singular accord between supercelestial ideas and subterranean behavior.

In less crystalline style she had observed somewhat the same thing and was puzzled by it: she recalled the strange case of Dr Foster, who had been positively identified at the burlesque, not once – which could have been attributed to his gathering material for a sermon – but several times. Furthermore he never mentioned it.

Over the wisdom of Montaigne she brooded, eventually reaching the conclusion that if supercelestial ideas were necessarily accompanied by subterranean beahvior it might be better to forego them both.

99 Gloves

She looked forward to Saturdays because on that day she was occupied with the distribution of used clothing at the Auxiliary charity center on Ninth Street. Usually she went with Madge Arlen. One week they would drive to work in the Arlens' Chrysler, the next week in the Lincoln, and when it was Mrs Bridge's turn she drew up before the garage where her husband parked. There she honked the horn, or beckoned if someone happened to be in sight, and shortly an attendant whose name was Hal would come out of the garage buttoning on a white duster and he would ride in the rear seat to the charity center. There he would jump out and open the door for Mrs Bridge, and after that he would drive the Lincoln back to the garage because she did not like it left on the street in such a neighborhood.

'Suppose you come by for us around six, or six-fifteenish, Hal,' she would say.

He always answered that he would be glad to, touched the visor of his cap, and drove away.

'He seems so nice,' said Mrs Arlen as the two of them walked into the center.

'Oh, he is!' Mrs Bridge agreed. 'He's one of the nicest garage men I've ever had.'

'How long have you been parking there?'

'Quite some time. We used to park at that dreadful place in Walnut.'

'The one with the popcorn machine? Lord, isn't that the limit?'

'No, not that place. The one with the Italians. You know how my husband is about Italians. Well, that just seemed to be head-quarters for them. They flocked in there by the dozen to eat their lunch and listen to some opera broadcast from New York. It was just impossible. So finally Walter said, "I'm going to change garages." So we did.'

The charity center had not yet been opened for the day. Mrs Bridge and Mrs Arlen walked between the counters piled high with sour, unwashed clothing, past the reform-school boys who were emptying sacks of clothing on the floor, and continued into the back room, which was reserved for Auxiliary members. Lois Montgomery was there, and Mabel Ong and Rebecca Duncan, along with several other ladies. They were having coffee and eclairs as they always did before starting work. Mrs Bridge and Mrs Arlen joined them.

After a while the doors were unlocked and the first of the poor entered. Behind the counters waiting to assist them were Mrs Bridge and her friends, all wearing gloves.

100 Marching with Dr Foster

For a few months Grace Barron worked at the charity center; then she quit, abruptly, without offering an explanation. Mrs Bridge was hurt by this, for it seemed unlike Grace Barron to be inconsiderate. Then, too, Mrs Bridge reflected, she had always been so concerned about the welfare of others; still she did have streaks of peculiarity, as, for instance, her attitude toward Dr Foster, whom Mrs Bridge considered not only one of the nicest men she had ever met, but also one of the most intelligent. Grace, inexplicably, was amused by Dr Foster.

Mrs Bridge regretted having told her about a rather unfortunate slip of the tongue which occurred at the start of the benediction on Palm Sunday. Dr Foster had said, 'With eyes bowed and heads closed . . .'

True, this was unfortunate, but, as she promptly added in defense of the minister, 'It could happen to anyone.'

Grace probably didn't hear; she was laughing hysterically. 'I knew I should have gone last Sunday,' she said, wiping the tears from her eyes, 'Oh, I'm so sorry I missed that!'

Then there had been that awful day when the elevator plunged into the bargain basement. It was a dark, rainy afternoon and Mrs Bridge had gone downtown and was browsing through the basement of one of the department stores in search of something humorous to give as a booby prize at a forthcoming card party. She was examining some celluloid toys when all at once there was a noise like a shot and a shrill singing whine and a rumble, and before she could understand what it was all about the elevator crashed not ten steps from where she stood. Later it turned out that the elevator had not fallen as far as everyone thought; in fact it had only dropped about six or eight feet. Even so, it made a great noise and most of the passengers dropped their parcels and one or two fell down. Mrs Bridge had not yet recovered from her surprise and was only looking rather blankly at the people in the elevator, who themselves were stunned into momentary silence and were looking blindly out of the cage, when someone began to scream for help. It was someone in the rear of the elevator, and presently this person fought his way through the other passengers and got to the front where he grabbed the cage and began shaking it.

'Why, Dr Foster!' said Mrs Bridge, and then there was so much confusion and so many people rushing around that she lost track of him.

He was not badly injured, as she had supposed he was; he had a sprained ankle. He went about on a cane for quite a while afterward – longer, in fact, than she had ever seen anyone employ a cane for a sprained ankle – and for several weeks more he hobbled and alluded dryly to his accident. Mrs Bridge was a little disappointed in him without knowing just why. However there was certainly nothing funny about the accident, and she was quite put out with Grace for laughing when she heard of it.

Her entire attitude toward religion was flippant, and Mrs Bridge did not think it was in very good taste. After one of the Auxiliary meetings she chanced to be nearby when Grace got on the subject of religion and said there was a rumor that after Christ was sentenced to death He turned to one of the soldiers and said, 'When am I going to learn to keep my big mouth shut?'

Mrs Bridge smiled courteously, as she never failed to do when someone told a joke, and though she did not believe God was planning to strike Grace dead, still she could not see there was anything to be gained by asking for trouble.

Frequently she attempted to interest her in religion, or at least in the habit of attending church, but the attempts were unsuccessful. It was a rare Sunday when she encountered Grace among the crowd on the church steps after services.

In the center of the church lawn stood a green wooden cupboard with a glass front. Each Thursday morning the janitor came out with a manila envelope full of white celluloid letters about two inches tall, and with these he composed the title of Dr Foster's forthcoming sermon. Mrs Bridge was pleased to see the Barrons' Cadillac parked in the lot one Sunday morning when the sermon was entitled: *Should We Go to Church?*

Naturally no one believed Dr Foster would decide in favor of the negative, yet Mrs Bridge could not help being irked when Grace whispered that she could hardly wait to find out. In a few minutes Dr Foster appeared and ascended to the pulpit. He was growing more stout and more dignified every year. Solemnly he gazed down upon the congregation. At such times Mrs Bridge thought he looked every inch the Man of God. She remembered seeing him one day on the Plaza; he had been studying himself in the mirror of a cigarette machine and she thought she had never seen him look more impressive. It was only at cocktail parties that he seemed unable to avoid little belches, after which he would stare with severity at the sandwich or cocktail in his hand.

'Should we go to church?' asked Dr Foster of his audience. He allowed a few seconds for everyone to ponder. 'Should we go to church?' he repeated. He cleared his throat, placed his hands on the sides of the lectern, and began.

The sub-title of the sermon was 'Unexplored Warehouses of the Cliff Dwellers.' The parable had to do with the fact that in plentiful years the Mesa Verde Indians stored part of their harvest in cliff houses and in time of famine they ate what they had saved.

A few minutes after noon Dr Foster was winding it up. 'We, of this more enlightened age, can surely benefit from the wisdom of those ancient savages. They learned to store their surplus against the time of dire necessity, and so it is when we go to church . . .'

A few minutes later he descended and strode magnificently through the swinging doors. The last they saw of him was the tail of his black and royal purple cassock. To Mrs Bridge he had seemed unusually eloquent and moving, and it was very strange, she thought, that throughout the sermon Grace was inattentive and listless. Afterward, on the steps, they talked for a little while.

'Grace,' Mrs Bridge said impulsively, and took her by the hand, 'is something troubling you?'

'No,' she whispered, with her eyes tightly shut. 'No, no, *no!*'

'There is!' cried Mrs Bridge. 'I know there is!' But at this point they were interrupted by the arrival of the men and whatever might have been revealed was lost.

101 Quo vadis, Madame?

That evening, while preparing for bed, Mrs Bridge suddenly paused with the fingertips of one hand just touching her cheek. She was seated before her dressing table in her robe and slippers and had begun spreading cold cream on her face. The touch of the cream, the unexpectedness of it – for she had been thinking deeply about how to occupy tomorrow – the swift cool touch demoralized her so completely that she almost screamed.

She continued spreading the cream over her features, steadily observing herself in the mirror, and wondered who she was, and how she happened to be at the dressing table, and who the man was who sat on the edge of the bed taking off his shoes. She considered her fingers, which dipped into the jar of their own accord. Rapidly, soundlessly, she was disappearing into white, sweetly scented anonymity. Gratified by this she smiled, and perceived a few seconds later that beneath the mask she was not smiling. All the same, being committed, there was nothing to do but proceed.

102 Joseph Conrad

She was wakened by the chimes of the grandfather clock in the hall. It was three or four in the morning. Her husband was sleeping easily, but gravely, as though exhausted. She awoke simultaneously with the knowledge of one morning many years before when she had been dusting the bookcase and came across an old, old red-gold volume. Taking it down she found on the flyleaf in dry, spidery script the name of Shannon Bridge, who was the uncle of her husband – an unambitious, taciturn man who had married a night-club entertainer and later died of a heart attack in Mexico, and upon whose death they had inherited a few books and charts. She had no idea what the charts were about, for she had not unrolled them, only stored them in the attic, and then one day, absently, since they were useless, she had discarded them; and as for the books, no one had read them, so far as she knew, though later she found Douglas examining them, and now at four in the morning she was lying completely awake, thinking of the time she had taken a book down from a shelf and had begun turning the brittle, yellowed pages. She stood beside the bookcase for quite a while, growing absorbed in what she read, and wandered, still reading, into the living room, where she did not look up from the book until someone called her, because she had come upon a passage which had been underlined, no doubt by Shannon Bridge, which observed that some people go skimming over the years of existence to sink gently into a placid grave, ignorant of life to the last, without ever having been made to see all it may contain; and this passage she had read once again, and brooded over it, and turned back to it again, and was thinking deeply when she was interrupted.

And Mrs Bridge remembered now that she had risen and had said, 'Yes, all right, I'm on my way,' and had placed the book on the mantel, for she had intended to read further. She wondered what had interfered, where she had gone, and why she had never returned.

103 Psychotherapy

Mabel Ong was going to an analyst. Mrs Bridge was surprised to learn this because Mabel in her tailored suits and with her authoritative masculine manner had always seemed the very picture of confidence. At luncheon club not long after Dr Foster's eloquent sermon on church attendance she found herself sitting next to Mabel, and by the time luncheon was over Mrs Bridge was convinced that she, too, needed analysis. She had, in fact, privately thought so long before her talk with Mabel. More and more it had occurred to her that she was no longer needed. Ruth was gone, so very gone – even her letters said so little – and Carolyn was almost gone, and Douglas, though still at home, was growing so independent, more like his father every year. Soon he too would be leaving home. What would she do then? It had been a long time, she felt, since her husband truly needed her. He accepted her, and he loved her, of this she had never had a doubt, but he was accustomed to and quite unconscious of love, whereas she wanted him to think about it and to tell her about it. The promise of the past had been fulfilled: she had three fine children and her husband was wonderfully successful. But Mrs Bridge felt tired and ill. She wanted help.

She surmised her husband would not be sympathetic to her idea of being psychoanalyzed, so, for a number of weeks before mentioning it, she planned the conversation. She meant to open with the direct, positive, almost final statement that she was going downtown the first thing in the morning to arrange a series of appointments. That certainly ought to settle the matter – he ought to be able to understand the situation. Possibly he was going to inquire how much it would cost, and she was uneasy about this, suspecting it was going to be expensive, with the result that she avoided finding out what it would cost. After all, in spite of his complaints, she knew, and he was aware that she knew, that they had plenty of money.

She tried to imagine all his objections to her idea, but really there was nothing he could say. He would simply be forced to agree. It had been years since she had asked him for anything, no matter how slight; indeed, every once in a while he would inquire if there wasn't something she wanted – anything for the house, or for herself. No, there was nothing. It was difficult to find things to buy. She had the money, but she had already bought everything she could use, which was why she often spent an entire day shopping and came home without having bought anything except lunch, and perhaps some pastry during the afternoon.

Having solved whatever objection he might make in regard to the expense, she concluded that all she had to do was let him know her intention. She kept putting it off. She rehearsed the scene many times and it always came out satisfactorily. The difficulty lay in finding the opportunity to begin. So it was that several weeks slipped away, then one evening after supper, as they were settling themselves in the living room, she with a bag of knitting and he with the stock-market page of the newspaper, she knew the time had come. She pretended to be straightening her knitting, but she was greatly occupied with marshaling her thoughts. He always got to the heart of a matter at once, wasting no energy on preliminaries, and she had to be ready for this. Just then he lowered the paper and she was terrified that somehow he had been reading her mind. Quite often he could, and this more than anything else was the reason she found it exceedingly difficult to defend her ideas. He was glaring at the newspaper.

'Listen to this: The Central has asked the ICC to investigate the circumstances of the sale of eight hundred thousand shares of stock, owned by the Chesapeake and Ohio Railway, to Murchison and Richardson last week.' He looked across the paper at her as if she were responsible.

'Well!' said Mrs Bridge in what she thought an appropriate tone. It would be unwise to annoy him at this point, but until he made it clear whose side he was on she could not say anything specific. Her expression remained intent and neutrally expectant, as though she wanted to hear more.

'What in God's name do those people think they're doing?' he demanded sharply.

'It certainly doesn't seem right,' she answered, still not certain whether the scoundrels were Central, or Chesapeake and Ohio, or Murchison and Richardson. Or, of course, he could be angry with the newspaper for having publicized it.

Mr Bridge had taken off his glasses and was staring at her.

'I don't know a thing in the world about it, of course,' she added hastily.

He resumed reading. A few minutes later he said, 'Allied Chemical: up four! Great Lord! What's going on here?' After this he was quiet for a long time, coughing once, shaking the paper into shape. Mrs Bridge, having noted it was almost time for bed, decided she must speak.

'Walter,' she began in a tremulous voice, and went on rapidly, 'I've been thinking it over and I don't see any way out except through analysis.'

He did not look up. Minutes went by. Finally he muttered, 'Australian wool is firm.' And then, roused by the sound of his own voice, he glanced at her inquisitively. She gave him a stark, desperate look; it was unnecessary to repeat what she had said because he always heard everything even when he failed to reply.

'What?' he demanded. 'Nonsense,' he said absently, and he struck the paper into submission and continued reading.

104 Pineapple bread

The following day being Thursday, Harriet's day off, Mrs Bridge prepared supper for herself and her husband. Douglas had telephoned a few minutes after school let out to say he was at a fraternity meeting and that as soon as it was over he and a couple of friends were going to get a hamburger somewhere and then were going downtown to a track meet in the municipal auditorium.

'What about your homework?' she asked.

'Homework,' he replied, giving a very final opinion of it.

'Well, I don't think you should stay out late,' she answered. 'After all, it's a week night.'

He said he would be home early, but early could mean any hour.

'All right now, don't forget,' she said. 'Your grades haven't been worth boasting about.'

'I'll get by,' said Douglas. 'Holy Cow!'

'Yes, well you just might Holy Cow yourself right out of graduating.'

With that the conversation ended and she went into the kitchen to start preparing a casserole, as she had done many, many times before. She moved around the kitchen slowly. She had plenty of time. The house was so quiet that she began to think of how noisy it had been when all the children were there, how very much different everything had been, and presently, remembering the days when she used to cook the meals, she went to the cupboard where the old recipe books were stored. Harriet occasionally referred to them, but otherwise they had lain untouched for years. Mrs Bridge began looking through them, seeing pencil notations in her own handwriting, scarcely legible any more. Her husband liked more pepper in this, no bay leaves in that – whatever he wanted and whatever he did not like was expertly registered in the margins, and as she turned through these recipes she thought how strangely intimate the faded penciled notes remained; they brought back many scenes, many sweet and private memories; they brought back youth.

Mrs Bridge grew thoughtfully excited. A glance at the electric clock on the stove panel told her there might be time enough to alter her plans for supper. She was thinking of fixing spaghetti for him, with the special sauce he had so often said was the best in the world. She had not fixed it for years. Harriet could not sense just how long to let it simmer, and without that particular flavor to the sauce there was not much point in eating spaghetti. A quick search of the refrigerator and of the cupboards disclosed there were not the right ingredients. She found some canned sauce and thought about improvising from it, but it would not be the same. He would taste the difference. And so, regretfully, she admitted it was going to be the casserole again. Next week they would have spaghetti. A little sadly she turned on through the cookbooks, and once more she had an idea. She had come across the recipe for pineapple bread and there was time for that and she was certain they had the ingredients – not only the pineapple but the chipped pecans, the raisins – yes, yes, she could do it.

She carried the bread to the table wrapped in a towel because it was still hot from the oven, and Mr Bridge, who, as he unfolded his napkin, had been looking at the casserole with resignation, now glanced with puzzled interest at what she was bringing him. His expression began to brighten. He smiled.

'Oh-ho!' said Mr Bridge, rubbing his hands together. 'What have we here?'

She placed it before him, too thrilled to speak, and hurried back to the kitchen for the bread knife.

'Well, well!' said he, accepting the knife, and he smacked his lips and shut his eyes for a moment to inhale the fragrance of the small plump loaf.

'Go ahead and cut it,' she said to him intensely, and waited beside the chair.

The first slice fell down like a corpse and they saw bubbles of dank white dough around the pecans. After a moment of silence Mrs Bridge covered it with the towel and carried it to the kitchen. Having disposed of the bread she untied her little ruffled apron and waited quietly until she regained control of herself.

A few minutes later she re-entered the dining room with a loaf of grocery-store bread on a silver tray. She smiled and said, 'It's been a long time, I'm afraid.'

'Never mind,' said Mr Bridge as he removed the lid of the casserole, and the next day he brought her a dozen roses.

105 Carolyn's engagement

Time was passing more rapidly than she thought; she was almost overcome when Carolyn appeared in the middle of the week with an engagement ring she had gotten the night before from a thin, shaggy boy with protruding teeth whose name was Gil Davis. He was a junior at the university. He was studying business management and working part-time in the dean's office.

Mrs Bridge, seeking a moment to recover from the shock, looked at Carolyn's ring and said, 'It's an opal, isn't it?'

'Gil doesn't have much money,' Carolyn explained. 'He told me he thought diamonds were absurd. And you know, Mother, he's worked for everything he owns!'

She was fascinated by this. She had never known a boy who was poor. In high school she had known boys who worked during summers and some who worked after school in order to have spending money, but none of them had been forced to work in order to eat and buy clothing. 'Well, I think it's lovely!' said Mrs Bridge, squeezing her hand. 'Does your father know?'

'No,' said Carolyn.

'Well, I'm afraid you'd better tell him, don't you think so?'

'Why don't you call him?' Carolyn suggested.

'This isn't my engagement,' replied Mrs Bridge.

Mr Bridge, being informed of his daughter's engagement, was outraged. He had never heard of any Gil Davis, and who did Gil Davis think he was? And as for Carolyn, there was to be no more of this ridiculous nonsense. She was to return that ring to that upstart boy, whatever his name was, and that was to be the end of the matter. Carolyn immediately burst into tears and threw her ring on the carpet. Her father had never talked to her like that before. When she returned to the university the ring was in her pocket. She had promised to give it back.

Gil Davis, being informed that his suit had been rejected, was also outraged. He was twenty years old and never before in his life

174

had he been the cause of any trouble. He looked at the ring, he looked at Carolyn, and then he ran out of the dean's office and ran all the way to the bus station, where he bought a ticket to Kansas City. He pushed his way past the secretary who wanted to know what his business was and he walked into Mr Bridge's private office without bothering to knock. He emerged at eight o'clock that night in company with his intended father-in-law; they ate sausage and buckwheat cakes together in a lunch wagon, both of them exhausted, and they had agreed he was going to marry Carolyn. So, for the second time, Gil Davis placed his opal ring on her finger and she wore the ring with a truculent expression.

'I know you two are going to be very happy,' Mrs Bridge said, hugging her. 'I'm so relieved everything worked out all right.'

Carolyn said, 'You do like him, Mother, don't you?'

'Why, of course, dear! He's awfully nice. It's just that he's so different from the kind of boys you've been used to.'

Gil Davis was aware of this fact; he quit the university because he saw he would need steady money and quite a lot of it as soon as he married Carolyn. He returned to his home town, which was located near the Oklahoma border in southern Kansas, and there he went to work for his uncle, who owned a dry-goods emporium. Carolyn wanted him to work in an aircraft factory where he could get overtime wages, but saw the sense of his decision when he told her his uncle was considering retirement.

The friends of Mrs Bridge were avid for information about Carolyn's engagement.

'Is her ring a blue or a white?'

'It's a lovely opal,' Mrs Bridge replied, facing the inquiries with her best smile.

'What a nice idea!'

'It's what Carolyn was hoping for,' Mrs Bridge countered.

'I understand he's not a Kansas Citian.'

'From Parallel,' she replied serenely, and scored a point by not explaining where Parallel could be found.

'It sounds quite far.'

'They'll be driving up for visits, I'm sure.'

'What does the father do?'

He was a plumber. Mrs Bridge had confronted herself with this fact a thousand times; there was simply no way around it. She imagined herself replying to this question, which, inevitably, would be asked, replying evasively that he was associated with a company that did household installations, and yet she knew in her heart she must speak the truth. It seemed to her that Carolyn's happiness depended on the acknowledgment of this condition, and, for better or worse, the acceptance of it.

Said Mrs Bridge – and her throat was so constricted she was afraid the words would lodge there – 'Mr Davis is a plumber.' She was astonished to see she had very nearly scored again, for she had spoken with such ease that one might almost believe everybody nowadays was marrying the sons of plumbers.

'I hear the boy is a Beta.'

'Well, no. As I understand the situation, Gil is of the opinion fraternity life can be a liability.'

'Oh, how true.'

'And how does he stand with the draft?'

His feet were as flat as ironing boards and his teeth were bad; he had been rejected as generally unsatisfactory. There was no sense going into detail, such details as Carolyn had given, and so she replied that he had been exempted for medical reasons. She believed he had had rheumatic fever when he was a child. In any event this sounded plausible, and was acceptable.

'You say he's in Parallel now?'

Mrs Bridge knew what was next. She nodded.

'I see. I didn't realize he'd already graduated.'

'According to what Carolyn tells me, in his opinion a four-year university education is actually less worth while than a certain amount of practical experience.' It had been badly put, she knew, and it was a retreat, but the business of the plumber had broken her composure.

106 Present from Douglas

Wedding gifts arrived. Day after day they arrived and Carolyn received enough silver to open a shop. She tore open the packages greedily and her blue eyes gleamed more brightly than the richest plate. Mrs Bridge, meanwhile, seated at her writing table with a notebook and fountain pen, dutifully jotted down what it was and who had sent it. Carolyn would be expected to memorize this list in order to be able to thank everyone personally and specifically: she would be expected to, but would she? Mrs Bridge was uneasy. She, herself, no matter how long it took, no matter how arduous the job, would have learned to identify every gift. She could only hope Carolyn would be as considerate.

There were a few awkward presents – a green bronze frog to be used as a doorstop, a queer desk lamp that resembled a pagoda, two or three novels and a book of Persian poetry, and from cousin Lulubelle Watts in Memphis a lifetime subscription to a magazine no one had ever heard of. There was one gift, however, worse than these. It was a present from Douglas. It was a toaster.

Douglas had delayed until the last moment because he hated to give or to receive presents. He liked his sister but he did not see where spending fifteen or twenty dollars would prove he wished her happiness. In deference to custom, however, on the next to last day he decided to buy a toaster because she had said she would need one. He walked to the Plaza – 'Nobody's using the Lincoln,' she had said, but he replied that he felt like walking – and on the Plaza he looked them over, hands in his pockets, while a salesman demonstrated. He was shown the most elaborate toasters that money could buy, but he was not pleased. The dials were set, the pointers turned, the levers pressed, the machine plugged in, the concealed tray that collected crumbs was removed, all for his benefit, but he was not pleased. At the conclusion of the demonstration he walked across the street to a dime store and bought a primitive toaster such as his parents had had when they were first married.

No one criticized the gift. Carolyn thanked him. Mrs Bridge exclaimed over how simple it was to operate, and indeed it was simple. Neither of them mentioned the four magnificent automatic toasters which had been delivered that same morning.

Of course the amount of money spent was not the important thing, everyone admitted that, and everyone said something really should be done to make wedding gifts more reasonable; all the same, people would want to know what Douglas had given his sister, and either Mrs Bridge or Carolyn would be obliged to point it out. Clearly it had not cost more than two dollars. Mrs Bridge was absolutely baffled by her son. Never in her life had she so wanted to shake him.

107 Carolyn marries

To southern Kansas Carolyn moved after the ceremony and a one-week honeymoon at Excelsior Springs. Mr Bridge had offered them a wedding trip to the Bahamas, but Gil refused, saying they would honeymoon on the money he himself had earned, so Excelsior Springs was the extent of it. Carolyn had wanted to see the Bahamas ever since she could remember. The wedding gift metamorphosed into one hundred shares of expensive, conservative stock.

Gil began working nights in order to convince his uncle that it was feasible to retire and leave the dry-goods business in his hands, the result being that Carolyn was lonely and bored, and became petulant, and frequently drove to Kansas City for the night after leaving a note pinned to the tablecloth. She would stay in her old room and, if there chanced to be a party that week end, she might remain in Kansas City until Monday. From the beginning she disliked Parallel and could not make up her mind whether she could stand living there.

'The golf course is pathetic, Mother,' she said one evening. 'It's a nine-hole public course – and by public I mean *anybody*, but anybody, even if they never *saw* a golf club before, can play there. I mean, really, how does Gil expect me to accomplish anything there? It'll absolutely ruin my game. The greens – there aren't any greens, Mother, they're as hard as wood and the grass is burnt to a crisp. It isn't any fun. Anybody can hit the ball three hundred yards, just about – they just go on rolling. My God! I mean, actually, Mother, you should see that place! I had no idea it would be like that.'

Mrs Bridge was extremely anxious for Carolyn to be happy. 'I should think it would be nice for a change,' she said.

Carolyn was not listening.

'Gil's a type, really. He *is*. He's a small-town boy, and it shows, Mother. He got simply furious when I tried to tell the barber how to cut his hair. I got so mad I wouldn't speak to him for three days.'

'Dear, I wish you wouldn't argue with him.'

'Listen, Mother, no man is ever going to push me around the way Daddy pushes you around.'

108 Alice

Subsequent events proved that Carolyn and her husband had their reconciliations, no matter how brief, for she very soon was pregnant.

She drove up from Parallel one snowy afternoon and said as she came in the door, stamping snow from her galoshes, 'You'll never believe this, Mother, because it's perfectly incredible.' And she said this repeatedly, as if to convince herself it was a dream. It was less than a dream, or more, depending, though she continued to exclaim for about three months, 'I mean, this is just insane!'

Eventually she grew accustomed to her situation and it appeared to Mrs Bridge that the marriage was going to work out all right. Gil and Carolyn were looking for a house in Parallel; their apartment would be too small when the baby came.

'But everything is so high,' said Carolyn. They were in the kitchen. It was Harriet's day off and Mrs Bridge was baking some oatmeal cookies to send to Ruth, and Carolyn was helping. 'We want something with a decent yard,' she went on, sliding a spatula under a row of hot cookies and transferring them to a towel spread on the drainboard. 'And Gil insists on a dry basement. That's the first place he goes. The real-estate agent no more than has the door open when Gil heads for the basement and I'm left standing there as big as an elephant. He's gone mad on turning out salad bowls on a lathe. A friend of his has a lathe. He says it calms his nerves, and so that's why he has to have a dry basement – so it won't rust the goddamned lathe. Really, how berserk can a man go?'

Mrs Bridge, carefully drawing a second tray of cookies from the oven, observed that there should be lots of pleasant homes in Parallel.

'Oh, there are, there are,' Carolyn mumbled, 'but you've got to check the neighbors.'

'I don't understand what you mean.'

'The niggers are moving in.'

Mrs Bridge slowly put down the tray of cookies. She did not know just what to say. Such situations were awkward. On the one hand, she herself would not care to live next door to a houseful of Negroes; on the other hand, there was no reason not to. She had always liked the colored people she had known. Still she thought affectionately of Beulah Mae and worried about her, wondering if she was still alive. She had never known any Negroes socially; not that she avoided it, just that there weren't any in the neighborhood, or at the country club, or in the Auxiliary. There just weren't any for her to meet, that was all.

'That reminds me, Carolyn. You'll never guess who I bumped into the other day. Alice Jones! We got on an elevator together.'

'My God! I'd absolutely forgotten that girl.'

'Don't you remember how you two used to play together? You were practically inseparable. I almost had to pry you apart at lunch time.'

'Did she recognize you?'

'Oh, right away.'

'What's she doing?'

'She's married now and she's working as a maid in one of the downtown hotels.'

'How many children does she have?'

'She didn't say.'

'Does she look the same?'

'Heavens, no! She's almost as tall as Douglas and she looked so black. It's such a shame.'

Carolyn became thoughtful, and finally said, 'I think I'd like to see her. Which hotel is she working at?'

'I've been trying to think. I knew you'd want to see her. And she told me which one it was.'

'Well, it doesn't matter, I guess. I don't know what we could say to each other, it's been so long.'

'How many years has it been?'

'Quite a few,' Carolyn answered, biting her lip. 'It's been quite a few years, Mother.'

Mrs Bridge turned off the gas in the oven and shut the doors.

109 Winter

The snow fell all night. It fell without a sound and covered the frozen ground, and the dead leaves beneath the maple tree, and bowed the limbs of the evergreens, and sifted out of the high, pearl-blue clouds hour after hour. Mrs Bridge was awakened by the immense silence and she lay in her bed listening. She heard the velvet chimes of the clock in the hall, and presently the barking of a dog. She had a feeling that all was not well and she waited in deep expectancy for some further intimation, listening intently, but all she heard before falling asleep was the familiar chiming of the clock.

110 Tuna salad

The next morning Lois Montgomery telephoned to say that Grace Barron had committed suicide.

In the days that followed Mrs Bridge attempted to suppress this fact. Her reasoning was that nothing could be gained by discussing it; consequently she wrote to Ruth that there was some doubt as to what had been the cause of Mrs Barron's death but it was presumed she had accidentally eaten some tuna-fish salad which had been left out of the refrigerator overnight and had become contaminated, and this was what she told Douglas and Carolyn.

To intimate friends, to those who knew the truth, which was that Grace Barron had swallowed over fifty sleeping tablets, Mrs Bridge talked more openly. They asked one another familiar and similar questions because, in many ways, Grace Barron was indistinguishable from anyone among them. Their problems had been hers, their position, their wealth, and the love they knew, these also had belonged to her.

'It came as such a shock,' Mrs Bridge heard herself say again and again. 'It's awfully hard to believe.'

She often wondered if anyone other than herself had been able to divine the motive; if so, it went unmentioned. But she herself had found it instinctively less than an instant after hearing the news: her first thought had been of an afternoon on the Plaza when she and Grace Barron had been looking for some way to occupy themselves, and Grace had said, a little sadly, 'Have you ever felt like those people in the Grimm fairy tale – the ones who were all hollowed out in the back?'

111 Old acquaintance

The country was now at war. Douglas had graduated from high school and wanted to join the Army. Ruth was gone; she seldom wrote. Carolyn, unable to get along with her husband, was coming home more frequently. And Mrs Bridge, lost in confusion, often lay down to rest awhile, and thought back to happier times. She saw that it was inevitable these things had come to pass, and she could not escape a feeling of unreality. One day, while shopping on the Plaza, she had recognized someone who used to live next door to her when she was a child. The woman was now evidently verging on old age, and Mrs Bridge, counting down the years as she observed, from a distance, the conclusion of the youth which was her own, felt a growing sense of despair and futility, and ever after that day she herself moved a little more slowly.

112 Home again

Sometime in the middle of the night Mrs Bridge awoke and knew Carolyn had come home. The house was absolutely still and yet she had no doubt; rising quietly so as not to disturb her husband she pulled on her quilted satin robe, found her slippers, and went along the hall to the room where the girls had lived. Sure enough the door was closed; ordinarily it was open. Mrs Bridge hesitated outside, listening, but heard nothing: she had expected to hear Carolyn sobbing.

'Dear, may I come in?' she asked. There was no answer, but she pushed open the door and saw Carolyn lying on the bed fully dressed with her hands clasped beneath her head. She was staring at the ceiling.

'Did you and Gil have another argument?' she asked, seating herself on the edge of the bed.

'I can't stand him,' she answered after a while.

'What was it this time?'

'He hit me.'

Mrs Bridge caught her breath.

'He did,' she repeated, with no apparent anger. 'He slapped me so hard I lost my balance and fell down.'

'You must have done something to provoke him. Didn't you?' she asked.

'Are you on his side?'

'I'm trying not to be on anyone's side, dear,' she said, and reached out to stroke Carolyn's head. 'It's just that I don't think Gil is that sort.'

'Oh, no? If you lived with him you'd find out different.' Tears had sprung into her eyes, and seeing them Mrs Bridge felt herself ready to weep.

'Do you know what he did afterward, Mother? He tried to make it up the way men always do.'

'Carolyn, there are some things about marriage that a woman has to—'

'Oh, no, don't tell me that! I don't want any part of that myth—I don't! Why, Mother, he didn't even know it was me. Do you know what I'm saying?'

'Why don't you tell me how it all started?' she replied, pulling the robe more tightly around her throat.

'It started at breakfast because I'd forgotten to get butter the day before, so he got sarcastic, and then he decided I didn't know how to feed the baby, and then he began yelling when he couldn't find his blue suit. Mother, he's been hounding me about that suit for two weeks. It's been at the cleaners and I've been so rushed with the baby and with the qualifying rounds at the club that I haven't had time to pick it up. He could have picked it up himself because he comes right by the cleaners every day, but he keeps saying that's my job. So, anyway, next he began shouting at me that if I spent less time playing golf and more—oh, hell, what's the

183

use? I mean, anyway, after he finally went to work I thought maybe it was partly my fault and so in order to make it up to him I got a baby-sitter to come over while I went to the beauty shop to have my hair set, and they couldn't take me right away and by the time I finally got through it was late and I didn't get home till after he did because I had to pay some bills and stop at the club to see if my entry had been posted. Well, I guess you can imagine what a foul temper he was in when his dinner wasn't ready for him, and he'd called the club and they'd told him I was there, even after I'd given strict orders to say I wasn't. Well,' she went on, after drawing a deep breath, 'he was furious and swearing. He'd thrown clothes all over the bedroom and even jerked out some of the drawers and turned them over on the bed because he couldn't find what he wanted. I told him the stuff hadn't been washed and he knew perfectly well the washing machine was broken. I guess he expected me to hand-wash everything. I mean, really, Mother, that's what he expected.'

'Well, I don't think it would hurt you to do some washing.'

'Oh, Mother, honestly! All he has to do is get the machine fixed.'

'Yes, I understand, dear, but perhaps if both of you were to try a little harder—'

'He said I didn't have the faintest idea what it meant to have to work.'

'Why, that's absurd!'

'He said I was spoiled, Mother. Is that the truth?'

'Of course not, dear. Why should he say a thing like that? Now I'm sure everything is going to work out all right, so why don't you get some rest? You'll feel better in the morning.'

'And do you know whose fault he said it was, Mother?'

113 Mr Bridge adjourns

Mrs Bridge was caught between wanting Carolyn home again for good, and wanting the marriage to succeed. The world was reeling, so it seemed, and she lost faith in tomorrow. Her ears rang with the frenetic song of war. She could not understand the slaughter and she was often frightened now that Douglas was gone. He had persuaded his father to let him join the Army before the draft caught up with him and now he was somewhere in Arizona. He wrote to her every week – cheerful, air letters, as though he had gone camping for the summer and would be back in time for college, and she could almost believe this was true. Then, without warning, she would be struck by the actual truth and she would feel lonely and helpless, and guilty over the happiness she experienced whenever Carolyn appeared. With Carolyn in the house – even in a foul humor so that she smoked and cursed without regard for anyone else – even then Mrs Bridge was comforted, for her presence was an arch to the past, and Mrs Bridge never tired of dreaming of the days when the children were small, and there had been peace, and so much to anticipate.

Often she sat up with a start, and after a desperate glance at the clock she would be ashamed to learn that two or three hours had gone by while she was thinking. She had given up working at the charity center; there were more than enough volunteers, particularly among the younger women, and the staring eyes of the people on Ninth Street had begun to haunt her. She often saw them in the middle of the night, the hungry, lost people.

And she was haunted, too, by recollections as inanimate and soulless as these unfortunate people, which surrounded her with undemanding, relentless attention, like a perfect circle of question marks – incidents, for the most part, comments she had offered, replies, attitudes, trivial circumstances which by all logic should have long since passed into obscurity, but which recurred persistently to trouble her. And always, or very nearly so, she overcame these doubts; and yet, even as she arose, secure in her convictions, she was aware she had not triumphed over them, nor destroyed them, nor pacified them, but only pushed them away for a little while, like nagging children.

Douglas came home on furlough; he got out of the taxicab looking much older. There was another soldier in the taxi to whom he waved good-by, and Mrs Bridge, waiting to embrace her son, heard him call in a resounding voice, 'Save a Jap for me, sergeant!'

'Who was that?' she asked.

'Fellow I met on the train,' he replied briefly.

'Didn't you want to ask him in?'

'I did, but he's on his way,' Douglas said, and throwing his duffel bag across one shoulder he pushed open the door and strode into the house.

'You've gained some weight,' she said, and she noticed, too, that he stood erect now, and there was a frankly adult look in his eyes. The most remarkable change, however, was the fact that he was beginning to grow a mustache – a reddish burr looking somewhat like a patch of sandpaper. Mrs Bridge thought it looked very silly, and not wanting to hurt his feelings she avoided mentioning it.

Mr Bridge, however, was neither reticent nor considerate of Douglas's feelings.

'For the love of Mike, what's that?' he asked, on first catching sight of the new mustache, but Douglas, very much to the surprise of his mother, neither flushed in embarrassment nor dropped his eyes.

'You think you could do any better?' he solemnly replied.

Mr Bridge laughed and clapped him solidly on the shoulder. 'How about a drink before dinner, soldier?'

'I could use one,' said Douglas, and away they went to the kitchen. Mrs Bridge heard them laughing, and Harriet's shrill laughter joining in.

Although she could not understand her son she was so pleased to have him home that she continually found excuses to be near him. So it was that she knocked on his door to ask if his socks needed mending. He told her to come in and look. She entered and found him standing in front of the bathroom mirror lathering his jaw. He was not wearing a shirt, only an olive green undershirt and khaki trousers, and she noticed a metal chain around his neck that he had never worn before.

'What on earth is this?' she inquired, approaching hesitantly, full of love and tenderness.

'Dog tags,' he said. He was amused.

She drew the chain up from beneath the undershirt, strangely and deeply moved to discover there was hair on his chest, and she held the tags in trembling fingers. She inquired about the data stamped on the dull brass disks, and he told her that one was his serial number, another his blood type, and so on.

'What is this "P"?' she wanted to know.

'Protestant,' he said. 'I told them I was a Buddhist, but they insisted I was a Protestant.'

'You did *what?*'

'We have to fill out forms all the time. Every form has a blank where you write down your religious affiliation. I always write Buddhist, but somebody always types it up Protestant. I don't know why.'

'Well, for goodness' sakes, that's an awfully odd thing to write. You're not a Buddhist.'

Douglas dipped his razor in the water. He was looking gently down on her in the mirror, white and foamy almost up to his eyes. She thought he looked inscrutable. She was bewildered.

'Well, I suppose you know what you're doing. Now hurry and finish shaving; Harriet will soon have dinner ready.'

She expected him to shave off the mustache, but he did not, and so several days later while he was leaning against the bookcase with Omar Khayyám in hand she remarked, 'You look like a perfect stranger.'

Douglas glanced down at her in a friendly way and said, without having asked what she meant, that he thought he would keep his mustache nonetheless.

But next morning, seeing it across the breakfast table, she knew it would have to go. Without a word she set down her orange juice and went upstairs to his room, where, in the closet, she found his Army cap. She put this on her head, and having touched up her graying curls at the mirror she marched downstairs and into the breakfast room swinging her arms stiffly. Douglas was not there. Harriet, stacking the dishes, gazed at her in astonishment. Mrs Bridge smiled at her bravely, and as serenely as possible under the circumstances. Just then she heard Douglas cough. It sounded as though he were in the living room. She turned around and marched through the hall and into the front room where she came to a halt in what she considered a military manner, and tried to click her heels.

'Attention, Private Bridge. March right upstairs this very minute and shave off your silly mustache.'

Douglas had been looking at the photograph on the dust jacket of Dr Foster's book of essays. He dropped the book on the sofa and crossed his arms. When it became obvious that he did not intend to speak, that he was simply waiting for her to leave, she pulled the cap from her head and stood in front of him uncertainly, rather humbly.

He was to leave from the Union Station at four o'clock the next afternoon, but a few minutes after three the telephone rang. It was Mr Bridge's office and the secretary was on the phone. Mr Bridge was dead. He had hurried into the office immediately after lunch and resumed work with a dictaphone. Sometime after that he rolled out of his swivel chair and sprawled on the carpet as dead as he would ever be. When the dictaphone cylinder was played they heard him say, 'It appears, therefore, the defendant—' and the squeak of the swivel chair.

'It was awfully good of you,' Mrs Bridge said, standing at the half-open door, telling each visitor good-by. 'Everyone has been so kind.'

114 Letter from a Buddhist

Douglas, having exchanged telegrams with the commandant of his camp, remained in Kansas City till after the funeral. Ruth had flown home from New York and Carolyn had driven up from Parallel; both of them were struck by the change in Douglas. Ruth had no difficulty in accepting him as the new head of the family, though he was nearly five years younger than she. Carolyn challenged him once or twice, half-heartedly. Neither of them expected their mother to make decisions. And to Mrs Bridge herself it seemed natural that he should become the authority. Harriet, keenly attuned to every situation, asked Douglas if she could have a raise; he said no. From that moment on she stopped calling him by his first name and referred to him as Mr Bridge, and his mother, hearing this for the first time, began to weep.

Soon, like birds abandoning a tree, they flew off in different directions. Ruth went back to New York, Carolyn to southern Kansas, and Douglas to the Army. The functions of the house were carried on by Harriet, and Mrs Bridge was left alone. She often went to Auxiliary meetings, and she went shopping downtown, and to the Plaza for luncheon, and to a number of parties, but she could no longer lose herself in these activities; the past was too much with her, and so she was frequently content to stay at home, waiting for the mail, or waiting for someone to call, remotely conscious of the persistent roar of the vacuum cleaner, no longer caring if Harriet smoked in the kitchen.

When she received the first letter Douglas wrote after returning to camp she thought how intimately it resembled the letters her husband used to write when he was out of town on business. There had been something quaint about her husband, an old-fashioned inclination which had caused him to begin his letters to her with, 'My dear wife . . .'

How strange that Douglas should write:

My dear Mother,
My father loved you above all else, and if he was apt to be rude or tyrannical it was because he wanted to protect you. He wanted so much for us all. He did not ever realize that what we needed was himself instead of what he could give us. On more than one occasion he and I discussed the family and its problems and in these talks I felt his constant preoccupation with your welfare after he was gone. I guess he knew he was not going to live much longer. He said he had never told you about the trouble with his heart.

There is nothing at all for you to worry about. You made him very happy during his life. I am quite certain that never once was he interested in another woman. My love to you, Mother, and to both my sisters. Tell Ruth when next you write her that I am anxious to hear from her.

Well, we have to go out on maneuvers now, but I'll write you again pretty soon.
With love, as always,
Douglas

115 All's well

Not long after this she was window-shopping on the Plaza when a young man in civilian clothes stopped and addressed her by name. At first she did not know him; then she saw it was Jay Duchesne.

'Why, I thought you were in service!' she said with a smile. Then she noticed he was missing an arm.

'I was,' he said, shrugging the shoulder where the arm had been.

'Oh, I'm sorry, Jay. I must have been asleep.'

'That's all right,' he answered cheerfully, and after a pause he said with a rueful grin, 'I'm one of the clowns you read about in the comics – the ones who never do anything right. I was always clumsy.' He took a package of cigarettes from his pocket, expertly shook one between his fingers and lighted it. 'How's old Red Dog these days?' he asked, blowing a stream of smoke.

'How is who?'

'Old Red Dog Doug. Gosh, I haven't seen the bum in years. What a character he is!'

'Why, he's in the Army,' she replied. She was disconcerted by the news that Douglas was a character; he had always seemed very normal to her, though a little more laconic than most boys.

'They bagged him, too? No kidding?' Duchesne laughed, puffed on his cigarette, and said, 'He'll give 'em fits.'

'He seems to enjoy it and he's doing quite well.' She was positive Duchesne was about to say he never heard of anybody doing well in the Army.

'Kidding aside,' he said. 'How times change. What about Mr Bridge? Dead and gone these many years, or still raking in the jack?'

'Mr Bridge passed away not long ago,' she replied stiffly.

Duchesne observed her for a minute, smoke curling from his nostrils. 'I'm sorry to hear that,' he said finally. 'He was a nice guy – once you got underneath the crust he was a real soft touch. Is Ruth still in the big city?'

'Yes. She's been there quite a while and is doing very well.'

'I can believe it. I always figured she'd wind up in Hollywood. She was sort of a glamour type, you know, but mysterious, like in these secret-agent movies.'

'Oh?'

Duchesne studied his cigarette. 'Look, Mrs Bridge, how's Cork?'

'Why, she's just fine.'

'Still married?'

'Of course!' Mrs Bridge laughed in displeasure. She noticed that Duchesne seemed rather disappointed.

'Why should you ask, Jay?'

'No reason,' he said, flipping the cigarette in the street. 'I think about her a lot, that's all. Tell her hello for me.'

'I certainly will. It's been nice seeing you again, Jay. You're looking quite well.'

'Things could be worse, Mrs B. In the hospital I couldn't go for it, but I know better now.' He took a deep breath and straightened up. 'So, anyhow,' he added, just before walking away, 'do give her the word.'

116 Remembrance of things past

Her album provided many comforting hours. There she could find her children once again, and her husband, too. He was standing in bright sunshine with one hand on the fender of the new Reo and Carolyn was sitting on his shoulders. There was Douglas showing off the baseball bat they had given him for his birthday. And there was Ruth in her first high heels, standing pigeon-toed and earnestly determined not to fall on her face. There, too, were her friends – Grace Barron waving from the high diving board at the country-club pool, Mabel Ong outside the Auxiliary clubhouse with hands thrust in the side pockets of her tweed jacket, Madge one snowy day in a Persian lamb coat with her galoshes unzipped, and Lois Montgomery looking presidential. Mrs Bridge wished she had taken more snapshots.

She had quite a few of the European trip. She had spent more than one enjoyable morning with a damp sponge on which to wet the mounting corners, the huge album lying open on the writing desk and the carpet all around her feet littered with negatives and with yellow drugstore envelopes. In went Trafalgar Square, Buckingham Palace, Piccadilly, the Thames, the changing of the Guard, and the ravens she had seen at the Tower of London. In went the Seine, the Arch of Triumph, an awning of Maxim's, Notre Dame, and Mr Bridge buying the *Herald Tribune* in front of the American Express. The pictures of the Riviera had not turned out well, though she could not imagine why, unless the light meter had not been working properly; the Riviera, whenever she thought about it, seemed so foreign, really more foreign to her way of life than Paris had been. Often she remembered the cliffs, the harbor, and the shining sea.

'I don't know whether this would interest you or not,' she would say to guests, picking up the album in both hands, and as she deposited it on her visitor's lap she would say, 'Now, just look at them until you get bored, but for heaven's sake don't feel obliged to go through them all.' And she would then hover nearby, anxious to know which pictures were being looked at. Often she would be unable to sit still; she had to look over the visitor's shoulder, reaching down now and then to say, 'That's the famous old cathedral you're always hearing about.' Or, 'That's the ocean, of course.' Or, 'This was taken from the steps of the National Gallery, and right there – directly behind the man on the bicycle – is where we ate lunch.'

But the pictures to which she returned most often for her own pleasure were those of her family: they evoked what she had known most intimately, and all she had loved most profoundly.

117 Hello?

One December morning near the end of the year when snow was falling moist and heavy for miles all around, so that the earth and the sky were indivisible, Mrs Bridge emerged from her home and spread her umbrella. With small cautious steps she proceeded to the garage, where she pressed the button and waited impatiently for the door to lift. She was in a hurry to drive downtown to buy some Irish lace antimacassars that were advertised in the newspaper, and she was planning to spend the remainder of the day browsing through the stores because it was Harriet's day off and the house was empty – so empty.

She had backed just halfway out of the garage when the engine died. She touched the starter and listened without concern because, despite her difficulties with the Lincoln, she had grown to feel secure in it. The Lincoln was a number of years old and occasionally recalcitrant, but she could not bear the thought of parting with it, and in the past had resisted this suggestion of her husband, who, mildly puzzled by her attachment to the car, had allowed her to keep it.

Thinking she might have flooded the engine, which was often true, Mrs Bridge decided to wait a minute or so.

Presently she tried again, and again, and then again. Deeply disappointed, she opened the door to get out and discovered she had stopped in such a position that the car doors were prevented from opening more than a few inches on one side by the garage partition, and on the other side by the wall. Having tried all four doors she began to understand that until she could attract some-one's attention she was trapped. She pressed the horn, but there was not a sound. Half inside and half outside she remained.

For a long time she sat there with her gloved hands folded in her lap, not knowing what to do. Once she looked at herself in the mirror. Finally she took the keys from the ignition and began tapping on the window, and she called to anyone who might be listening, 'Hello? Hello out there?'

But no one answered, unless it was the falling snow.

Mr Bridge

For
Elizabeth McKee

I was the world in which I walked, and what I saw
Or heard or felt came not but from myself;
And there I found myself more truly and more strange.

Wallace Stevens

1 Love

Often he thought: My life did not begin until I knew her.

She would like to hear this, he was sure, but he did not know how to tell her. In the extremity of passion he cried out in a frantic voice: 'I love you!' yet even these words were unsatisfactory. He wished for something else to say. He needed to let her know how deeply he felt her presence while they were lying together during the night, as well as each morning when they awoke and in the evening when he came home. However, he could think of nothing appropriate.

So the years passed, they had three children and accustomed themselves to a life together, and eventually Mr Bridge decided that his wife should expect nothing more of him. After all, he was an attorney rather than a poet; he could never pretend to be what he was not.

2 Family portrait

Each morning as soon as he walked into the office he glanced at the photograph of his wife and children which stood on the desk in a silver frame. He had placed the picture exactly where he wanted it, so that it never interfered with his work but at the same time he could see the family as often as he liked. Later pictures had been taken but this one pleased him best: Ruth was five years old, Carolyn three, and Douglas was a baby. The girls were seated on the studio couch, one on either side of their mother, who was holding Douglas in her lap. The photograph was orderly, symmetrical, and serene.

One Monday morning when he entered the office he noticed that the photograph had been moved. Evidently the woman who cleaned the office over the weekend had forgotten where it belonged. He put it back where he wanted it. Then for a few minutes he remained motionless in his swivel chair and stared at the picture; and he wondered again what would have happened to him if he had never met this woman who became his wife. He felt profoundly obligated to her. It seemed to him that the existence of the family was a mysterious accomplishment to which he had contributed very little. She had done this, somehow, almost by herself. He had provided the money and he had made decisions, but these things appeared insignificant when he compared them to what she had done; and he reflected on some lines from a letter by a famous man which he had read not long after meeting her: *Thou only hast taught me that I have a heart – thou only hast thrown a deep light downward, and upward, into my soul. Thou only hast revealed me to myself; for without thy aid, my best knowledge of myself would have been merely to know my own shadow – to watch it flickering on the wall, and mistake its fantasies for my own real actions. Indeed, we are but shadows – we are not endowed with real life, and all that seems most real about us is but the thinnest substance of a dream – till the heart be touched.* These lines had impressed him so that he copied them and kept them a long time; he had often been on the point of reciting them to her because they expressed his own feelings with such lucidity and tenderness.

The idea of life without her caused him to move restlessly.

Then, because it was time to begin work, he cleared his throat, blew his nose, and rang for Julia.

3 In the counting house

Occasionally he went to the bank around the corner from his office in order to look at his securities. Before going down to the vault in the basement he usually stopped to see the president, Virgil Barron, whom he had known for several years. They lived not far apart in the Mission Hills district, and both were members of a group that reserved a round table for lunch in the Terrace Grill of the Muehlebach Hotel. After visiting with Barron for a few minutes he would walk downstairs, ask for his safe-deposit box, and carry it into one of the walnut-paneled cubicles. There, after placing the long black metal box in the middle of the table, he locked the door, put on his reading glasses, opened the box, and began to examine the stock certificates and bonds.

Each bond and each stock certificate was neatly folded to fit into a business envelope. On each envelope he had listed the contents: the certificate numbers, the number of shares, the date purchased, and the amount paid. On the back of each envelope he had noted the recommendations of his broker to sell or hold, together with the date and the selling price. If he had accepted the broker's advice and sold a particular security he made a note of this. But he seldom sold anything, because it seemed to him that if one invested in a substantial, well-managed corporation it should almost never become necessary to sell. There would be exceptions, the most prudent investor must be prepared to admit that times change; even so, as he reminded his wife every now and then in order that she should have this principle irrevocably planted in her head by the time of his death, it is better to trade too little than too much.

Frequently while he was looking through his securities – sometimes reading the italicized print which set forth the conditions, but more often gazing at the handsome heavy papers as though they were exhibits in a gallery – he would remember the bad judgment of his father, and a frown of displeasure would crease his face. Several thousand dollars had been wasted on penny gold mines, on the schemes of inventors, and similar speculations. Now there was nothing but one bulky envelope stuffed with these testimonials to folly: certificates of corporations with names like Amazon Bonanza and Del Rio Silver King, and handwritten promises to repay loans. These were folded as his father had folded them many years ago. Most of the companies were defunct and the few that existed could not be found on any exchange, and the men who had promised to repay the money were dead; but it was not much trouble to keep the documents and it might be foolish to destroy them. However, it gave him no pleasure to consider them. They angered him and left him with a feeling of embarrassment for his father's naïveté.

Otherwise, the fact that his father had left him nothing did not trouble him. An inheritance would have simplified things and it was a shame the money had been squandered; beyond that Mr Bridge seldom thought about it. And in one respect he intended to benefit by the foolishness of his father: he would not repeat his father's error.

So he bought shares in companies that he considered essential. Metropolitan public utilities seemed the safest because their services were indispensable and their monopoly was guaranteed; but he had also bought into several food and drink corporations with long records of uninterrupted dividends, and he had bought small amounts of somewhat more speculative companies such as American Tobacco and the Union Pacific Railroad. All of these, he thought, were manifestly solid concerns, and during periods of fluctuation on the stock exchange he observed with pleasure and satisfaction the stability of his investments.

He had said to his wife: 'When the time comes, India, that you are alone, do not sell these stocks. These are sound corporations with fine records and they will not let you down.'

She had promised to keep them and to pass them along to the children.

He had said to her: 'These securities are worth a nice little sum of money today. They ought to be worth a great deal more in years to come.'

Ordinarily he brought with him the latest issue of the *Wall Street Journal* and spent some time jotting down current prices on a scratch pad in order to calculate the value of his holdings; then he would consider the provisions of his will and ask himself whether a few changes should be made. At present almost everything had been assigned to his wife, yet perhaps this was not the wisest policy. Might it not be wiser to apportion the stocks: a certain number of shares to each of the children upon his death, the remainder to her? Naturally this would reduce her income, which was most important, but at the same time the children would be given a degree of independence. Thirty shares of American Tobacco, for instance, might be willed to each of the children, thus providing them with a quarterly check. Or the entire Tobacco holding might go to Ruth, an equivalent holding of General Foods to Carolyn, and some shares of Bethlehem Steel to Douglas. Or, because the dividend was liberal, it might be best to leave Bethlehem in the name of Mrs Bridge. Douglas, being young, might be better endowed with a stock that displayed a somewhat more favorable growth pattern. These were things to be considered.

A copy of the will was in the safe-deposit box, and though he knew every word of it he sometimes read it through, searching for possible points of contention. The logic and clarity of the will were pleasing to him; the measured cadence of the sentences he had composed was reassuring, as though the measure of his mind must be respected when it was read aloud at some future date. Often he read to himself particular passages from the will, imagining the delight and surprise with which it would be heard for the first time by his wife and by the children, not merely for the precision of language but because they had no idea of the value of the investments.

Only once had he shown her the contents of the box. Then he had pointed out an envelope containing five one-hundred-dollar bills to be used in case of emergency, and had unfolded a few certificates and gone over them with her so they would seem familiar; but he had minimized the total worth of the documents in the box. Women tended to behave curiously where money was concerned. She was not extravagant, at least she had not been extravagant so far; if anything she was quite the opposite, worrying mildly about the cost of almost everything. Still, change was in the nature of women and no good could come of letting her know his exact worth.

The fact that she knew so little about these securities apparently did not trouble her; since that day she had never inquired, or hinted, or shown the faintest sign of wanting more information. He was puzzled by this. He had expected her to ask a great many questions, but she had merely looked attentive. He suspected she had not understood everything he attempted to explain; he remembered her perfunctory smile and how she nodded each time he paused. But at least she did know of the existence of the box and she knew what was in it.

The children had not yet been informed, although he meant to show them, one at a time, as they grew older. It pleased him to anticipate the time when he could go over all of the securities with the children, pointing out what he had paid for each and comparing this price with the current market value.

So he meditated as he unfolded his certificates, absently gratified by the parchment quality of the paper, and checked them against the notations to make certain everything was in order, and studied the earnings reports, the forecasts, and the dividend news reported in the *Journal*. Sometimes he would read a market letter or a corporation analysis which he had brought along in his briefcase;

but more often he spent these tranquil moments in the basement of the bank examining the handsomely engraved certificates and contemplating the satisfaction they would give after his death.

4 Two women

He seldom spoke to his wife about what went on at the office or in court. Before they were married and for a while afterward she had inquired, doing her best to appear interested, trying to comprehend the life he lived apart from her; but he had answered briefly because he knew she did not really care, so that as time went by she asked less and less, and now it had been reduced to a ritual like a fragment excerpted from a play. She would greet him at the door, glance at the briefcase, and put on an expression of dismay or resignation, saying, 'Now truthfully, Walter, couldn't whatever it is wait till tomorrow?' By this she demonstrated her concern for his health and reminded him that he did not need to work such long hours for the family's benefit. They had plenty of food, a nice house, and money enough to pay the bills. Then he would reply that he was only planning to work a little while after dinner or that he was going to finish a few things which should have been taken care of a week ago, or he might remark that it was Julia's fault. Julia was to blame for saddling him like a burro with more than he could carry during the day. Then she answered that she was going to call Julia in the morning and tell her to cut down on the amount of work.

This familiar and lifeless scene was not as unnatural as it appeared; after all, he himself did not care what happened at the house during the day. There was no more reason for her to be curious about his work than for him to be concerned with groceries, laundry, getting the children to school, and whatever else she did. Yet it would seem rude, almost brutal, to drop the pretense and admit that neither particularly cared what the other was doing. A display of interest, however shallow, made life easier.

Julia, on the other hand, did not need to pretend. She cared vitally about the progress of each case, and about such things as the rumor that a new federal courthouse might be built; and as the years went by he found that he was discussing these matters as intimately with Julia as he had once imagined he would discuss them with his wife. This, too, he reflected, must not be unnatural; no doubt other men had found themselves living a similar divided life, involved with two women almost equally.

He was grateful that they got along well together. Julia was quite a pretty young woman, but so far his wife had shown no jealousy. Perhaps she sensed that he was not attracted to Julia, and occasionally he wondered why he was not. Julia's features were regular and delicate and she had a charming smile. She walked gracefully. Her figure was trim. She never slouched or scratched her head or chewed a pencil. She dressed modestly, as women should, and did not smoke. She was intelligent and clean, and impudent to the point of mild impertinence. She ought to be physically inviting; it was curious that she was not, yet he could feel no desire for her. Somehow the idea of putting his arms around her was disagreeable.

Those evenings when they worked later than usual he drove her home instead of letting her take the bus. She lived in an ugly gray building just off Valentine Road, sharing an apartment with a much older sister who was crippled by arthritis. Each time he drove her there he felt uncomfortable and obscurely guilty, and after watching until she was inside the door he continued toward Mission Hills with a sense of relief. Her misfortune was not his fault. The salary she got was comparable to what she could earn anywhere else, and every few months Mrs Bridge invited her to the house for dinner.

Except for these occasions when he escorted Julia home he seldom thought about her. He did not know whom she was seeing at night, if anybody. He did not care. She might possibly be planning to get married, although she had given no hint of this. If she did decide to marry it would be all right, providing she did not have a baby.

These two women were growing around him like strands of ivy, but the feeling of entanglement was not disturbing; it seemed to him that these persistent female tendrils were supporting and assisting him.

205

5 Dinner at home

Around dinnertime it usually occurred to Mr Bridge that there were, in fact, three women on whom he depended and Harriet was not the least of them. She was such a marvelous cook that he resented the occasions when he and Mrs Bridge were invited out. There were traces of the South in her cooking. Such dishes as jambalaya appeared on the table, and frequently she served barbecued ribs which he loved with a love he held for very few things on earth. She could prepare sugar-cured ham with red-eye gravy far better than any restaurant, and hot biscuits and honey, and turnips which tasted like no other turnips, and candied yams with the flavor of marshmallow. She never used a cookbook. She knew. Sometimes while he was eating he would torment himself by trying to decide whether Harriet or Julia was more indispensable.

Every night he looked forward to his dinner and he was sorry when Thursday came around, which was Harriet's night off. On Thursday there was apt to be macaroni casserole, or leftovers from Wednesday.

He concealed his dismay at these Thursday suppers, and told himself it was not his wife's fault if she no longer cooked as well as she did when they were first married; after all, cooking requires practice like everything else, and since Harriet had taken over the kitchen there was not much for Mrs Bridge to do. Once she had been quite good, never in a league with Harriet, but there had been a time when she could make excellent little puddings and special kinds of bread to go with the fried chicken and the pot roast. She could bake an agreeable cherry pie, a rich banana upside-down cake, and crisp tarts, and she knew how to make chili without using too much tomato sauce. He had never been dissatisfied with her cooking – even now it was not bad – but on Thursday nights he could not overcome a sense of weariness as he plunged his fork into the casserole.

6 The tip

Each year on their anniversary they went out to dinner. He insisted on this because it was traditional, although he knew she would just as soon stay home. Sometimes they went to the Mission Country Club, sometimes they went downtown to one of the big hotels or to a restaurant they had heard about. One year they decided to try a supper club near the Warwick Theater which the Barrons had recommended, and they were not disappointed. The food was excellent, there was nothing wrong with the service, and the atmosphere was pleasant. After dinner they lingered awhile listening to the music and they got up several times to dance. Then it was time to go home so Mr Bridge signaled for the check. It came to eleven dollars and twenty-five cents. He examined it to be sure they had not been overcharged and that the addition was correct. Then he laid three five-dollar bills on the tray. The waiter, bowing and smiling, inquired in a practiced murmur whether there would be anything else, and Mr Bridge was astounded to realize he meant to keep all of the money.

'You will bring me the change,' he said.

When the change was brought to him he counted it and found that it was correct. He put two dollars into his wallet, twenty-five cents went into his trousers pocket, and he left one dollar and fifty cents on the tray. Then he stood up, the waiter held the chair while Mrs Bridge got to her feet, and they walked out.

As they were driving along Ward Parkway he considered what had happened. He was afraid his wife had been embarrassed.

He said, 'Maybe I should have let that fellow get away with it. After all, another two dollars wouldn't break me.'

She replied that she thought he had done exactly the right thing.

'I've had waiters pull that stunt on me before,' he said, to justify himself. 'They take advantage of people every chance they get.'

She agreed, and told him about a very similar experience on the Plaza when she was having lunch with Grace Barron.

'My Lord,' he muttered, 'that fellow was hoping for thirty per cent!'

'He did seem awfully pushy,' she remarked. 'Next year we'd better try someplace else.'

7 No oil

According to the mileage on the speedometer it was time once again to have the Reo lubricated. The company recommended a lubrication every one thousand miles and he did not like to drive farther than this without having the job done. He suspected it was not necessary quite so often; however, he did not want to take a chance on damaging the motor. The company also recommended a change of oil every thousand miles and he had accepted this without thinking about it, but now the idea began to irritate him: very possibly the auto manufacturers and the petroleum industry were conspiring to sell the public more oil than the cars required. He decided there was no reason to change the oil each time the car was lubricated. As long as the filter was functioning the oil should be all right.

At the garage where he parked he looked around until he located the manager, whose name was Jerry Buckworth. He was wearing his usual blue smock with *Jerry* stitched in white script above the pocket, but Mr Bridge addressed him formally because he was the manager.

'Good morning, Mr Buckworth,' he said.

The manager took the cigar out of his mouth and replied, 'Good morning, Mr Bridge. What can we do for you?'

'I would like to have the Reo greased.'

'When will you need it?'

'Six would be soon enough. Don't change the oil.'

'We'll have her for you,' the manager said.

Mr Bridge nodded and walked out of the garage.

That evening when he returned to pick up the car he was met by the manager, who explained apologetically that the oil had been changed.

'I told you not to,' said Mr Bridge.

The manager explained that he had forgotten to tell the mechanic.

'Well,' Mr Bridge said, 'I am not going to pay for that oil.'

'What we can do is this,' the manager said, 'we'll let you have it at cost.'

Mr Bridge shook his head. 'I intend to pay for the lubrication, nothing more. This mistake is not my fault. I distinctly told you. I will not be charged for something I did not order. I have been parking here for six years and nothing of this sort has happened before. Why does it happen now?'

'It was our fault,' the manager said. 'We'll take care of it.'

And that was how it ended.

8 Lester

Whenever he went to the garage to pick up his car it was brought out of the stall by Lester. Lester did not depend on tips for a living. He got a salary, and few of the garage patrons tipped him, but Mr Bridge always handed him fifty cents. Parking cars day after day was not much of a life, and not only was Lester colored, he was cross-eyed. Mr Bridge knew nothing else about him, not even his last name, but he liked Lester and he was sure the garage attendant returned this feeling – which had nothing to do with the fifty cents a day. They could not become more friendly than they were, yet it was a satisfying relationship they had, and Mr Bridge occasionally wondered if there was anything else he could do to make life a little easier for Lester.

One afternoon when he was met by a strange attendant and did not see his friend anywhere he was puzzled. He asked if Lester was sick. The new attendant replied that he had been hired just that morning and did not know.

Mr Bridge pointed to the stall where his car was parked. 'Get me the blue Reo,' he said. Then he walked to the cashier's window, where he saw Mr Buckworth discussing something with the cashier.

'I notice you have a new man,' he said. 'What's become of Lester?'

'Lester's not with us any longer.'

'Now don't tell me you fired him!'

The garage manager cleared his throat and looked at Mr Bridge uneasily. 'They tell us he cut somebody up last night. You know how they are when they get to drinking. Him and some other nigger got in a fight. We don't know what about. We found out this noon after Lester didn't show up for work. They got him in city jail.'

'Great God,' said Mr Bridge softly.

'Too bad. Lester was a good worker. He was with us a long while. But I'll see Bob takes care of you.'

On his way home Mr Bridge tried to believe what he had been told, but not until he saw it in the evening *Star*, a small article on the fourth page, could he accept it. Lester's full name was Lester Leroy Titus. He was forty-six years old. He lived in a hotel on Wabash and he was an ex-convict. He had served ten years in Leavenworth prison for armed robbery.

He pointed out the article to his wife and asked if she had seen it. She had not, but after reading it she said, 'Honestly, there's so much crime these days.'

He realized that she had not recognized the name so he told her who it was. She often parked in the garage while she was downtown shopping.

'Oh, my word!' she exclaimed, drawing back with a shocked expression. 'Oh, I simply can't believe it!'

'I didn't either.'

'He seemed so nice.'

'Yes, he was,' Mr Bridge said. 'He certainly was. He was one of the nicest and most dependable Negroes I have ever known.'

'Do you suppose you could help?'

'I doubt if I could do much. Apparently he's got a temper and now he's got to pay for it. Furthermore, I cannot afford to get mixed up in something like this.'

'He was always so helpful. It's such a shame.'

'Those people!' Mr Bridge said, shaking his head. 'Time and time again. If it isn't a knife, it's a razor.'

9 Trouble in the road ahead

About a month after Lester dropped from sight Mr Bridge was in his study rewriting a brief when there came a tap at the door. He recognized it – somewhat like the tapping of a bird, very different from the way the children requested admittance – and told his wife to come in. The door opened halfway. She peeped in, afraid that she was disturbing him. He had never been able to get used to this hesitancy; she behaved as though she were interrupting Einstein. He was at work, true enough, and the door had been shut for a purpose, but still she was his wife and if the matter was important enough for her to interrupt him he wished she would do so with more assertion.

He asked what was on her mind, and she replied that it was about Harriet. Harriet had asked for an advance of twenty-five dollars.

He frowned. Borrowing money was a bad policy. He himself had not had to borrow for quite a few years, not since he first went into practice and had no clients. Borrowing was hateful and degrading, and as a rule the people who wanted to borrow money were just too lazy to earn it. In a nation as prosperous as the United States almost anybody who was willing to work should be able to earn enough to live on. Granted, there were bad times and exceptional circumstances. Anyone could have an accident or be struck by a disease. There were unusual cases, true. But as for Harriet wanting to borrow twenty-five dollars before she was entitled to it, that did not sound reasonable. She must have been squandering money.

Why had she asked for this advance?

Mrs Bridge did not know.

What became of last month's salary?

Mrs Bridge did not know. 'I agree with you one hundred per cent about borrowing,' she added, 'but I do think it would be a good idea if you spoke to her. She's never asked for an advance before.'

'I'll listen to the story,' he said.

And a few moments later Harriet appeared at the door. He told

211

her to come in, and gestured at the leather couch. She seated herself primly, feet together, hands folded in her lap.

'Now, what's all this about wanting to borrow?'

'Well, as a matter of fact,' said Harriet 'I do wish to request a small sum in advance of my monthly wages. I presume Mrs Bridge has informed you?'

'She has.'

Then in an obviously rehearsed statement Harriet said, 'I ought to make plain it is not a life-or-death proposition. It is simply a matter that I have a number of special items of personal nature I wish to purchase between now and next payday. I was hopeful this could be arranged somehow.'

Mr Bridge said, 'What you do with your money is not my affair, but if you find it necessary to ask for an advance it strikes me that you may not have been handling your money too wisely.'

'Emergencies do crop up,' said Harriet.

'I don't mind telling you I think it's a poor policy. Borrowing money is asking for trouble.'

'I fully agree,' Harriet said, sounding very much like Mrs Bridge. 'One can't help disapproving. However, there is a situation come up the other day which is making life difficult.'

'Oh?'

'May I speak frankly?'

'By all means.'

'Well, if I may say so frankly, this situation I refer to is dislikable even to mention, so I prefer not to get into detail, if you don't mind.'

'Spare me the details. But under the circumstances I think you had better give me at least a general idea of what this is all about.'

Harriet compressed her lips and frowned at the rug. 'Well, as everybody is aware, I have this relationship with Mr Talbot.'

'I know nothing whatever about your personal life.'

Harriet was still sitting with her ankles pressed together and hands folded. 'I am sure you must be acquainted with Mr Talbot. He has come by the house here a number of evenings on my night off to pick me up.'

'Couperin,' Mr Bridge said. 'That's who you mean.'

'That happens to be Mr Talbot's first name, yes.'

'How does he enter into this?'

'Well, I hate to say so on account of our relationship, but if the truth be known he is responsible. This whole thing is on his account, as you see.'

'No,' said Mr Bridge, 'I don't see.'

'I was about to explain. May I speak frankly?'

'Go ahead.'

'Well, as I was saying, Mr Talbot and I, we have had this relationship when I am off in the evenings for some time now. I forget just how long, except it has been some time.' she paused and gave him a significant look.

'Go on.'

'I was fixing to. Mr Talbot he has this unfortunate problem about money and things of that nature, if you follow me. He got this special difficulty keeping his hand out of other people's pocket. He has got hisself in trouble with the law on that account, along with one or two gentlemen I could name, although they do say he is getting better about it.' She pulled a handkerchief from the pocket of her uniform and began fanning herself.

'He has stolen from you, is that what you are telling me?'

'Not precisely.'

'But he has been stealing, has he not?'

'No sir. His friends they sincerely believes he means to pay back. It is just that some is more impatient than others. There is this one friend of his happens to have this extremely bad nature. According to what they say, he has told Mr Talbot either you gets me that money tomorrow midnight or there is trouble in the road ahead.'

'When did he say this?'

'Well, let me think. That must have been about yesterday, as I recall.'

Mr Bridge leaned back in his chair. 'By midnight tonight, then?'

Harriet nodded miserably.

'The twenty-five dollars you want to borrow is not for yourself, but for this man you run around with. Is that correct?'

'Yes, sir.'

'A few minutes ago you told me it was for personal expenses. You told me there were some items you wished to purchase for yourself. Now you give me a different story. Which am I to believe?'

Harriet was busily patting her forehead with the handkerchief.

'Suppose this twenty-five dollars is not repaid. In your opinion, what will happen?'

'Well, it does come to a bit more than just that.'

'More? More, you say? How much more?'

'Let me think. There is all these claims being made which makes it difficult. However, according to what I hear, it's likely about a hundred dollars, I believe. Mr Talbot, though, he claims he still got some of it left yet and we feel if there is twenty-five dollars added to what he has not spent that will do for the time being. In fact, he has talked the situation over with this friend of his and that is the idea.'

'But if neither of you can find the twenty-five dollars?'

'I just don't know,' Harriet said. 'I just don't know, Mr Bridge.'

'Has this man threatened Couperin?'

'I would call it that, yes. There has been these threats, yes. Quite a few.'

'Harriet, I don't mind telling you I don't like this. I don't like anything about it. I don't intend to become involved in it. Surely you can find the money somewhere else.'

'We done asked. Everybody we know, only nobody don't help. Everybody tell us the same—don't want to get theirselves mixed up in nothing.'

'I don't blame them.'

Harriet's eyes were glistening. 'He promise he won't never do it again.'

'I wish I had more confidence in Couperin's promise. If you want my opinion, you would be better off if you stopped seeing that fellow.'

She buried her face in the handkerchief and wept without making a sound.

'Borrowing is bad business. You will never get a clearer demonstration of it than you are getting right now. I am sorry, Harriet, but I am not going to lend you the money.'

After she left the study he remained for quite a while in the same position, leaning back in the chair with his chin resting on his fingertips while he thought about the problem; and he thought about Lester, and a number of other experiences with Negroes.

10 Senator Horton Bailey

Harriet had been putting on an act, he decided, and he suspected he would hear no more about it. Days passed and he became convinced he was right because she went about her duties with no sign of animosity, and on Thursday he noted that Couperin came by for her as usual.

But the problem of debts turned up again after Mrs Bridge remarked while reading the evening paper: 'I see your friend Horton Bailey is in the news.'

'Friend?' he replied, putting stress on the word.

'Oh, just because you disagree with his politics! Honestly, Walter, what would this country be like if we all agreed upon everything?'

'His politics are his business. It so happens that I do disagree with the man on that score, but I have other reasons for disliking him. Perfectly valid reasons.'

'I thought the two of you got along very well. You mention him every once in a while.'

'I have known the man since the World War but I don't recall ever saying that he was a friend of mine.'

'I'm mistaken then,' Mrs Bridge said. 'All right, your "acquaintance" Horton Bailey is in the news again. He's being talked of as a future presidential candidate.'

'I heard that on the radio.'

'Apparently a great many people think quite highly of him.'

'They don't know him.'

'Now stop being such a boor,' she said rather coquettishly. 'Just what information have you that none of the rest of us have?'

'For one thing, the man doesn't pay his debts.'

'Oh? How do you know?'

'Because he has never repaid me. That's how I know.'

'Horton Bailey owes you money?'

'Years ago I lent that man five hundred dollars. To this day he has not repaid one cent of it, nor said one word about it.'

'Really? I had no idea. That's hard to believe.'

'Believe it or not, it's a fact. After the Armistice he came back here and started a men's clothing store at Ninth and Walnut. There used to be a lunch counter across the street, and I don't know how many times I saw Horton Bailey sitting at the counter because nobody was in his shop. I gather that he went around trying to borrow from everybody he could think of and finally he got around to me. I never cared for the fellow and I was having a difficult time myself, but he sounded desperate, so I let him have it. That was the last I saw of it.'

'I'm sure he just forgot,' said Mrs Bridge.

'He did not forget. He is a "deadbeat" – that's what he is.'

'Now, Walter, you're not being fair. Have you asked for the money?'

'No, nor do I intend to. The man is what he is. I happen to know what he is and I want nothing further to do with him. I hope to God such a man never becomes President of the United States. I am no great admirer of Herbert Hoover, but at least Hoover appears to be a man of some personal integrity.'

'Well, I confess I'm shocked,' Mrs Bridge said. 'I can't believe he would do a thing like that. I really think you ought to mention it. Surely it would be worth knowing whether or not he's forgotten.'

'I will not speak to him about it,' said Mr Bridge. 'I know the man. I know he is completely unprincipled. He came around begging, and I supposed he would have the decency to repay me when he was able, but I was wrong. He's no good. He never was any good – he was not even a good businessman – and he never will be any good. I don't care how many millions of people he is able to persuade, Horton Bailey will never again persuade me of anything. I have already listened to the man once too often. He is a liar and he is a cheat. He belongs in prison. Instead, he is a United States senator.'

'I wish I'd never mentioned it.'

'I don't mind your mentioning it. I've never had any reason to tell you how the man swindled me. It's a thing of the past. I learned my lesson. Beggars are beggars regardless of what else they may be. Since you asked why I didn't like the fellow, I told you. Furthermore, I suspect I wasn't the only one he took to the cleaner's.'

'It's a shame,' Mrs Bridge said as she folded the newspaper. 'I suppose the best we can hope for is that he's turned over a new leaf.'

'When that happens,' Mr Bridge said, 'I will be the most surprised man on earth.'

11 Forgive us our debts

On his way home a few days later, reasonably content with life, as he drove past the Congregational Church he glanced at the sign on the lawn and there he saw spelled out in white block letters for the benefit of anybody who got within a hundred yards of the church the title of Dr Foster's next sermon: FORGIVE US OUR DEBTS.

He continued driving but he was no longer so content. The sign had reminded him of Horton Bailey. He could not understand how a man could go through life year after year pretending that a debt did not exist. He thought he would not mind so much if Bailey at least had the decency to allude to it; but the senator, on those occasions when they happened to meet, slapped him on the shoulder and pumped his hand and said not a word about the five hundred dollars.

The longer Mr Bridge thought about Horton Bailey the angrier he got. He considered sending a letter requesting payment, perhaps demanding payment. Yet he knew he was not going to do this, he could not to do it unless the money was absolutely necessary; and the realization of this made him all the angrier so that by the time he reached home he had ruined his appetite.

12 Prohibition

When there were guests Mr Bridge went into the kitchen to mix drinks because Harriet did not know how. Carolyn usually followed him to the kitchen and watched while he took the bottles out of the cupbaord and measured the liquor. When he had finished he would reach for another glass and look at her inquiringly, and he was always surprised that this did not amuse her. He had played this game with Douglas, who responded by hiccuping and staggering around, and he had teased Ruth, who held out her hand and probably would drink it. But Carolyn's attitude puzzled him.

One evening when the Arlens and the Lutweilers had been invited to dinner he was measuring gin for the martinis when Carolyn said, 'Daddy, you're breaking the law.' She took a step backward as though she expected him to slap her.

He said after a few moments, 'No, it is *not* against the law.'

She walked out of the kitchen. He did not see her again until the next day. Ordinarily she liked to sit around listening to the adult conversation.

He waited for her to bring up the subject again, but she did not. He began to reproach himself because his tone had been sharp and he decided it might be best to have a talk with her, so one night he suggested they go into the study. Obediently she followed him upstairs. He shut the door and sat down at his desk.

'I wanted to talk to you about Prohibition,' he said. 'You remember the evening when Mr and Mrs Lutweiler and Mr and Mrs Arlen were here?'

She nodded.

'I did not break the law,' he said, and tapped the desk for emphasis. 'The Eighteenth Amendment to our Constitution prohibits only the manufacture, sale, and transportation of intoxicating beverages. It does not specifically prohibit the use of such beverages. Now, I am not scolding you,' he went on. 'Please don't misunderstand. This so-called "law" – this amendment to our Constitution – is absurd and it will be repealed before much longer. There's no doubt about it. This law came into being through the short-sightedness of a few people a good many years ago. Let me it explain it this way: Some people became very distressed about public drunkenness, and they were quite right, so they banded together and eventually became powerful enough to force this legislation through Congress. However, they were not wise enough to foresee the consequences. What has happened is that Prohibition has encouraged bootlegging, because you cannot tell people how to live their lives. That is the great danger of government. A certain amount of government is necessary, but Thomas Jefferson was correct in saying that we ought to have as little government as possible. This country at the present time has too much government. The government interferes with the rights and privileges of private citizens. It's getting worse every year. The labor unions, for example, are forcing more and more people to do whatever the union leaders say they should. This is an example of poor government and the President of the United States does not have sense enough to put a stop to it. These left-wing unions are wrecking our national economy. Lord only knows where it's going to end. However, to get back to what we were talking about – I don't approve of bootlegging. I dislike doing business with these people. At the same time, I do enjoy a cocktail before dinner and your mother enjoys a small glass of sherry. You have never known either of us to behave badly after a drink, have you?'

Carolyn sat rigidly on the edge of the couch. She was biting her upper lip. Her face was as hard as the face of a doll. He sighed and leaned back in his chair.

'You're acting silly. I don't expect you to understand this Prohibition nonsense, and since you don't understand it I don't think you ought to set yourself up as a judge of anyone's conduct. Some cranky old men and a bunch of foolish women are responsible for this situation. I don't know how much longer we will have to put up with it, but until this amendment is repealed I intend to have a drink when I feel the need of one. I work very hard at the office so that you and your mother and brother and sister will have enough to eat and a decent place to live, and a drink now and then relaxes me. There is no harm in it.'

He had explained his position and he knew he was right.

'Are you disappointed in us?' he asked. 'Are you disappointed in your mother because she enjoys a small glass of sherry?'

Carolyn would not respond.

For a long time they confronted each other. Finally the silence became unbearable, so he let her go.

13 Life begins at forty-three

One evening when they had been invited out he decided to wear a suit he had not worn for several months. When he pulled on the trousers they felt tight. He could not understand this because he did not think he had been gaining weight; however, to be sure he walked into the bathroom and stepped on the scale. He peered at the dial and found he weighed no more than usual, perhaps a pound or so, but not enough to make the pants uncomfortable. He took them off and looked at them suspiciously. After a few moments he put them on again. But again they did not fit, so he once more took them off and sat down on the bed to think.

Presently he stood up, holding his pants in one hand, took a deep breath in front of the mirror, and observed his chest and his waist. Naturally one's body changed shape with the passage of time and he was no longer twenty, but he was not seventy. He could see no change in his body. It had always been a lean body, generally supple and not ungraceful considering its length, never a body that caused women to turn around, yet it was not bad – it was not bad, it was Lincolnesque, he thought, and he felt proud of it. And because it looked the same as always he did not know why his pants would not fit.

He went back to the bed and sat down again.

He thought about the Mission Country Club where he had paid dues for a number of years. He had not used the club very much. There was a swimming pool and he had intended to stop by for a swim after leaving the office; and there were tennis courts and he thought he would find time for tennis. Then there was the golf course. But he had remained at the office every afternoon until it was too late. That was the way it had been, and the weekends mysteriously slipped away.

He tried to remember the last time he had gone swimming. It had been the year before last, or perhaps the year before that; and he had not once used the tennis courts or the golf course. Occasionally there was a party or an event of some sort, otherwise he almost never visited the club. His wife went more often because her women friends liked to spend afternoons at the pool, and of course as the children grew up they would be using the club facilities, so it was worthwhile to retain the membership. But he ought to be using it himself. Certainly it was his own fault if he did not; he could arrange to leave the office earlier and go for a swim, play tennis, or do whatever else he felt like doing. Yet somehow this was impossible. He knew he could not quit work at three o'clock or four o'clock. Some men did this and he resented the fact that they did; they ought to keep working until five or six.

Mr Bridge frowned at his pants. He lifted them and gave them a shake in case they were getting wrinkled. Then he relapsed into thought.

If it was not feasible to go to the club at least he could do calisthenics in the bedroom. Many people did that, and no doubt it was beneficial. Five or ten minutes every morning ought to produce results. Then, too, it would be easy enough to go for a brisk walk around the block every evening. And downtown there ought to be more walking and less taxi riding.

Mrs Bridge came into the bedroom. She looked at him sitting on the edge of the bed in his shorts with his trousers across his knees.

He said to her: 'Did you send these to the cleaner's?' If she had sent the pants to the cleaner's they might have shrunk, which of course would explain the situation and make calisthenics unnecessary.

'I haven't touched them,' she said. 'Do they need to be cleaned?'

'No,' he said. 'I was just wondering.'

'Is a button missing?'

'No. Nothing's wrong,' he said.

Then he put on his trousers for a third time and decided he could get through the evening, which he did; but as soon as he got home he took them off and handed them to her, saying they ought to be let out a little.

14 Thumper

The children wanted a pet rabbit. Carolyn in particular was pleading for a rabbit. Now Douglas and to some extent Ruth had joined the familiar chorus. A rabbit would not be any trouble, they would take good care of it, feed it, clean the pen every day, and so on and so forth. For a while Mr Bridge avoided saying yes or no and hoped that the clamor would diminish. He was not anxious to have a rabbit around the house. It would get sick and die. Or the children would tire of it, and then what? But Easter was approaching, and he sensed that his wife was on their side, so at last he conceded: he handed her a five-dollar bill and said all right, since a rabbit was what they wanted, get them a rabbit.

Easter morning the children wandered around the house and the yard with little wicker baskets looking for the chocolate eggs Mrs Bridge had bought and for the hard-boiled eggs which they themselves had decorated and which she had hidden. In the garage Carolyn found the rabbit. His pen was an orange crate with a piece of chicken wire across the top and he was nibbling a shred of lettuce when she saw him and let out a screech of pure joy.

They named the rabbit Thumper. He was a healthy, mildly inquisitive, normal rabbit, utterly useless, and they spent the rest of the morning pushing lettuce and carrots at him. Mrs Bridge went around collecting the undiscovered hard-boiled eggs, somewhat puzzled that they had managed to find all of the chocolate eggs. Mr Bridge, after contemplating the children and their rabbit for a few minutes, went back the house to read the Sunday paper.

But while he was reading the paper he wondered again what would happen. He suspected that the rabbit would catch distemper or pneumonia. The previous Easter the children had begged for some baby chicks, so Mrs Bridge had bought a dozen at the grocery store, but they had not lived long. They were dyed as bright as Japanese lanterns and probably the dye had penetrated the skin. At any rate, they began falling over. All twelve were dead within a week, and he had a persistent feeling that the rabbit was not going to have much better luck.

Thumper expired sooner than he expected. Before noon. Jock, the Sealyham from the next block, came trotting into the garage and was driven mad by the sight and odor of the rabbit. Douglas kicked at the Sealyham and grabbed it by the collar, Ruth swatted it with a broom, Carolyn screamed and ran into the house for help; but by the time Jock was dragged out of the garage the rabbit was almost dead. It lay on the stained and pellet-spotted newspaper and its ribs went up and down like bellows. The water cup had been turned over, the lettuce was scattered. The Sealyham had lunged against the crate so hard that several of the slats were splintered.

The dog had not gotten its teeth into the rabbit, but Mr Bridge, bending down and looking closely at the rabbit's eye, guessed that death was on the road. Carolyn, weeping, pleaded with him to get a bottle of limewater, for she had heard somewhere that limewater was a sovereign cure for ailing rabbits. But neither limewater, nor any other remedy, would save this Easter bunny.

About thirty minutes later Thumper was dead. Mrs Bridge took the children into the house.

That a creature could die of terror, and nothing except terror, was something Mr Bridge found difficult to believe. Yet this was precisely what had happened. It disgusted him a little. He disliked weakness. He wrapped the carcass in a page of newspaper and threw the bundle in the garbage can. He did not blame the dog, which had acted according to nature. And if the dog had not destroyed the rabbit something else would have gotten it. Pets were difficult to keep in a city. The dog itself had been hit and nearly killed by a car a few months ago.

So be it, he thought, as he put the lid on the garbage can. The day may come when I will wish for a death as painless and quick.

15 The dream

Douglas, winking significantly, stood on the roof of the house. Ruth, a black-haired grandmother, lay voluptuously on her back in a garden while thirty or forty children crawled over her body like bugs.

He awoke. His forehead was damp. He felt chilled and sick at his stomach. Trembling, he got out of bed, went into the bathroom, and looked at himself in the mirror. Then he sat on the toilet and held his head in his hands. The dream meant that the children were going to grow up and live as they pleased, leaving him to grow old and die. He tried to recall if Carolyn had appeared in the dream, although that was not important: the inference of two children was enough. He did not want to die and there seemed to be no reason that he must. He was happy, everybody in the family was happy, therefore this life ought to continue indefinitely. Suddenly his heart began flopping back and forth. He could feel it throbbing beneath his ribs like a fish at the end of a line. Protectively he cupped his hands over his heart, expecting a terrible hot stroke. But after a while the violent beating subsided.

He waited a few minutes, then he got up and washed his face and remained standing in front of the mirror. He wondered if he ought to wake his wife and have her drive him to the hospital; however, since there was no pain, he decided he was all right.

He thought again about the dream. He could imagine no other interpretation. Sooner or later he was going to die, while the children went on living.

'Are you all right?' Mrs Bridge inquired. She stood at the door of the bathroom. He had been staring so intently into the mirror that he had not seen her.

'Should I call Dr Stapp?' she asked.

'I have a slight stomach upset,' he said. 'Go back to bed. I'll be there soon. You have nothing to worry about.'

16 Struggling upward & other works

A few nights later he was wakened again in the middle of the night, this time by the realization that his wife was not in bed. He opened his eyes and listened. The house seemed unnaturally quiet. He turned his head on the pillow and looked out the window and saw that it had begun to snow. Just then she returned, slipped off her robe, and got into bed.

'Carolyn was crying,' she whispered.

'What about?' he whispered.

'She was afraid a star might fall.'

He smiled and shut his eyes. He remembered the fears he used to have. He remembered that he had cried himself to sleep many nights because he believed that on the day he became twelve years old he would be forced to leave home and seek his fortune. He could not recall how he had gotten this idea but there was a picture in his mind, which must have come from some magazine or illustrated book: a boy was leaving home with a stick over his shoulder and a few things tied up in a bandanna on the end of the stick. The boy's parents stood in the doorway of a cottage. The mother was weeping, the father was trying to comfort her, and the boy, too, was very sad. Now it seemed as ludicrous as Carolyn's fear, but once upon a time nothing had been more real.

17 Thayers's drugstore

Every week a large picture puzzle appeared in the window of Thayer's: an elaborate drawing of a jungle filled with an intricate assortment of nearly concealed birds, beasts, and hunters. The neighborhood children looked for these figures and reported to the druggist how many they had found, and every Saturday somebody won a silver dollar. Ruth, when she was younger, had entered this contest from time to time but never won the prize. Now she was no longer eligible. Carolyn, however, had begun to win the dollar often enough that Mr Thayer looked up sourly from his work of filling prescriptions each time she walked into the drugstore.

At last Mr Thayer had had enough. One Friday afternoon when she located every animal, bird, snake, butterfly, pygmy, and hunter in his jungle he disqualified her. Carolyn was dumbfounded; she glared at him and her face turned red, then she ran out of the drugstore hysterical with rage and ran all the way home and told her mother what the druggist had done. Mrs Bridge was disturbed not only because Carolyn was in such a state of emotion but because she, too, felt the druggist had been unfair. Not knowing exactly what to do, she waited until her husband came home from the office.

He listened to what she said, then he called Carolyn into the study and listened to her account. He inquired if she did not think she had won often enough. Maybe, he suggested, she ought to let other children win the prize.

Carolyn rejected this. She wanted her money.

Mr Bridge realized the problem was not going to be solved as simply as he had thought. Carolyn obviously had no intention of sharing the wealth. She had discovered the joy of money and she was not about to relinquish this luxury to which she was becoming accustomed, certainly not in exchange for some neighborhood utopia where each boy and girl had a dollar. She wanted all of it. Her face was tight and pinched. Suddenly she burst into frantic sobs. He opened his arms. She rushed to him and clung to him, crying bitterly while he stroked her head and patted her shoulder.

When she had exhausted herself he asked if she knew what the word 'avarice' meant. She did not, so he said: 'I want you to go downstairs and look in the dictionary. Find out what the word means. Then come back and tell me.' She asked how to spell it. He spelled it for her and she went away.

Very soon she was back. She stared at him reproachfully. They discussed the matter some more. She was sullen and peevish. She was not yet reconciled to what had happened, but he thought the point of her rage had been deflected because she was no longer accusing the druggist; her quarrel now was with the implication that she was greedy.

He reflected, too, on the alacrity and the imagination with which she defended herself. Whatever qualities Ruth and Douglas might have to recommend themselves, it was becoming clear that Carolyn was the cleverest of the three.

18 The pony

Not long after Mr Thayer disqualified her for winning too many of his jungle contests Carolyn entered another contest, this one sponsored by the Golden Grocery Stores to promote a new brand of ice cream. Any child who bought a quart of Golden Ice Cream was given a map of the world. The countries and the oceans were to be colored and the map returned to the neighborhood store. Prizes would be awarded for the best coloring. First prize was a deluxe bicycle loaded with accessories or a Shetland pony named Jiggs. The bicycle and Jiggs were photographed side by side on the entry blank. There were two second prizes, ten third prizes, and one hundred fourth prizes. Carolyn decided she would be satisfied with first or second, which was a five-tube radio, so she came home from school one afternoon carrying a quart of strawberry ice cream, the map, and the entry blank.

After some deliberation she went to work with a set of colored pencils. They were prettier than wax crayons, and watercolors would cause the paper to pucker. Every night for about three weeks she worked on the map. She worked carefully, and when it was done it was very nicely done – even her brother admitted this. Her mother announced that she was sure to win the contest, but her father reminded everybody that there would be quite a few maps colored just as neatly. Carolyn thought about this. She resented her father's remark but she knew it was true. Then it occurred to her to emphasize the boundaries of each country with india ink. She consulted the rules. Outlining boundaries was not specifically prohibited. She bought a lettering pen in the dime store, went over the map with it, and was pleased with the result. The colors appeared much brighter by contrast with the black borders. There was, of course, the possibility of being disqualified again, but there was only one way to find out. She completed the entry blank and delivered it and the map to the grocery.

At ten o'clock on a Saturday morning the telephone rang. Carolyn was alone in the house except for Ruth, who was still asleep. When she answered the telephone a man inquired if her name was Carolyn Bridge. She said it was and he said he was Mr Denny, the Golden Ice Cream contest director, and he congratulated her for winning first prize. She did not believe him. She thought it was a trick. However, after talking to him a few minutes she was convinced and told him she would take the bicycle. She already had a bicycle, but she did not particularly want a pony and it would be nice to have two bicycles.

Mr Denny said the prizes were to be awarded next Saturday at noon at the Golden Grocery on Linwood Boulevard. Carolyn said she would be there, Mr Denny said he looked forward to meeting her.

This conversation ended just as Harriet returned from next door. Carolyn told her the good news and announced that she was going to celebrate by making a pan of chocolate-nut fudge. She was at work on this when Douglas and his friend Bobby Tipton came into the kitchen to get a bottle of root beer, so she told them about winning the contest. A few minutes later Ruth wandered downstairs looking for breakfast, and she too was informed. Then Mrs Bridge got back from shopping and reacted skeptically.

'Corky, you aren't teasing, are you?' she asked.

'No. I won,' said Carolyn.

Mrs Bridge set her packages on the kitchen table. 'Well, dear, that's wonderful,' she said as she began to pull off her gloves, 'but are you sure?' Then Carolyn explained again who Mr Denny was, and at last Mrs Bridge felt reasonably convinced. She hugged Carolyn and congratulated her, and said, 'It must have been quite a surprise!'

'No. I thought I'd win,' Carolyn said. She went back to chopping nuts for the fudge.

'Have you called your father?'

'I didn't want to bother him.'

'I don't believe he'll mind,' Mrs Bridge said. She picked up the telephone. 'Let me see if he's there.'

He was and she handed the telephone to Carolyn.

'Well! Well!' he said after hearing the news. 'That must have been a surprise, wasn't it?'

'No. I thought I'd win,' Carolyn said.

'Oh,' he said. 'Now, Cork, tell me. When you first talked about this thing I recall you saying there were two first prizes. Is that correct?'

'A Shetland pony and a bicycle.'

'So I thought. Since you have a bicycle why don't you take the pony?'

'I don't know how to ride.'

'Riding a pony is no trouble at all,' he said enthusiastically. 'When I was a boy I used to go riding on the farm with my cousin. I believe I've told you about that. It was great fun, Carolyn. In my opinion you've made a mistake.'

'I already told Mr Denny I wanted a bike.'

'Give me his number,' Mr Bridge said.

'I don't know it.'

'What's the name of the outfit sponsoring this thing?'

'Golden Ice Cream. I don't know how to ride a pony.'

'I'll teach you myself,' said Mr Bridge.

'Okay,' Carolyn said doubtfully. 'But where are you going to keep him?'

'I'll look into the matter. I expect we can make arrangements to stable him not too far away.'

'Do I have to pay for his food?'

'Of course not. I'll take care of the expenses. I'm going to call up that fellow and tell him you've changed your mind.'

'His name is Jiggs.'

'You told me his name was Denny.'

'Jiggs is the pony.'

'All right,' Mr Bridge said after this had been straightened out. 'You're going to enjoy riding, Cork. It's great fun.'

'I guess I will.'

'I know you will. Now, is your mother there?'

'She went upstairs. Do you want to talk to her?'

'Tell her I'll be home later than I expected and the rest of you are not to wait dinner on me. Julia was late getting to work and everything has been thrown off schedule.'

'Okay,' Carolyn said. 'I sure don't see you very much.'

'I'm sorry, sweetheart, but I have a great deal of work. Now be a good girl and I'll call this fellow right away. Good-by.'

'Good-by, Daddy,' she answered somewhat wistfully.

Mr Bridge had Julia locate the contest director. Mr Denny was sympathetic and promised that Jiggs the pony would be waiting for Carolyn next Saturday.

Mr Bridge could not attend the presentation ceremony because he was again spending Saturday at the office, but everybody else went to the grocery store – Mrs Bridge, Harriet, and all three children. Mr Denny himself was there. He looked rather like the leader of an orchestra. He was a slender young man wearing two-tone shoes, loose gray slacks with a sharp crease, and a British blazer with a gold crest on the pocket. Having shaken hands with everybody he asked them to call him Alfred, which nobody did.

After it was over and Carolyn had been photographed sitting tensely in the saddle, Jiggs was led back to his carrier and driven to the Waldo Stables, where Mr Bridge had rented a stall.

Jiggs remained at the stables for several months. Then Mr Bridge sold him to a farmer for thirty dollars. Carolyn had gone to visit her pony only twice. Ruth had gone out a number of times and come home nervous and excited, her clothing damp with perspiration, her eyes bright, and her long black hair undone, which displeased her mother. Douglas had not been to the stables at all. So it was that Jiggs did not have much to do and got fat eating oats. Mr Bridge got tired of buying oats and the farmer wanted a pony for his children. Everything considered, it seemed sensible and perhaps inevitable that Jiggs should be sold. Carolyn was satisfied with her thirty dollars and not much more was said about it.

Once in a while something would remind them of Jiggs. They would wonder how he liked being on the farm, and they spoke of driving to Harrisonville some Sunday afternoon to say hello. But the Sundays slipped away and they never went.

Mr Bridge often thought about the pony. The lively little creature reminded him of days he had almost forgotten, and it saddened him to realize he would not see Jiggs again – the cottony coat, the tossing head with its large metallic eye, the flecks of foam on the leather bridle – or hear again the imperious stamp of the tiny hooves.

19 Bleak day

Coming home late from the office one wintry Thursday he noticed the lights on in the dining room, which meant that the family was eating. After parking the Reo he let himself in the back door and stopped at the dining room. Douglas was not there.

Mrs Bridge said he had been invited to have dinner with Bobby Tipton. Then she added, 'I trust you have no objection.'

'No, I have no objection if he wishes to have dinner with one of his friends. How are the rest of you?'

'Just fine, as usual,' she responded, smiling at the girls. 'They were simply famished, so we took the liberty of starting.'

Ruth said, 'Daddy, what's wrong?'

He looked down at her curiously. 'What makes you think anything is wrong?'

She glanced at his briefcase and he realized that he was swinging it back and forth.

'Oh, dear, *is* something the matter?' Mrs Bridge asked.

He walked into the hall, where he took off his gloves and his hat and coat and put them in the closet. Then he returned to the dining room.

'A youthful client of mine was awarded a certain sum of money for personal injuries this afternoon but the judge took it upon himself to reduce the amount.'

'Really?' she exclaimed. 'Why, I had no idea they could do such a thing!'

'They can and they do. One thousand dollars is all that boy is going to get. One thousand dollars,' he repeated, and picking up a spoon he began to eat his soup.

'I sure could use a thousand dollars,' Carolyn said.

'It is far from adequate,' he answered shortly. He sighed and pushed the bowl of soup away.

'Was it snowing downtown?' Mrs Bridge inquired.

'Of course it was snowing downtown. It snowed here, didn't it? It snowed most of the day and the weather bureau predicts more of the same tomorrow.'

'I suppose getting around was a chore.'

'Getting around was next to impossible. I waited fifteen minutes for a cab. Good God, I thought I was never going to find a cab.'

'Do you have a headache?'

'I have had one since noon. How far is Douglas from here? Where does that Tipton boy live?'

'Oh, not far. Just the next block.'

'I don't want him walking home alone in the middle of a snowstorm. He might get lost.'

Ruth said, 'He won't get lost. He knows where he lives. Stop worrying, Daddy.'

'Now you listen here, young lady: I am in no mood for an argument. I am the one who decides whether or not your brother is old enough to walk home by himself.' He had spoken more harshly than he intended. He pushed at the plate of lamb stew his wife set in front of him.

'If you want me to, I'll walk over to Tipton's and get him,' Ruth said.

'If those people invited him they should have had the decency to offer to bring him home.'

'I'm sure they will, if the snow starts again,' Mrs Bridge said.

A few minutes later somebody knocked at the front door. Ruth answered it, and there stood Douglas accompanied by Mr Tipton.

After the front door had been shut Mr Bridge said, 'Did they feed you enough? How about some dessert?'

Douglas said he didn't think so, because he had eaten three pieces of chocolate pie at Tipton's.

'You are tracking snow on the carpet, my young friend,' said his mother. 'Go into the kitchen and take off your shoes.'

'Maybe later I'll eat dessert,' Douglas said as he started for the kitchen.

'Pigs is pigs,' Carolyn remarked.

'We will have no more of that,' Mr Bridge said, and after a moment he went on: 'In fact, you may go to your room.'

Carolyn was startled. 'What did I do?'

'You heard me.'

She turned to her mother, but Mrs Bridge said, 'You'd better obey your father. I'll come see you in a little.'

'Daddy—' Ruth began.

'And you! Both of you. Right now. March.'

They looked at their mother, who shook her head helplessly. They got up and walked out of the dining room.

Mr Bridge found himself very much alone at the opposite end of the table from his wife. He had not wanted this. He had been looking forward to a comfortable evening with his family. Now it was ruined. He began drumming his fingers on the table.

She asked if he would care for anything else, and he searched her voice. But she was not sarcastic. In all that time he had known her she had not once used herself that way.

'No. No, I can't eat tonight. Take some dessert to the girls when you go to see them. That business in court has thrown my whole day off.'

'I do think you're overworking,' she remarked. 'Why don't you take up a hobby? Other men do. Virgil has quite a stamp collection, you know.'

He went on as though she had not spoken: 'I represented a boy who suffered irreparable injury because of negligence on the part of his employer. That boy will never again lead a normal life. The compensation was not unreasonable. So far as that goes, to my mind it is difficult to contemplate any sum which might be called "unreasonable" after somebody's life has been virtually destroyed. Be that as it may, the jury agreed that the sum requested was not unfair. This amount, however, was deemed excessive and reduced to the point of mockery by a judge who is totally incompetent. That boy, incidentally, is not quite nineteen years old, so he may anticipate a good many more years in his present condition.'

'It's a shame. The judge should have realized.'

'The judge did not realize because he happens to be a fool.'

'Can't anything be done?'

'I intend to appeal the judgment. However, what this means is more work for me, and I am not taking a fee for this case. What an appeal means is that I must invest more time and effort in a charity situation. I already have spent more time on it than I can afford to.'

'Oh,' she said uncertainly. 'Well, of course I don't understand the ins and outs of the case, but it does sound as though the judge was unfair.'

'Just what would you consider "fair" in this life?' he demanded.

And hearing himself speak to his wife so rudely and so foolishly, he put down his knife and fork and held his head, which was pounding like the ocean.

20 Cadillac

That winter he decided he could afford a Cadillac. For some time he had been thinking about this, but there were two considerations. First, of course, was the expense. The second was more difficult to evaluate because it had to do with taste. Cadillac quite unmistakably symbolized success, and he did not want anybody who observed him in a Cadillac to assume that he was boasting. So, wanting one, he had told himself it would cost too much. But there came a day when he stopped at an agency to get the brochure, and he arranged for a salesman to bring a Cadillac to the house so he could take the family for a ride.

It was a splendid Saturday afternoon, clear and cold, when the luxurious black machine glided into view. The fat tires squashed sensuously over the icy ruts in the street. Behind the wheel, profoundly aware that he was representing Cadillac, sat Mr Pulliam the salesman.

After shaking hands with Mr Bridge, tipping his hat to Mrs Bridge, and speaking to the children, Mr Pulliam presented the keys. Then he stood on the front step patting one of the neighborhood dogs and chatting with Harriet while the family went for a drive through Mission Hills.

They were gone about twenty minutes and when they returned Mr Pulliam inquired confidently whether they had enjoyed themselves.

'Yes, we did,' Mr Bridge replied.

'You will never buy a finer automobile,' Mr Pulliam said.

Mr Bridge frowned. The Cadillac was impeccable, but Mr Pulliam annoyed him. He turned to the family and said, 'Well, speak up. Do you like it, or don't you? I'm not the only one who's going to be using it. Shall we see about buying this or look around for something else?'

'It's okay,' Douglas remarked without much enthusiasm. He had no objection to the car. He was willing to ride in it.

'Well, I certainly like it,' Mrs Bridge said, modulating her voice to express both her appreciation of the Cadillac and her knowledge that it was terribly expensive.

'What about you two?' Mr Bridge asked Carolyn and Ruth. He had nearly made up his mind. He was pleased that his wife and son liked the car. The cost troubled him, but he knew he could manage and he felt that the time had come to indulge himself. In the past he had denied himself many things in order to make certain that the family was deprived of nothing. Now, because he had worked hard and was succeeding, and because there were enough securities in the bank so that they would suffer no hardship if he died unexpectedly, he thought he would buy this enormously gratifying piece of machinery.

'It's gorgeous,' Ruth said, and touched the fender with a finger-nail.

'Many of our owners prefer three initials,' Mr Pulliam observed, pointing to a small metal plate near the door handle. 'Although you may prefer two.' He smiled.

Mr Bridge ignored him because he had interrupted when Carolyn was ready to speak. Furthermore, the suggestion about the initials implied that a decision had been made.

Mrs Bridge and all three children knew the salesman had mis-calculated. Mr Pulliam looked around helplessly.

Carolyn knew it was her turn to speak. She said in the voice her mother often used, 'Oh, it's awfully nice.'

'I'll have to think this over,' Mr Bridge said. 'Give me your card in case I decide to call you.'

Mr Pulliam smiled desperately. He opened his mouth to try again, but after looking up at Mr Bridge he realized that whatever he said would make matters worse. He smiled once more, handed Mr Bridge the card as though handing over his sword, slipped into the Cadillac, and drove away stamped with defeat.

For a few minutes Mr and Mrs Bridge remained standing on the driveway to discuss the situation.

'He was so sure of himself,' she remarked.

'They're all alike, every last one of them,' he answered. 'If we decide on a Cadillac I'll go through some other agency. And Lord knows I won't have my initials on it.'

He continued to think about the Cadillac, but he could not forget·the salesman; and the suggestion that he should advertise himself by putting his initials on the door was so offensive that several weeks after the demonstration he bought a Chrysler. The family liked it, and he himself did not feel quite so conspicuous. He concluded that he had made the proper decision.

21 Locusts

Gradually the low sky of winter began to lift. Beneath the shrubbery and in dark, cold corners the snow hardened into ice, but everywhere else it was melting. Icicles grew from the eaves, dripping and shining during the day while great pleats of snow skidded from the roof and thundered softly into the drifts.

Then one afternoon a breeze floated through the rose trellis, birds sailed overhead, and it was April. Harriet left the kitchen door open. The laundress strung clothesline in the back yard. Ruth and Carolyn oiled their roller skates and Douglas quit wearing the helmet he had worn nearly every day since October. Mrs Bridge placed her fur coat in storage. Mr Bridge, with no regret, carried the big flat-bladed snow shovel to the basement, where he hung it on a nail in the wall behind the furnace. He inspected the window screens. He rolled the lawn mower back and forth and sharpened the blades, and he sharpened the clipping shears.

And then it was summer.

Nothing spoke so persistently of summer as the ceaseless rasping song of the locusts – not the whirring lawn mowers or the morning twitter of sparrows in the birdbath or the shouts of boys playing baseball, the monotonous buzz of houseflies, little girls skipping rope on the sidewalk, not even the ephemeral moths bumping with mild anxiety against a screen. No noise welled from the green heart of summer like the buzzing of the locusts. Each afternoon they began when the hottest part of the day was over, and they did not stop until late at night, unless there was rain.

One evening on the porch he was reading the *Star*. His wife was sewing buttons on a shirt. Carolyn was reading a book. Douglas sprawled on the floor drawing pictures in a tablet with a box of crayons. Ruth lay on the swing doing nothing. In the dark trees the locusts sang.

Carolyn looked up. 'Mother,' she said, 'where do they go when summer is over?'

'The locusts? I'm not sure, dear. Ask your father.'

Mr Bridge lowered his newspaper. 'They live only a few weeks, Carolyn.'

'How do they make that noise?'

'Oh, goodness, I used to know,' her mother said. 'Let me think. We were taught in school.'

He waited for her to remember, but she could not, so he said, 'They are not rubbing their wings together, as most people thing. They produce the noise by the vibration of a membrane situated near the abdomen. And as I recall, Carolyn, it's only the male who "sings" – if you care to call it singing. I'm afraid this just about exhausts my knowledge of them. It's been quite a while since your mother and I were in school.'

But she had noticed that they began in unison, not one after another. She asked how they knew when it was time to begin. He answered that this was a mystery.

'It's so beautiful,' Ruth said. 'It's like they had an orchestra with a conductor. I could lie here and listen forever.'

Mrs Bridge said, 'They always let us know evening is on the way.'

'It sure is funny you never see them,' Carolyn said. 'I looked, only I couldn't find any.'

A few minutes later Mrs Bridge remarked, 'Don't you wonder how many there might be in that old elm? Suppose we guess.'

Mr Bridge discovered that he could not read any more, though he continued holding the paper. He listened to his daughters and his wife and he observed his son, but he no longer understood what was being said; as he listened to their voices and to the seasonal music of the insects the problems which had troubled him during the day did not seem important, and he reflected that he had practically everything he ever wanted.

22 You don't love me

It happened one warm Sunday afternoon while he was on his hands and knees in the yard with a can of poison. She came out of the house to watch, at least he assumed she had come out to watch his progress in the unending battle against the snails. For about ten minutes she stood around saying nothing, plucking nervously at her necklace. Then all at once she cried in a voice he had never heard before: 'What people say about you is true!' Mr Bridge reared up on his knees and gazed at his wife in amazement. He thought she had gone out of her mind. Her face was pale. She breathed noisily. She was furious about something, there was no mistaking the fact.

'Walter,' she said, making an obvious effort to control herself, 'I insist on a divorce. Right now. At once. Do you understand?' Before he could answer, she stamped her foot and rushed into the house.

He put down the snail poison carefully so it would not tip over and destroy the new grass. Then he stood up, brushed off his trousers, and followed her. She had gone upstairs. She was in the bedroom. The door was locked. He tapped at the door but there was no response, so he went downstairs to the kitchen and opened a bottle of beer. After this many years of marriage she had gone berserk. He sat down at the kitchen table to drink the beer and consider what he should do next, when he realized that she was glaring at him from the pantry.

'I thought as much,' she cried in a soft, fierce voice. 'You've never cared about me. Just look at you! Look at yourself! Drinking beer!'

'Now for Heaven's sake, India,' he said. 'Stop acting ridiculous. You know perfectly well I care for you.'

'I don't expect you to understand. You've never understood. Lois told me she had never seen a man so wrapped up in his own affairs. Half the time you don't know if I'm dead or alive.'

'Why, that's not true,' he said. 'That simply is not true.'

'Go right ahead,' she remarked when she saw him glance at his beer, which was foaming pleasantly near the rim of the glass. 'Go right ahead. I'm the last person on earth to spoil your pleasure. We can discuss the divorce after you've enjoyed yourself. I can wait. I don't mind waiting. My life has been spent waiting on you and the children. None of you have been aware of it, but that's all right. I realize you've written me off.'

He patted the chair next to him. 'India, won't you sit down?'

'Thank you, I prefer to stand. Lois read my horoscope the other day. It says "Your emotional destiny is to lend courage, strength, truth, and tolerance to the world. Express your idealistic love nature fearlessly but sensibly so that you command respect as well as love from those dear to you." That doesn't make the slightest difference to you; not that I expect it to, because you are completely wrapped up in your own affairs. The office, the office, the office, the office! I'm not blaming you, Walter. You are what you are. It scarcely matters if we see you only at the table. We can get along without you.'

However, she did sit down beside him, and when he put his arm around her she did not throw it off.

She never explained what he had done wrong, and after thinking quite a lot about this incomprehensible fit of hysteria he decided the best procedure was to ignore it.

23 Call me Avrum

'Mr Bridge, is it not?'

A squat, bald Jew dressed in an expensive blue pinstripe suit skipped out of a doorway with an umbrella hooked over his arm. Mr Bridge stopped walking and looked down at him suspiciously. The suit was an attempt at good taste, but it failed because it was obvious. He carried a copy of the *Wall Street Journal* but he held it so that it could be noticed. On his plump, pink, manicured little finger sparkled a diamond ring. Mr Bridge looked again at the umbrella. There was no reason to be carrying an umbrella. The sun was shining, no rain had been forecast. This man was not to be trusted. Whatever his business, he was shallowly successful, and the business probably was marginal. He had the air of a slum lord. He could be a political lobbyist or a North End liquor wholesaler. He might be an osteopath or a cut-rate dentist. He was not a corporation executive or a reputable businessman. Whatever he did, he was not to be trusted. He was shrewd. He was repugnant. He was an opportunist. Under no circumstances should he be trusted, no matter what he said or did or suggested. He had stepped suddenly out of nowhere, wanting something, because that was the sort he was. He thought himself urbane and thought he had stepped away from his heritage as nimbly as he had skipped out of a doorway; whereas in fact everything he did, everything he wore or carried, and each affectation, revealed his nature, his background, and his ideals. His manner and his education had been picked up like pennies on the sidewalk. This was a man who had not seen the inside of a university because his parents lacked the means, and he had neither forgotten this nor forgiven his parents their poverty. Possibly he had made money, but he was not *nouveau,* no matter how many diamonds he had collected; this man's goal in life was to emulate the newly rich.

So, without a smile, Mr Bridge inspected him.

And the ingratiating voice responded: 'Rheingold is the name, Mr Bridge. Avrum Rheingold.' He was offering his card. MIMM, ZACK & RHEINGOLD. Stocks and bonds. Then he was offering to shake hands.

Mr Bridge was about to return the card and decline the extended hand, but Avrum Rheingold was alert.

'We have a mutual acquaintance, Mr Bridge, the great psychiatrist Dr Alexis Sauer. Am I wrong to think you are joining him for lunch today at the Hotel Muehlebach?'

As a courtesy Mr Bridge slipped the card into his pocket. And because the hand was still there like an object in a dream he accepted that, too. The hand was moist and fleshy, as he expected. It curled affectionately around his own. He could hardly restrain a shudder. It occurred to him that Rheingold's hand felt like the tongue of a cow, and again he had to control a shudder. The hand was almost licking him. He heard the broker praising Alex Sauer in the most egregious terms. The flattery was intolerable. He withdrew his hand, which came away stickily. He wanted to wash it. His hand felt moist and unhealthy, as if during those few seconds it had become infected.

'What this man has done for my wife you would not believe. You would not believe a word, Mr Bridge, I'm telling the truth. He is a genius. A marvel. A wonder-worker. My wife is not the same woman. Such skill. It's my great privilege to counsel him on financial matters.'

Mr Bridge glanced at his watch.

'I know how busy you are,' said Avrum Rheingold. 'To a man like yourself minutes are jewels. I could not resist the opportunity to shake hands. You have been pointed out to me, Mr Bridge. I noticed you at once. Everybody does. Who wouldn't? In a crowd you are the first person everybody sees. Why is that? It's a gift, Mr Bridge. A gift of the gods. Plus hard work. It shows. You are a man among men, like your dear friend Dr Sauer. I have observed you together and said to myself sincerely "Avrum, this is a rare and beautiful sight. A great legal mind, a great psychiatrist." I don't hesitate to say this, because everybody knows it's the truth. I'm detaining you. I know how a man like yourself extracts life from each minute. It's my good fortune to make your acquaintance. Please call me Avrum. It's noon. You are on your way to the Muehlebach. I have a small favor to ask. Be kind enough to offer my respects to Dr Sauer, the savior of my wife. Such a man. Believe me, you should have seen my wife two years ago.'

Mr Bridge nodded, wondering if the sweetish odor came from Rheingold, or from something in the street.

'Good-by. Good-by.' He almost bowed.

Mr Bridge continued to the Muehlebach. There was nothing about Rheingold which could be considered attractive, and after descending the steps to the Terrace Grill he stopped at the men's room to wash his hands before going in to lunch.

Alex Sauer was at the table with Simon Lutweiler, Russell Arlen, and a friend of Arlen's. Sauer evidently had arrived early and was in a hurry, because he had begun eating.

'Alex,' he said, 'I was stopped on the street by someone who is a great admirer of yours. A person named Rheingold.'

At this moment the great psychiatrist was gnawing a turkey leg. He paused, wiped the grease from his chin, and exclaimed 'Ah ha!' But that was all he said, so Mr Bridge refrained from giving an opinion of the man.

24 EK

On the recommendation of his own broker, who was a different kind of man, and having himself spent a considerable amount of time reading recent statistics concerned with potential, yield, dependability, sales, and earnings, Mr Bridge one Monday morning added to his portfolio with the purchase of twenty shares of Eastman Kodak. The company had been in business for quite a while, it had paid dividends every year since 1902, and he had concluded that in spite of the almost frivolous nature of its merchandise Eastman Kodak was here to stay.

Eastman Kodak was on his mind most of the day, and after leaving the office he stopped at the newsstand to buy a copy of the evening paper. He turned to the daily listings and was shocked to find that E Kodak had dropped five points. Fluctuations were to be expected, but such a fall as this was abnormal. His first thought was that he had been swindled; yet Eastman was a reputable firm and the broker was a conscientious, honorable man with whom he had done business for fifteen years, so there was little likelihood of manipulation. All the same, in print was the disagreeable fact: down five. Eastman had neither risen nor fallen five dollars in a single day for a long time. It was as though the company had merely been waiting for him to buy before the price dropped.

Frowning, with the *Star* folded and stuffed into a pocket of his raincoat, he pulled on his gloves, settled his hat on his head, picked up his briefcase, and started walking toward the garage. He had worked late. Julia had gone home two hours ago. Now the streets were dark. A damp wind was blowing. It was a depressing night to be out and he looked forward to his comfortable home.

At the corner a voice behind him said: 'Stick 'em up!'

Mr Bridge continued walking. He did not believe what he had heard. Either he had not heard what he thought he heard, or if somebody had ordered him to put up his hands it must be a joke.

The command was repeated, and there were footsteps.

Mr Bridge stopped walking and turned around. Coming toward him was a red-eyed, unshaven man with one hand thrust into the slit pocket of a shabby trench coat.

Mr Bridge said impatiently: 'What is it you want?'

'Give me your money,' the man said in a hoarse voice, and he made a threatening gesture.

'Don't be ridiculous,' said Mr Bridge, and walked away.

While driving home he contemplated the incident. Evidently it had been a serious attempt to hold him up. The man might very well have had a gun concealed in his pocket, and it was possible that he was desperate enough to have used it. However, he could not become alarmed as he thought about it any more than he had been alarmed at the time. He felt nothing except a sort of exasperation. The man's presumption was extraordinary. If he had no money he should get a job like everybody else.

25 Kansas City Power & Light

The years were falling over like ducks in a shooting gallery, and it seemed to Mr Bridge that he had scarcely taken aim at one when it disappeared. Now another year was all but gone. However, it had been a good year. He was not dissatisfied. He had worked hard, harder than most men, but the work had been rewarding. He was acquiring more than he needed, quite a lot more. And yet most important was the happiness he sensed around him. He believed that his wife was happy and the children also, and because of this he felt their happiness within himself.

Christmas Eve he lay awake until he was sure everybody in the house had gone to sleep; then he got out of bed, put on his robe and slippers, and went into the study. He shut the door, turned on the desk lamp, and unzipped his briefcase. In a large manila envelope were the Christmas gifts. He folded them and slipped them into business envelopes which he addressed – one to his wife, one to each of the children, and one to Harriet. On the back of each he wrote 'from Santa'. Then he switched off the lamp and went downstairs to the living room. Moonlight from the east windows flooded the bushy green spruce and the heap of brightly colored packages. He surveyed this tranquil scene and it pleased him. He approached the Christmas tree, took five paper clips from the pocket of his bathrobe, clipped the envelopes to the branches of the tree, and returned to bed.

Next morning after breakfast the family gathered in the living room to open presents. For a while the business envelopes hung unnoticed among the peppermint candy canes, the tinsel, and the sparkling ornaments. But then Carolyn discovered them, saw that one had her name, and tore it open. She unfolded the certificate avidly, not certain what it was but sensing that it was valuable.

'Oh, goodness! My word!' Mrs Bridge cried when she opened

her envelope. 'This *is* Christmas!'

Douglas looked skeptically at the certificate he had gotten.

'It's ten shares of stock in the Kansas City Power & Light Company,' Ruth told him. 'Thank you, Daddy.'

'You're welcome,' he answered, laughing. 'But it appears to me as if it came from Santa Claus.'

'That's right!' Mrs Bridge said, pointing to the back of the envelope. 'Well, thank you, Mr Santa!'

'Thank you,' Carolyn said. She was reading everything printed on the certificate.

'Thanks,' Douglas said. He was more impressed by the baseball glove and the hockey stick.

'Don't lose these,' Mr Bridge said, wagging his index finger in mock anger. 'They're worth quite a bit of money. I'll put them in my safe-deposit box for you.'

'Oh, yes, please,' Mrs Bridge said, and handed him her certificate.

Ruth handed him the one she had received.

Douglas shrugged and gave back the one he had gotten.

'I want to keep mine,' said Carolyn.

'If you want to, you can. It's your privilege,' he said. 'But if you lose it we will have to go through a considerable amount of red tape to have another certificate issued.'

'All right, here,' she said after thinking the matter over.

'I certainly do wish to thank you,' Harriet said.

'You're most welcome, Harriet,' he said. 'Would you like me to hold yours, or can you take care of it?'

'Well, if it is not too much of a problem, I would appreciate you keeping mine in the safe deposit also.'

'I'll be glad to,' he said, and reached for it. 'Any time you want it, let me know.'

While the rest of the packages were being opened he sat holding the five certificates firmly in both hands. He did not want them to get misplaced so that they might be burned in the fireplace with the tissue paper and empty boxes when the room was cleaned up. A few minutes later he carried them upstairs and put them once more in the manila envelope, which he zipped into the briefcase.

26 Paper hat

New Year's Eve the Montgomerys gave a party. Mr Bridge did not want to attend. He disliked New Year's Eve, and after listening to football games on the radio all afternoon he wanted nothing more than to spend the evening in bed reading travel brochures and a mystery novel he had gotten for Christmas. However, they were obligated to go because they had turned down a previous invitation from the Montgomerys, and the invitation to this had been sent so far in advance that another rejection would be embarrassing.

The party was exactly what he had feared it would be. Just before midnight the butler broke open boxes of confetti, streamers, paper hats, horns, whistles, and other noisemakers. Mr Bridge got behind the piano where he sipped a glass of champagne and hoped he would not be noticed until the worst of it was over, but his wife found him.

Gaily she cried, 'Don't be an old stick-in-the-mud! Tonight you're going to put on a paper hat and enjoy yourself!'

'I will not wear a paper hat,' he said. 'That's final.'

'Oh, goodness, we all feel silly,' she replied, adjusting the peppermint-red hat she had chosen, 'but everybody's wearing one.'

'I am not everybody,' he said.

'You certainly aren't,' she said. 'But can't you make an exception on New Year's Eve?'

'No,' said Mr Bridge.

27 Purple crayon

If Carolyn proved to be the most intelligent of the children, Douglas was growing up to be the most obdurate. To persuade him was as difficult as it was simple to command him; in the depths of his soul some recalcitrance was rooted which could neither be examined nor assuaged. If he was about to be punished he would argue against it, not very effectively, and finally accept it without comment, leaving no doubt that he considered himself undefeated. Punishment failed because he either knew he had done wrong, in which case the punishment seemed unnecessary and therefore ridiculous, or he remained convinced that he had been treated unjustly. Neither his mother nor his father knew quite what to do. Strange wood was growing; both of them sensed it.

'What in the world have you on your hands?' his mother demanded.

Douglas gazed at the backs of his hands, which were blotched with purplish marks, as though he observed nothing unusual. He said it was crayon.

'Crayon!' she exclaimed. 'Young man, if you think for one instant you can sit down at the table without washing those hands, you have another think coming. Hop to the kitchen right now.'

'Let me see those hands,' his father said.

Douglas obediently walked around the table. Mr Bridge took his son's hands in his own and looked closely at the curious marks. He turned the hands over and looked at the palms, which were clean.

'How did you get this?' he asked.

Douglas said he had gotten the crayon on his hands during geography class, but he did not explain.

'Let's hear the rest.'

'What rest?'

'How did you get these marks?'

After a long silence Douglas said: 'From a ruler.'

'Go on.'

'Ye cripes,' Douglas said, and rolled his eyes. 'It's a little bit of purple crayon. You act like it was the end of the world. It was just Miss Breuhauf, that's all. She got sore and gave me the business with her ruler. I guess it had a little purple crayon on it.'

'Do you mean to say,' his mother asked with a shocked expression, 'she struck you with a ruler?'

'Don't worry. He deserved it,' said Carolyn.

'A fat lot you know,' said Douglas. 'She probably did worse than that to you when you had her class.'

Mr Bridge was still examining his son's hands. The skin had not been broken. He said, 'Does she make a habit of this?'

'Sure,' Douglas said. 'She loves to beat up kids. She gives somebody the business all the time. Rodney Vandermeer got it last week. If she gets sore she gets good and sore.'

'Do your hands ache?'

'Not too much. They swelled up at recess but they're okay now.'

'I simply cannot believe this,' Mrs Bridge said. 'She ought to be reported.'

'Don't report her,' Douglas said patiently. 'She'd just take it out on us. She's nutty as a fruitcake.'

'Why did you provoke her?' his father asked.

'I didn't.'

'Spitballs,' said Carolyn.

Douglas sneered. 'How do you know so much? Were you there?'

'No. But I know somebody who was.'

'That will be enough, both of you,' Mrs Bridge said. 'Corky, eat your salad.'

'Well,' Douglas said, 'am I supposed to wash my hands, or not?'

'Yes. Go do it,' said Mr Bridge, and with a thoughtful expression he began to whet the carving knife. Carolyn probably was right, very probably Douglas did deserve to be punished for whatever he had done; but he did not like the idea of a teacher who made a habit of beating children.

Later that evening he stopped by his son's room to talk about it some more.

Douglas had assumed the matter was ended, and he was bored. He admitted, after questioning, that he had been trying to antagonize the teacher, and he did not seem to feel that he had been mistreated. Yes, he said, it hurt while she was beating him. Then he said, 'She thought I was going to try and jerk my hands away, so she grabbed hold of them, but I just let her do whatever she wanted. She sure got mad. I thought she was going to have a heart attack. She kept asking if I was sorry. That's what she asks kids when she beats them up.'

'Did you apologize?'

Douglas laughed. 'Shoot, no.'

'Why not?'

'Because that's what she wanted.'

'What did you tell her?'

'Nothing.'

'Where did this take place?'

'In the front of the room.'

'In view of the other children?'

'She usually takes the girls into the cloakroom, but she likes to give it to the guys where everybody can see.' After a meditative pause he added, 'I don't think she'll do it to me anymore.'

'Why do you think that?'

Douglas struggled to answer, but could not find the words. At last he said, 'I just got a hunch.'

Mr Bridge had been sitting on the edge of the bed with his arms crossed. He stood up, told his son good night, and walked downstairs. He was no longer particularly concerned about the teacher, because Douglas had almost destroyed her. Very possibly she had never before encountered a child whose will was greater than hers. It was not likely that she would be the same again. She must have understood while she was beating him that she was losing, and knowing the child was aware of this must have made it very hard for her.

As to the effect of this punishment on Douglas, Mr Bridge was not sure. He suspected that the beating had affected Douglas, too, though, not necessarily for the worse. There had been that odd quality in him, like the resiliency of ironwood, as he described what happened. This quality might be useful to him when he grew up, and what the woman had done was to nurture it. At any rate, he had not been damaged. Like a young Trojan he had displayed his wounds in public. Probably, if left alone, he would not have washed his hands for a week.

28 *Stiff lower lip*

Whenever he thought about his son's confrontation with the teacher a thin smile touched his face and he reflected that Douglas had inherited much of his own temperament. This more than anything else assured him that he did indeed have a son. Not even the physical resemblance – the lank body, the bony Anglo-Saxon features, and the dry, reddish hair – none of these irrefutable signs persuaded him as deeply as certain temperamental characteristics which he could recognize as his own. And of these the most unmistakable was that despotic obstinacy which could not conceive of surrender, no matter what the cost. He knew this in himself. So he smiled as he considered it in his son.

29 Barbarians

Rodney Vandermeer and Douglas were expelled from school for two days. They had run amuck for no comprehensible reason. First, they had rushed into the girls' dressing room in the gymnasium, shouting and terrorizing the little girls. Summoned to the office of the principal and severely reprimanded, they were contrite. But at lunchtime they had somewhere found a box of F.D.R. campaign buttons; they bent the pins straight up and scattered the buttons on the classroom seats. Again they were taken to the principal, who ordered them to bring their mothers to school for a talk. But they were no sooner released from the office this time than they ran around to the rear of the building and urinated against the wall, in plain view of the policeman at the corner.

Mrs Bridge was bewildered. Mr Bridge listened silently to her account of everything that happened. He could not make sense of it either. He said he would have a talk with Douglas.

Douglas was brought into the study, but he did not know why they had done what they had done. He mumbled, he scratched his neck, he picked at the braces on his teeth, he scraped his shoes together, examined the pencil he was carrying behind his ear, and could not explain. He did not even remember whose idea it was to invade the girls' dressing room, nor could he remember which of them had first thought about the campaign buttons. They had just felt like doing it, that was all.

The buttons were serious. The other two acts were foolish and vulgar, but if one of the children had seated himself on a pin there would have been real trouble.

'Somebody might have been badly injured,' Mr Bridge said. 'Weren't you aware of that?'

'We only left them in the girls' seats,' Douglas answered.

249

And suddenly the various outrages were linked. It was not incomprehensible after all, only a little bizarre.

30 Boxtops

According to Douglas there were a number of worthwhile things one could get in exchange for cereal boxtops, and in his room in the bottom drawer of his desk where valuable possessions were kept, along with a Roman candle left over from the previous Fourth of July, a bottle of nails, a deflated rubber basketball, a bronze coin bank in the shape of a book with a leatherette cover, and other choice items – there in the bottom drawer he maintained a cache of boxtops. From time to time, when he had accumulated enough, he would mail some of these boxtops to the company and in about ten days would receive the premium. He had gotten a balsawood glider kit which he had assembled, but the glider lodged high up in an oak tree on its maiden flight and was still to be seen months later. He had gotten a mustard-colored ocarina, known as a 'sweet potato', on which he played unrecognizable melodies. He had gotten a Tom Mix cap pistol with a glaring red holster, but had mislaid the gun so that now he had only the holster. He had gotten a pair of aluminum spurs which dragged the ground whenever he attached them to his tennis shoes, and a horsehair lasso, and a fishing reel – the line was now irrevocably snarled – and a bicycle pump that leaked, and a reproduction of *Custer's Last Stand*. He had in mind several other premiums. He desperately wanted a blow-gun with six darts, a battery-powered model of Sir Malcolm Campbell's *Bluebird*, a periscope, an incense burner, and most of all a fur-lined aviator's helmet with tinted goggles.

Nobody else in the family saved boxtops; even so, it took a long time to get a premium. He had been considering this, together with the fact that in almost every house in the neighborhood somebody ate cereal, which meant, presumably, that hundreds of boxtops were going to waste. If he could get hold of these boxtops he could order most of the premiums in the catalog. The question was how to get them. At first he thought of going from house to house asking for them, but the idea of ringing doorbells and explaining what he wanted was embarrassing. Finally he decided to follow the trash collectors who came around every two weeks.

He did not mention this to his friends Tipton and Vandermeer, because they might cut in on the route; nor was there any point in mentioning it at home, either to his parents or to his sisters or to Harriet. If his mother or his father found out what he was doing there might be trouble. He did not think there was anything wrong with the plan, but just the same he did not mention it.

Every other Saturday morning as soon as he had finished breakfast, without telling anybody where he was going he went out the kitchen door, jumped the hedge, and trotted away. He cut through the vacant lot, climbed the fence behind the Edison house, trotted down their driveway, crossed Stratford Road, and at the corner of Fifty-ninth Street he squatted beside one of his favorite telephone poles to wait for the truck.

He came home in time for lunch, with his pockets bulging.

At first he felt uncomfortable as he followed the truck through the neighborhood, but after several trips he began to feel that the trash collectors accepted him, and after a while he learned their names – Vince, Steve, and Dom. Dom was the friendliest, occasionally speaking to him and calling him 'kid'. Dom was also the thirstiest; he often stopped at the water faucet outside somebody's house and drank from his cupped hands. Then he usually blew his nose while holding his thumb against it and wiped his thumb on his pants before going back to work. Douglas was impressed by the way the trash man blew his nose and tried it himself a number of times when nobody was watching, but finally gave up and continued using a handkerchief.

One April morning when the truck stopped in front of his own house he thought it must be about time for Dom to have another drink, so he inquired. He explained that this was where he lived and he volunteered to get a glass of ice water from the kitchen. The trash man said he could drink from the outside faucet. Douglas said it was no trouble to get a glass of ice water, and he went into the kitchen and opened the refrigerator. Harriet, who was rolling dough for a piecrust, watched him suspiciously. Douglas said he was not hunting for something to eat, he was not going to spoil his lunch, he was getting some ice water to make the trash man a drink.

251

Harriet said, 'He can get his drink through the hose.'

The trash man, who was standing just outside the screen door, heard this and started edging away, not certain whether the cook or the little boy had more authority. Douglas saw that he was about to leave and told him to wait. He stopped and stood with his hands on his hips, ready to walk either way.

Harriet said, 'Oh, all right then, here let me find you a glass.' She wiped the flour from her hands, opened a cupboard, and brought down a jelly glass.

'Get him a real one,' Douglas said.

'This here will do,' she said. 'Give me that ice.' She took the tray and held it under the hot water until several cubes dropped into the sink.

'I can do it,' Douglas said.

Harriet ignored him. She put some ice in the glass, filled it with cold water, and handed it to him. Douglas knew she was being rude and he was concerned.

'Come on in, Dom,' he said.

The trash man stayed where he was. 'Bring it out here, kid,' he said.

'Come on in,' Douglas repeated. 'This is my house.'

The trash man deftly opened the screen door and slipped inside. Douglas gave him the water and he began to drink, pausing after a few swallows to wipe his lips on his sleeve.

Just then Mr Bridge entered the kitchen. In a fraction of a second he interpreted the scene: the unknown man – a laborer – with a glass of water, Douglas, and Harriet. During the first instant the one thing he did not understand was why the man was inside the house. But he sensed no danger. The man was a working man of some sort, not a tramp. Everything was all right. Still, it was curious that he had gotten inside the house.

'Good morning,' Mr Bridge said without hesitation and with no change of expression. He had come into the kitchen to see if there was any French mustard, which he liked. His wife had mentioned that they were nearly out of French mustard, and he had come into the kitchen to find out for himself how much was left. He took down the tin of powdered French mustard from the spice shelf, pried off the lid with a knife, and peered inside. Then he replaced the lid, put the mustard back on the shelf, and walked out of the kitchen.

Nobody moved or spoke while he was there.

31 *The gardener's child*

He had known for a day or so that his wife was concerned about something, and he waited. When she was ready to tell him, she would. One night she did. As they were undressing she said, 'Walter, I hate to bother you, but I'm afraid I need your advice. It's about Alice Jones?'

'Alice Jones?' he asked. 'Who is Alice Jones?'

'You know. The colored child who used to be around here on weekends. The gardener's child. Jones. That gardener who works next door. She and Carolyn were quite friendly. They've begun drifting apart now, but she was here last week and apparently invited Carolyn to a party. The thing is, I'm not sure I've done the right thing. I told Corky it wouldn't be a good idea. I honestly didn't know what to do. It's been on my mind ever since. Alice is such a sweet child.'

He was inspecting his shoes to see if they needed new soles. He continued turning them over while he said, 'What sort of a party?'

'I haven't the foggiest notion. The two of them were on the porch talking, and Corky came into the sewing room to ask if she could go. I suppose I could drive her down and pick her up after the party is over. What do you think?'

'It sounds to me as though you've already settled the matter.'

'I feel so guilty. I wouldn't hurt Alice's feelings for the world.'

'Where do those people live?'

'Thirteenth and Prospect, I believe. I understand it's a mixed area, though I've never been there. Do you suppose it would be safe?'

'Safe?'

'Would it be safe for Carolyn to go down there for an hour or so?'

'Yes, of course it would be safe, as long as that colored girl invited her. However, I don't want her fooling around in that neighborhood. I have no objection to the girl visiting Carolyn here

253

at the house when her father is working next door, but that's the extent of it. These situations get worse, not better. I don't want Carolyn to get in the habit of visiting that end of town.'

'I'm sure she wouldn't make it a habit. This was a special occasion.'

'It makes no difference. Carolyn doesn't belong at Thirteenth and Prospect any more than you or I do. Those people resent us.'

32 Summer in Georgia

In July of that year a weekly news magazine printed a photograph of a lynching. The Negro was chained to a tree. He was naked to the waist and his back was crisscrossed with the marks of a lash. Around him stood a crowd of whites. Mrs Bridge, when she saw this picture, was stunned; she carried the magazine to her husband and enquired in a faint, bewildered voice: 'What on earth makes people behave that way?'

The picture irritated him because its publication was unnecessary, but he concealed his reaction. He studied the contorted body and the glistening black face. Then he examined the crowd. There appeared to be at least fifty men – mostly farmers, to judge from the overalls – armed with clubs and guns, and quite a number of boys. Most of the men were grinning. Several of the boys had struck comic poses for the camera. The photograph evoked a sense of the South: he could nearly feel the oppressive heat and hear the hoots of laughter and the jokes and shouts and lewd suggestions as the lash went whistling through the air and exploded against the Negro's skin, the cheers and the clapping, the barking dogs, and the guns popping wildly in the pine forest.

Suddenly he remembered that his wife had spoken; he blinked, glanced up, and discovered her staring at him with a frightened expression.

'There are many fine people in the South,' he said. 'What did this fellow do?' He placed his index finger on the Negro's head. 'Tell me, what was this fellow doing that he shouldn't have been doing? I have spent a certain amount of time in the South. I once spent several days in Atlanta and I never met more courteous people.'

33 *Underground*

That was the summer a group of neighborhood boys dug a cave in one of the vacant lots. Douglas was not allowed to dig, presumably because he was too young to be granted such a privilege, but after the cave was finished he was sometimes permitted inside. Mr Bridge did not altogether like this, and one Sunday he decided to have a look at the cave. He thought he could locate the entrance, because Douglas had described how it was camouflaged.

As he was walking along the street toward the vacant lot he began thinking about his own boyhood. He remembered how important it had been to have a cave, or a platform in the fork of a tree, or a shack to use as a club-house, and how necessary it was to keep the entrance hidden or locked. More time had been spent on locks and burglar alarms than on anything else. He had not thought of these things for a long time, and they began to bring back other memories. He remembered the farm near Joplin where he often went to visit his cousin Reed, and the odor of apples moldering in the orchard, the dried grapevine they tried to smoke, the dying fox they found one evening on the riverbank, the plump and stupid hired girl whose name was Lizzie or Tillie – so many years had passed that he was no longer sure of her name. The nipples of her breasts stood up like raisins beneath her dress. And he could see again his aunt and uncle seated side by side on the swing, gliding calmly to and fro, never speaking, never moving, while bats and barn swallows darted after insects in the summer twilight. Now and then an automobile could be seen bouncing along the dirt road to town, and the ragged sputtering of the motor carried clearly across the silent fields. All of this came back to Mr Bridge like the unforgotten taste of hard green apples. A generation had passed. Not ten years, or fifteen years. A complete generation. The old folks were gone. Uncle Senn with his drooping frontier mustache. Aunt Christine with her ivory locket and blue-veined hands. Reed owned the farm now and had four sons, three of them older than Douglas.

The cave was not easy to find. He pushed through the weeds and was wondering if he had gotten into the wrong lot, when suddenly he heard voices underground. He stopped and looked around, because the entrance must be very close, but he could not see it. Then he found the dead bush and beneath it the outline of a sod-covered door. He had planned to tramp back and forth on top of the cave, but now because it was occupied he thought he should not.

The bush quivered, the trap door tilted, and the startled face of Rodney Vandermeer appeared among the weeds. Just as quickly he disappeared under the bush. There was more subterranean conversation. Silence. Once again the trap door opened. This time it was Douglas.

'Hello there,' said Mr Bridge.

'Hello,' Douglas said.

'I've been wondering how substantial this thing is. I didn't want the roof falling in on you.'

'It won't fall in.'

'Ah? What makes you so sure?'

'Some of the guys ran a wheelbarrow full of bricks over it.'

'I see. Well, these things can be dangerous if you don't watch out. Have I disturbed you?'

'Oh,' Douglas said, 'I guess not. We knew somebody was up there.'

'You could hear me walking around, could you?'

'Easy.'

'Are you having a meeting?'

After a pause Douglas said, 'I don't get you.'

'Isn't this some sort of a clubhouse? Don't you have meetings here?'

'It's just a cave. You want to come in?'

'No. But thank you. How many of you are in there?'

'Right now?'

'Yes.'

'I don't know.'

'What do you mean you don't know?'

'Well, I guess there's six or seven.'

256

'My Lord, how big is that place?'

'It's pretty deep,' Douglas said. 'You can stand up if you want to.' He had been holding the trap door above his head, but his arms were beginning to tremble; he lowered the door until it rested on his head. 'We're sort of crowded, though. I guess you'd get your pants muddy if you tried to squeeze in.'

'I expect I would. Who else is in there?'

'Tipton, and Rod, and the big guys, and some guy from Overland Park. He's a friend of one of the big guys. He plays quarterback on the Overland Park High School team.'

'Ah ha. Now tell me, is this the only entrance?'

'Yes, but they're talking about digging a rear escape.'

'That sounds like a good idea.'

'We caught a snake here yesterday.'

'What kind?'

'Just a garter snake. At first we thought it was a rattler. He's about a foot long.'

'You've kept him?'

'He's in the cigar box. We're going to try and catch a live mouse for him to eat.'

'I don't believe garter snakes eat mice.'

'That's what the guy from Overland Park says. But we thought he might anyway.'

After a lengthy silence Mr Bridge said, 'I didn't mean to interrupt.'

'That's okay,' Douglas said as the trap door began sinking, 'let me know if you want to come in sometime.'

34 Discretion

'Just say some guy really had it in for you and yanked out a pistol,' Douglas proposed. 'What would you do?'

Mr Bridge had settled down to read the stock market reports. 'I would do as I was told,' he replied as he opened the paper.

'What if he wanted your dough?'

'I would give it to him, naturally.'

'You'd let him get away with it?'

'I would remember what the man looked like and report the robbery to the police as soon as possible.'

'Can they get your dough back?'

'Not often.'

Douglas thought this over, then he said, 'I don't know what I'd do.'

'You should do the same. If you are ever held up, you give the fellow whatever he asks for. After that go straight to the police.'

'If they can't get your dough back what good does it do?'

'Chances are it will accomplish nothing. The point to remember is that if you are ever approached by a thug with a weapon you must not argue or attempt to fight. Chances are that if you do as he tells you, you won't get hurt.'

'If he wasn't a big guy maybe you could get his gun.'

Mr Bridge lowered the newspaper. 'Now, let me tell you something. My grandfather was shot to death by a bandit because he refused to give up his money.'

Douglas knew that his father seldom joked, but here was a bit of information so extraordinary that he felt obliged to put on a cynical face.

'It's a fact,' said Mr Bridge. 'It happened aboard a train in the state of Delaware just after the turn of the century. I was a child at the time, but I vividly recall my father talking about it. My grandfather owned a brick factory in southern Delaware. He made a good deal of money and employed, I believe, fifteen or twenty workmen. In those days they didn't have banks in every town, so if a man wanted a considerable sum of money he was often obliged to make a trip to get it and carry it himself, which was risky business. I suppose a number of men were robbed. At any rate, once a month my grandfather was in the habit of taking an overnight train to the town where his money was banked. He would withdraw enough to pay his employees and then take the train home again. Well, sure enough, some fellow found out about this, and in the middle of the night he awakened my grandfather, pointed a gun at him, and demanded the money. Instead of doing what he was told, my grandfather while lying in the berth attempted to kick the bandit, with the result that the fellow shot him. He died the next day.' Then he added: 'It was extremely foolish of my grandfather. By attempting to save a small amount of money he forfeited his life.'

'How much did the guy get?'

'I have no idea. I imagine it would have been several hundred dollars, which in those days of course was worth a good bit more than it is today. However, the amount he lost is irrelevant. What is important is that by attempting to save some money he lost his life.'

Douglas scratched his head but he did not say anything.

'Have I made my point clear?'

'I guess so.'

'All right,' Mr Bridge said as he lifted the newspaper. 'Kindly make a note of it, my friend.'

35 New clothes

'I'm nearly at wit's end,' Mrs Bridge admitted one evening while seated at her dressing table. 'I've tried everything under the sun.'

He suspected she was referring to the problem of getting clothes for Douglas. Douglas did not like new clothes. All summer he had wandered around looking unpressed and ragged, and he saw no need to change his appearance just because school was opening. She had said 'You can't keep acting like a tramp forever,' and he had said 'Nobody's going to know the diff.' Then she had said 'Do you want people to think we're halfway to the poorhouse?' and he shrugged. This problem came up each September, but it seemed to be getting worse as he grew older.

'Take him to Altringer's and turn him over to the salesman who got him dressed last year,' Mr Bridge said.

'I dragged him there yesterday. Mr Yanofsky can't do a thing with him this year. I feel so sorry for that poor man. He tries so hard. I just hope the other boys behave better than Douglas. He brought out goodness knows how many suits, and Douglas managed to find fault with every single one of them. I could cheerfully have strangled him.'

Mr Bridge was tired and did not want to get involved. He pulled off his shoes, wiggled his toes, and yawned.

'I'm trying again tomorrow,' she continued. 'I've told him we're going to that new shop on the Plaza. I certainly hope they have something that will intrigue him. It might help if you simply laid down the law. He ignores me. I might as well argue with the moon.'

'Remind me before I go to the office. I'll talk to him.'

'I do wish you would.'

'Why didn't he like the suits at Altringer's?'

'Not a thing in the world was the matter with them. Several of them were very nice. He was being obstinate. He pretended that one was too tight and another was the wrong color. He went out of his way to find fault with whatever Mr Yanofsky showed him. Honestly, Walter, I'm starting to wonder if there isn't something wrong with him.'

Mr Bridge yawned again and rubbed his eyes. 'Douglas will get over it. I did.'

'I can't imagine you ever behaving like a wild Indian.'

'I did, though.'

'Really? The other day Grace Barron said she just knew you were wearing a suit and tie the day you were born.'

'Oh, she did, did she?' he asked, and thought about the comment for a few moments. 'Well, I'm afraid I must be what I am, for better or worse. If I were to try to answer all the attacks made on me, this shop might as well be closed for any other sort of business.'

36 Yuh, yuh, yuh

Not long after the opening of school a SOLD sign was posted in the vacant lot. Except for this the lot appeared to be as public as ever. Weeks went by and whoever had bought the lot did not come around to inspect it, nor were there any complaints about the cave, so that after a while the sign seemed to belong and its significance was nearly forgotten. Dogs, cats, birds, mice, rabbits, butterflies, and insects shared it with the neighborhood children, and the weeds grew higher.

But one morning while Douglas was at school a tractor drove into the lot and promptly ripped off the roof of the cave. When he returned to the house at dinnertime he was very depressed. Bitterly he asked: 'Why didn't they let anybody know? At least we could have got our stuff out. The cigar box is gone. And Tipton's harmonica and a lot other stuff.'

'I would like to have seen somebody's face,' Mr Bridge remarked, 'when that cigar box was opened and a snake slithered out.'

'Good Heavens,' Mrs Bridge said. 'Were you keeping a snake?'

'We had some money and marbles and coupons and a Scout knife and a lot of other junk in there besides,' he said. 'That dirty old guy on the tractor stole everything.'

'How do you know?' Mr Bridge asked while testing the blade of the carving knife.

'It's gone, isn't it? Who else could have swiped it?'

'I'm afraid that argument won't stand up in court.'

'You don't care because you didn't lose any stuff.'

'You are making a bit too much of this. How much money was in the box?'

'Over a dollar. And the Scout knife was worth plenty. And we had all those coupons and marbles. And there was a lucky chestnut and some more stuff, too.'

'Did you hunt for the box? That fellow driving the tractor may not have stolen it. He may not have known it was there.'

'It's gone,' Douglas said with a grim face.

'Well, I do think he's right,' Mrs Bridge said. 'They should have told the boys they were planning to start excavating.'

'Pass your mother's plate,' Mr Bridge said to Ruth, and then he continued: 'Yes, it seems to me they should have, or could have. I don't believe it would have been much trouble to make a few inquiries and find out where the boys lived.'

'Why don't you sue them?' Carolyn asked her brother.

'You think it's one big fat joke,' he said. 'It's not funny.'

'Listen to me, young man,' Mr Bridge said. He paused for emphasis, the carving knife and the heavy silver fork poised above the roast. 'In this life we lose a great many things. Many things that we love and cherish and hope to keep forever are taken from us without our permission. There are times when litigation is in order, but unfortunately no court of law has yet existed which is capable of restoring to us those properties which we consider genuinely valuable. What you and your companions lost today – or what may have been stolen from you – is altogether inconsequential.'

'Yuh, yuh, yuh,' Douglas muttered.

'Furthermore, I think it is high time you made a pronounced effort to speak the English language.'

'Okay, okay,' said Douglas.

37 *The pistol*

'He's found your gun,' said Mrs Bridge one evening not long before Halloween.

Mr Bridge had just gotten home. He was standing in front of the hall closet taking off his gloves.

'Why on earth he was poking around beneath the mattress I don't know,' she continued, 'but I walked into the bedroom this afternoon and there he was.'

'What did he say when you caught him?'

'Not a word.'

Mr Bridge remained standing where he was when she had first spoken. He had meant to show the gun to Douglas some day and explain why it was kept under the mattress, but he had planned to wait until Douglas was much older.

'How did he know about it?'

'I haven't the foggiest notion. I really wish you wouldn't keep it there – it gives me the willies.'

'Somebody must have told him it was there.'

'Don't look at me,' she replied.

'You must have mentioned it without realizing it.'

'I certainly have not. As far as I'm concerned it simply does not exist.'

'What was he doing with it?'

'Sitting on the window bench pointing it at different things. Apparently he didn't hear me walk in.'

'Was it cocked?'

'Heavens. I wouldn't know.'

'Did he have the cartridges?'

'I didn't ask. I certainly hope not.'

'Didn't you look?'

'It never occurred to me. I just told him to put it right back where he found it and that I was going to tell you about it as soon as you came home.'

Mr Bridge took off his hat and slowly placed it on the closet shelf.

'I hardly think your gun is necessary,' she went on in an obviously rehearsed tone of voice. 'There don't appear to be any burglars in this neighborhood, and with the night watchman making the rounds I'm sure you'll never have any use for it.'

'Ask Harriet to fix me a highball,' he said, and went upstairs to the bedroom, where he opened the bottom drawer of the dresser and slipped his hand beneath the folded pajamas. He felt the two cardboard boxes. He took them out and opened them. The stubby little bullets had not been disturbed. They were tightly fitted together like tidbits of food, just as they had come from the factory. Evidently Douglas had not found them. He lifted one of the bullets out of the box with his fingernails, looked at it for a few seconds, and slid it back into place. He shut the boxes, put them under the pajamas, closed the dresser drawer, and went downstairs.

Mrs Bridge was in the living room selecting some records to play on the phonograph. 'You'll speak to him, won't you?' she asked.

He nodded. 'Where's my highball?'

'Coming.'

'I need no more days like this,' he said, and sank into his chair with the evening paper but did not begin reading until Harriet brought him the drink.

After dinner he led Douglas to the bedroom, lifted a corner of the mattress, and picked up the pistol.

Douglas said, 'I was only looking.'

'How did you know it was here?'

'I sort of knew.'

'Did one of your sisters tell you?'

'How would they know?' he asked contemptuously.

'They sometimes help Harriet make the beds.'

Douglas did not say anything.

'Well?'

'I forget.'

'I am not satisfied with that answer. How long have you known about this gun?'

'A couple of years, I guess.'

Mr Bridge lowered the gun in astonishment. 'Did Harriet show it to you?'

Douglas clamped his mouth shut.

'So!' Mr Bridge murmured. 'So! And what else has she shown you?'

'Nothing.'

'What about the bullets?'

'Have you got some?'

'Now, I want you to understand me. This thing I am holding is not a toy. This is not to be played with. Ever. Is that clear? Do you understand me? This weapon is extremely dangerous. You are not to touch it. You have your own room. I do not want you poking around in here.'

'Okay,' Douglas said, and hitched up his belt.

'You are to promise me.'

'Holy smoke, okay. I promise. I was just looking at it for a couple of minutes. You act like I was going to rob a bank or something.'

'If you were to fire this gun and hit somebody I would be in a great deal of trouble.'

'Yeah, but how about me? If I knock some guy off they'll take it out on me more than you.'

Mr Bridge gestured impatiently. 'You are not to touch this pistol without my permission. Is that clear?'

'I already promised.'

'All right. Now I am going to show you where the bullets are, so there will be no reason for you to be curious. And no reason for you to come rooting around in here again.' He walked to the dresser, opened the bottom drawer, and pointed. 'Under these pajamas,' he said. He lifted them so that Douglas could see the two boxes. 'Do you want to look at them?'

Douglas sucked in his breath and nodded. Mr Bridge opened one of the boxes, pulled out a bullet, and handed it to him.

'They sure are greasy,' he said after a few moments.

'The grease prevents corrosion.'

Douglas continued to examine the bullet.

'Look at it as long as you like, because I do not want you coming in here again unless I am with you.'

'If I ask first, can I look at them and the gun again?'

'If you ask. Under no other circumstances. Furthermore, you are not to tell your friends about this. I want that understood.'

'I won't tell.'

'All right. Now, have you any questions?'

'How come you got it?'

'It was issued to me while I was serving in the Army.'

'How many Germans did you get with it?'

'I have never fired this gun except during target practice.' He could see that Douglas was puzzled. 'Few men in military service engage in actual combat. The majority are kept busy providing food and clothing and ammunition and any number of other things for the few who are unfortunate enough to be assigned to the trenches. Let me put it this way: the Army functions like a timber company which requires the service of a great many people doing office work so that a relatively few men may go into the forest to chop down trees.'

'Is that all you did?'

'Essentially, yes.'

'Then how come you got a gun?'

'I have wondered about that myself many times. As I say, it was issued to me along with quite a number of things for which I had no subsequent use.'

'Did everybody get issued one?'

'I don't know.'

'Didn't you shoot even one German?'

'No, thank the Lord. The only Germans I saw were prisoners.'

'I thought you fought in the war. I told Vandermeer and Tipton you killed a lot of Germans.'

'I'm sorry to disappoint you.'

Douglas was silent for a while. Then he said, 'It's okay.'

'I could show you some souvenirs of the war.'

'Like what?'

'Well,' Mr Bridge said, raising his eyebrows, 'I'd just have to think about it. Yes, sir, I'd just have to try to remember what I have in my trunk.'

'That brown wood one with AEF on top?'

'That's the one. I brought back quite a number of souvenirs. But of course I don't know whether or not you're interested. However, if you are, I suspect I might be able to find a trench knife, and I might even be able to find some bayonets. Then there might be some Iron Crosses, and some pictures of the men in my unit, and – let's see now, what else? We just might find a German officer's helmet with a metal spike on top, and my old khaki uniform with the puttees. Have you ever seen puttees? Those were something! Trying to wrap those puttees around your legs when you were in a hurry.'

'What kind of bayonets?'

'All kinds. French. German. American. The French bayonet still has traces of blood in the grooves.'

'Where'd you get it?'

'I bought it from a French poilu.'

'Can we look now?'

'No, no! Not now,' Mr Bridge said, laughing.

'Why not?'

'Because I don't feel like opening my trunk right now. Those things will keep. I'll show them to you some day, because you've promised me you are not going to touch this pistol again. Are we clear about that?' And when Douglas nodded he went on, 'Very well. Now I'm going to replace this exactly where it was. It will always be here. At some future date, when you are a grown man, it will belong to you.'

'To keep?'

'To keep. But guns are not meant for boys.'

'You don't need to tell me five hundred times.'

'I want to make sure there is no confusion about this. I do not want any possible misunderstanding about this. I assume Harriet found the gun while she was changing the sheets, but she had no business showing it to you. I am going to speak to her about it. In the meantime, there is no sense mentioning this to your sisters.'

'Don't worry,' Douglas said. 'They wouldn't know which end the bullets come out of.'

'You aren't to touch these cartridges again.'

'I heard you the first time. I'm not going to touch them with a ten-foot pole.'

'All right. We understand one another.'

'When are you going to show me what's in the trunk?'

'That depends on your behavior,' Mr Bridge said.

He lifted a corner of the mattress and laid the gun on the springs while his son watched attentively.

38 Halloween

A sergeant at the Sixty-third Street police station telephoned to say they were holding Douglas. Mrs Bridge, who had answered the telephone, gasped 'Oh, my word!' and hurried into the living room where her husband was stretched out on the sofa listening to Nelson Eddy sing 'Ah, Sweet Mystery of Life.' She knew how much he enjoyed Nelson Eddy and she did not want to interrupt. He was awake, she knew, but his eyes were shut and he was going to be annoyed. Grasping her beads, she leaned over and said, 'Walter?'

He opened his eyes and looked up at her. He had been irritated by the ringing telephone and he could not help feeling annoyed with her too, although she would not have interrupted unless the call was important.

Mrs Bridge, hopeful that he might be able to hear what she was saying and listen to Nelson Eddy at the same time, said in a subdued voice: 'The police.' Then she straightened up doubtfully.

He glared at her because he could not understand. He had been dozing, and he was not sure he had heard what he thought he heard. But then he remembered that it was Halloween.

In the breakfast room he picked up the telephone and said 'Yes?', and heard just about what he expected to hear. 'All right,' he said when the sergeant finished, 'I'll be there in ten minutes.'

Mrs Bridge had followed him and stood by anxiously. She said, 'I hope it's nothing serious.'

'That unholy trio,' he said. 'I should have guessed.'

'Oh, goodness, not again!' She knew he was referring to Douglas and his friends Rodney Vandermeer and Bobby Tipton.

'They turned over a can of garbage on Mr Knapp's porch.'

'Not really!'

'I am afraid it is all quite real,' he answered more sarcastically than he intended. He was still annoyed that the music had been

267

interrupted; he looked forward to Nelson Eddy and Jeanette MacDonald each week at this time. Now the evening had been ruined.

'Shall I come along?'

'No. I'll take care of it,' he said, and went to the hall closet to get his hat and coat.

Het Vandermeer was already at the station. The father of the Tipton boy, whom Mr Bridge did not know, arrived a few minutes later. The victim, Mr Knapp, was also there. They listened to the sergeant; they listened to Mr Knapp; and finally it was agreed that no charges would be lodged if the boys apologized and cleaned up the garbage by seven o'clock the next morning.

On the way home Douglas said moodily, 'I guess I better get up about five.'

'Consider yourself lucky,' said Mr Bridge.

Neither of them spoke again. The night was cold and windy. Clouds were scudding across the moon. Dead leaves fluttered out of the darkness like moths and clung to the windshield of the Chrysler for an instant before disappearing. Douglas turned up the collar of his jacket.

As they came within sight of the house Mr Bridge asked, 'Are you glad to be home?'

'It's better than a police station,' Douglas said. 'Old man Knapp sure can run. I never figured an old geezer like that could run as fast. He must be about a hundred.'

'He was chasing you, was he?'

'Why else do you think we ended up in the police station?'

'I've been wondering about that. How did he manage to catch all three of you?'

'He never did catch me or Vandermeer. We outran him. But he was gaining on Tipton, so Tipton tried a short cut through McGreevy's back yard, except he forgot they had a clothesline and just about strangled himself. That's how Tipton got caught.'

Mr Bridge parked the Chrysler in the garage and turned off the motor. Then he said, 'You and that other boy, did a police car pick you up?'

'No. We got to the end of the block and waited, only when Tipton never showed up we figured old man Knapp had got him, so we went back.'

'That's how he caught you?'

'No. We saw him hanging on to Tipton's collar, so we gave ourselves up. Then he had Mrs McGreevy call the cops.'

'Why did you surrender?'

'Who knows?' Douglas replied with a shrug. 'We just decided to.'

After a few moments Mr Bridge said, 'Well, here we are. Let's go in,' and he opened the car door. Douglas got out the other side, and they began walking toward the house.

'Dad,' Douglas said, 'when you were a kid did you ever do anything like this?'

'I imagine I did. I've forgotten, it's been so long. I suppose I did. Yes, I expect I must have done a few things similar to this, although I'm quite certain nobody ever caught me.'

'I could've got away without any trouble.'

'I know,' Mr Bridge said. He found his house key and opened the door and held it for his son to go in. 'I have one bit of advice: do a first-rate job on that garbage tomorrow morning.'

'Nobody needs to tell me,' Douglas remarked as he entered the house. 'Also, thanks for getting me out of jail.'

'You're welcome,' said Mr Bridge.

39 Daiquiri for Harriet

Sunday noon, about an hour before dinner, Harriet walked into the living room carrying the silver tray on which there was a small glass of sherry for Mrs Bridge and a whisky sour for Mr Bridge. After he had tasted the whisky he smacked his lips and wagged a finger at Harriet and told her she did not know what she was missing. She grinned but said nothing. She did not drink. She would not take so much as a glass of wine with her meals. When she was first interviewed she had said she did not drink. He had been skeptical, and for months after she came to work he expected to find some evidence that she had lied; but months went by and then years went by while there was no indication that she ever took a drink. This puzzled him. In her room she kept a Bible which she often read, she attended church every week, and she liked to sing hymns in the kitchen; yet her refusal did not seem to be based on religion. Evidently it was a personal thing: she preferred not to, just this and nothing else. He had taught her to mix a few simple cocktails so he no longer had to go into the kitchen to do it himself, and she did not mind mixing them, but she never tasted them. If he teased her about this she answered simply that she did not care to.

Now he remarked as he had many times before that a drink would do her good. Then Harriet said a daiquiri might be nice, and it was as though a spell had been cast on the room.

After a long silence Mr Bridge set his whisky sour aside, stood up, and beckoned to her. 'Come along,' he said. 'I intend to make this one myself.' He led the way to the kitchen followed by Harriet, the children, and finally by Mrs Bridge; and there they stood around and watched while he mixed Harriet's daiquiri. When it was ready he placed it in the center of the tray, picked up the tray, clicked his heels, and presented it to her.

She accepted her first drink with immense poise. She sipped it while everybody waited.

'Well?' he asked. 'What do you think?'

'This is really very good,' she said.

'Praise the Lord,' he said.

They marched back to the living room and resumed their places. Harriet took a seat at the end of the sofa, holding the daiquiri delicately with her slender fingers.

'So you like that, do you?' he asked.

'Well, yes,' she answered. 'I must say I do.'

40 Harriet and Carolyn

Harriet's status began to interest Carolyn, and the fact that her ancestors presumably were slaves brought to America from Africa made her all the more fascinating. One morning when the two of them were in the house alone Carolyn ordered her to sweep the back steps, where several maple leaves had fallen during the night. Harriet refused. Not only did she refuse, she answered that she was going to tell Carolyn's mother.

Mrs Bridge learned about the squabble as soon as she got home.

Carolyn wanted Harriet fired. Harriet responded by threatening to quit. She had no intention of quitting, she was perfectly satisfied with her position and did not want to lose it, but she felt that under the circumstances her threat was justified. Then, too, she had been thinking about asking for a raise, and her bargaining position might be strengthened if her employers believed she was ready to quit. As to the possibility of being fired, she knew Mr Bridge well enough to know he would not even consider such a thing.

Mrs Bridge did not know what to do, so she took the problem to her husband.

He listened. He thought it over. He suspected Harriet was bluffing. Except for Carolyn's absurd behavior she had no legitimate complaint. She was adequately paid and she knew it. She had a comfortable room of her own next to the kitchen, she had a day off each week and occasionally an extra day off if there was a bona-fide reason. She got a liberal gift at Christmas and a two-week paid vacation every summer. She could, of course, find another job in the neighborhood without much trouble, because she had a good reputation; all the same he thought she was pretending to be more insulted than she actually was. She must have some other reason for threatening to quit. He could not guess what that might be, but for the moment it was irrelevant. The problem, he decided, was not Harriet. The problem was Carolyn.

And the more he considered her foolish command the more it exasperated him because her behavior was a reflection upon himself, as though in some way he had not communicated to her his own sense of personal dignity. He sent for her. He lectured her for quite a while, and at last he concluded: 'You will treat Harriet courteously. She is not your property, nor is she mine. President Lincoln once said "It is no pleasure to me to triumph over anyone". Remember that, Carolyn, as long as you live. And now let us hear no more of this.'

41 Onward, Christian Soldiers

Once a year Dr Foster came to dinner. He arrived at seven and he departed at ten. He never forgot to bring a little gift – flowers, a box of salted nuts, hard candies, or a bottle of sherry made by the monks in California. One year he brought a copy of a book of essays he had written, which were published by a local house. Mrs Bridge already had bought and read his book, and she had told him how much she enjoyed it, but evidently he had forgotten; or possibly there was a surplus and he worried that the unsold copies might unceremoniously appear on a department-store bargain table. For whatever reason, there were now two copies of Dr Foster's book in the house, both copies autographed. Mr Bridge had read a few pages. Dr Foster mentioned Mankind frequently, and almost every page contained some reference to faith or hope. The essays were modestly confessional, confessing to such sins as the desire when he was a boy to run off with a circus; but, as he noted, he had managed to overcome this temptation. Mr Bridge had not opened the book a second time. There was nothing specifically wrong, except that it was dull. It was remarkably dull. The man seemed to possess an exceptional gift for being dull. Sentence after sentence had been hauled to the surface as though he had cranked them out of a cistern in a bucket. And like most men who are incurably dull he considered himself lively, and was under the impression that everybody talked about him; consequently he was twice as dull in person as he was in the pulpit, or when he commenced an essay: *I take pen in hand* . . .

The annual dinner, therefore, was an evening to be dreaded. Three hours in the man's company was suffocating. How or why the custom had started, he could not remember. The minister's salary no doubt was small, so he did not eat well, and presumably he very often ate alone; perhaps for some such reasons Mrs Bridge pitied him and invited him to dinner. It seemed altogether unnecessary. The man had chosen that sort of life. If that was what he wanted let him have it.

But he said nothing, and each year when his wife reminded him that Dr Foster was coming to dinner again on a certain evening he merely nodded. If only the minister held some violent prejudice, no matter how preposterous, then at least he would be worth talking to. But he had no prejudice, or if he did he had buried it beneath a haystack of piety. Indeed, he was so careful not to offend anybody that he seldom offered an opinion about anything; and whatever he said, he qualified, chuckling and coughing into his fist. Bland was the word for him. He was a fifty-year-old Boy Scout. He had no more sinew than a dish of custard. He could no more be despised or hated than he could be loved or respected. He was a cross to be borne when necessary and avoided whenever possible. His ingenuous neutrality was disgusting, but principally he was a bore, that was all. He was such a bore that he was careful never to talk about himself, always about what he supposed must be interesting to other people. Sports and politics ought to interest a man, so each time he came to dinner he tried out these topics. Then he tried gardening, antique collecting, silverware, church social activities, charity drives, and P.T.A. with Mrs Bridge. And, predictably, he made a great point of talking to the children. The only thing to be grateful for was that he had enough decency to refrain from mentioning religion.

Three hours of this once a year should not be unbearable, but certain years it was, and Mr Bridge weakened before ten o'clock and retreated to the bedroom with the excuse that he had to get up early. There he would change into his pajamas, brush his teeth, put on his reading glasses, and settle himself in bed with a mystery or with the stock market reports until the noise of the front door closing told him that Dr Foster was gone for another year.

42 *Home from the office*

One evening not long after Dr Foster's annual visit Mr Bridge came home later than usual and was met at the back door by his wife, who said, 'We decided to begin. I hope you don't object. The children were starved.'

In a tired voice he answered that he had expected to get away from the office earlier.

'You sound utterly exhausted,' she remarked as she untied her apron. 'I really am going to call up Julia and give her strict orders to stop loading you with so much work. Goodness knows other men don't keep these hours.'

For years she had been threatening to call Julia – as though Julia had anything to do with it. Julia, no doubt, would have been happy to work shorter hours.

'What's become of Harriet?' he asked.

'She wanted tonight off instead of Thursday. There's some sort of a big "do", I gather. She was all dolled up. A man came by for her a little while ago.'

'Does she still run around with that fellow on a motorcycle?'

'This one had a car. I don't know if it's the same one or not, I didn't see his face. He just tooted for her, and away they went.'

'What's on the menu?'

'Macaroni casserole. And fruit salad for dessert.'

He tried to conceal his dismay. He wondered if Harriet could be persuaded to give up her night off in exchange for a raise in salary.

'All right. Fix me a scotch,' he said, and went upstairs to wash his face and change clothes. When he came down and walked into the dining room he was saluted by his son.

'Oh-ho,' cried Douglas, 'guess what the cat drug in!'

'Shut up, you simpleton,' Carolyn said.

'Now, now, both of you,' Mrs Bridge interrupted. And to Douglas she said, 'That's hardly the way to speak to your father.'

'Mother,' Ruth said, holding her head with both hands, 'the way you keep after him it's no wonder. He was just trying to be funny. Is that such a dreadful crime?'

'He's got a stupid sense of humor,' Carolyn said. 'He's a complete dolt.'

Mr Bridge listened indulgently. He was pleased to hear their voices and to see their faces; it was for them he had spent these long days at work, and because he heard the affection beneath their bickering he did not mind how they pretended to insult each other.

'Make a pile of dough today?' Douglas was asking.

'Not enough to keep you properly clothed, I'm afraid.'

'Oh, and that shirt isn't six months old!' said Mrs Bridge, who had followed his glance.

'Yuk, yuk, yuk,' Douglas said, stretching his arms above his head to show how short the sleeves were.

'Unanimously voted most likely to flunk,' said Carolyn.

'Daddy, how *was* the day?' Ruth asked.

'I doubt if my days interest anybody at this table,' he laughed.

'Now, you know that isn't true,' Mrs Bridge said, pretending to scold. 'We all care about your work. I don't know how many times I've asked, and the children too, but getting information out of you is like pulling teeth.'

'It's a fact, Pop, it's a fact,' Douglas said.

He noticed that the girls, prompted by their mother's question, were watching him politely; he suspected that all three of the children had been told to show some interest.

'Well,' he said, 'since you ask, more of the same. There is a Latin phrase which pretty well sums up the situation: *Unius dementia dementes efficit multos.*' He smiled at Ruth, who was studying Latin at school, but she was suddenly busy with her food. And in a little while the conversation had turned to other things.

He sipped the drink, feeling too tired to eat, and wondered why he could not talk to the family about his work. At first when the children were small it was not possible, but now? What was there to say? They had asked, it was true. And whenever they asked, whether the questions were sincere or not, he had answered elliptically, turned the offer into an ironic joke. Why? He knew that he did want to confide in the family. Now they were asking. Why had he rejected the chance? He felt that he was close to understanding; then something intervened like a shade drawn down. After all, they could not possibly care about the testimony of a streetcar conductor involved in a traffic accident on the eighteenth of September of last year. The exchange with Judge Hibler made little sense out of context. Or Julia's observation about the mechanic with the infected tattoo. None of this would make sense at the dinner table. They might listen, but it would be a strain.

No. No, he thought, as he peered into his glass, there is almost nothing I can say to them. My life is cut in half. The halves remain side by side in perfect equilibrium like halves of a melon. I suppose the same is true of most men. Or are they somehow unlike me? Are they able to share themselves?

The question was familiar. He had asked it many times.

I know very little about other men, he thought, although I go through life assuming that I do. I know only myself, but I do believe I know myself. What I am, as well as what I am not, I think I know, even if I may not know exactly what I would like to be. In any case, whatever I feel or think or see or believe is a consequence of my own sensibility, not that of some other man. I believe what I believe, and I have not yet believed a single thing only because it was believed by others, nor do I intend to. I can be grateful for this, at least: that I have kept myself. I have not once dressed up in a costume. There may be stronger consolations, but not many. Be that as it may, I cannot live differently than I do. Whatever the reasons for this, good or bad, they exist. Evidently that is enough. So, early tomorrow, I must get up again to do what I have done today. I will get up early to do this, and tomorrow and tomorrow and tomorrow, and there is nothing to discuss.

43 Handful of change

That night, before hanging his trousers in the closet he took the change out of his pocket and left it on the dresser as he always did, but the next morning he forgot it. When he came home in the evening the coins had disappeared. He supposed his wife had picked them up, but she said she had not touched the money. She had noticed it on the dresser after he left for work, but she had left it where it was. She suggested that Harriet might have put the money in a dresser drawer while she was cleaning the bedroom, but he had looked in the dresser drawers. The coins were gone. He walked into the kitchen and found Harriet filling a tray of chocolate éclairs with whipped cream. He asked if she had seen the coins. Harriet thought for a minute, then said she had not. There was no money on the dresser when she went upstairs to make the beds. She was sure of this, she said, because she had straightened the things on top of the dresser and surely would have seen any money lying there. He asked if anybody else had been in the house during the day. Harriet said that as far as she knew nobody except the children had been in the house. He did not want to ask the children; if one of them had taken it he, or she, ought to mention it. So he waited, thinking that when they were all together at the dinner table somebody would speak up. But during the meal nobody said anything, and he realized he had waited too long. To ask about it now would sound like an accusation.

Later that night Mrs Bridge asked if he had found the change. He answered that he had not, and indicated by his tone that he did not want to talk about it again. However, he continued to think about the missing money. He wanted to believe that Harriet had stolen the coins. There was no proof that she had not. The incident troubled him because it never was resolved. It bothered him like a small sore which healed underneath a scab; and this, too, disappeared at last. But it left a little scar.

44 Season's greetings

Christmas that year was memorable because of a card from Senator Bailey. They had never before gotten a card from him.

'He's up for re-election,' Mr Bridge answered when his wife wondered why they had been included on the senator's mailing list. The sight of the card and the thought of Horton Bailey irritated him. 'The man is a "deadbeat", as I've told you before. I have no use for him whatsoever. I wouldn't cast my vote for Horton Bailey if he was the only candidate on earth. The man is no good. He's no good, I tell you. He never was any good. He never will be any good!'

'My word, you sound so final,' she said, and pinched his arm.

'I have no respect for a man who welshes on a debt. And that *is* final.'

He could imagine Bailey's response if the debt was mentioned – the false heartiness; the harsh, loud laughter; a vigorous, professional slap on the back. Then another booming laugh out of the freckled Irish face as though both of them agreed it was beneath their dignity to talk of such a thing as an old debt. The debt would never be paid. It would never be honored; and every time he thought about this his thin features seemed to become even thinner, and he appeared to be contemplating a repulsive spectacle.

After his first glance at the Christmas card he avoided looking at it. He felt like throwing it in the fireplace, but sensed that his wife was flattered by it. Not everybody received a Christmas card from a senator. She had never said as much, yet he suspected this was how she felt, so he left it where she had placed it on the mantel beside the little painted wooden crèche and the celluloid angels.

45 The squirrel

Christmas Day a little before noon Mr and Mrs Bridge were standing in the front yard under the old elm tree. The elm was dying, although the previous summer a tree surgeon had lopped off several branches and done whatever else he could to save it. Both of them were fond of this tree. They did not know how old it was, but very probably it had stood rooted to this spot for at least half a century. They considered it sadly and talked about whether they should have it cut down, because it might break and crash against the house. The bark of the tree was dry and thick, cracked into corky brown ridges. The limbs protruded lifelessly. Silhouetted against the freezing blue sky, it was clear that death lived within the tree.

While they were standing next to it Douglas appeared around the corner of the house carrying a large gray squirrel. He was holding the squirrel by the tail so that it hung down like a rag. The paws extended stiffly from the limp, swaying body as though the animal was reaching for something. In his other hand Douglas carried the air rifle he had gotten just that morning.

Mr Bridge observed the squirrel with surprise because he had assumed the air rifle was not powerful enough to kill anything much bigger than a caterpillar. He saw a red bead gather on the squirrel's nose and drop like a ruby into the snow. Then he realized that his wife was watching; she was waiting to see what he would do about this.

The front door opened. Carolyn came out of the house. She looked at the squirrel with distaste because it was dead, and folded her arms as she had seen her mother do when something was wrong.

Douglas, for his part, was disconcerted. He had not expected to walk into an audience. Rather uncertainly he held the squirrel up for inspection, in case anybody wanted a closer look.

Mr Bridge knew he was expected to judge the situation. A gun, a hunter, a dead animal. But because he did not know exactly how he felt, he did not know what attitude to take; he felt only the presence of his wife and his daughter forcing him toward a resolution with his son. This silent female insistence annoyed him. He spoke to his son sharply: 'Now that you've shot it, what do you intend to do with it?'

Douglas thought this over. Then he said, 'Can't we eat him?'

Carolyn made a face and a gagging noise.

'We have meat enough for the table,' said Mr Bridge.

'I was thinking if we wanted him we could fix a stew, maybe. Only I want his pelt.'

'So you think you are going to skin it, do you?'

Douglas murmured and nodded. He jiggled the squirrel, and another drop of blood sank into the snow.

Mr Bridge felt the increasing pressure of the two women. They were not going to speak. They were going to wait. They had done this before when they disapproved of something. According to them, a little animal had been killed for no reason, that was all there was to it. They understood nothing beyond that, and they wanted the killer punished. But Mr Bridge began to feel the obstinate power of his son opposing them with the male conviction that it is right to kill animals. Now he was expected to rule in favor of one of these philosophies.

To his son he said, 'Have you ever tried to skin a squirrel?'

Douglas answered that he had cleaned fish. He and his friends with the reluctant assistance of grasshoppers and worms had pulled a number of small perch and sunfish out of Crystal Lake. A few of these specimens were large enough to eat, so Harriet had fried them for his lunch.

'Cleaning a fish is not the same as skinning a squirrel,' said Mr Bridge.

Then Douglas grew stubborn. 'How do you know? Did you ever skin one?'

Mr Bridge replied that he had.

'Well, I can too,' the boy said, and he held the dead squirrel confidently. At his belt was a Boy Scout sheath knife.

'What will you do after that?'

'What do you mean?'

'What will you do with the skin?'

'I'll stretch it on a board and hang it in my room.'

'Oh no,' his mother said. 'Oh, no, you will not, young man. I put my foot down.'

'No?' he asked with a challenging expression. 'No?' he repeated. 'How come? He's mine, isn't he? I killed him, so he belongs to me. I can do anything I want with him.'

'Eat it,' Carolyn said. 'The fur and the claws and the tail and the ears and everything else. I hope you choke. I hope you die.'

'Nobody wants to listen to you,' he muttered. 'Get lost.'

'Take his gun away and don't give him any allowance.'

Mrs Bridge put one arm around Carolyn's shoulders. 'Now, now, just calm down. Your father will do whatever is best.'

Mr Bridge said, 'Suppose you and I strike a bargain, son. I will allow you to skin the squirrel, and you do as you please with the skin. Tack it to a board and hang it in your room, if you wish. However, there is one condition.'

Douglas looked up at him suspiciously.

Mr Bridge folded his arms and went on: 'You must leave it there until I say you may get rid of it.'

'Is that all?'

'That is the condition.'

'What's the catch?'

'There is no catch.'

Douglas thought this over. He poked some holes in a snowdrift with the muzzle of his gun. At last he said, 'What happens if it starts to stink up my room?'

'You heard me. You will keep it until you have my permission to throw it away.'

Douglas' eyes suddenly filled with tears. He gave the elm tree a savage kick, and he said just loud enough to be heard, 'I guess I can bury it somewhere.'

46 Happy days

Now another year was ending. The year had been good and he regretted the end of it, but he felt pleased that it was concluding without sickness in the family and with indications that the worst of the Depression might be over. The children were growing up nearly as he hoped they would and his wife was content. These were the important things. Secondly, he could feel the burden of his work, and this also was good.

Roosevelt, of course, was a poor choice, a man who already had damaged the structure of the economy, very possibly the worse president since Ulysses Grant. And if the voters responsible for him had not yet acknowledged their mistake they would be forced to soon enough. The unions were out of hand, Communists had gotten desks in the Labor Department, and there was the threat of increased taxes. These things were the result of Roosevelt's New Deal, and the implications were serious. Mr Bridge considered the future of the country and often discussed it. He found other men as angered and frustrated as he was himself, all of them helpless to alter this current of socialism. However, if one could imagine that Roosevelt and his left-wing advisers did not exist, or believe they would be thrown out of office at the next election, or at least come to their senses and modify their programs – well, then, life could not be much better.

The clouds that hung over Europe were not blowing away, yet nobody would forget the lesson of the World War. Nobody would be quick to start another war. And if that did happen it was not likely to involve America. Too many people remembered.

Meanwhile there was much to be thankful for. Money was not plentiful, and there was suffering; but for the majority of men who were industrious enough to work, who did not stand around on street corners complaining and waiting for the government to feed them, there was enough.

At midnight on New Year's Eve at the country club a champagne glass shattered in the fireplace and the orchestra played 'Auld Lang Syne'. Mr Bridge lifted his glass in response to the toasts and remarked, as he brushed a sprinkle of confetti out of his hair, 'Happy Days!'

47 Cousin Lulu's estate

Not long after New Year's a letter arrived from an attorney in Tennessee stating that Mrs Bridge and her children had been named to share in the estate of Lulubelle Watts, recently deceased. Mrs Bridge was very much distressed. 'Poor thing,' she said again and again. 'I had no idea Lulu had passed away.'

'Was she the goofy one?' Douglas asked.

'That's the woman. That *is* the woman,' his father said.

'Well, she was sweet,' Mrs Bridge said. 'Oh, dear, I should have been nicer. The poor thing. I do feel guilty.'

'You were as nice to her as anyone could be. You have nothing to reproach yourself for. That woman was a borderline case. In my opinion she would have been better off in a mental institution.'

'How much do I get?' Carolyn asked.

'Now, Corky, I don't know how much you "get", or how much any of the rest of us will "get". It doesn't matter. We have enough to eat and we should be thankful. There are more important things in the world than money. Poor Lulu. I feel terrible. Whenever she wrote she asked about everybody. She thought so much of all of us, and she remembered everybody's birthday. She never had a family of her own. I really should have invited her to visit us more often.'

'Once was enough,' said Mr Bridge.

'I'm afraid it was a bit hectic,' Mrs Bridge admitted. 'But of course her health wasn't good. It just seems to me that I didn't do as much as I should have.'

'Under the circumstances, you did as much for her as anyone could reasonably be expected to do.'

'I suppose you're right. I just feel so sorry for her.'

'Well, it's too bad, but it happens to us all sooner or later.'

'Cut the gloom, will you?' Douglas said.

Mrs Bridge sighed and shook her head. Reluctantly she picked up the letter. 'How do I go about answering this?'

'Give it to me,' he said, and took it from her and put it in his pocket. 'I'll have Julia type up a response in the morning and bring it home for you to sign.'

Not long after that the word came back from Tennessee: Mrs Bridge was to receive $2,222.22 while each of the children would receive $333.33.

'That woman,' said Mr Bridge when they got this news. 'If I told you once I told you a dozen times – that woman would have been better off in an institution.'

'I believe she was interested in astrology,' said Mrs Bridge.

'I know what I want,' said Douglas. 'A racing bike. Can I?'

'*May* I,' his mother said.

'It's your money,' his father said. 'If that's what you want. What about you two?' he asked the girls.

Ruth said she was going to buy clothes.

'And you,' he asked Carolyn, 'as long as the others can't think past tomorrow, what are you going to do with your windfall? Squander it?'

Carolyn said, 'I want an oil well.'

'Who doesn't?'

She was not amused. 'You told Mother you almost made a million dollars once.'

'I said that? I don't think so. I think you must be mistaken. I'm sure I never told your mother such a thing.'

'You did so,' Carolyn said.

'Oh my, I'm starting to remember,' said Mrs Bridge. 'Years ago. Corky, you can't remember anything that far back. Surely you can't.'

'Yes, I do,' said Carolyn.

'Well, I don't,' said Mr Bridge. 'You'll have to enlighten me.'

'It had something or other to do with your friend Henry Gutekunst. When he first moved to Oklahoma.'

'Henry Gutekunst,' he exclaimed, looking incredulously at Carolyn. 'You couldn't have been more than five years old when Henry Gutenkunst moved to Oklahoma.'

'Younger than that,' Mrs Bridge said, patting Carolyn on the back.

'I remember,' Carolyn insisted. 'You told Mother you'd be a millionaire if you had any sense.'

Now it had begun to sound familiar. He listened while Carolyn repeated what he had said. He was astonished. She seemed to be reading or reciting rather than remembering. She scarcely hesitated. He recognized certain words he often used, and the rhythm of his speech, and it brought back a moment he had nearly forgotten. He had read aloud an article from the financial page of the *Star*. Henry Gutekunst had found oil in a field a few miles south of Tulsa. It was the first of many wells he brought in. Gutekunst was now a multimillionaire. Six months before the first strike he had suggested going into partnership.

Carolyn went on: 'You said to Mother prospecting for oil was the quickest way on earth to lose money. You said that's why you didn't give Mr Gutekunst any money when he offered you a partnership.'

'You might be correct,' he said. 'I must admit I'm impressed by your memory. And it's true that if I'd taken up his offer I'd be wealthy by now. However, that's long past and has nothing to do with the present situation. My friend Mr Gutekunst did become wealthy, but he was the fortunate exception. For every man like Henry Gutekunst who does strike oil there are hundreds upon hundreds of men who lose every cent they own. They throw away their money on a wild-goose chase. I've seen it happen, I can tell you. I've seen it happen too often.'

'But you said you were sorry you didn't give him the money.'

'Had I known in advance that there was an enormous oil field exactly where Henry Gutekunst thought there was, naturally I would have invested. Certainly I wish I had known, Carolyn. The trouble is that we have no way of determining these things in advance. He could just as easily have lost his shirt.'

Mrs Bridge said, 'It was a nice idea, Corky, but of course your father knows best. You wouldn't want to lose your money, would you? Then, too, although three hundred and thirty-three dollars is an awful lot, I'm just not sure if it would be enough to do whatever it is you wanted to do.'

Mr Bridge said, 'Let me make a suggestion. I think we can solve this problem. Cork can be part-owner of thousands of oil wells. Now, how does that sound?'

Carolyn was suspicious.

'I happen to know of a number of fine, well-established companies in the oil industry. Standard of Indiana is one. Texaco is another. We can get a few shares of stock in one of those companies. Your money will be safe, and each time your company brings in a well you'll own a bit of it. What do you think?'

'Why, that's a good idea!' said Mrs Bridge.

Everybody looked at Carolyn.

'How about it?' Mr Bridge asked.

'I want one of my own,' she said.

Mr Bridge was beginning to get annoyed. 'I'm sorry, but you cannot have one all to yourself. You don't have enough money. And if you did have enough I would not allow you to invest in any such foolish venture, so you might as well get used to the idea. Money is not something to be thrown away. Money doesn't grow on trees. I have worked hard for what I have, and as you grow older you will realize that this is ordinarily the case. The Henry Gutekunsts of this world are few and far between. Henry, as a matter of fact, worked very hard to earn the capital he had to start with, and furthermore he did not just happen to locate that field overnight. He invested not only his savings but a great deal of time and effort. As a geologist he was obliged to work for other men for a number of years before branching out on his own. I am in a position to know how hard Mr Gutekunst worked. He deserves his wealth. But at the same time he was extremely fortunate. The chances are he would not be so fortunate again. As of today he is solidly entrenched in the Oklahoma oil industry and it is reasonable to assume that his corporation will continue to bring in profitable wells, but nothing is certain, and it is conceivable that his fortunes could take a turn for the worse. In any event, Carolyn, regardless of this man's success, your position is altogether different. You have a nice little bequest from your mother's cousin, and I think that over a period of time if we invest this in a reliable company with sound management and a good history it should do very nicely for you.'

'Oh, all right,' Carolyn said.

'There now,' Mr Bridge said. 'That's settled.' He turned again to Ruth. 'Are you going to spend all of your inheritance on clothing?'

Ruth said she wanted to think about it. He looked at her for a few moments and it occurred to him that he did not care how she used her money. He did not know why he felt this way. Logically, it was she much more than Carolyn who needed a lesson. Carolyn was not extravagant or foolish, and despite the impracticality of wanting to buy an oil well with three hundred dollars there was nothing wrong with her thinking. In fact, it was a remarkably mature thought. It was a thought that would not occur to Ruth.

'As you wish. Think it over,' he replied. 'You're not a child anymore.' For an instant their eyes met; he saw a darkness which he could not comprehend. He sensed that she loved him with a passion which was almost sensual. Her love was different from Carolyn's.

To Douglas he said: 'A racing bike. All right. After that, what?' Douglas shrugged. Except for the bicycle he did not care what was done with his money, so they agreed to put it in the bank.

Then Mr Bridge turned to his wife, curious as to what she wished to do with her inheritance. Often she went shopping, yet she never bought very much. Presumably she did not want to seem extravagant. Now, however, she had money of her own and could buy almost anything which appealed to her. He waited, smiling down at her indulgently with his hands thrust into his pockets, and she began to look anxious. She was trying to think of something she wanted.

It occurred to him that she went shopping merely to use up time. The children were in school, or when they were not in school they were busy with their own affairs. Harriet took care of the house, did the cooking, and ordered groceries. A laundress came once a week to do the washing and ironing. There was not much else to be done. She did not have any way to occupy herself. As he became aware of this it seemed grotesque. He himself had too much to do. Days were not long enough. Yet for her the days had grown too long. That was why she went shopping. He perceived this so clearly that he could not imagine why he had failed to perceive it earlier.

He waited a little longer. She was still attempting to think of something she wanted. At last he said, 'For the time being, do you want me to handle it?'

'Yes! Would you please?' She was obviously relieved.

'Shall I buy some securities for you?'

'That sounds fine. Whatever you think best.'

'All right then, I guess we've settled cousin Lulu,' he remarked. It was not quite the proper thing to say, but nobody noticed.

48 Nevacal

Avrum Rheingold, as though scenting the money, turned up next day at the Muehlebach luncheon table. Dr Sauer had invited him. Mr Bridge, trying to conceal the aversion he felt, said very little and avoided looking at the broker; it seemed to him that Rheingold was, if possible, more repulsive than when they had first met. He was the color of veal and he smelled of lotion. A diamond stickpin glittered on his tie. His veined skull reflected the lights of the Terrace Grill, and what remained of his hair appeared to have been dyed blue and was brushed forward in a bizarre attempt to hide his baldness. He resembled a decadent Roman senator, or perhaps just an unctuous fat man who thought of himself as senatorial. Avrum Rheingold licked his lips. His small brown eyes glistened while he inspected the food. His jowls quivered. He belched with anticipation. His teeth were discolored. This was the man Alexis Sauer trusted to conduct stock market transactions.

Munching radishes, swallowing coffee, buttering rolls, heaping beans and mashed potatoes on his fork with the assistance of his knife, pausing only to pick his teeth, Avrum Rheingold discoursed on the merits of a company called Nevacal. Priced at four times earnings, with such a potential, at three dollars and fifty cents a share it was a steal. Gold mines in Nevada, land in California. A beautiful little company growing like a beanstalk.

Mr Bridge did not ask any questions about Nevacal. He had never heard of it. He knew it would have no rating with Standard and Poor's, it would not be listed on the New York exchange, and certainly it paid no dividend. These things being so, and quite apart from his mistrust of the broker, he knew he was not going to drop a single dollar into it. He wondered if Sauer had invested. This was not impossible; in fact, it was possible that not only had Sauer invested in this will-o'-the-wisp, he had invited the broker to spread the gospel.

Some days later he was shocked to learn the effect of Avrum Rheingold's recommendation: four members of the round table had bought shares of Nevacal. Only Virgil Barron had not; and when they discussed this they agreed that it was, at best, a dangerous speculation. Beyond that it could be a deliberate fraud. Barron knew something about Avrum Rheingold. The broker's reputation matched his appearance.

That evening Mr Bridge looked in the paper. As he suspected, the company was unlisted. The next morning he telephoned his brokerage firm to inquire about it. After some delay, during which he was twice asked to spell the name, a quote was obtained. The price had risen to four dollars. He said he did not want to buy any stock, he was merely curious about the price.

A week later he called again. Nevacal was selling for approximately six dollars a share. He hung up the telephone in a bad humor. The price of Nevacal would drop as sharply as it had risen, he was positive of that.

He did not call the brokerage office again, because it would be embarrassing to inquire three times about Nevacal without buying any, but at luncheon when the conversation got around to the stock market he inquired in a jocular tone if anybody knew how Nevacal was doing. Everybody knew. He was the only one at the table who did not know. It was selling for nine dollars. Virgil Barron had reconsidered and bought some.

Mr Bridge laughed. He advised them to sell out while they were ahead.

Alex Sauer said he was in close touch with Avrum Rheingold. Rheingold believed it would go higher.

'Suit yourselves, but don't say I didn't warn you,' Mr Bridge remarked, and he tapped the table for emphasis.

The following Friday there was an item in the *Wall Street Journal*. Nevacal had reported a three-hundred percent increase in profit over the previous fiscal year. Management was predicting further gains for the year ahead. The stock, still unlisted, was quoted at eleven dollars a share.

Mr Bridge knew it would go down. It was due for a severe setback.

But it continued to go up, and finally Avrum Rheingold passed the word. The time had come to sell. Everybody in the group sold out, very well satisfied because they had quadrupled their money, all except Virgil Barron who had jumped aboard after the train was moving.

'You got away with it,' Mr Bridge addressed them. 'More power to you. My personal opinion is that if you keep pulling stunts of this sort you are headed for trouble.'

He had not mentioned Nevacal at home, because it did not concern the family – except that if the shares had dropped in value he meant to cite this as an example of irresponsible investing. Unfortunately Nevacal had done just the opposite, so there was no sense discussing it. To do so would only encourage the children toward similar speculations when they were old enough to take an interest in such things. Instead, as soon as he observed during a brisk market rally that Kansas City Power & Light had scored a fifty-cent advance he pointed this out to the children, reminding them that they should always pay attention to basic values.

49 Fleur-de-lis

He felt no particular obligation to instruct or prepare the girls for their future except to make certain they were neat, polite, truthful, modest, and adequately educated; the rest of the business could be handled by their mother. Once out of school they might work at one job or another while waiting to get married, and if they spent a year or so doing something trivial it would not really be a waste of time. Quite the opposite. Better a couple of years in an office typing letters and running errands than an impulsive marriage ending in divorce. But for Douglas to squander his time at one meaningless task after another would be ridiculous. Accordingly, he planned to speak to his son about the future, to encourage him to start thinking about it, and by delineating not only the rewards but the liabilities of his own career he hoped to provide some suitable points of reference. He wished to impress upon his son three things which he felt that he himself had achieved: financial security, independence, and self-respect. In his mind these were of supreme importance. They stood together like the points of the fleur-de-lis.

50 The family tree

In the bedroom in an ordinary black picture frame was a letter appointing Henry Thompson Bridge a colonel in the Army. The letter was dated 1812 and it was signed by James Monroe, who was then Secretary of State. Mr Bridge could not recall the first time he had seen this letter, which had belonged to his uncle, but he had been fascinated by it as long as he could remember, and his uncle had willed it to him. Now, although the letter had been hanging in the same place in the bedroom for quite a few years, he was still aware of it, and he thought it may have been this document which first caused him to become curious about his ancestry, with the result that he had commissioned a genealogist to do some research. The genealogist eventually brought him a little history of his predecessors, which he had read many times, and considered, and which he had shown to his wife and the children. He was somewhat disappointed that they did not find it as fascinating as he did himself. It was understandable, of course, that his wife would be less interested in his forbears than she would be in her own; he had been thinking of employing the genealogist again to do a similar paper on her family, which might be a nice surprise for her birthday. As for the children, they ought to be interested, and he hoped they would be when they were older. Carolyn did show signs of curiosity, but Ruth and Douglas were singularly unimpressed.

He had told them that in Delaware there was a town named after their great great-grandfather, and that the brother of this man was at one time the lieutenant governor of Ohio. Another ancestor was a Scottish earl who owned a castle which still stood near the village of Auldearn by Moray Firth. What did they think about that! Another ancestor was a major in the Revolutionary War. Another was the fourth president of Hamilton College. Another was recommended to President Hayes for appointment as the American ambassador to Mexico, although for some reason he did not get the appointment.

They listened to all of this with very little comment. Finally Douglas inquired about horse thieves.

Well, Mr Bridge answered, no doubt the family had its share, because few families have not had their black sheep, but their names were not recorded for posterity. Why? Why was he asking?

No reason. Just asking, Douglas said.

51 New neighbors

On the lot where the cave used to be there was now a red-brick Colonial house with French windows, with six square white pillars fronting the portico, and a brass lion's head on the door. The garage, which was a smaller replica of the house except for the pillars, had room for three cars. Throughout the winter, regardless of bad weather, the workmen had been there. Now the house was almost finished.

'I can't help wondering who'll move in,' Mrs Bridge said. 'Nobody seems to know.'

'Whoever they are, they've got money,' he said. 'Great Lord, the amount that place must have cost!'

Carolyn asked if they had seen the weather vane atop the chimney – a copper rooster. Douglas remarked that the workmen were building a barbecue oven in the back yard.

Ruth said, 'I hope they're more exciting than the rest of the people in this neighborhood.'

'We ought to be finding out very soon,' said Mrs Bridge.

The new family moved in on the first day of May. Their name was Snapper. Leo Snapper was short and swarthy, with a long, straight nose and quick, reddish eyes like the eyes of a fox. His wife Edith was taller, thin as a mannequin, with elaborately coiffured pearl-gray hair. She walked with a cane, as though she did not see very well. They had two daughters several years older than Ruth whose names were Judith and Olivia, and there was an Oriental chauffeur.

Carolyn said, 'Are they Jews?'

Mrs Bridge replied: 'I don't see what difference that makes. Do you?'

'No,' Carolyn said. 'I just wondered.'

'How come they never say hello to anybody?' Douglas asked.

'That's not our affair,' his mother said. 'But goodness, doesn't she look like the Empress Josephine with that hair?'

'I wonder what business that fellow is in,' said Mr Bridge more to himself than to anybody else.

'I was asking Lois,' Mrs Bridge said. 'I believe it's import-export.'

'They got a dog,' Douglas said, 'only it's a poodle.' He was disappointed about the dog because a poodle was an indoor, informal sort of dog. Except for the weather vane, which he liked, and the remote possibility that he might be invited to a barbecue, he was generally disappointed with the new neighbors.

'I saw their cars,' Carolyn said. This, she felt, was the notable thing about the Snapper family. 'They leave the garage doors open to show off. I'm not sure what one of them is, but two of them are Cadillacs.'

'One's a Cad,' Douglas said wearily. 'One's a Buick. One's a this year's Olds. You can tell from the fenders a mile away.'

Ruth was disappointed that there were no sons in the family; however, the haughty sophistication of Judith and Olivia almost made up for this. She wanted to get acquainted with them. She hoped they would introduce her to the men they knew.

'Well,' Mr Bridge observed, 'just as long as they're decent people. That's the main thing.'

'Oh, I'm sure they are,' said his wife. 'I think we have an awfully nice neighborhood.'

'I do, too,' he said. 'Let's hope it stays that way.'

52 LS

He had spoken lightly about the Snappers, but he was apprehensive. Three cars seemed unnecessary and therefore pretentious, and the copper rooster was absurd, and the woman's hair style was flamboyant. A conservative, cultivated family with less money would have been preferable to a vulgar millionaire. Then, just a few days after the Snappers moved in, the weather turned warm and their awnings were put up. Leo Snapper had his initials on the awnings. The initials could be read half a block away.

'Lord, what next,' Mr Bridge said, shaking his head.

His wife lifted her hands. 'My stars, I couldn't agree more! Isn't that the limit?'

'I won't be the first bit surprised,' he said, 'if those people set a flagpole in their yard.'

Douglas, who had not been listening closely, heard this and glanced at his father with sudden interest, because a flagpole would be a good thing to climb; but then, reading his father's expression, he understood the remark. 'I think they're okay,' he said. 'Mr Snapper's a good guy.'

'Oh?' Mr Bridge asked. 'What makes you say that?'

'Vandermeer's glider sailed over the fence the other day and Mr Snapper didn't get sore. He sailed it back.'

'Well,' Mr Bridge said, smiling a little, 'time will tell. I don't care for the man's taste. Otherwise, I have nothing against him.'

And as he thought about this statement he decided it was true; the new neighbors were gaudy, but after all that was not a serious offense. He could not feel cordial toward them, and he did not care to know them better, but perhaps their entrance into the neighborhood would not make any difference.

53 The regatta on Ward Parkway

The major event of the month of May, as far as Douglas was concerned, was not the arrival of the Snapper family but the sailboat race on Ward Parkway pond. Scheduled for Sunday, May 31st, it was open to all boats built in the manual training classes of the public grade schools. Ribbons would be awarded to the first twelve boats to sail across the pond. Douglas had been working on his boat since February, but still it was not finished. Several times he had asked his mother if she could drive him to the pond on Sunday the 31st, and each time she promised she would.

'Providing you ever get that boat finished,' Mr Bridge said to tease him. Then Douglas insisted he would finish the boat. When asked what color he intended to paint it he said white, as though anyone should know. Boats sail better when they are painted white. His father did not believe this, and asked who had told him such a thing. Douglas did not know, but it was true. Everybody knew white boats went faster. He was asked how many boys in his class were building boats. There were eight or nine, he thought. He was not sure.

'Vandermeer's making one,' he added, 'but I don't know if he'll get finished on account of he keeps doping off.'

'Not "on account of". We say "because".'

'Okay, okay! So anyhow, Mr Teale got sore at him the other day and threw an eraser at him, except it hit another kid.'

Mrs Bridge glanced anxiously at her husband. Every once in a while she heard of teachers throwing things, or slapping a child, or otherwise behaving strangely, and at every such report she became alarmed.

'Mr Teale's really got a terrible temper,' Douglas went on. It was clear that he wished to make the manual training class sound as adventurous as possible. 'Whenever you dope off he throws things. All of a sudden – *pow*! He hit Tipton with a piece of chalk last week.'

'That could put somebody's eye out,' Mrs Bridge said. 'Has he thrown anything at you?'

'Well, sure. He throws stuff at every kid in class. Usually it's just a wad of paper, unless he gets good and sore. I stay out of his way if he looks sore.'

'That's using your head,' said Mr Bridge.

'Are you coming to the race, Dad?'

'Am I invited?'

Douglas made a face and Mr Bridge laughed.

'All right, you finish that boat and I'll go watch the race.'

Douglas answered disdainfully that he could finish the boat in two or three days, but he wanted to do a good job. 'Some guys do it any old way,' he said. 'Sutton Boggs finished his up yesterday, but if he enters it in the race it'll probably sink.'

Mr Bridge began to realize the importance of the sailboat. Thinking back, recalling the number of times Douglas had mentioned the boat, he wondered if it had assumed some significance that the boy was not aware of. Never before had he worked so laboriously at anything. Never before had he shown the least pride in anything he did; yet now there was pride shining in his eyes as he described how he planed the spars and how he had planed and sanded the deck until it was so thin that he could almost see light through it. He had cut the keel from a sheet of tin, and Mr Bridge remembered the evening when he had drawn a picture of the keel and explained how he had screwed lead weights to the bottom, filled the screwholes with putty, and then sandpapered the putty so that not a mark remained. Now, listening again to his son talk about the sailboat, he reflected that Douglas without quite knowing what he was doing had begun work on his life.

He decided not to tease his son any further. 'If you are concerned about finishing it,' he said, 'maybe you should spend some time working on it after school.'

Douglas answered seriously that he had been thinking about this, but he was afraid to ask Mr Teale's permission.

'Are you afraid he would laugh at you?'

'I thought he might get mad.'

'I doubt it,' Mr Bridge said. 'Why don't you ask?'

Douglas said he might.

'Do any of the other boys stay after school to work on their boats?'

'No,' he said. 'They don't care what they're doing. They clear out as soon as the bell rings.'

'If you expect to have a first-class product you must be willing to pay the price. Good merchandise isn't found in a bargain basement. Cheap goods are cheap because the workman did just enough to get by. There's nothing criminal about that, in fact it happens to be the way a majority of people live their lives – doing just enough to get by. Just enough to get by, that's all.'

'Yeh,' Douglas said.

'I'm not urging you to work after school, understand. If you want to play marbles or basketball or whatever, that's your privilege. So long as your grades are satisfactory I ask nothing more. Do as you please.'

No more was said about it, but Mr Bridge listened, and later that week Douglas hinted that he was staying after school to do some work on the boat. His parents knew it was nearly finished when he bought a piece of white cloth in the dime store and borrowed his mother's shears to cut the sails. She offered to hem the sails on her sewing machine, but he refused. He said he would do it by hand, which he did, and he managed to sew on the brass curtain rings which would hold the sail to the boom. Harriet instructed him in the use of the flatiron so that he was able to iron out the wrinkles and flatten the puckered stitches. And then very carefully he rolled up the finished sails and took them to school.

'He's dying to win that race,' Mrs Bridge said.

Mr Bridge had not thought much about the race. Douglas was hoping to win, of course. That was taken for granted. But he had not talked about it, he talked mostly about the boat. This began to seem rather strange.

'Oh, he's talked to me about it,' Mrs Bridge said. 'He's obsessed with the idea of a blue ribbon. Really, Walter, I'm beginning to get alarmed. There will be so many boats, and I just don't know what might happen if he doesn't win.'

'Well,' Mr Bridge said, jingling the coins in his pocket, 'Abraham Lincoln observed that in this sad world of ours sorrow comes to all, and to the young it comes with bitterest agony because it takes them unawares, whereas the older have learned to expect it. If Douglas is defeated in that race he must accept his defeat with grace and with dignity.'

'I suppose,' she replied; but he did not think she had been listening.

On the afternoon of the race Ruth and Carolyn had better things to do, so Mr and Mrs Bridge together with Douglas, who was carrying his boat in his arms, got into the Chrysler and drove along Ward Parkway to the pond. There they found an unexpectedly large crowd made up almost entirely of boys with their parents. The pond was dotted with boats. Other boats lay on the grass like captive pelicans. More boats arrived every minute.

'I didn't think there'd be this many,' Douglas said with an expression of dismay.

'I just know you're going to win,' his mother said, but she did not sound convincing. There were too many boats.

Mr Bridge said, 'I don't see how they expect to hold a race with all these things. Great Scott, they'll bump into each other.'

Douglas nodded. 'Yeh. Especially with this wind.'

'Isn't that Bob Tipton?' Mrs Bridge asked.

'Yeh, I saw him. That's him.'

'That is "he".'

'Okay, okay,' Douglas said, and looked down at the boat in his arms.

Bob Tipton walked over. He was chewing a wad of pink bubble gum.

'You entering?' Douglas asked.

'Might as well,' Tipton said.

'Where's your boat?'

'My folks have got an eye on it. There sure are a lot. Jeez, Doug, I never figured there'd be this many, did you?'

'Nope,' Douglas said. 'Is Boggs entered?'

Tipton nodded and blew a balloon of gum that exploded and clung to his upper lip.

'I bet Boggs sinks,' Douglas remarked thoughtfully.

'Could be,' Tipton said. He pulled the gum off his lip and stuffed it into his mouth. 'Some guy on the other side has got a real beaut.'

'What school?'

'Don't know,' Tipton said. 'I think he got help. No kid our age could get the deck as perfect as that. I guess his manual training teacher worked on it for him. Sure looks that way.'

'Did he try it out yet?'

'Don't think so,' Tipton said.

'Maybe it only looks good. Those boats that look so hot don't always sail fast.'

'Could be.'

'They're awarding twelve ribbons, so we got a chance.'

'They ought to award about fifty,' Tipton said.

A few minutes later Douglas said to his parents, 'Me and Tipton are going around on the other side and get ready. I'll meet you here afterwards. Maybe if you get closer to the bank you can see better.'

Mrs Bridge answered that they could see well enough from where they were, but Mr Bridge took her by the arm. 'Good idea. We'll move up.' And as Douglas and his friend were disappearing into the crowd he called after them, 'Good luck to you both!'

The race did not start for another half-hour. Then not many of the spectators were certain it had started, but more or less all at once the flotilla was drifting away from the opposite bank. The breeze had grown stronger. The little boats nudged each other and began floating in different directions, rocking and listing, except for a few which locked sails and clung together with sodden desperation. Here and there one fell over and lay on its side while others flopped upside down like feeding swans so that only the hull and the keel could be seen above the water. But out of this wallowing armada sailed several stout boats – firm on their course with sails billowing, cheered by the crowd. Onward they sailed, dipping their bowsprits as if headed for the New World. Among them the boat Douglas had built could not be found.

The boat Douglas built was eventually located in the exact center of the pond where it stood as solemn and motionless as a stork. Occasionally its sails trembled, the brass curtain rings knocked delicately against the boom, and the boat listed a few degrees, as though contemplating the race and perhaps wondering whether or not it ought to compete. But then with a little shudder it would resume its stance.

Over a period of minutes the boat was observed to drift, but it refused to sail. It leaned and it rocked against the waves and it quivered, and once it turned completely around. But that was all. Whether it had sailed by itself to this point in the middle of the pond, or whether it had been pushed or towed or merely followed another boat, nobody could say, because of the confusion at the start. But there it was, no matter how it had gotten there, and there it evidently planned to remain, possibly forever. On the shore stood its maker with a green felt button-studded crown set somewhat crookedly on his head, standing there alone in corduroy knickers, a new sweatshirt showing a flag and the triumphant legend ALL AMERICA, and frayed tennis shoes and no socks, with his arms dangling at his sides as though they were broken, staring out to sea.

The great race did not end with much more finality than it had begun. It disintegrated. There were rumors of disagreement about the winner because several boats touched shore at the same time. But none of this concerned Mr and Mrs Bridge. They walked around the pond and they stood on either side of their son, who acknowledged their presence without a word and continued to stare at the fruit of his hands, which by now had again turned around and seemed to be contemplating the perils of a return voyage.

'Anyhow,' he said, 'it didn't sink.'

'And it's the prettiest one here,' said his mother as she slipped an arm around his waist.

Fifteen minutes later the boat had drifted halfway to the south end of the pond, but no closer to either shore. Mr and Mrs Bridge and Douglas followed it.

'Lots of them didn't get across,' she said.

But the boat heard this and faced them with sails flapping in vast astonishment.

'I'm just sure it'll come back before much longer,' she said.

Douglas answered quietly. 'Sooner or later.'

So they waited, watching other boats that drifted around the pond, and commented on these; and they looked at the boats floating on one side dead in the water as if they had been torpedoed, and at the white keels standing up here and there like freshly painted tombstones.

'I guess a couple went down,' Douglas said.

'Oh, what a shame,' his mother replied. She took off his crown and smoothed the tangled hair with her fingers and set the crown back on his head.

Then, against the dying breeze, out of some magical perversity with which it may or may not have been imbued by the spirit of its maker, the boat that Douglas built was seen to come to life. With both sails bent and full, and the pennant fluttering as though some ancient mariner at the helm could not rest until the journey ended, the marvelous boat bore straight toward them.

'Here it comes,' Mrs Bridge cried, and she clapped her hands.

Douglas nodded.

They watched, and as it approached them the boat sailed more cautiously; yet there was no doubt that it intended to reach the shore.

Mr Bridge asked Douglas if he was hungry.

'Hungry?' he answered without looking up.

'I was thinking that after your boat comes in the three of us might go somewhere for a banana split.'

'All right,' Douglas said. He knelt on the bank to wait.

54 Semi-pro

Mr Bridge felt guilty about the boat race even though he knew he was not responsible for that melancholy afternoon. He did not know why he felt a sense of guilt, but he could not escape from it, and it caused him to attempt something which he realized was foolish. For weeks Douglas had been after him to get out into the middle of the street with a baseball bat and hit a few grounders for the benefit of Rodney Vandermeer. Rodney Vandermeer's father had been a semiprofessional ballplayer and was in the habit of knocking the ball around for his son and Douglas and Bobby Tipton and any other neighborhood children who cared to play. Douglas therefore, was anxious to demonstrate that his father was equally handy with a bat.

Mr Bridge could not remember the last time he had hit a baseball. He thought it had been at least twenty years ago. He had used every excuse he could think of to avoid making a spectacle of himself in the middle of the street. He had hoped to get through the summer, and perhaps by the following summer Douglas would abandon the idea; but not long after the boat race, when Douglas once again brought up the subject, he succumbed. Very reluctantly he accepted the bat, and after a last desperate look at his wife he followed his son out the door.

The bat felt exceedingly strange in his hand. The weight of it, and the smooth little handle. He read the trademark. He waved the bat in small tentative circles as they proceeded to the street. He knew he should expect a bad half-hour. The important thing, of course, was to hit the ball. He would not be expected to hit it farther than the Vandermeer boy's father. Neither of the boys would be expecting that.

Douglas shouted 'Here he is!' and Mr Bridge saw not only Rodney Vandermeer but three other boys sprawled in the shade of an oak. Just then another boy dropped out of the tree, where he had been hanging from a limb like a sloth. Mr Bridge saw the five boys scrutinizing him as though never in their lives had they observed anything so remarkable.

Douglas ran to join them, leaving him with the bat and ball.

The boys were getting to their feet without enthusiasm, and one of them was looking at him with absolute contempt. He thought there was something wrong with the boy's joints, because he stood as though he was made of rubber. He was a round-shouldered, bandy-legged boy with a face like a sheep. He was chewing a twig. A first baseman's glove dangled from his left hand, slowly opening and shutting like a lobster's claw.

Douglas yelled, 'Okay, Dad!'

The boys wandered into the street. Rather indolently they took up their positions. They were not excited. They just stood in the street and waited.

Mr Bridge considered the ball. It occurred to him for the first time that the ball was not going to be pitched to him. He was supposed to toss it in the air and hit it as it dropped. He remembered doing this when he was a boy, but now he was not sure which hand held the bat and which hand tossed the ball. He decided to toss the ball with his right hand, and if that did not work he would try it next time with his left hand.

'Rod, you take the first one,' Douglas said very clearly.

Mr Bridge tossed the ball into the air and clutched at the bat with both hands. The ball dropped to the ground sooner than he expected.

'Okay,' Douglas said, smacking his fist into his glove. 'Any time you're ready, Dad.'

Mr Bridge did not want to look at the peculiar boy, but he could not help himself. The boy was simply resting on those spidery legs. There was no sign of intelligence on his face.

'Give us a high fly,' Douglas called, and sank into a crouching position with his hands on his knees to show that he was prepared to leap in any direction. The other boys stood in a row. Their attitude was respectful but they were not particularly alert.

Mr Bridge tossed the ball into the air again, higher this time so that he would be ready when it came down, and as it came down he chopped at it and felt a quick pain in one wrist while the ball dropped between his feet like a dead bird.

Douglas was silent. The street was silent. There was not a sound.

Mr Bridge worked his wrist to see if it had been injured. It was all right, so there was nothing to do but try again. This time, with a sense of unspeakable relief, he hit the ball. It went bouncing up the street, Douglas screamed 'Take it, Clyde!' and with a feeling of horror he realized that the strange boy was Clyde.

The ball rolled up to Clyde. There it stopped. Clyde leaned over, scooped the ball into his glove, and with a practiced flip sent it arching down the street. Mr Bridge dropped the bat, and as it struck the concrete he knew he should not have dropped it; too late he remembered that it was all right to drop a bat on a playing field but never on concrete. But there was no time to look after the bat, because the ball was almost upon him. It bounced once and hit him in the chest.

'Give us another grounder,' Douglas shouted. Obviously he had concluded there was no chance of a spectacular high fly.

Mr Bridge swung again and the ball went hopping up the street toward Douglas, but Douglas pretended to be unable to judge it and screamed for another boy to handle it. This was easily done. Once more the ball came flying back and he managed to stop it with his foot.

Now, with two out of three to his credit – not counting the time he had neglected to swing – he began to feel more confident, and after another grounder he contrived to hit the ball some distance in the air. It did not get as far as any of the players, but still it did show improvement; Rodney Vandermeer fielded it and popped it into his glove several times, which Mr Bridge interpreted as a compliment. He laughed and waved at the boys to move backward. It seemed to him that all he had needed was a little practice. He was convinced that he could hit the ball regularly. Very soon he ought to be able to hit a long high one.

But on the next attempt he missed and felt something definite happen to his spine, and right then he decided that what he was doing was ridiculous. He did not think he had hurt himself, but he did not intend to swing the bat again. 'I'm sorry, boys,' he called, 'I'm afraid you'll have to get somebody else.' There was not much point in trying to explain. It would sound like an excuse.

Douglas walked part of the way toward him and said, 'I guess the rest of us are going to stay out here and take turns a while. Anyway, thanks a lot.'

'We're having an early supper,' Mr Bridge said. 'Don't stay too long.' He leaned the bat against a tree, waved good-by to the players, and started towards the house. On the way he experimented with his spine, bending slightly forward and turning cautiously from side to side.

'Home so soon?' Mrs Bridge asked as he came in the door.

He eased himself into a chair and took off his glasses. 'Yes. It's been too many years. I tried to tell Douglas, but he kept insisting.'

She smiled. 'I'll bet it did you loads of good.'

'No, it did not do me loads of good,' he answered sharply. 'I embarrassed him in front of his friends. I knew this would happen. I tried to tell him, but he refused to believe me.'

'Well, I doubt if it matters a great deal.'

'Oh, yes it does,' he said. 'Yes, indeed it does. Make no mistake about that.'

'Really? I can't see why.'

'You were never a boy. That's why.'

55 Golden gloves

Douglas spent most of his summer playing baseball, but he also took up boxing, and although he had mentioned this at home nobody thought much about it until he walked into the kitchen with a bruised eye and asked Harriet for a piece of beefsteak. Instead of giving him the steak Harriet reported the matter to Mrs Bridge, who, after peering at the eye and tentatively touching the skin with her little finger, led him into the study where Mr Bridge was at work. He, too, inspected the eye. Then he leaned back in his chair.

'Well, well, well,' he said, 'you have what we used to call a "shiner".'

'It's awfully swollen,' Mrs Bridge said. 'Don't you think we ought to call Dr Stapp?'

'How does your eye feel?' Mr Bridge asked.

Douglas said, 'It's not bad. I just want a piece of beefsteak.'

'And how did you happen to acquire this decoration?'

Douglas had explained to Harriet and then to his mother that he had been boxing in Tipton's garage with Huggins, the Tipton chauffeur. He thought it was unnecessray to explain again, but he did so because he knew that otherwise he would not get the steak. He had been boxing with Huggins and Huggins caught him with a left jab. That was all there was to it.

Mr Bridge did not like the idea of his son boxing with somebody's chauffeur. Douglas replied that he was not the only one. Bob Tipton and Rodney Vandermeer had also boxed with Huggins because they were having a round-robin tournament. Then he added that Huggins had given Rodney Vandermeer a bloody nose.

The smile disappeared from Mr Bridge's face. 'Go on,' he said.

Douglas shrugged. There was nothing more to tell.

'Whose idea was this tournament?'

'Mine. We were just going to have it with three of us, but after Huggins finished washing the car he was sitting around watching, so we invited him to join. He didn't want to at first, but finally we talked him into it.'

'This was your idea?'

He grinned. 'Yeh. It sure was some bright idea. Huggins really has got a left. But Tipton got pasted harder than either one of us – he almost got knocked colder than a cucumber. He was weaving around all over the garage like he was punch drunk.'

'Where is this man now?'

'Who?'

Mr Bridge gestured with annoyance. 'The chauffeur.'

'I don't know. He doesn't live at Tiptons', so maybe he's gone home. Or maybe he's still there. How the heck am I supposed to know? Anyway, what's the diff?'

'What's the telephone number at that place?'

Douglas hesitated. He knew he had said something wrong. He could see that his father was angry but he could not guess exactly why. He thought it had something to do with the chauffeur. Plaintively he said, 'It wasn't Huggins' fault, for cripes sake.'

'You have a nasty black eye, your friend Rodney had his nose bloodied, and the Tipton boy was nearly knocked unconscious. I have heard more than enough. If you know the Tiptons' telephone number, give it to me. If you don't, I will look it up.'

'Wait a minute,' Douglas said. 'Will you please kindly relax and listen a minute?'

'Be quick about it.'

'Huggins didn't smack Tipton. Rodney did.'

'Let me get this straight. The Tipton boy was almost knocked unconscious. Who hit him?'

'I just told you. Rodney. Rod got him with an upper-cut.'

'I see. But your friend Tipton also boxed with the chauffeur, is that correct?'

'Sure, because that's what a round-robin means. Everybody's got to box against everybody else. How many times do I have to explain? Only they didn't do much except spar around. They hardly touched each other. Huggins didn't have anything at all to do with Tipton practically getting kayoed. I mean, for cripes sake, if you don't get it by this time I give up.'

He was telling the truth, there could be no doubt of it; even so, Mr Bridge was not satisfied. The fact that the third boy had not been injured by the chauffeur seemed to indicate that the man was not deliberately trying to hurt them. At the same time it was all very suspect. 'I don't like this,' he said. 'Not one bit.'

'Holy cow! If you're going to box you sort of expect to get pasted on the kisser once in a while, unless you're some sort of professional world's champ.'

'I certainly don't like it either,' Mrs Bridge said.

Douglas sighed. 'Nobody was trying to kill anybody. We were all kind of pulling our punches, only once in a while like I just said there's sometimes you can't help getting one square in the kisser. You should have seen the one I landed on Vandermeer's bread-basket. It knocked the wind clear out of him. He was doubled over for about ten minutes.'

Mr Bridge rocked around in his chair while he considered. Finally he said, 'It sounds to me as though this business got completely out of hand.'

'Maybe. Sort of,' Douglas agreed.

'Now, you listen to me. If you want to box with your friends – with boys of your own age and size – I have no objection. But no more of this black-eye bloody-nose nonsense, do you understand? And absolutely no further boxing with that chauffeur. Or with any other servant under any circumstances. Is that clear? Do you hear me?'

'I'd have to be pretty deaf not to.'

'Very well. Suppose we drop the matter. And now I have some work to do.'

'Uh, well . . .' Douglas said.

'Yes? What is it?'

'Can you tell Harriet to let me have a piece of beefsteak?'

'If you are convinced that's what you need, all right.'

After Douglas had left the study Mrs Bridge asked if the meat would do much good, and Mr Bridge replied that he did not think so.

56 Crosby

Looking through the bills at the first of the month he noted that Douglas had charged eight Bing Crosby records at the Plaza music store. He mentioned this to his wife.

'Really?' she said. 'Why, he oughtn't to be doing that. I'll speak to him. After all, he does get an allowance. He can pay you back.'

'Never mind, it isn't important,' he said, and opened another envelope.

A few minutes later she looked up from her magazine and said, 'That's odd. It just occurred to me. He never plays them.'

'If he doesn't play them why did he buy them?'

'I can't imagine. I suppose he does, but for some reason it seems to me that Carolyn is the one who puts them on the machine.'

Mr Bridge picked up the statement from the music store and looked again at the sales receipt which Douglas had signed; then he handed the receipt to her, and as she studied it an expression of bewilderment came across her face.

'What's the matter?' he asked. But she did not answer. 'That's his signature, is it not?'

'Oh, I suppose it must be,' she said so weakly that he could hardly hear her.

'Is it? Or isn't it? You know his handwriting better than I do. Is that his signature, or not?' But still she hesitated. 'Do you recognize it?' he insisted.

'I don't pretend to be an expert,' she said, and touched herself on the forehead as if she was about to faint.

'Listen to me. Who signed this receipt?'

'There must be an explanation.'

'There is, and I intend to have it. Where is Douglas?'

'In his room, I believe.'

Mr Bridge got up and started toward the steps. She called his name. He turned around.

'What are you planning to do?'

'Before doing anything I intend to ask a few questions.'

'There's some mistake, I'm just sure.'

'I hope so. We will not have any monkey business in this house.'

Douglas was lying on his back on the Navajo rug. He was holding both legs straight up in the air. His face was contorted and his eyes were squeezed shut.

Mr Bridge asked what he was doing.

He replied through clenched teeth that he was trying to see how long he could hold his legs up.

'Why?'

'Because,' he gasped, and sucked in his breath.

'Is there some reason you never play your Bing Crosby records?'

Douglas gradually lowered his feet to the floor. For several moments he lay quietly with an agonized expression. His brow wrinkled as though he might be thinking. 'It really gets you in the gut,' he said. And then: 'Who says I got any Bing Crosby records?'

'You bought eight this past month.'

After a long silence Douglas said, 'Nope. Not me, boss.'

'You did not?'

'Bing—' he said, and cleared his throat. 'Bing Crosby records?'

'Bing Crosby records.'

'Old boo-boop-a-doo?'

'Did you or did you not charge several records at the Plaza music store recently?'

To show that he was mystified Douglas scratched his head. Then he said in a plaintive voice, 'No, I didn't. Will somebody please tell me what in the zook this is all about?'

'Where are your sisters?'

'Search me.'

'Have they gone out?'

'Who cares?'

The girls were not in their room, so Mr Bridge went downstairs and pushed open the swinging door to the kitchen. Harriet was alone in the kitchen. She was drying dishes while listening to jazz on the radio. She turned down the volume until it was inaudible and went on wiping a dish while she watched him with a neutral expression.

'I am looking for the girls. Have you seen them?'

'I sure haven't,' she said promptly, almost enthusiastically, very much relieved that her radio program had not brought him into the kitchen. 'Well, hold on though, let me think a minute. Ruth, she went somewheres a little bit back. Movies, if I recall, she and her friend Dodie. Carolyn, now, I don't know. Wait, I do believe. Here it comes to me – she's 'cross the street.'

'When she gets home, tell her I want to speak to her.'

'I will. I sure will. Soon as she puts one foot in the door.'

He left the kitchen, walked through the breakfast room, and was about to go upstairs when he noticed a light was on in the basement recreation room. He went down a few steps and looked. Carolyn was on the chaise longue with her hands behind her head and her feet crossed.

'I got home a couple of minutes ago,' she said. 'I came in the front door.'

'What were you doing across the street?' he asked pleasantly.

'Patsy and I were talking. Do you want anything special?'

'No,' he said before he could prevent himself. He did not know why he had said this, nor why he had smiled. He saw that she was observing him closely. He went down the rest of the steps and approached the chaise longue in a serious manner.

'Daddy, I overheard you talking about those records.'

'Oh? You did, did you?' He sensed that she was trying to control the conversation.

'Why didn't you come to me first?'

'Now, just one minute,' he said.

'I'm sorry. You may not believe me, but I really am.'

'What are you sorry about?'

'You know.'

She had managed to confess without actually admitting anything and before being accused. He looked down at her with an expression of annoyance.

'I'm not sure I do know.'

She reached up and took his hand. 'Haven't I apologized? What more do you want, Daddy? Am I supposed to take those records back to the store? If that's what you want, I will. Whatever you say.'

She had signed her brother's name to the receipt. To call this 'forgery' sounded absurd, yet that was what it was. He wondered if she would have mentioned it if she had not been caught.

She was watching carefully. 'I was meaning to tell you. Honestly I was, but Daddy at times you're impossible.'

He wanted to pull his hand away, but he could not; so soon she would be grown. Soon she would belong to another man.

'Carolyn,' he said in a supplicating voice, 'how could you do it?'

She withdrew her hand and refused to look at him, as though he were the one who had betrayed a trust.

57 Beefcake

Ruth had been pasting pictures of movie stars on the walls of her closet. Mrs Bridge, discovering this, was greatly displeased on two accounts: first, because the closet would need to be repainted after the pictures were scraped off, and second, because all the pictures were of men. She was so displeased that before speaking to Ruth about the matter she consulted her husband. He did not care how Ruth decorated the closet. Mrs Bridge mentioned the expense and the inconvenience of repainting. He was not sure this would be necessary. She invited him to have a look at the closet, the better to understand the problem, so he followed her to the girls' room. Mrs Bridge opened the closet door and began pushing aside the sweaters, blouses, slips, skirts, coats, and everything else Ruth had stuffed into the closet, and at last he observed that what she said was true: movie stars were peeking at him from everywhere. Some were in swimming trunks, some were on the golf course, some were pictured at home, others were merely beaming at the camera. There they were, dozens of them glued to the wall. He contemplated them. He was bemused by the rows of blinding white teeth, the rather benevolent and universal stupidity shining from the featureless faces of these totems. He said he could not see any reason to scrape them off the wall. Ruth would get tired of the pictures. In another year or so she would be sick of them and of her own accord would ask if the closet could be repainted, whereas now she would raise a fuss if the pictures were removed. Let her alone, he advised. After all, Ruth was the only one who had to look at them.

Mrs Bridge, still very serious, at last agreed, but added that she felt it was setting a poor example for Carolyn.

So the collection remained, and gradually increased as though the handsome gentlemen were multiplying spontaneously.

58 The fight

It was all over by the time Mr Bridge came home, and he would never have learned about it except for the scratches on Carolyn's cheek. She had made the mistake of calling her sister a slut – for what reason he did not ask – and the fight started immediately. Ruth had no marks on her face, and beyond this she wore the complacent air of the victor. Mr Bridge was surprised. It had never occurred to him that in spite of their frequent arguments they would actually get into a fight; but they had, and he was further surprised by the result. Ruth was two years older and a little taller, but Carolyn was much sturdier, much more solid. Then, too, it was always Carolyn who had temper tantrums and broke things; Ruth folded herself up like a bat in a cave when she was angry. But on this occasion she had flown out of the cave and Carolyn ran away shrieking. At all events, it was over. Carolyn would carry the scars for several days as reminders of her bad judgment, otherwise the affair had a curiously remote quality, perhaps because he had not been a witness to it nor heard Carolyn's screams. No serious injury had been sustained by either party, and since any sort of punishment would only revive the scene he let it pass without much comment. Thinking about it, he was secretly a little pleased. He could not bring himself to lay a hand on Carolyn when she became objectionable, but he suspected Ruth might have taught her a lesson. Whether or not it would have any permanent effect was something else.

59 In the garden

Saturday morning he saw Ruth in the back yard getting ready for a sun bath. She had spread a beach towel on the grass near the rose trellis. She was as brown as a Mexican from loitering around the pool at the country club, but evidently she did not think she was brown enough. She untied the straps of her bathing suit, opened a bottle of suntan oil, and began smearing oil on her arms and legs while he watched from the bedroom window. He noticed for the first time that she had become a woman; her body had lengthened and softened. He watched attentively while she poured oil into the palm of her hand and stroked the oil on her skin. Her flesh gleamed in the morning sunlight like varnished cherrywood. Presently she finished oiling herself and lay down on the towel with her arms outstretched as if she had been dancing and fallen exhausted in that position.

Just then Mrs Bridge entered the bedroom. He turned from the window, caught her by the shoulders and kissed her, forcing his tongue between her teeth. She pulled away. He caught her again and pushed her toward the bed while she murmured doubtfully.

60 Do you remember . . . ?

'Do you remember,' she asked, 'that evening on my parents' front porch before we were married?'

The question demanded some kind of response. He had worked late at the office and was tired, and he disliked this sort of coercion. He tried to think of what to say. He did not know which evening she was referring to. They had spent quite a number of evenings seated on the swing on the front porch of her parents' home. These times had been pleasant and it was there he had made up his mind to ask her to marry him, but the proposal had been made in the parlor so she must be referring to another evening. He could not imagine which one.

She smiled almost drowsily. 'You talked about Robert Ingersoll. You admired him. You told me he was one of the greatest men on earth.'

'Oh good Lord,' Mr Bridge remarked, and waved his hand to disparage whatever he had said that long ago.

'You were so young. I've never forgotten. And before you went home you read some verses from *The Rubáiyát*. You had a little leather-covered book of poems with a green ribbon for a place mark. I've often wondered what became of that little book. What did you do with it?'

'I have no idea,' he said. He hoped she would not go on reminiscing. He sat on the edge of the bed to take off his shoes.

'Ever since that night I've loved *The Rubáiyát*.'

'I'm afraid young men of a certain age are apt to get carried away.'

As though she had not heard him, she said, 'Walter, I'm sure there's a copy of *The Rubáiyát* in the bookcase in the breakfast room.'

'Oh, now. Now, wait just a moment,' he said, sitting erect with a strained expression and a shoe in one hand.

'I suppose it *is* silly.'

She wanted him to try to recreate a moment twenty years past. He thought about it. Of course he could go downstairs, get the book, and read a few verses to her. Nobody would ever know, and this would please her. But there was no way of guessing what this might lead to. He glanced at her, wondering if she was beginning to indulge herself in memories of the past. If so, it was unhealthy. Memories should be left undisturbed.

'Never mind,' she said. 'I can see you don't want to.'

'I'll get the thing,' he said, 'if it means a great deal to you.'

'No. No.' She was embarrassed.

'It's up to you. Yes or no?'

'No, I don't want you to. It was foolish of me.'

'I'll get the thing if that's what you want.'

'No. Let's forget it. I should never have mentioned it. I don't know what came over me.'

He took off the other shoe and walked across the bedroom to the closet, where he placed them just inside the door as he did every night. He felt that he ought to say something. He rubbed his chin and coughed. 'I wasn't aware those verses had such an effect on you.'

Apparently she had regained control of her emotions. 'It must have been a combination of things. It was such a lovely night – it was summertime. Do you remember the azaleas by the porch?'

'The azaleas by the porch. No, I can't say I do.'

'I don't know why I was so impressed. Perhaps because you were the first boy who ever paid much attention to me.'

He did not like to hear this. He remembered how concerned he had been that she might be seeing somebody else. Now she made it sound as though nobody else wanted her. 'India, stop this nonsense. I could recall offhand the names of several young men who found you extremely attractive.'

For a little while she was quiet. She appeared to be thinking. Then she said, 'Walter, tell me the truth. Did you find me attractive?'

He frowned. 'What on earth has gotten into you? All at once for no good reason you behave as if – I don't know what. You were an attractive girl and you are today an attractive woman.'

'Am I?'

'You are indeed.'

She looked at him playfully. 'Would it hurt so much to tell me once in a while?'

'I'm afraid I'm not good at that sort of business.'

'You used to be.'

This was both flattering and embarrassing. He pretended to hunt for something. The night seemed unusually still; he glanced at the window and saw trickles of water darting along the glass.

'Tell me, Walter, because I need to know. Do you love me?'

'Love you? Of course,' he answered. Just then he heard the boom of thunder overhead, the house almost trembled, and the rain increased.

'Before we met, were you in love with somebody?'

'No.'

'Have you been in love since?'

'What?' he asked, incredulous. She rushed over to him and slipped her arms around his waist.

'I'm being silly,' she whispered.

'I should say you are.'

'Do you mind?'

'India, just what in the name of sense . . .?'

As soon as he said this she released him. She walked to her dressing table where she sat down and began to take the pins out of her hair. The pins dropped into a heart-shaped porcelain tray which she had kept on her dressing table since they were married. He did not know where she had gotten the tray, he assumed it had belonged to her mother or her grandmother. He had never paid any attention to it. Now he stared at it and at the black hair-pins summarizing twenty years of marriage.

'Time has such a way of going by,' she said. 'I suppose that must be the reason.'

He watched her fingers deftly locating and drawing out the hairpins and dropping them in the tray, and he felt bewildered. Why had she chosen this night to grow nostalgic? They had spent the evening reading and listening to the radio while Carolyn put together a jigsaw puzzle on the card table and Douglas in his room worked on a model airplane. Ruth and her friend Dodie were at the movies. In the kitchen Harriet was chatting with somebody. There had been nothing unusual about this evening; it had been all but identical to hundreds of others.

61 Happy birthday

Before going to the office he wrote a check, which he left on the breakfast table underneath her napkin. That night when he got home she thanked him for it, showed him what the children had given her, and remarked that it had been a very nice birthday. He wished her many more. Then he suggested that they go for a drive after dinner. The weather was sultry and a drive should be pleasant. She agreed.

They started off along Ward Parkway, turned west on Huntington Road as far as the state line, and from there they drove slowly north past the Mission Hills golf course and the tennis courts until they came to the highway. At this point he turned toward the Plaza. In front of the United Motors display room he pulled over to the curb. In the window under a spotlight a sleek green Lincoln was parked.

She sensed immediately that he had bought it for her. The check he left on the breakfast table had been for five dollars, and all day she had been puzzled because ordinarily he spent so much on gifts. Now it was clear. He had planned a surprise.

He patted her knee and said, 'Happy birthday, India.'

She looked at the automobile with an expression meant to indicate that she could not believe such good fortune.

'Walter, you must be joking! You can't be serious!'

He laughed. 'If you're not satisfied we'll give it back.'

'Don't you dare!' she cried. 'Oh, my word! I'm overwhelmed! I didn't expect anything else. I assumed the check was my present.'

'That was simply a trick to throw you off guard. Apparently it succeeded.'

'Goodness! I should say.'

He laughed again. 'All right. Let's hope the car proves satisfactory.'

'Walter, it's beautiful. Just simply beautiful. I don't know how to thank you.' She leaned over and kissed him on the cheek. 'Thank you!'

'You're very welcome,' he said. He opened the glove compartment of the Chrysler and took out a manila envelope. 'Here are the papers.'

'Oh,' she said, accepting the envelope. 'Well, thank you again.'

From the inside pocket of his suit he took another envelope. 'Now, this is your insurance. Herbert Scott is your agent.'

'Do I know him?'

'Probably you have met him. His office is in my building on the eighth floor.'

'His name sounds familiar. Wasn't he the man we met at the Barrons' cocktail party a few months ago?'

'I don't recall him being there; however, he might have been.'

'The man I'm thinking of had just returned from a fishing trip in Canada.'

'Gene Herbert. This is Herbert Scott. They have no connection.'

'I suppose the name must be what confused me.'

Mr Bridge unfolded the contract. He held it up to the light from the display window and studied it. 'I think this coverage ought to be more than adequate. You will be fully insured in event of bodily injury to one or more than one person. Property damage. Medical. Comprehensive. Collision. That should pretty well cover it. These other clauses are not worth worrying about.'

'It sounds adequate,' she said, staring at the contract to prove she would pay attention to everything concerning the new Lincoln.

'These insurance people throw in whatever they can think of, if you don't watch them. The important clauses pertain to bodily injury and property damage. In the future, if anything should happen to me I don't want you to neglect these clauses. I've known Herbert Scott for a good many years and he is perfectly reliable, but he's getting on, and there may come a time when you will be dealing with a younger man who is interested only in the premium. As long as I am alive I will handle this for you, but when the time comes for you to do it yourself I want you to remember to maintain maximum coverage on property damage and bodily injury. The chances are you will never be involved in a serious accident; nevertheless, it's a good idea to be covered.'

'I think that's true,' said Mrs Bridge.

'All right. Now, we are going to need your signature right here.' He pointed to the line where the contract was to be signed, uncapped his fountain pen, handed it to her, and held the contract flat on the seat while she signed. After this was done he blew on the ink, folded the contract, put it back in the envelope, and slipped the envelope into his pocket. 'I'll drop this off at Herbert's office tomorrow at lunchtime. So, I think that pretty well takes care of the situation. All you have to do is bring the Reo in here tomorrow, tell the fellow who you are, and he will give you the keys and you can drive it away. Leave the Reo with these people. They are taking it in trade.' He looked again at the Lincoln.

She also turned to look at it. 'Walter, it's beautiful. I can't thank you enough.'

'Well, I'm glad you're pleased,' he said, and they drove home.

62 How much?

From time to time the family inquired about his work, somewhat perfunctorily, to be sure; just the same they did make a point of asking, and he thought he should acknowledge their show of interest.

'All right,' he began, as though somebody had just that moment inquired, 'the other day an incident took place which you might care to hear about. Would you, or would you not?'

'Oh, I should say!' Mrs Bridge replied, and put down her knife and fork to prove how very interested she would be in this revelation.

The children continued eating.

'You may not believe I'm telling the truth,' he said in a warning voice. 'But the fact of the matter is that last Thursday I was approached on the street by a man I had never seen before. At least to the best of my knowledge I never had seen this fellow. He stepped right up to me as bold as brass. And he knew who I was, though I cannot imagine how. Somebody must have pointed me out to him.'

'So? What'd he want, a handout?' Douglas asked.

'I'll get around to what he wanted in a moment. Keep your shirt on. As I say, to the best of my knowledge I never had seen this person before. The first thing I knew, he was walking along beside me as if he had dropped straight down out of the blue.'

'My word!' said Mrs Bridge while selecting a roll from the silver basket Harriet was carrying around the table. She placed the roll on her butter plate. 'Tell us what happened next.'

'I think I'll make a long story short,' said Mr Bridge. 'Briefly, what it amounted to was that this fellow proceeded to offer me a bribe. There, now! You inquire every once in a while about my work, so what do you think of that?'

'Horrendous,' said Carolyn.

He looked at her and firmly shook his head. 'This is not a joke. I was offered money. Two thousand dollars.'

Douglas rocked back in his chair and slapped himself on the face. 'Oy Oy! Two grand!'

'Oh, goodness, that *is* something. I trust you didn't accept,' Mrs Bridge said. And she began buttering the roll.

'I most certainly did not.'

Ruth asked what he was supposed to do in return for the money.

'Grind the face of the poor,' Douglas muttered, and Carolyn jabbed him with her elbow.

'I was asked to do a thing I have not the slightest intention of doing, now or at any time in the future.'

'Uk, yuk, yuk!' said Douglas.

'Mother,' Carolyn said, 'can you please excuse him from the table? Why do we have to put up with him? Daddy's trying to tell us what happened, and this moron keeps interrupting.'

'Ho-ho-ho, who's talking!' Douglas said. 'Old fat frumpy rumpy, in person.'

'We'll have no more of that,' Mrs Bridge said instantly. 'You certainly will be excused from the table.'

Douglas clasped his hands. 'Velly solly, velly solly. Numbel one boy excluse, pliz.'

'Behave yourself,' his mother said. Then she returned the conversation to her husband. 'What a dreadful experience that must have been! You read about these things, but you simply can't imagine them happening.'

Ruth asked if there were any witnesses.

'As far as I know, there were none,' he said.

'How come you didn't take it?' Douglas asked.

Mr Bridge considered his son. Then he said, 'You do not let yourself get mixed up with such people. Not under any circumstances.'

'For two thousand smackeroos? Ho, ho, ho!'

'Explain yourself.'

'Everybody's got his price.'

'Where did you hear that?'

'I don't know. It's true, though. Everybody's got his price. So what's yours? Fifty grand?'

'I have no price. I am not for sale.'

'How about a hundred grand?'

Douglas and his father looked at each other for a long time.

'Holy cats,' Douglas mumbled, 'it was a joke.'

'I don't care for your sense of humor. Hereafter find a more appropriate subject.'

'Solly. Excuse again, pliz.'

63 The dawn patrol

With his friends Tipton and Vandermeer, Douglas went to see *The Dawn Patrol*, and before the movie ended all three of them had sworn to become pilots. It was obvious to them that aviators were in every possible way infinitely superior to other men.

Just two things were required to become pilots: money, of course, for flying lessons, and their parents' permission. After the show they agreed to arrange for these things so they could go to Fairfax Airport the following Saturday to take the first lesson.

As he wandered home Douglas reasoned that if he could get permission he could raise the money. There was not much left of his inheritance from crazy Lulu; however, there were the ten shares of stock in the Kansas City Power & Light Company. That ought to be enough. So the important problem was how to get permission. As he walked from the streetcar line to the house he was arguing aloud with his father. His argument was successful: his father admitted he was right and not only gave permission but offered to pay for the lessons. This was the way the argument ought to go, he could think of no reason it should not go this way; nonetheless, he decided to approach his mother first. She would tell him to speak to his father, because that was how she always responded to certain kinds of questions; just the same it would help if she could be persuaded. And it would make very little difference if she could not be persuaded.

She did not believe he was serious. She told him that if he was still anxious to become a pilot when he was twenty-one years old – well, they could discuss the matter again. He reminded her that he would not be twenty-one for another nine years. She then suggested he talk to his father.

He went outside and climbed a tree in order to meditate. He plucked at the bark and dangled his feet and considered his argument. From where he sat he could see into the study. As usual, his father was at the desk working on some papers and turning the pages of a big book. Without knowing just why, he knew it would be a mistake to suggest selling the Kansas City Power & Light stock to pay for flying lessons. The money must be raised some other way.

After about fifteen minutes he climbed halfway down, dropped the rest of the distance to the ground, landing on all fours, picked himself up, brushed off his pants, and returned to the house.

Mr Bridge listened solemnly to his son's proposition: if he could borrow enough for flying lessons he would repay the money out of his allowance with fifty per cent interest; furthermore, he would get a job raking leaves after school and shoveling snow as soon as it began to snow, so all the money would be paid back very soon. He was talking fast. The first request, which was for permission, had been slipped in as though it was of no consequence, as though both of them understood this permission was going to be granted. The emphasis was on the money.

'Now, what you say is all very interesting,' Mr Bridge remarked when his son stopped talking, 'and I have no doubt you intend to do whatever you promise toward paying me back. But there is another aspect of the situation which perhaps we ought to discuss.'

Douglas attempted to look puzzled.

Mr Bridge leaned back in his chair. He formed a steeple of his fingers and asked: 'How old are you?'

Douglas gestured vaguely. He had been expecting this. He hooked his thumbs in his belt to give himself courage, and he said, 'There's one thing you didn't think about.'

'Which is?'

'If Tipton and Vandermeer and me take flying lessons we can get to be the youngest pilots in the country.'

'I have a bit of sad news,' Mr Bridge said.

'What?'

'You are not going to be the youngest pilot in the country.'

It was all over, of course; he knew he had never had a chance. But because he had nothing further to lose he decided to keep trying. He asked if his father had seen *The Dawn Patrol*. Mr Bridge had not. This answer somehow proved beyond doubt that all was lost. He scratched the back of his neck and took a deep breath. He could not think of anything else to say. He scraped at the rug with his toe.

'Ah,' Mr Bridge said. 'Ah ha! I begin to see.'

'It's about these English guys and these Germans. It's at the Uptown. I thought maybe you saw it.'

'Your mother and I seldom go to movies. When did you see it?'

'I just got back.'

'And it was about airplanes, was it?'

'Yeh, it was about the World War. These guys were dogfighting all over the place, and then this one German guy flew over the field and dropped this other guy's scarf and helmet after he shot him down.'

'It sounds like a good show.'

'Yeh. They had these old rickety crates. But you don't care anything about planes.'

'Why do you say so?'

'Just don't think you do,' Douglas mumbled without lifting his head.

Mr Bridge studied his son for a few moments. 'I have no romance in my soul. Is that what you mean?'

Douglas thrust his hands into his hip pockets. The word 'romance' made him uncomfortable. He said, 'I just asked to take flying lessons is all. I don't see anything wrong with that.'

'There is not a thing wrong with it except your youth. When you are grown you may take all the flying lessons you can stomach. You may discover you don't care much for them. Flying can be an exceptionally disagreeable experience.'

'How would you know?' Douglas demanded. 'What do you know?'

'Let's have a different tone of voice,' Mr Bridge said. 'I didn't like that.'

'I'm sorry,' Douglas said. 'But you don't know the first thing about planes, so how do you know what it's like?'

'I've been up.'

'I don't mean in a big transport. I mean like those planes they had in *The Dawn Patrol*, where they did Immelmann turns and loops and stuff. Being in a transport doesn't count anything. That's about the same as being in some old box-car.'

'That is not what I'm talking about,' Mr Bridge said. 'I went up in a French observation plane.'

Douglas looked to see if his father was telling the truth or joking; when he saw that it was true he was silent with astonishment.

'Oh, yes indeed, I did,' Mr Bridge asserted. 'A young French flying officer took me up. We flew over Paris. As a matter of fact I came very close to losing my life.'

Douglas wiped his nose on the back of his hand to conceal the awe and the amazement he felt.

Mr Bridge went on: 'I can still see the insignia on the fuselage and I can remember the noise of that motor as clearly as though it was yesterday. Shall I tell you about it?'

Douglas nodded.

'Well, it was during the war. I happened to be stationed near an airdrome and I wanted to go for a ride. I had never been off the ground. In those days not many people had. So one morning I bought some cigarettes and hired a taxi to the field and explained what I wanted to one of the French officers who spoke English. He introduced me to this young lieutenant about my own age, who agreed to take me up in exchange for the cigarettes. This young Frenchman didn't speak a word of English, however, and that fact very nearly cost me my life. I was not aware there was such a thing as a safety belt. Or if I did know I must have assumed it wasn't necessary. At any rate, I simply climbed into one cockpit, he climbed into the other, some fellow cranked up the motor, and then we took off. Well, we had no more than gotten off the ground than this French pilot began all sorts of gyrations, apparently trying to give me a good ride. By this time I had realized something was wrong but there was nothing I could do about it. I had no way of telling him I was not buckled in. I had no choice but to hang on to some metal bars in the cockpit and trust to luck. Well, as I say, this Frenchman evidently thought I was enjoying myself, because every time I shouted at him to stop he would do some other trick. He turned that little airplane completely upside down at one point — right over on its back! I don't mind admitting I was scared half out of my wits. I can recall to this day the sight of the Seine River above my head. It was quite an experience, believe you me! I thought my arms were going to be pulled out of their sockets. I'm not going to forget those few moments as long as I live.' Mr Bridge paused, remembering the flight.

Douglas watched him with grave respect.

64 Ground glass

Pat, the Tiptons' Irish setter, ate a ball of raw hamburger mixed with ground glass. Three other dogs in the neighborhood had been killed this way during the past several months, so there was little doubt that whoever was doing it either lived or worked nearby. The police came around and made a show of talking to people and driving back and forth in the patrol car just as they had done on the previous occasions, but then they went away and everybody knew that was the end of the investigation. The setter had been a somewhat raffish individual with an amiable bark that alarmed nobody. It followed the postman every morning and was a well-known dog. There was no reason to kill it.

From time to time the children had pleaded for a dog, but Mr Bridge was reluctant. If a car did not get the animal, distemper would, or something like this. He thought again of the baby chicks that died, and the pet rabbit, and a turtle Douglas had found somewhere and brought home, which crawled around and around the box he put it in and finally died, perhaps from boredom. There had been other little creatures the children insisted on keeping: baby birds that had fallen from the nest, toads, grasshoppers, guppies, and so forth. But one after another they escaped or died. Pets were difficult to keep in a city. So he had resisted whenever they begged for a dog. If a turtle died, or a toad, one could feel a slight regret and that was all. But a dog – if a dog lived with the family for a long time and then was killed, the shock of its death was deep. He remembered the grief he felt as a child when his dog went mad one summer and had to be shot. He did not think the enjoyment of owning the dog compensated for the grief he felt over its death, which he could remember thirty years afterward. He did not want the children to go through the same experience.

And now the Irish setter had been killed. He had petted it and tossed sticks for it to chase, and he was sorry about what had happened but he was not surprised. He shook his head noncommittally when his wife talked about it. She was dismayed and could not imagine why anyone would do such a thing.

He did not try to answer, except to repeat what he had said

before: keeping pets in the city was almost impossible. As to who killed the Tiptons' dog, he had no more idea than the police, so he did not give an opinion, although he suspected it might be one of the Negroes who worked in the neighborhood.

65 Liberal arts

'Oh! I forgot to tell you,' Mrs Bridge remarked. 'Harriet received some awfully exciting news today.' And as Harriet was at that moment serving the mashed potatoes, some acknowledgment was necessary.

'Is that so?' he inquired. 'Well, well, let's hear about this.'

'Actually,' said Harriet, 'it's nothing.'

'Why, it most certainly *is* something,' Mrs Bridge retorted.

'All right, if you must know,' Harriet said while offering the potatoes to Carolyn, 'it's my nephew, Junior Dewes.'

'No more,' Carolyn said.

Harriet gracefully lifted the dish and moved around the table to Ruth.

'No thanks, I'm on a diet,' Ruth said.

She offered the potatoes to Douglas, who began to load his plate for the second time.

'Well, as I was saying to Mrs Bridge earlier this evening, I received this long-distance telephone call placed by my sister Dorothy Dewes at Cleveland, Ohio. She took sick a while back and has felt poorly ever since; however, she seems to be improving somewhat. At least, that is what I am informed.'

Mr Bridge was buttering a biscuit. He said, 'That's fine, Harriet. I'm glad to hear it.'

'Yes, it is good news, of course. However, the news with regard to my nephew is he has become the receivient of a four-year university or college scholarship, whichever he chooses. So you can understand why my sister Mrs Dewes, as well as her husband, was thrilled to death.'

'I should imagine!' Mrs Bridge said enthusiastically, as though hearing about it for the first time. 'And you told me he was applying for admission where?'

'Harvard is the college he wishes to attend. However it is very difficult to be accepted there, so he don't know if they will take him. Though naturally he is extremely hopeful.'

'Harvard?' Mr Bridge asked. 'Harvard is where the boy wants to go to school?'

'Yes. Junior feels it is a school of extremely high quality with good teachers and all that.'

'Oh, I should say!' Mrs Bridge agreed. 'And he intends to study what?'

'The liberal arts. He wishes to get his degree of Bachelor of Liberal Arts.'

'I hope for his sake everything works out,' said Mr Bridge.

'We expect it will, because his grades is the highest that's been recorded in his school at Cleveland since the year 1921.'

'Your nephew must be exceptionally bright, if what you say is true.'

'Oh, yes. Junior was always very intelligent and extremely scholastic. He has been given these various tests they give to prodigal children and he scores very high. He taught hisself to read a little bit when he was six years old.'

Having offered the potatoes to everybody, she then asked if there would be anything else. For the moment nobody wanted anything, so she returned to the kitchen.

Later that evening Mr Bridge wandered restlessly around the bedroom while his wife sat at the dressing table stroking her face with cold cream.

'I didn't realize she had a nephew that old,' he said. 'The boy must be nearly the same age she is.'

'Not quite. Harriet looks younger than she is. She's twenty-four or twenty-five, if I'm not mistaken,' Mrs Bridge answered thoughtfully. 'Of course, I suppose her sister could be any age.'

'There are plenty of decent colored schools.'

'Yes, I imagine,' she said, dipping her fingers into the jar of cream.

'Why doesn't the boy pick one of those schools? Why the devil does he want to go to Harvard?'

'Goodness, I'm not the person to ask,' she replied. She continued stroking the cream on her face. 'But it's hardly a mystery. Harvard is such a fine school.'

'It *is* a fine school. A very fine school. It's a very fine school indeed.'

Because of his tone she paused. She glanced at him in the mirror. 'If Harriet's nephew wishes to attend Harvard don't you think he has every right to?'

'Junior Dewes, or whatever his name is, has the right to apply for admission. He does not necessarily have the "right" to attend Harvard.'

'Well,' she said, 'of course, it isn't up to me. I haven't the faintest idea whether or not they're going to accept him. I suppose that's up to the Board of Trustees, or whoever makes these decisions.'

'If you want my opinion, that boy is asking for trouble. Why does he want to attend Harvard? There have been any number of Negroes who became respected, influential men without going to a white school. Look at George Washington Carver! Look at Booker T. Washington! Lord, these men managed to get a fine education without doing what this boy in Cleveland wants to do.'

She paused again, watching him in the mirror, and finally said, 'I had no idea this would upset you so. I wouldn't have brought up the subject.'

'No good will come of it,' he said as he paced the bedroom pulling at the tassels of his robe.

66 *High school album*

Under the impression that his name must be Solomon, Mrs Bridge brought him a family argument to settle. At considerable length she explained what had happened; even so it was confusing. As nearly as he could discover, Carolyn, without asking permission, had taken a pair of scissors and had clipped a number of pictures out of Ruth's high school annual. Five pictures. Five pictures of one boy. Being presented with the evidence he studied it: five rectangular photographs about the size of a postage stamp featuring a plump, mealy-faced youth with prominent ears and a foxy grin whose name was Hayden Seitz. In each photograph Hayden Seitz was grinning. As Mr Bridge pondered this example of his daughter's taste in young men he began to feel depressed. It was doubtful if a less promising specimen could be found anywhere in the album. All the same, she was infatuated; there was no question of this, because she had mutilated Ruth's book. Ruth was in a rage, having slapped her younger sister; now Carolyn was crying but she too was enraged, not only because of the slap and because Ruth had grabbed her by the hair but because, as Mrs Bridge explained, not satisfied with hair-pulling and slapping, Ruth had called Carolyn 'a dreadful name'. So there was chaos and disorder in the house, as there had been once before when the girls could not abide each other, and he was expected to do whatever ought to be done. It was that simple.

The phrase his wife had used made him curious, though under the circumstances only two or three names seemed likely. He thought about inquiring, but decided not to. After all, the name was irrelevant. What was relevant was that it was dreadful; and from this description he concluded that his wife did not intend to repeat the word aloud. So, with the idea that sometime in the future when all of this had been settled and nearly forgotten he might ask Ruth just exactly what she had called Carolyn, he rocked around in his swivel chair and deliberated. What he must decide was which of them should be punished, and how, or whether both of them deserved punishment. There seemed to be no way out of the situation. His wife had not been able to handle it, and now, because she had let the girls know that she was going to tell their father, they were waiting to see what he would do.

He asked where they were. They were standing in the hall just outside the study. They were not speaking to each other. Carolyn was sniffling. They were waiting to be admitted, each confident of vindication and looking forward to the other's punishment.

Having ordered them brought into the study, he listened to two more accounts of the atrocity committed by Carolyn and the vengeance exacted by Ruth, after which he announced that he did not intend to punish either of them, because they had punished themselves. This thought had come to him while he was listening to their stories, and it pleased him. No doubt Solomon could have done better, but on the whole it was not bad. Not bad at all.

The girls gazed at him doubtfully. They had not expected this. Their case had been carried to the supreme authority in the expectation of a decision which they might accept, or which they might appeal. But the supreme authority had refused to accommodate them: he had returned their sins to them, and the contemplation thereof. They were not sure if they approved of this.

Mr Bridge in his swivel chair, rocking back and forth while his fingers formed a steeple beneath his chin, regarding his truculent, unsatisfied daughters, experienced a moment of epiphany. He had supposed he was being no more than clever, he had thought he was merely extricating himself from an uncomfortable situation when he returned their wrongdoing to them. Instead, he had touched a truth half buried like a root in his path, stumbling over it – the futility of punishment. But at once his instant of enlightenment lay in ashes while logic reasserted itself, pointing out that from the beginning we have believed in punishment, we have ordained it, therefore this precept of society must be valid.

So the vision came but then was gone, and he found himself troubled by a problem far exceeding that of his quarrelling daughters.

67 Moment musicale

Most of the radio programs he enjoyed were conveniently scheduled on Saturday and Sunday evening: Jack Benny, George Burns and Gracie Allen, 'Gang Busters,' 'The Chase and Sanborn Hour' with Don Ameche and Edgar Bergen, 'Amos 'n Andy,' 'The Kraft Music Hall' with John Scott Trotter's orchestra and Bing Crosby, and 'The American Album of Familiar Music' starring Frank Munn. If he and Mrs Bridge had been invited out, he felt mildly resentful because there was nothing he liked better than to relax in the living room after dinner while listening to this familiar and reassuring cycle of programs. Each week there were guest artists: Grace Moore, Deanna Durbin, James Melton, Dennis Day, Jessica Dragonette, Lanny Ross, Rosa Ponselle, John Charles Thomas, Lawrence Tibbett – and he enjoyed them all. They sang 'Bendemeer's Stream' and 'Isle of Capri' and 'Ave Maria' and selections from the famous operettas such as *Blossom Time*, *The Desert Song*, *Naughty Marietta*, *The Chocolate Soldier*, *Roberta*, *The Vagabond King*, and *Sweethearts*. And of all the programs the one he liked best was 'The Bell Telephone Hour', where he could usually count on hearing Nelson Eddy. He thought, and often remarked, that Nelson Eddy had the finest voice he had ever heard. Indeed, 'The Bell Telephone Hour' was so gratifying that at times he had difficulty concealing the emotion he felt.

Slumped in his chair beside the fireplace, he listened without a word, eyes half shut, to the voices soaring from the substantial walnut console. Occasionally he considered writing a letter to let the people in New York know how much he appreciated their program; but the idea of identifying himself to strangers was unacceptable, so he did not write. In the chair, comfortably dressed, sometimes in pajamas and bathrobe and carpet slippers, surrounded by his family after a Sunday-night meal of cold chicken and beer, or, in winter, of homemade chili and scrambled eggs and bacon, he half-slept and listened, unperturbed by anything except the knowledge that after a while the program was going to end. Now and then he opened his eyes and looked at his watch to see how much of the hour remained.

He knew that eventually the hour would end forever. The network might run into financial problems, the show might be canceled for any number of reasons, or somebody might be hired to replace Nelson Eddy. And even if none of these things came to pass, still the hour would end because the children were growing up; they would spend their Sunday evenings elsewhere, so it would not be quite the same.

The first to become restless was Ruth. She examined her fingernails and sucked her lip. Then one evening she excused herself before the program was over, saying she wanted to visit Dodie.

After she left the room he remarked that she seemed to be losing interest in music; but Mrs Bridge said no, quite the contrary, during the past few months Ruth had grown extremely fond of music. She was borrowing records from the school music department; she brought them home and played them in the afternoon, and she was talking about trying out for the chorus.

He asked what sort of records she brought home. Mrs Bridge said they were classical. He asked why Ruth never played them in the evening when he was at home, and she replied that perhaps Ruth was afraid of disturbing him. Nonsense, he said, he would like to hear them. Mrs Bridge said she would mention it.

When Mrs Bridge told Ruth that her father would like to hear some classical music she became excited, and during the next few days she spent hours listening, trying to decide which records to play for him. Her mother reminded her that he seldom stayed up late because he went to work very early and he liked to read in bed for a little while before turning out the light. Because of this she ought not to play many records. If he asked for more, well, that was a different matter.

The following Sunday evening after 'The Telephone Hour', which concluded with a duet from *The Merry Widow*, Ruth began to play the records she had chosen.

Midway through 'Calm Sea and Prosperous Voyage' Douglas got up and walked out.

During the opening bars of 'Eine Kleine Nachtmusik' Carolyn walked out.

Mr and Mrs Bridge, doing their best to remain attentive, sat on the sofa like wax figures. They listened to the overture to *Tristan*. They listened to 'E' grave il sacrifizio'. Next came a sonata for two pianos. Mr Bridge could take no more hammering. 'The Telephone Hour' had been quite satisfying, but this music Ruth played not only bored him, which he could have endured, it picked at him. He had to restrain himself from striding to the phonograph and snapping it off. He placed his hands on his knees to indicate that he was ready to stand up and leave. Then he did stand up.

Ruth had been stretched out like a leopard on the carpet in front of the phonograph. When her father got to his feet she stiffened.

He paused a few seconds to show that he was still listening to the piano sonata. Then he said, 'Well, folks, I've got a full day tomorrow, so I'd better say good night.'

Mrs Bridge put on an expression of concern. 'Oh, must you?'

He laughed. 'Business before pleasure, unfortunately. And Julia expects me in the morning bright and early.'

'Yes, I suppose. You do need some sleep. Well, I'm sure Ruth doesn't mind. Do you, dear?' she asked, smiling at Ruth.

Ruth pretended not to hear. She was turning a knob to adjust the tone.

He felt uncomfortable. He considered sitting down again, but this might make the situation worse. 'Some night when I have time I'd like to hear more,' he said; but Ruth pretended to be unaware of anything except the music, so he affected a yawn, loosened his tie, and added, 'Good night, all.'

'Good night,' Mrs Bridge said. 'I'll be along as soon as this record is over. Unless, of course, Ruth has some others she'd like to play. I'm enjoying them so much.'

'Listen as long as you like,' he remarked affably. His daughter was still ignoring him, so he walked out of the living room and started up the steps. On the landing he paused to wind the grandfather clock, and while he was doing this the sonata ended. He heard his wife say, 'Thank you, dear, it was lovely.' Then Ruth spoke, but too softly to be understood, and her mother replied, 'I'd love to. Right now, though, I'd better sew a few buttons on your Dad's shirts. You know how he is about loose buttons.' Ruth did not say anything else.

He continued to the upper hall, where he stopped to look out the window. The moon was shining through the leaves of the maple tree and the house was quiet.

68 Coppélia

Very seldom did a ballet troupe perform in Kansas City, a situation which Mr Bridge regarded with profound indifference. He had never been to a ballet, he had never considered going to a ballet, and when he chanced to notice in the *Star* that a New York company had scheduled two nights in the municipal auditorium he reflected that they would probably lose money. Not enough people cared for this type of entertainment. He was bemused by the announcement. Whoever was responsible for booking the troupe knew very little about Kansas City.

Several days later it occurred to him that he was continuing to think about the ballet. He asked himself why he had not forgotten it, and he realized that he wanted to do something for Ruth. He did not think he had behaved badly by going to bed before she finished playing her records; even so it had been awkward, and he wanted to make it up to her. Probably she would enjoy seeing a ballet.

When he inquired if she would like to go she gave him a look which stirred him deeply. He felt again as he had felt when he saw her lying in the garden with the morning sun gleaming on her skin.

She would love to go, she told him. Her eyes were radiant. She asked if he would buy tickets for the second night so they could see *Coppélia*. Somewhat puzzled, he agreed. Obviously she had learned something about ballet; he could not imagine how, or when, because as far as he knew it had never been mentioned at home. Perhaps it was being discussed in one of her high school classes.

'What about your mother?' he asked. 'Would she like to go with us?' But he saw the disappointment, and told her they would go by themselves.

The performance was not in the main arena as he assumed it would be, but in one of the small auditoriums ordinarily used for business conventions. The program was shorter than he expected and unlike anything he ever had seen, but he found it rather agreeable. The girls were graceful and attractive with their hair tied in a bun, the music was pleasant, and the costumes and the scenery were quite colorful. The male dancers, however, made him restless. He did not know what attitude to take toward them. They were altogether professional, yet whenever he watched them he felt dissatisfied.

On the way home she wanted to know what he thought of the ballet. He told her he liked it.

He never said anything further about the ballet, but he could not forget those muscular young men bounding around on the stage. Very often he realized that he was thinking about them, and each time this happened he discovered a frown on his face. For young girls to spend their lives dancing seemed perfectly natural, they were charming; and although he did not intend to go to another ballet he admitted that watching them dance around in time to the music had been a pleasure. But the male dancers puzzled him. No doubt they were necessary for the show, and he could not think of any specific reason the young men should not be dancing; all the same he did not quite like it.

69 Hair shirt

Another thing he did not forget about that night at the ballet was the spectacle of Dr Sauer wearing brilliant yellow socks. The psychiatrist had taken a seat in the middle of the first row; there he sat with his legs crossed, and the socks so bright they almost made a noise. They were not merely yellow, they were the yellowest possible yellow. Mr Bridge, who invariably wore black silk socks with garters and black shoes, was astounded but not particularly surprised, because Dr Sauer had turned up in the Terrace Grill of the Muehlebach wearing a green-checked vest with glass buttons, cordovan loafers, striped Italian trousers, and other such items. Frequently he wore a large, loose, blue Spanish beret, which he had bought one summer in Valencia.

During intermission they met in the lobby. Mr Bridge introduced Ruth.

Later she remarked, 'He's mad!' and Mr Bridge laughed because that was his own opinion.

'Did you notice those socks?' he asked.

And Ruth said, 'They're great! I wish you'd wear something jazzy.'

He tried to imagine himself wearing a pair of yellow socks. He could see himself wearing them at home, as a joke, but that was all. He tried to imagine wearing them to the office, and he had no trouble seeing the expression on Julia's face.

Whether it was Ruth's comment or only the sight of the yellow socks, he did not know, but not long after the ballet he found many things reminding him of them. Each time he saw a pair of socks of any color he was reminded of Dr Sauer's socks, or if he saw anything yellow, even a banana. It was annoying. And inevitably, the more he determined to forget them, the more often he discovered himself thinking about them.

In an effort to rid himself of them he thought about them deliberately; and doing so he remembered the psychiatrist commenting at lunch one day that it is not what a man does that he later regrets but what a man has failed to do.

Then it seemed probable to Mr Bridge that Alex Sauer had had a desire for yellow socks and rather than meditate on this he had gone straight out and bought them. Rather than risk some later regret he had simply bought them. There might be some sound psychological principle here. Indeed, he reflected, there might very well be considerable merit in this. He recalled how often he had denied himself some inconsequential object he wanted, denied himself a slight pleasure or satisfaction for no truly reasonable reason but only because his heritage argued against indulgence. Yet how rational was such an argument?

Without confiding to anyone what he had made up his mind to do, he took to pausing in front of shop windows in the hope that he might see something he wanted, which he meant to buy at once. He hoped that when he found the object he was seeking it would not be too expensive, or too ridiculous; however, it should be expensive enough to cause discomfort, and mildly absurd. It should be a thing which previously he would never have considered buying. And still it must be desirable, because this was intended as a little exercise in liberation, not one more punishment.

He looked at fur-lined gloves, suits, neckties, fedoras, and camel's-hair overcoats. He looked at wristwatches that glowed in the dark, unusual cufflinks, stickpins, rings, and jeweled fountain pens. He did not want any of them.

He decided to look for something larger. He began to contemplate sports cars, which were a possibility because they had the advantage of being rather outrageous and yet were recognized as a permissible indulgence, and he found two or three which appealed to him. However, that was a lot of money to invest in what was essentially nothing more than an experiment so he decided not to buy another car.

One more week went by. He felt discouraged and a bit foolish, thankful nobody knew what he was doing. Also, it was galling that after examining most of the merchandise in dozens of store windows he could not find anything he wanted. He began to feel resentful toward Dr Sauer, whose fault this was. The preposterous search was using up time – here a moment, there a moment. He calculated that he had wasted two or three hours.

One day at the Terrace Grill while grinding pepper into his salad he inquired about the yellow socks. What had become of them? Had they been thrown away? No, no, no, the psychiatrist answered as if it were a perfectly natural question, those socks had not been thrown away and if Mr Bridge would like to see more of them he would wear them tomorrow. Mr Bridge said that would not be necessary, he just happened to think of them for some reason, he was merely curious.

On his way back to the office he stopped at Woolf Brothers clothing store and picked out a red-plaid wool shirt which he did not like. He asked the clerk to giftwrap it, and he took it home and after dinner produced it and announced to the family that he had bought himself a present. While everybody watched, he opened the box.

There was not much reaction to the shirt. It was not grotesque. Not at all. His wife remarked that it was quite attractive and as winter was coming on it should be very practical and comfortable to wear around the house or in the yard. He had not expected this. He had thought there would be some laughter; then he himself could join in the fun and explain how he happened to buy it, all because of Dr Sauer's socks, so the entire business could be finished. But because nobody thought the shirt was amusing he could not make a joke of it; he was obliged to pretend he had bought the shirt because he liked it. Carolyn asked him to put it on. He did not want to, but he took it out of the box and went upstairs to the bedroom where he put it on. It scratched.

He wore his new shirt the rest of the evening while he read the *Star* and the *Wall Street Journal* and listened to the radio; and that night he hung it in the closet, knowing that every time he opened the closet door and saw the shirt he was going to be annoyed. He began to estimate how long he must leave it hanging in the closet before he could say he was tired of it and suggest giving it to the Salvation Army.

70 So soon?

Ruth mentioned that she had seen Dr Sauer at the Paseo football game. Mr Bridge asked if she had spoken to him, and she said they had had a long talk after the game.

He was amused. 'Did you indeed? And what have the two of you in common?'

'More than you think,' she replied in a manner he could not interpret.

'What sort of person is he?' Mrs Bridge inquired. 'I've never met him, though I've heard enough tales.'

'He reminds me of an owl,' she said. 'He smokes like a stove and he's totally out of his skull. I mean, really!' Having supplied this description, she added that she thought Dr Sauer probably could dance very well, although she did not explain why she thought so. With a quizzical expression she turned to her father. 'He said something actually sort of weird. He said I was going on a dangerous trip.'

'Pay no attention, the man is eccentric,' Mr Bridge replied.

However, he continued to think about this remark. He was afraid he knew what it meant.

71 Juliet

The high school drama department was planning to present an abbreviated production of *Romeo and Juliet* during the Christmas holidays. Tryouts were soon to be held. Ruth, hopeful of getting the heroine's role, practiced at home, wandering through the house with a tormented expression while reading aloud from *Four Tragedies*. Occasionally she would stop in the front hall before the mirror, fling the hair out of her eyes, catch her lower lip between her teeth, and wrinkle her brow; and after observing herself for quite a long period of time she would continue wandering and reciting.

Douglas mimicked her. She ignored him.

Carolyn went to their mother demanding that she make Ruth quit, because the performance was 'too utterly sickening for words.' But Mrs Bridge, pleased that Ruth finally had decided to take part in some school activity, refused to interefere.

Ruth sometimes passed through the kitchen wearing one of her Juliet expressions and went out the back door and toured the yard while Harriet, vastly entertained, smothered her face in her hands.

Mr Bridge kept silent. If Ruth wanted to try out for the play, all right, or if she did not, all right. He agreed with Harriet that she looked ridiculous walking back and forth in the yard reciting Shakespeare, and probably the neighbors were talking; however, it was none of their business, and besides, it was normal for a girl of Ruth's age to behave melodramatically. He doubted she would get the part. He had not read the play since he was in school, he had not much cared for it then and had not looked at it again, but he recalled a certain simplicity underlying the florid romanticism of Juliet which was not in the least like Ruth. Still, he wanted her to win the role. Often he listened and watched while she was practicing.

Suddenly one night, as though she knew how he felt, she asked if he would read the part of Romeo, and without hesitation he agreed. Carolyn groaned, Mrs Bridge began applauding, and Douglas, who had been reading *Model Airplane News*, promptly fell out of his chair and sprawled on the carpet clutching at his heart.

After a lengthy conference between the principals as to which speeches were to be read and which omitted, they took their places, facing each other in front of the fireplace, Harriet was invited in from the kitchen, and Mrs Bridge snapped off the overhead light.

Mr Bridge adjusted his glasses and cleared his throat. With *Four Tragedies* opened at page forty-two he began to read, running his index finger along the lines: 'He jests at scars that never felt a wound. What light through yonder window breaks? It is the east, and Juliet is the sun. Arise, fair sun, and kill the envious moon, who is already sick and pale with grief, that thou her maid are far more fair than she. Be not her maid, since she is envious. Her vestal livery is but sick and green, and none but fools do wear it. Cast it off. It is my lady. O, it is my love.'

'Aye me!' Ruth cried, stepping forward.

'She speaks,' Mr Bridge said. 'Oh, speak again, bright angel. Now,' he continued in the same tone, 'am I to read the remainder of this passage or not?'

'No,' Ruth said. 'That's another place where Mr Billis decided to cut. It's supposed to be marked. Let me see.'

He handed the book to her. They consulted again. The reading resumed.

'O Romeo, Romeo! Wherefore art thou Romeo? Deny thy

father! And refuse thy name, or if thou wilt not, be but sworn my love, and I'll no longer be a Capulet!'

'Shall I hear more?' Mr Bridge inquired. 'Or shall I speak at this?' He cupped one hand behind his ear.

Ruth moaned and swayed. 'O 'tis but the name that is my enemy! O, be some other name!'

'I take thee at thy word.'

She stepped away from him. She tossed her hair and sighed. 'My ears have not yet drunk a hundred words of thy tongue's uttering! Yet I know the sound! Art thou not Romeo and a Montague? How camest thou hither, tell me? And wherefore? The orchard walls are hard to climb!'

Mr Bridge frowned at the next lines. 'With love's light wings did I over-perch these walls.'

Douglas made a strangling noise; Mrs Bridge reached down and tapped him on the shoulder.

'By whose direction found'st thou out this place?'

'By love, that first did prompt me to inquire. He lent me counsel and I lent him eyes.'

'Dost thou love me? O, gentle Romeo, if thou dost love, pronounce it faithfully.'

'Lady, by yonder blessed moon I vow, that tips with silver all these fruit-tree tops.'

'O, swear not by the moon, the inconstant moon, that monthly changes in her cycled orb, lest that thy love prove likewise variable.'

'According to my copy, that word is "circled" rather than "cycled".'

'Go on!' cried Ruth. 'Oh, go on! Go on!'

'All right. Let me see, now,' Mr Bridge said, hunting for his place. 'Ah, here we are. After "likewise variable" Romeo speaks again: What shall I swear by?'

'Do not swear at all! Or, if thou wilt, swear by thy gracious self, which is the god of my idolatry! And I'll believe thee.'

'If my heart's dear love—'

'Well, do not swear. Good night. Good night! I hear some noise within.' She leaned toward the fireplace as though listening, then straightened up with an agonized expression and said, 'Stay but a little while. I will come again.'

'Ruth, that was awfully nice,' Mrs Bridge said.

Ruth said desperately, 'Mother, it's not over!' and brushing the hair out of her eyes she pretended to be staring down from the balcony. 'Three words, dear Romeo, and good night indeed! If that thy bent of love be honorable, thy purpose marriage, send me word tomorrow, by one that I'll procure for thee – I mean, procure to come to thee, where and what time thou wilt perform the rite, and all my fortunes at thy foot I'll lay, and follow thee my lord throughout the world. Romeo!'

'My dear?'

'At what o'clock tomorrow shall I send to thee?'

'At the hour of nine.'

'I will not fail! Good night, good night! Parting is such sweet sorrow that I shall say good night till it be morrow!'

'Sleep dwell upon thy eyes, peace in thy breast,' Mr Bridge recited, and closed the book. 'Would I were sleep and peace, so sweet to rest.'

In the lamplight Ruth was gazing up at him, but he saw that she did not recognize him. Her eyes were luminous, her lips carried a sensual smile. She hardly seemed to breathe. He was alarmed, and wondered who she thought he was. He had listened to the alien words she spoke and he had responded to them, yet never believed their meaning; now she was possessed, in his image, by the soul of a man who lived four centuries ago.

72 Tijuana

Ruth asked to borrow two hundred and fifty dollars. She would not say why she wanted the money. He refused to consider giving it to her without first knowing why she wanted it. At last she said one of her girlfriends was flying to Tijuana and needed company. He said he would not let her have the money. Then he inquired, jokingly, why her friend wished to go to Tijuana, and Ruth answered that her friend was going to have an abortion. Before he knew what he was about to do he jumped up from behind the desk and slapped her across the mouth; then he sat down again as though nothing had happened, and Ruth walked out of the study. He noticed with astonishment that the hand which had slapped her was dancing around on the desk as if it was attached to a string. He seized it with his other hand and bowed his head. He could not believe he had struck her. His fingers burned at the memory. When she was a baby he had held her in his arms while she was falling asleep. There were nights when nothing more than the knowledge of her existence had been enough to waken him so that he had gotten out of bed and gone to the crib to watch over her.

73 Marijuana

Shortly before ten o'clock on Harriet's night off the telephone rang. Moments later Mrs Bridge entered the living room with a worried expression. 'For you,' she said. 'Somebody by the name of Lieutenant Adessi.'

Mr Bridge abruptly lowered the newspaper. Adessi was on the narcotics squad.

'I believe that was the name,' she said, clasping her hands. 'Don't you know him?'

'Yes, I know him.'

'You seem surprised.'

He got up without answering and went to the telephone.

'Sorry to bother you,' the officer said.

Mr Bridge waited.

'You employ a Miss Harriet Rodgers?'

'Go on.'

'She was picked up a short while ago.'

'I appreciate you calling me. I'll be there in twenty minutes.'

When he returned to the living room Mrs Bridge remarked, 'You just wonder why people telephone at this time of night.' But then she noticed his face. 'Oh, dear, was it important?'

'I'll be going out for a while,' he said, and went to the hall closet for his hat and coat.

Harriet had been crying. Her features were puffy, her make-up was smeared, and she resumed crying the instant she saw him. He ordered her to get control of herself, which she did, but she broke down again an hour later on the way home. Sniveling and choking with emotion, she continued to insist that she had been an innocent bystander, a victim of circumstances, it was all a terrible mistake, the whole affair was Couperin's fault, and so on and so forth.

Mr Bridge listened to as much of this as he cared to, and while they were driving out Pershing Road he told her there was no point in discussing it any further. 'I do not want to hear any more,' he said. 'I believe I can manage to get you out of this, so you may as well stop blubbering. But I am not going to bat for this man you chase around with. He will have to pay for his foolishness. I refuse to get myself involved any further. And I want you to remember,' he added, shaking a finger at her, 'I have placed myself in a position I dislike. I dislike it very much indeed. Should anything of this nature happen again, ever, you are through. Is that clear?'

She assured him it would not happen again. Then she went on with a sanctimonious air, 'That Couperin, I could just kill him. As far as I personally am concerned he ought to be locked up in jail the rest of his days. Trouble is his middle name.'

Mr Bridge was disgusted by her fickleness. Not two hours earlier she had been very much a part of Couperin's big evening.

'It was on account of that automobile,' she said as though reminiscing about a vacation. 'Since he got hisself that Pontiac he is just plain uncontrollable. You'd think a person would learn, finally. Not him, though. Well, at least I am glad to say I surely have learned my lesson.'

'I hope you have,' Mr Bridge said.

They drove through Penn Valley Park and up Broadway and she was all right, but then she started to sniffle.

'Now, you stop,' he said. 'I have had more than enough.'

'Feel so ashamed.'

'It has been disagreeable and humiliating for us both.'

She sobbed into her handkerchief. 'That Couperin.'

In a voice that was almost a shout Mr Bridge said: 'Shut up!' which was an expression he had not used for many years.

As they were turning into the driveway she wiped her nose, coughed rather delicately, and fluffed her hair with her fingertips. Evidently she was getting organized for an appropriate entrance, in case Mrs Bridge or the children should be in the kitchen to greet her.

'I wish to thank you again,' she said.

'All right,' he answered, guiding the Chrysler into the garage.

'I frankly do not know what might have become of me in that there police station without assistance.'

'I could tell you.'

'As you know, this was my first police experience. However, they were very nice and gentlemanly, I must say.'

'Let's hope this is your last experience with the police.'

'I'm perfectly sure it will be,' she said. 'Somehow they do leave a person mortified to death.' Then, having once more touched up her hair, she inquired: 'Shall we go in?'

74 The primrose path

During the holiday season Harriet was observed to put away several daiquiris, and Mrs Bridge was of the opinion that she was becoming much too fond of them. Mr Bridge answered that an occasional snort was not going to do her any harm. If she had taken this many years to get around to it she was not apt to become an alcoholic.

But Mrs Bridge said, 'I believe I'll speak to her. I found two glasses on the drainboard the other day. I think two in one day is one too many.'

He slipped an arm around her waist and suggested they stop worrying. The idea of Harriet drinking too much amused him, and the next time he saw her with a daiquiri he told her that she had better have another because nobody can walk on one leg.

75 Harriet's system

After being warned by Mrs Bridge, Harriet resolved to quit drinking. Mrs Bridge had not spoken severely, nor even pointedly, yet there could be no mistake, it was a warning. Furthermore, it was humiliating. Not more than that, but it certainly was humiliating. She did not think her position was in danger, she had been employed too many years to be dismissed lightly; she was sure they knew this. However, a word to the wise was sufficient.

Some time went by while she considered the best way to stop, and finally she decided that instead of giving up the daiquiris all at once she should give them up gradually in order to avoid a shock to her system. She felt that her system had become accustomed to a daiquiri or so every now and again. A suitable program should be to leave a few sips in the glass, and leave a few more sips each time. That would be easy, and the body fluids would not be disturbed and remorseless. She devised this program one stormy Tuesday night while doing the dishes. Mr and Mrs Bridge had gone to a party at the Lutweilers and would not come home until late. Ruth was visiting Dodie. Carolyn was in the basement. Douglas had gone to his Scout meeting.

She began to sing. One song after another came into her head. She sang 'Ananias' and 'Standing in the Need of Prayer' and 'Ezekiel Saw the Wheel'. Lightning flashed, thunder rolled, windowpanes rattled. Rain poured against the side of the house. She sang 'Just a Closer Walk with Thee' and 'Jacob's Ladder' and 'Blessed Assurance' and 'Wade in the Water' and 'Precious Lord' and 'There Is Balm in Gilead'. Feeling a bit exhausted by so much song, she decided to refresh herself with a daiquiri. Then she resumed singing, and she sang until midnight.

76 Witch doctor

Dr Sauer was at the Lutweiler party wearing his yellow socks, and as his trousers were cut two inches short the yellow socks could be seen drifting here and there as though they possessed a life of their own.

'I don't understand that man,' said Mr Bridge. 'I do not for the life of me understand that fellow.'

Mrs Bridge, trying to defend him, suggested that perhaps short trousers and bright socks were the style in Europe.

'And what about the girl he's with? This Genevieve, or whatever her name is.'

'She must be his daughter, don't you suppose?'

'His daughter is back East at some boarding school. Who in the name of all that's holy this girl is, I have no idea.'

Before the party was over they found out. Genevieve was a student at the Kansas City Art Institute. Genevieve, unable to put up with life in Chillicothe, unable to live with her father because he owned a hardware store and with her mother because she was her mother, had fled to Kansas City, where the streets were paved with gold and a girl could study art without being nagged about it and nagged about marrying Howard Bagley. Howard Bagley thought the hardware business had a great future. Genevieve revealed all. She announced that she had been a mess when somebody told her about Dr Alexis Sauer. Now everything was fine.

On the way home Mr Bridge said, 'Well, I warned you about Alex. Take him as he is, or not at all.'

'Oh, I found him awfully entertaining,' she said. 'His face reminds me of someone, though I can't think who.'

'Lenin, that's who.'

Mrs Bridge was startled.

'That's who it is,' he said. 'Everybody notices it, and they never can think who he looks like. But that's who. In my opinion he cultivates the resemblance deliberately, Lord knows why.'

Mrs Bridge said, 'I'm sure he wouldn't do that.'

'I'm sure he would.'

A few minutes later she said, 'I just wonder if he'll be happy with someone that age.'

'I doubt very much indeed if he's planning to marry that girl.'

'Oh, really? Well, I suppose he can't be blamed for not wanting to rush into a second marriage. They say his wife was impossible.'

'I never met the woman. I don't see how she can be any more impossible than he is.'

'They must have been quite a pair. The *Star* certainly made hay out of the divorce proceedings.'

He did not answer. The divorce had been uglier than most. He did not want to discuss it.

'Madge was telling me she heard he cared more for his art collection than for his wife. I suppose it must be quite extensive.'

'Alex travels a great deal. I expect he's picked up things from various countries.'

'Apparently the Lutweilers have been quite close. Helen was

telling me the Sauers' house was simply crammed with art objects of every description.'

He suspected that for some reason she wanted to become better acquainted with the psychiatrist. Sauer was a pudgy, balding little man with a noticeable cast in one eye and moist lips the colour of fresh liver. He should not be interesting to women, yet his former wife was beautiful and now there was this pretty young girl, Genevieve. He recalled, too, hearing the wives of other men discuss Alex Sauer with obvious fascination. It did not make sense.

'Madge tells me he's considered one of the most briliant analysts in the country.'

Mr Bridge did not say anything.

'He *is* clothes-conscious,' she remarked a trifle critically, but at the same time there was approval in her voice.

He thought about the psychiatrist's clothes. The gaudy vests with glass buttons were almost insulting. The European suits and the shoes with crepe soles. The Tyrolean hat he frequently wore as though he was vacationing in downtown Kansas City. The Spanish beret. It seemed to Mr Bridge that all of this was an affectation. He shook his head resentfully. The flamboyant apparel exemplified the mistrust he felt for psychiatrists and for their profession, which was not far removed from the absurdities of fortune telling, astrology, ecclesiastic ritual, and lucky dice.

77 Happy Easter

Easter weekend Dr Sauer and Genevieve flew to New Orleans to amuse themselves, and they did not return to Kansas City until the following Thursday. He telephoned his office Monday morning to cancel the appointments for that day, he telephoned again that night to cancel the Tuesday appointments. He telephoned again to cancel everything on Wednesday.

Mr Bridge, hearing about this, was exasperated. No professional man was entitled to behave in such a fashion. Nobody with any self-respect could jeopardize his reputation by flying to New Orleans with a woman who was not his wife. If he did, he should be discreet, and he certainly should return in time for his Monday appointments.

Secondly, it was rumored that he had gotten into a card game and had won twelve hundred dollars. Mr Bridge did not altogether believe this rumor. Very possibly Sauer had gotten into a card game, in fact it was probable. Being as clever as he was, he might well have won some money, but not twelve hundred dollars. Conceivably, he had won fifty dollars or so, and the story had grown as such stories do. Given a little more time, the figure would be twelve thousand.

Mr Bridge discovered that he was more outraged by the gambling than by the fact that Dr Sauer had taken the girl along. It was wrong to have taken this girl to New Orleans, it was irresponsible, he should not have done it; but twelve hundred dollars, if true, was as much as some men earned in a year.

Dr Sauer, like a good gambler, would not say yes nor would he say no when asked about this famous excursion. He laughed and he laughed. Mr Bridge, listening, glanced across the table at Virgil Barron with a look of inquiry, on the chance that Sauer might have made a large deposit in the bank: very greatly to his astonishment he met the banker's eye. So it was true. Then Mr Bridge joined the conversation for the first time.

'Well, Alex, regardless of whether you did or did not win, if you enjoyed yourself, that's what matters.'

'Jesus Christ, Walter,' the psychiatrist snapped, 'You can be so God damned stuffy.'

'My guess is that none of us is quite what he might choose to be. Call it a defect, if you will. It's simply that I happen to subscribe to certain fundamental truths.'

'Gamblers always lose? Would that be a fundamental truth?'

'In my opinion, sooner or later they do.'

Dr Sauer reached for the wine bottle and said that in his opinion, the later the better.

'Since I amuse you,' said Mr Bridge, 'go ahead. Gamble at cards or on horses or anything else. Behave as you please. Far be it from me to lay down the law for other men. As far as gambling is concerned, I feel under no compulsion to shut down the card games and racetracks and the rest of it. Free enterprise, even for such a borderline industry, is one of the cornerstones of this country, and it appears to me that a degree of license is advisable. A man ought to be allowed to do as he wills, so long as he does not infringe upon the rights and liberties of others. However, if you gamble, be prepared to accept the consequences. And I do happen to believe you will lose, should you decide to tempt fate again. Assuming you did win a certain amount on your trip to New Orleans, I say more power to you. But you have entered a fool's paradise. The law of averages exacts its toll. Whoever gambles is a fool — a fool! Make no mistake about it.'

His voice had been rising while he spoke. At nearby tables people were beginning to turn around. He noticed this and stopped. He removed his glasses, polished them on his napkin, and continued eating lunch.

78 Bawdy story

Out of a sense of propriety women were seldom discussed at the round table; nor was religion discussed, because nobody was interested; nor politics, because this led to arguments. But one day the psychiatrist told a joke about a girl from Chihuahua. Everybody laughed except Mr Bridge. Simon Lutweiler asked if he had heard the joke, but Dr Sauer interrupted:

'Walter would cut his throat before he'd laugh at a dirty joke.'

'I confess I have never been able to find anything amusing about smut,' said Mr Bridge.

'Have you tried?' asked Dr Sauer, and once again everybody laughed except Mr Bridge.

79 Wild party

Possibly inspired by the success of their New Orleans trip, Genevieve and Dr Sauer moved into an apartment building on a hill overlooking the Plaza and soon afterward announced that they were holding open house. When asked if she would care to attend this event Mrs Bridge replied that she would not miss it for the world.

'Lord only knows what it's going to be like,' he told her. 'I expect half of Kansas City will be there.'

And so it seemed when they arrived. They could hear the noise before they got out of the elevator.

'It sounds like pandemonium,' she remarked, adjusting her silver-fox stole.

'Don't say I didn't warn you. This fellow likes to put on a show. I have no idea what we're getting into.'

Mrs Bridge smiled and insisted she was looking forward to it.

Nobody greeted them at the door, but the door was wide open and since it was ridiculous to stand there ringing the bell they walked in. They could not get in very far because of the crowd. The air was warm and smoky and at first they thought something was on fire. Leading his wife by the hand, Mr Bridge pushed ahead and found their host playing the drums while the drummer had a drink. Somewhat later they had a chance to talk to him. And, after a while, they belonged to the party and found many people they knew. The Arlens were there and the Montgomerys were there. Avrum Rheingold was there eating and drinking everything in sight. He mentioned a nice little company, the Poseidon Corporation based in Tampa, Florida, selling sea horses by the thousands. This little company was growing like a beanstalk. Avrum Rheingold hinted it could be worthwhile to meet for lunch one day.

The Hodges were there with a lady from New Zealand who did not stop talking. Dr Foster was there, a drink in his hand, chuckling genially at whatever was said. The Koeppels and the Lutweilers were there. Mabel Ong in her familiar tweed suit, with a volume of poetry under her arm as usual. The Ralph Porters just back from another European vacation; they had not cared very much for Denmark. Grace and Virgil Barron were there. Edith and Leo Snapper appeared; however, they were difficult to talk to. Her imperial manner and her royal coiffure disconcerted Mrs Bridge, and there was something furtive about Leo Snapper which Mr Bridge disliked. The Beckerle sisters arrived in ancient beaded velvet gowns which looked as though they had been packed in a trunk for half a century, and Judge Chisholm stopped by for a little while.

But by far the majority of the guests at the open house were strangers.

'Well! That was a three-ring circus if ever I saw one,' she remarked while they were driving home. 'My word, it was a struggle to turn around.'

'Great God, that music,' he said, shaking his head in disbelief. 'It sounded like a traffic jam. Horns blowing all over the place. I don't see how a person can enjoy that.'

'I agree one hundred per cent, but I suppose some people must like it. Otherwise they wouldn't listen. However, it certainly was bedlam. I did like some of his "objects d'art" though, didn't you?'

'Nothing I'd care to put in our living room.'

'Oh, well, neither would I. But I thought some of it was intriguing. Grace and I visited the Nelson Gallery last week, and several of Dr Sauer's things reminded me of paintings and sculpture we saw in the gallery.'

'You can have the whole bunch, and welcome to them. He must have invested a small fortune in that stuff. I wouldn't profess to know why. It's beyond me.'

'I'm not defending everything he has, but I do think it would be good for you to take an interest in art.'

'If half that junk Alex has collected is "art" I'm a Fiji Islander. Any time you want to go look at it you're free to call up Alex or his little friend. They'd probably be delighted to give you the grand tour. So help yourself. But if you want my opinion, the children did better when they were five years old. Any one of them could paint a better picture right now than most of the stuff Alex has hanging on the wall. I don't pretend to be a connoisseur of art. I never have. I don't care for it very much, and Lord knows I haven't the time, but I'm not afraid to say what I think. And I think most of that stuff is junk, junk pure and simple. So there you are.'

'My word, you sound so provoked!'

'Furthermore, I don't believe he likes the stuff either. In my opinion it's all a pretense, right along with his checkered vests and Italian suits and the rest of that nonsense. That's why I sound "provoked", as you call it. Lord, if he had a Rembrandt or one of those Dutch sitting rooms where the people are recognizable human beings I could see the point of paying good money. But this African primitive business and these surrealist or cubist schools, or whatever they're called nowadays – it's too much for me, I tell you. And I'm willing to bet you a dollar to a doughnut that fifty years from today you won't find hide nor hair of it.'

'I feel the same way,' Mrs Bridge said. 'My only point was that I did find it interesting for a change.'

'Suit yourself. Any time you want to look at it, call up Alex. You and Grace Barron hop right over there and admire it to your heart's content. One more thing – those Negroes. There's another example for you: he invited those people for one reason, and one reason only.'

'You know perfectly well they're friends of his.'

'I know they are. But I also know he invited them because they're black.'

'Now, Walter, that simply is not fair. You can't possibly know he invited them for that reason.'

'As you like. As you like,' he replied in an uncompromising voice.

'They didn't bite anybody.'

'I have not criticized those people in any way. I am talking about Alex. And the next thing you know, he'll be inviting them to lunch at the Muehlebach.'

'I doubt if he'd go that far.'

'You don't know the man. I do.'

'I scarcely know him at all. Perhaps you're right. In any case, I am awfully glad we went to the affair. And if you'd acted a bit more sociable you might have had a good time yourself.'

'I did have a good time,' Mr Bridge said. 'I don't need to trot around shaking hands with every Tom, Dick and Harry in order to prove it.'

'I know, but you see so much of Stuart and Virgil and the other men that I should think this would have been an opportunity to meet somebody new.'

He replied that he knew more than enough people already.

80 Wastebaskets

That summer Ruth applied for a job with a local company called Blissco, which produced an assortment of household and office novelties. The founder and president of this company was a young man named Harry Bliss, who hired Ruth as soon as he saw her. When he discovered that she could not take shorthand and could barely operate a typewriter he put her to work painting phoso-phorescent floral designs on wastebaskets, an item he invented at that moment.

Her parents were pleased that she had found a job, because they had expected her to spend the summer as usual, tanning herself beside the pool at the country club and loitering with Dodie in a booth at the Walgreen drugstore. They agreed the job would be good for her. She did not like to work, she had never done much work of any sort. She slept late and always seemed to be lying around the house.

From what she told him about the company Mr Bridge surmised that Blissco might not last very long, but if it was able to pay her salary every week he could see no harm in allowing her to paint wastebaskets. If Carolyn had taken such a job he would have been impatient, but Ruth did not have Carolyn's brains. Of course it was absurd that anybody should spend a summer decorating wastebaskets; however, it would keep her occupied, and as he thought of the way men must look at her he concluded that it might be prudent to keep her in an office where she was more or less out of sight. She was now seventeen, and he did not like to consider what might happen. She lacked not only the intelligence but the armor of Carolyn, who, at fifteen, already had learned to defend herself like a porcupine.

Ruth spoke constantly and rather foolishly about her job – what a marvelous company it was, how lucky she was that Mr Bliss had given her a job in spite of her inexperience, how brilliant he was, and of the opportunity it offered to begin a career as a commercial artist. But one afternoon when the temperature downtown rose to ninety-eight degrees and Julia had an attack of nerves and dizziness Mr Bridge decided to quit work earlier than usual; when he got home he discovered Ruth lying on the porch swing, wearing shorts and a halter. She was reading a movie magazine. He could not understand why she was there instead of at work, so he asked what she thought she was doing. She squinted up at him as though this question did not make sense. He asked why she was not on the job. She scratched her breast and answered that she had quit several days ago.

'I thought you knew,' she added. 'Didn't Mother tell you?'

Nobody had told him. He sat down, laid his briefcase across his knees, loosened his collar, and took out a handkerchief to wipe his forehead. Ruth had placed the electric fan on the table beside the swing where she could get the benefit of it, otherwise there was no breeze at all. The sun was blazing. The grass in the yard smelled like hay. The birds and the locusts were silent. The entire neighborhood was silent. Nothing moved. He could almost hear the roaring of the sun. He had no sooner patted his forehead than it felt damp again. 'Now, what is all this?' he demanded. 'Start from the beginning. Do you or do you not have a job?'

Ruth dropped one bare foot to the floor and gave the swing a leisurely push. He observed that she had painted her toenails, and apparently she had been shaving her legs because there was a patch of adhesive tape on her shin. Her indolence was exasperating.

'You have quit, I take it. Did you quit merely because you happened to feel like quitting? Am I entitled to quit because there are times I would rather loiter on the swing and drink lemonade?'

'It's so hot,' she murmured. 'Let's not squabble. Ask Mother if you want to know why I quit.'

'I am asking you, not your mother. And I want an answer, and I want an answer fast. Do you hear?' Everything about the day had been unsatisfactory, and her attitude was the culmination of it. She was lounging around the house two-thirds naked; she knew what he thought of this, yet there she lay – idly swinging herself, sipping lemonade, and reading a movie magazine.

'Do you hear?' he repeated. 'I am talking to you. I have had just about enough for one day.' His heart was beginning to flutter. He frowned and slipped one hand inside his coat.

Ruth was almost wallowing in the swing while the breeze from the electric fan swept across her body. She continued sipping lemonade through a green straw. Her eyes were nearly shut. A drop of water wriggled down the side of the glass and plopped on her stomach.

'If you must know,' she murmured with a foolish smile, 'Mr Bliss was always – well, it's just too gruesome to try to explain. I mean, you can get mad at me if you want to, but I actually don't think you'd want me to keep on working there. I mean, really, I don't think I should.'

Mr Bridge considered this information for a few moments. Then he said, pointing to the lemonade pitcher, 'Suppose you pour me a glass of that while I take a shower and change clothes.'

81 The laborers

That summer another member of the family concluded it might be time to go to work. Douglas, either bored with life at the country club or stimulated by his elder sister's example, went out one Saturday morning to look for a position suiting his talents, came home late in the afternoon, located his parents in the back yard, and announced that on Monday he was starting to work as a garbage man. Then he began dancing back and forth as though he was in vaudeville, lifted his baseball cap, and bowed.

Mr Bridge, who was worried about the condition of the yard which was thick with dandelions and crab grass, was not sure he had heard his son correctly. 'Stop prancing around,' he said.

Douglas clutched his heart and collapsed on the lawn.

'All right, now. Behave yourself,' his mother said.

He sat up, put his cap on backward, and explained that he had gotten a job as a helper. He would be paid three dollars a day and would be given his lunch. Ordinarily a route took eight hours, he said, but with a fast driver, if everybody on the truck worked hard, a route could sometimes be finished in five hours. So he might earn a full day's pay in five hours. How many jobs were like that?

Mr Bridge asked what his duties would be. Douglas replied that he would follow the men while they were emptying the cans and clean up whatever they spilled.

'Oh, well, I just don't know about this,' said his mother, who had been listening uneasily.

Mr Bridge agreed. He told Douglas he would have to find another job. Douglas promptly flung his arms wide apart to indicate despair.

'For the love of Mike, why? I mean, why? I mean, what's the matter? I don't get it!'

'I don't want you to come home smelling like a pig.'

'So we're too ritzy to let me work on a garbage truck?'

'Not at all,' Mr Bridge said with a thin smile. 'I have done manual labor myself. From the time I was old enough to know what money was I knew that if I wanted it I had to earn it. My parents never had enough to give me an allowance. You don't know how lucky you are. And, as a matter of fact, there were plenty of times when I was a kid that it never occurred to me to keep what I earned. I handed it over to my parents without question so they could buy enough to keep us alive. You seem to be under the impression that because we live in a decent neighborhood and have plenty to eat I do not know what poverty is all about. Nothing could be further from the truth. I tell you this: I *do* know it. I know the smell of it and the sight of it and the anxiety of it firsthand, and I thank the good Lord that you and your sisters and your mother have had no such experience. I hope you never know what it means, because it is not very pleasant. It is not fun. It is not amusing. I do not look down on laboring men. We are not too "ritzy", as you express it, for you to work on a garbage truck this summer. However, there are other jobs available. You will have to find something else. You may take any sort of work you wish to, provided it is legal and reasonably clean. I do not mean you cannot get your hands dirty, but there is no necessity for you to clean sewers or pick up garbage.'

Mr Bridge paused; but then he continued, moved by the memory of things he had not thought about for a long while: 'I used to get up before dawn to work on an ice wagon pulled by a couple of old broken-down nags. Lord, I'll never forget. I worked until time to go to school. And I don't mind letting you know it was not very agreeable chipping and carrying ice at five or six o'clock on a January morning with the snow coming down in blankets and a north wind howling. To this day I remember the sight of my fingers

354

raw and bleeding. And many's the morning I sat down at my school desk with my fingers too stiff to hold a pencil. That was no fun, let me tell you, but I did it without complaint. I never thought I was too "ritzy" for hard work. Never. As Abraham Lincoln once observed: "I am not ashamed to confess that twenty-five years ago I was a hired laborer".'

Douglas was bored.

'All right, I won't lecture you. Go out and find yourself a job. It's what you need. But you are not going to work on a garbage truck. Is that clear?'

'Right-o,' Douglas answered with heavy sarcasm.

Mr Bridge gave him one brief, significant look to indicate that he had heard this and did not want to hear any more. Douglas shambled into the house to telephone his regrets to the garbage men.

Mr Bridge resumed his survey of the weeds in the yard.

But while he contemplated the dandelions his thoughts went back to the time he had been working on the ice wagon. He thought of the black-leather vest which buckled at the waist and hung down almost to his knees like a garment from the Middle Ages, and the iron tongs, the rag he strapped across his shoulder so the cakes of ice would not be quite so painful, the grizzled old man whipping the struggling horses up the wintry hills, the bumping wagon, the dampness, and the sleet bouncing off the long blocks of ice. He lifted his right hand and considered the palm. He rubbed his thumb across his palm where the calluses used to be. Now the hand was as soft as the hand of a surgeon.

82 Bleh!

A few days later Douglas reported that he had a job in the produce department of Horkey's Grocery. He was to run errands for the produce manager, sweep the floor, keep the vegetable bins stocked, spray the lettuce, shuck the corn, and so forth. It was legal, it was reasonably clean.

Before long everybody was sick of hearing about life in the produce department, and the threatening figure of the produce manager appeared regularly at the dinner table.

'I mean, and that's just a single little example,' said Douglas one evening after a lengthy account of the boorishness, lack of imagination, stinginess, unintelligence, and hypocrisy of the produce manager. 'What I mean is, well, listen, like today for instance, you know, we get this great huge shipment of lemons, see. Really, there was about ten billion lemons, at least. So anyhow this imbecile manager decides he better do something fast, because they're just sitting there blocking traffic, and he can't think of anything better so he decides to make somebody take them out of the crates and put them in littler boxes, so naturally I happen to be the first poor sucker he catches sight of, so he has me sorting these lemons for about a thousand hours. I almost didn't get any lunch. I'm just sorting these lemons from about nine o'clock this morning, see? Well, and so anyhow after a while this dumb cluck can't figure out anything to do himself, so he naturally has to stand around watching me. There's this waste barrel, see, where the bad fruit goes. The rotten fruit you throw away because you can't sell it and if you leave it in with the other stuff, why, pretty soon the rest of it gets rotten.'

'Come to the point,' his father said.

'I am, for gosh sakes. If you'll just let me finish. I was just about to tell you what happened. So I'm there sorting these lemons and naturally I throw some of them away, so this produce manager comes marching over and picks up one of them I just dumped in the waste barrel and he says I just threw away the day's profit! He wasn't kidding, either. That's really what he said. He said "You threw away the day's profit". I thought he was kidding.' Douglas looked at his father to gauge the effect of this information.

Mr Bridge looked around the table to see if anyone was ready for another piece of chicken.

'Anyhow, this lemon I threw away had a lot of white mold all over it, so nobody was going to buy it, that's a cinch. Not exactly all over, I guess actually it wasn't as bad as some of them, but it was going to get rotten in another day or two, so that's how come I threw it away. But this dumb cluck practically has to hit the ceiling. He goes marching around like Captain Bligh just holding this lemon up between two fingers for everybody in the produce department to look at, like it was the crown jewels or something, and says if I don't know how to do my job right he knows how to find somebody who does. Wow! I mean, how stupid can anybody get!'

'Were you paying attention to what you were doing?'

Douglas was insulted by this question. 'Sure I was! Even suppose it was a fairly good lemon, is that any reason for a person to hit the roof like he did? What's one lemon?' He took a deep breath as though he was about to begin another speech and quickly said, 'Listen, Dad, I been thinking maybe I ought to quit. If I could get in some other department besides produce it wouldn't be so bad, but this big, fat slob that manages produce thinks he knows everything, and he doesn't know his—' Douglas hesitated. 'Doesn't know beans. Then old man Horkey has to come in about twice a week and peer around to find out if everybody's doing their job right, and then this produce manager falls all over himself bowing and scraping and saying "Oh, oh, oh, g-g-good morning, Mr Horkey!" It's enough to make me puke. So like I say, I've been thinking I'll quit because he's probably planning to fire me anyhow.'

'Young man, you listen to me,' said Mr Bridge. 'You have a job and you will do your best to keep it. We are not going to have two quitters in this house.'

'If Ruth can quit her job, why can't I?'

'We will not go into that. You will do as I say.'

'I could get a better job that would pay better.'

'I doubt that.'

'You do?' Douglas said defiantly. 'Why?'

'Jobs are not easy to find these days. You may not have an important job, but there are quite a few grown men in this country who would be delighted to have it.'

'They sure can have it.'

'Once or twice in the past,' Mr Bridge said, 'I have heard you use that tone. I have warned you about it.'

'I'm sorry,' Douglas said. 'But is that all business is? I mean, one lemon? Is a person supposed to work his head off all day and make about two cents?'

'The man exaggerated. He was attempting to point out to you that you should learn to work conscientiously.'

'Ye cripes!'

'And that is an expression I have heard more often than I care to.'

'Okay, okay. It's just that this whole thing is so stupid, if you ask me. All that work for one lemon.'

'You may or may not like your job, but I want you to keep it until school opens.'

'You're kidding.'

'Because if you do not, son, I will cut your allowance in half.'

'You expect me to sort lemons the rest of my life?'

Mr Bridge did not bother to reply.

'Bleh!' Douglas said.

'I mean it.'

'Ye cripes,' Douglas muttered. 'I know you mean it.'

83 Stockings

Ruth was ready to go out for the evening. Her mother commented on how nicely she was dressed. Mr Bridge agreed, but he noticed that she was not wearing stockings. He told her to go upstairs and put them on. She said it was too hot to wear stockings.

He said, 'Don't tell me how hot it is! I have seldom been as uncomfortable in my entire life as I was downtown today. Court was like an oven. However, I presented myself as I invariably do despite the heat because it is important to appear respectable. And you will not leave this house looking like a tramp from the North End. You may stay at home and dress as you please, or you may go out when you are respectably dressed. Take your choice. I have nothing further to say.'

She gave him a baleful stare but went back up to her room. She was gone a long time. When she came down she was wearing stockings, but her attitude seemed different. He thought he knew why: she was planning to take them off as soon as she got away.

'And keep them on,' he said, pointing his finger at her so she would know he was not joking, and from the furious way she set her hands on her hips he knew that his guess had been correct.

84 *4 a.m.*

His eyes opened and focused quickly, because something was wrong. The house was silent. At his side his wife breathed deeply and calmly. He could not hear anything except the ticking of the grandfather clock in the hall and the wind soughing through the trees, but he thought somebody was downstairs. He got up, put on his robe and slippers, took a box of bullets out of the dresser, and emptied the bullets into his pocket. He slid his hand under the mattress and pulled out the gun. He loaded it and cocked it and started walking slowly along the hall, pausing every few steps to listen. He was standing at the top of the stairs when he heard somebody groan.

He placed one hand on the rail to steady himself and started down. At the bottom of the steps he raised the gun and looked around the corner into the living room. The drapes had been drawn apart. Moonlight spilled through the east window and he could see a man lying on top of Ruth. She opened her mouth and kicked her legs like a frog. The man lifted his head. He groaned again. She pushed at his face, and as mechanically as figures in an old film they rolled away from each other. She got to her feet briskly and pulled down on her skirt. She brushed the hair out of her eyes and stepped into her shoes. One of the sofa cushions was lying on the floor. She picked it up and dropped it on the sofa. At that moment the clock began to chime. Mr Bridge wondered if he was asleep; he blinked and looked around, because he thought he remembered the sound of the front door closing. The man had disappeared.

Ruth was calmly buttoning her blouse, which was undone half-way to the waist. He gazed at her in disbelief. She ignored him and went on buttoning her blouse. He remembered that he had brought the gun; he looked at it and saw that it was in his hand, and the weight of it convinced him that he was awake.

'What were you planning to do?' she asked.

He put the gun in the pocket of his bathrobe and sat down in the nearest chair. It seemed to him that he had been a fool. He was a fool to suppose that he could prevent things like this from happening.

Ruth went on in the same sardonic voice: 'He begged me to go to a hotel, but I wouldn't. So here we are. Here we are, you and I.' She crossed her arms and looked down on him with an expression of indifference or contempt. 'Promise me one thing. Don't let Mother know. It would probably kill her.'

Mr Bridge realized that he was attempting to cry, but he had not cried since he was a child. He began to cough.

'Things are different now,' she said, and she approached and brushed his ear with the tip of her little finger, but her face was hard. Her eyes were not asking forgiveness.

'No,' he said, shaking his head. 'Some things never change. Love and respect and human decency – these never change. Your mother and I have these things.'

'Good for you.'

'No,' he said firmly. 'Without these none of us could go on living.'

Ruth shrugged. She did not seem to be listening. He looked up at her helplessly.

'What about this man? Are you planning to be married?'

'Oh God,' she murmured with a gesture of impatience. 'I never saw that ass before tonight. Times have changed since you were young.' Then she added, 'And besides, you've probably forgotten how it used to be.'

He shook his head again. 'I have not forgotten what it means to desire a woman. I am still able to feel great desire for your mother.'

'I don't want to talk any more,' she said. 'I'm exhausted. I'm going to bed.' She ran out of the room and up the steps.

85 Sweet shit

For three days Mrs Bridge had been in bed with a cold. Now she was well enough to receive visitors, though she remained upstairs. Most of her friends came by bringing a book or flowers or some fresh fruit, and among these visitors was Mildred Cox, who had moved into the neighborhood only a few weeks earlier and whom

Mrs Bridge did not know very well.

When Mrs Cox departed, Carolyn, who saw her to the door, returned to the living room and remarked in a voice nearly indistinguishable from her mother's: 'Well, wasn't that sweet!'

Then Ruth said, 'I am so sick of that word. She's sweet. It was sweet. Now wasn't that sweet? Everything is sweet. Shit!'

Carolyn looked immediately at their father.

He was in his chair beside the fireplace. On his lap lay a vacation brochure from the Manitoba tourist bureau and he had been thinking about a fishing trip next summer. This agreeable prospect, together with the flames crackling around the logs and the autumn wind humming beneath the eaves of the house, had lulled him so that at first he did not hear what Ruth said. At last he lifted his head to look at her. From the emphasis she had placed on the word he knew she had said it deliberately. She was defying him. In the firelight her oblique eyes were glittering. She had never been more beautiful. He was shaken by the sight of her, and he knew he loved her in a way he could not ever love the other children, perhaps because she was the first, or because of the strange darkness in her which he could feel also within himself.

'We will have no such language in this house,' he said. He thought he saw a flicker of amusement on her face before she turned away.

86 Silver

There was more silver that Christmas, and silver pleased Mrs Bridge more than anything else. Through the years she had bought a good many items of silver, and for her birthday and on her wedding anniversary and every year at Christmas she received other silver articles, so that the house was getting fairly full of silver. To Mr Bridge it looked like a shop. There was silver just about everywhere. In the dining room a pair of elaborate silver candelabra with spiraling arms stood on the cherrywood cabinet, where the best silverware was kept. Between the candelabra rested a large rectangular silver platter on which there was an antique-silver coffee urn, a chased-silver cream and sugar set, an ornamental-silver ladle, and a triangular silver cake knife. On the opposite side of the dining room stood a long Chippendale serving table, which was almost never used for that purpose, but which functioned as a display table for an eighteenth-century silver wine mug with a gold stem, a silver bonbonnière, a blue-enamel cigar box with silver filigree, a nutcracker, an inkstand, a condiment set, a snuff-box, a pitcher, a Revere tray, two vases and several pieces of cutlery. In the kitchen Harriet maintained a supply of the necessary serving trays and bowls, covers and compotes, utilitarian knives, spoons, forks, ice tongs, the ice bucket, and a few other articles. Of course there was silver elsewhere in the house. Silver could be found upstairs and downstairs. In the basement recreation room was a silver whisky decanter she had discovered at an auction, and another platter, and a tea tray which she did not like very much, and another cream-and-sugar set, a pair of nut or mint dishes shaped like swans, and a drawer full of knives and forks and spoons. In the master bedroom on the chiffonier stood another set of candelabra, which he did not like very much, though he said nothing about it. In the breakfast room there was silver, in the hall hung an oval mirror with a fantastic silver frame, and in the living room was quite a lot of silver. And while opening the back hall closet in search of a sweater he had not worn for a long time he came upon a silver vase hidden like a lost Easter egg behind a hatbox. Mrs Bridge had forgotten about it, too, but she was pleased that he had found it. She polished it herself, and then she arranged a place for it on the mahogany sideboard next to a tiny silver bell with a delicate tone.

As usual, many of the Christmas presents that year were silver. A carving set from the Montgomerys, who evidently did not remember that they already owned three such sets. A soup tureen from the Barrons. A client of Mr Bridge, hearing that his wife liked silver, stopped by on Christmas Day with two dozen sterling cocktail picks. From another client came a heavy silver picture frame. From the Van Metres, an engagement calendar with a silver lid. A brooch from the Beckerle sisters. Avrum Rheingold, keeping his finger on the pulse of Mr Bridge like the shrewd doctor of stocks that he was, took the liberty of sending her a silver-plated fish knife together with his best wishes for a happy and prosperous New Year. Mrs Bridge was delighted.

After the holiday debris had been cleaned up and papers and boxes and ribbons were burning cheerily in the fireplace and Harriet was going over the carpet with the vacuum cleaner, Douglas took time off from his own presents to survey his mother's latest acquisitions. She had, he said, made out like a burglar, and Mr Bridge privately agreed.

87 California Sunshine

Feeling the need of some sort of moderate physical activity, Mr Bridge decided he would clean out the garage. After changing into old clothes he put on his fishing hat and a pair of cotton gloves and walked through the kitchen, where he paused just along enough to sample a kettle of turkey soup simmering on the stove. Then he stepped outside and inhaled deeply. A high veil of clouds grayed the sun and the wind blew steadily from the north. He clapped his hands to frighten some chickadees hopping around on the frozen earth and proceeded to the garage in good humor, amusing himself by walking into his breath which was visible in the wintry air.

He opened the garage door and stepped inside but instantly hesitated, sensing that he was not alone. He snapped on the light but did not see anybody. A cat or a dog might be under one of the cars, so he got down on his hands and knees and looked, but nothing was there. Somewhat puzzled, he got to his feet ready to admit he had been mistaken, when he felt again a strong intuition and glanced up and discovered his son almost directly overhead straddling a plank which lay across the rafters.

'Well!' he exclaimed. 'Good morning up there!'

Douglas nodded but did not speak. A cigarette dangled from the corner of his mouth and he was holding a magazine. The magazine made Mr Bridge suspicious.

'What do you have there?' he asked.

Douglas shrugged and murmured. Occasionally he climbed up into the garage rafters and stayed there awhile, but Mr Bridge had never thought this particularly strange because he remembered how he used to enjoy climbing. He had attempted to explain this to his wife, who did not like their son going up into the rafters or very

363

high up in trees; but women could not understand because they lacked the instinct, or urge, or need, or whatever it was that impelled most boys and a good many grown men to climb things, to get as high as possible. There was a peculiar airy excitement in reaching for a branch or a foothold. And a thick pleasure flowed like syrup through the blood. However, these things could not be explained; either you understood, so that no explanation was necessary, or you could never understand. But now something else was going on. Mr Bridge stood just inside the garage door and squinted up into the diagonal shadows.

'What are we having for lunch?' Douglas inquired, swinging his feet. The cigarette still drooped from his lip, but he was sliding the magazine out of sight.

Mr Bridge said, 'Come down here.' He snapped his fingers.

Douglas pretended bewilderment. He blew a large cloud of cigarette smoke.

'Come along. Be quick about it. Bring that with you, whatever it is. No more of this nonsense.'

At last he got up, his arms outstretched for balance, and walked the rafters like railroad ties until he reached the wall, lowered himself to the top of the stepladder, jumped over the hood of the Chrysler and nearly landed on the snow shovel.

The title of the magazine was *California Sunshine*. It consisted of pictures taken at a nudist camp.

'Where did you get this?' Mr Bridge demanded. 'And throw away that cigarette.'

Douglas expertly flipped his cigarette out of the garage. He said he had gotten the magazine downtown. 'I think I just put my knee out of joint when I jumped,' he added, grimacing and rubbing his knee. 'It sure hurts. You better call Dr McIntyre.' However, as this did not distract his father, he began to stamp his feet and blow on his fingers and he said, 'Wow, it sure is cold. It must be about zero.'

Mr Bridge was turning the pages three and four at a time. 'How long have you had this thing?'

Douglas stuffed his hands into his hip pockets and leaned against the fender of the Lincoln.

'Couple of weeks, I guess. I don't know. I forget. Why? What difference does it make?'

'Get rid of it.'

'Get rid of it?' he echoed in a squeaking voice.

'You heard me.'

'It cost fifty cents.'

'You made a poor investment. We won't have this sort of junk around the house.'

'Well,' Douglas said, 'I can't just dump it in the trash.'

'If you can't, I can,' said Mr Bridge, and he did.

88 Watering the flowers

Spring came earlier than usual. High overhead the Canadian geese streamed northward. In the yard pale shoots of grass appeared unexpectedly. Neighborhood boys threw baseballs back and forth. Little girls uttering shrill cries roller skated up and down the sidewalk.

The arrival of spring pleased Harriet. She did not like winter. Winter created retractions in the blood and noticeably interfered with the system. But now warm weather was on the way, so she sang as she worked while robins and sparrows and a pair of glossy blackbirds fluttered through the arbor and alighted from time to time on the rim of the birdbath. And when she had finished cleaning up the kitchen and hidden the newly baked cinnamon tarts where Douglas could not find them and vacuumed the carpets upstairs and downstairs and made the beds and telephoned for groceries, she thought it might be pleasant to spend a while outside. It might be nice to spend half an hour watering the flowers. Since nobody else was home she changed from her white uniform into a halter and plaid skirt, which she was not supposed to wear, and presently she stepped outside with a daiquiri in one hand.

She turned on the water, picked up the hose, and wandered back and forth humming and chatting with herself while she sprayed the begonias, the tiger lilies, the chrysanthemums, the hollyhocks, a side of the garage where it was streaked with dirt, and Goethe, the Edisons' German shepherd, who gave her a bleak look before trotting away, and several robins which did not mind very much.

Soon the daiquiri was gone. She stepped inside just long enough to prepare another, then she took up the hose again.

She sprayed the kitchen steps and the basement steps, the trunk of the old elm and the evergreens, and the irises planted beside the porch, and about half of the yard, and a number of windows, and when everything in sight was wet she directed the hose nearly straight up to see if she could create a rainbow, which she did. She waved the hose and the rainbow drifted. She felt pleasingly damp and refreshed. She hung the hose over the clothesline while she went inside to fix another daiquiri and after sampling it she floated outside just as the Chrysler turned in the driveway. Mr Bridge was home early.

She held the kitchen door open for him, but he stopped before entering the house. He stared at the hose hooked across the clothesline with water pouring from the nozzle. He looked at the dripping trees, at the flooded basement steps, the sparkling flowers, the wet garage, the pools of water on the driveway, and at Goethe who had returned and now sat observing the scene from the shade of the hollyhocks like a saturated coyote. He looked at the glass in her hand, and he said:

'What is going on here?'

Harriet said, 'Well, I have been watering.'

'Indeed?' he asked.

'Yes,' Harriet said. 'Things seemed to require it.'

He remained standing on the back step. Once more he looked around. The Edisons' dog regarded him with deep attention, obviously waiting to learn what would happen next.

He said, 'Harriet, I think everything has been watered sufficiently.'

'Well,' Harriet said, 'it does appear that way.'

Then he said, indicating the daiquiri, 'If by any chance you are not planning to drink that, I believe I might. This has been a rather difficult day.'

89 Mrs Paul A. Cornish

Turning through the evening *Star* he noticed on the society page a photograph of Mrs Paul A. Cornish, whom he had never met, although he was acquainted with her husband. Frequently she appeared on the society page for one reason or another – at a benefit for crippled or retarded children or at the opening of a flower show or having luncheon with friends or attending a reception for somebody. She did not look as young as she used to. She had gotten stout and she wore her hair differently now, in a chignon which emphasized her classical features but at the same time pointed out the damage of the years. He noticed that she had begun wearing glasses. Perhaps she always had, but not in a photograph; they were attached to a little chain looped around her neck so that she could let them rest on her bosom whenever she did not need them. This more than anything else seemed to signify the end of youth. Yet these changes did not make her less attractive, and as he observed her cool patrician face he felt mysteriously close to her. If, years ago, before either of them had married, he had crossed a certain street or waited for the next elevator – what then?

However, life had not turned out that way. This seemed strange to him. Strange also, that during these years they could have lived so near each other, a few blocks apart, yet never met. Probably she must know his name as well as he knew hers. Indeed, she might very easily know him by sight. Someone might have pointed him out to her in the Terrace Grill or at a party. Logically there was no reason they should not become friends.

All at once he realized that his wife was watching. He lowered the paper and looked at her.

'What absorbs you so?' she asked.

'Oh,' he replied with a laugh, 'just keeping up with society,' and after another glance at Marlene Cornish he turned to the financial section.

90 In the Aztec room

Not long after graduating from high school Ruth asked if she might come downtown to have lunch with him. He agreed, and they set a date. Why she wanted to meet him for lunch he did not know. He supposed there was a reason. She must want something.

They arranged to meet in the Aztec Room of the Westport Hotel. He had first suggested Wolferman's Tea Room because most women liked it – the place was invariably filled with women who had come downtown shopping – but Ruth made a face. Then he mentioned the Drum Room at the President; however, she assented so listlessly that he asked where she would like to eat, and she suggested the Aztec Room. He had been there only once, years ago, for some purpose long since forgotten, but he remembered that he did not like it. The Westport was only four blocks from the Muehlebach, yet in those four blocks another kind of life appeared. In that neighborhood, in that hotel, and in the Aztec Room itself there was something cheap and stale and oppressive, almost sinister. He remembered a trio of Mexicans in sleazy silk blouses and the sequined bandstand and women in their thirties or forties who loitered around the bar as though waiting for messages. On one wall hung a painting of a nude woman done in phosphorescent paint on black velvet and above the piano were several hammered-tin masks with feathered headdresses. The ash trays were black onyx. The matchboxes gave the telephone number of the hotel. Everything about the place was unpleasantly suggestive, and he had never expected to be there again. However, that was where she wanted to have lunch, so that was where they would go.

He arrived a few minutes early. The Aztec Room had not changed. He recognized the stale odor, and there were the women at the bar. He thought of waiting outside and telling her they would eat somewhere else, but the headwaiter was beckoning.

He had just unfolded his napkin and picked up the menu when Ruth entered. She saw him and began sauntering toward the table as if she were in a public park. People watched her, which annoyed him. She did not come directly to the table but walked a little out of her way; it seemed to him that she wanted to be noticed by two men who were at a table in a corner. They appeared to be Italians, although one of them had a Jewish nose. They were young and dressed expensively but in poor taste. Their suits were almost identical. Each had a handkerchief folded into the breast pocket so that the points were visible. The collars of their shirts were prominent. The sleeves were too long. They wore diamond cufflinks. These men were coarse, and perhaps dangerous. One of them, who had obviously had smallpox, was picking his teeth with a matchstick. They were a familiar type in this neighborhood. They had nothing in the bank, but plenty in their wallets. They could be found in certain cocktail lounges at any time of the day. They would pay the check with a large bill and leave a large tip. He studied them until he was sure he could recognize them anywhere under any circumstances, because he was convinced she knew them. However, when she strolled by their table they paid no attention.

The food was not bad, at least there was this to be grateful for; he ate without saying much, waiting for her to indicate the purpose of their luncheon together. Finally, while they were eating spumoni, she said she was not happy in Kansas City. She did not feel at home in the community which always had been her home. The friends she had known all her life were not important to her. She did not want to get married to some boy she had known a long time and become nothing but a housewife. She wanted more out of life than raising children in the suburbs of Kansas City while her husband climbed the ladder. She wanted to move to New York. She wanted to get into theater work. She had a talent for acting. She wanted to attend a theatrical workshop and try out for Broadway plays. If she stayed in Kansas City she could never become an actress. Nobody in Kansas City cared about theater or any of the other arts. There was some Little Theater work but not much; besides, she did not want to act in local productions – not in Kansas City, although that would be all right in New York.

As soon as he found out what she wanted he felt relieved. He had been afraid she was in trouble. He had been reluctant to admit a thought which he could now dismiss quite easily; he had been afraid she was involved with the people who infested this place.

About the acting, he was skeptical. He had seen small evidence of this talent she claimed. She had not gotten the part of Juliet, and although this did not necessarily prove she lacked ability it confirmed his own opinion. She had reduced the balcony scene very nearly to farce. If she could do that to Shakespeare she would probably destroy a lesser playwright. Possibly the talent for acting had missed the family entirely. He himself had never cared much for plays, nor had his wife. Nor had Douglas. Carolyn once played the part of the Virgin Mary in a children's Christmas play, but her characterization was unremarkable: for about fifteen minutes she sat absolutely motionless on a three-legged stool and pensively considered a lightbulb in a cradle. Never was there a more rigid Virgin. Ruth's Juliet leaned heavily on the other side of the scale, with much flinging of hair, sighing, murmuring, pleading, wetting of lips, and so forth. And regardless of her ability, acting was reputed to be among the most difficult ways to earn a living.

However, he reflected, he knew next to nothing about such matters, and it was at least possible that she could succeed. Maybe she deserved a chance. There was little to be gained by discouraging or forbidding her. The hour for this might come when she herself had learned how difficult it was. Then she might welcome his disapproval so she could give up and try something else without feeling humiliated.

He asked what her mother thought of the idea. Ruth answered that she had not mentioned it at home, and he was surprised because the children never came to him first. For money or for permission to use the car they were accustomed to asking him, but that was all. For everything else they went to their mother. He felt oddly moved, and took off his glasses and slowly polished them while Ruth continued talking, attempting to convince him she would be safe in New York. An older sister of Nathalie Blakely lived in New York and was married to the vice-president of an advertising agency. Nathalie was writing to her sister. And so on, and so on.

Mr Bridge listened to his daughter's voice, but what she said was irrelevant. She would not be around much longer. What Alexis Sauer had predicted was about to come true. Ruth was going away. He could prevent this, if he chose, but only for a little while. Finally he told her he would think it over, and they must find out how her mother felt; but he knew she would be leaving, and he knew he must allow it.

91 *Houyhnhnm*

Soon she was gone. Each evening when he returned from the office he hoped to find her at home, or to hear that she had called from New York saying she was coming home; and each evening he inquired if there had been a letter. She wrote seldom, and briefly, addressing the letters to Mr and Mrs Walter G. Bridge, and although these letters were meant for them both he knew that she wrote with her mother in mind.

But one day there was a letter for him at the office. He hesitated before slitting the familiar lilac-tinted envelope; he was holding it in both hands like a gift when Julia marched in carrying her stenographic pad. He said he would be ready in a moment and as she returned to the outer office he opened the letter, sniffed the perfume, and then began to read. She had found a job with a women's magazine, so that was good news, yet he sensed there was more to the letter than this announcement. On the fourth page she got around to it; she wanted money for an avant-garde magazine called *Houyhnhnm*, which was to be published by some new friends of hers. The first issue already was laid out, and as soon as there was enough money it would be printed. A corporation was being formed. 'Friends of Literature and Art' were cordially invited to buy shares of stock in this company at five dollars per share. Ruth was positive he would like to buy at least one hundred shares. As soon as the magazine was a success – as soon as it had a national reputation, plenty of advertising, and a big subscription list – the Board of Directors would decide how much of a dividend to pay the shareholders. This was a marvelous opportunity to make money, the magazine was going to be a tremendous success because so many talented people were working on it, and she hoped he would send the five hundred dollars as soon as possible. The certificates had not yet been printed because the printer insisted on his money in advance; but she was sure there was not going to be any problem because *Houyhnhnm* already had more than a dozen one-year subscriptions and one two-year subscription, and her friend Steve Cook, who was the advertising manager, had an appointment to see the vice-president of one of the big publishing houses about the possibility of a full-page ad.

With the letter she enclosed a mimeographed sheet announcing the imminent publication of this magazine, described as a 'long-awaited Quarterly of New Writing, Ideas & Art,' listing the contents of the first issue, a partial table of contents for the second issue, and giving biographies of the editors. Glancing through this information he noted that the editor-in-chief and at least two other members of the staff, judging from their names, were Jews. When anything having to do with art or music was announced there were Jews involved. Why this was, he did not know, but he faintly resented it. In any case, he had made up his mind about *Houyhnhnm* the instant he realized what it was. He dropped the mimeographed sheet in the wastebasket.

Then he read Ruth's letter again, not for what she was telling him about her job or the avant-garde magazine but because it came from her. He thought he would keep the letter in his desk instead of taking it home. Months might pass before she wrote to him again at the office.

The magazine, of course, would fail. The so-called corporation would never pay one cent to anybody. Shares of *Houyhnhnm* would always be as worthless as they were at this moment. Yet he wanted to send her the money. But that was buying her love, which he could not do. When he answered the letter he wrote that they could discuss the magazine's prospects while he was in New York; he was coming East on business in about two weeks, would be in New York for approximately three days, and looked forward to seeing her.

92 7:42 a.m.

He arrived in New York after midnight, so he did not telephone her; he took a taxi from the station to his hotel and after leaving a call for seven thirty he brushed his teeth, wound his watch, and went to bed. The next morning soon after getting up he dialed her number, but a boy with a lisping voice answered. Mr Bridge apologized because he thought he had gotten the wrong number. Then the boy inquired if he was Ruth's father. He said he was.

'Well, I'll shake that lazy thing,' said this voice.

Mr Bridge, unable to believe what he was hearing, gripped the telephone and waited. He heard mumbling and what sounded like the boy giggling. Then he heard Ruth cursing.

'What is going on there?' he demanded.

Nobody answered.

Finally Ruth said hello. She sounded more asleep than awake.

'This is your father,' said Mr Bridge with his fist clenched on his knee.

After a long pause she asked, 'Daddy?'

'Yes!'

'Is that you?'

'Yes!'

'My God. Are you here?'

'Yes!'

'In Manhattan?'

'I am in Manhattan and I want to know what is going on in the place. Do you hear me?'

There was another pause. Then she said she had not expected him until Friday and asked when he had arrived.

'Last night. Evidently you've forgotten the information in my letter. What's going on there?'

'Here? Oh, that's Bobby.'

'I do not know what this is all about, but we are not going to discuss it on the telephone. How soon will I see you?'

'Oh God,' she said yawning. 'Let me think a minute. Daddy, I'm half asleep. I was up most of the night.' She spoke to Bobby. Mr Bridge heard her say 'Sweetheart, make some coffee.' Then she was back on the line.

'What kind of a place are you in?' he asked, trying to control himself.

'I'm sorry. Bobby was chattering. What did you say?'

'Is someone in that apartment with you?'

'Bobby is here, Daddy. You just talked to him. Don't you remember?'

'I warn you Ruth,' he said, 'I shall want a complete and satisfactory explanation of this situation. I do not understand what is going on, but I do not like it one bit. Is that clear? I gather you have some sort of extension to your telephone, or this person has access to your apartment. I want an explanation, and it had better be a good one. Now, at what time shall we meet?'

After another conversation with Bobby she suggested they meet in the Algonquin lobby at six.

Mr Bridge was in the lobby at five thirty. He expected her to bring Bobby; but a few minutes after six she entered by herself, smiled as though nothing was wrong, and kissed him on the cheek. She asked how everybody was at home. He said they were fine. Douglas was growing rapidly, taller every day. Carolyn was playing golf all the time. And their mother, too, was fine – except for occasional headaches – and very busy with some sort of charity organization in the North End. Everybody was fine. Harriet. Julia. Everybody. And he waited for an explanation of the man in her apartment, but apparently she was not going to mention it. Nor did she show the least sign of embarrassment or guilt.

He began: 'Ruth, I consider myself reasonably broadminded. However, you have not told me what this person was doing in your living quarters when I telephoned this morning. I have allowed you to come to New York alone at a very early age. I have begun to think it may have been a serious mistake.'

Ruth slowly tamped out her cigarette while she listened. Then she said, 'Bobby affects people that way.'

'Come to the point. I want an explanation and I want it this instant. Not later. Not at your convenience. Now.'

'But you heard him. Couldn't you tell?'

'I heard something I did not like. Now you are going to tell me what that fellow was doing in your apartment at a quarter to eight in the morning. And be quick about it. My patience is running out.'

'I let him sleep with me last night.'

'I have had just about enough,' Mr Bridge said. 'Just about enough.'

'So have I.'

'You are not yet twenty-one. Until you are twenty-one you will listen to me.'

'For Christ's sake. Why do you think I left Kansas City?'

Mr Bridge was stunned. She had never spoken like this.

'Stop living in the past,' she said. 'Don't you know what year this is? This isn't the first of the century any longer. Do you expect me to live the way Mother lived?'

'Your mother has always lived a decent life. I thank the Lord that's not a thing to be ashamed of. I don't know what sort of life you are living.'

'I don't know either. I need to find out.'

'By sleeping with men?'

She had been leaning toward him, her eyes gilded with anger. Now she drew back. 'You don't – oh good God! Are you serious? Do you actually think little Bobby made love to me?'

'What else am I to think?'

'There are times when you sound like Mother.'

'If this person was not – as you call it – "making love", what was he doing in your apartment overnight? Why was he there? That's what I want to know.'

'He had a tiff with his lover. He came over about twelve and asked if he could stay with me.'

'Are you telling me this man is homosexual?'

'Well, if he isn't,' Ruth said, 'I never hope to see one.'

He shook his head. 'I do not understand these things. I am not ignorant of them, but I have never been able to understand them. Where did you meet this person?'

'At times you are positively incredible.'

'I insist on knowing.'

'This "person" works in the office. He's been very sweet to me. He's one of the sweetest boys I've ever known. When I first got here I don't know what would have become of me if it hadn't been for Bobby.'

'Your mother and I did our best. Apparently our best was not good enough.'

'Oh, stop the crap. You're driving me wild.'

'As I am sure you know, I can compel you to return to Kansas City.'

'And both of us know how much good that would do. Don't we?'

He continued as though she had not spoken: 'I shall let you remain here on one condition. You are going to promise me there will be no more of this sort of thing.'

'No more of what? Letting Bobby stay at my place?'

'Exactly.'

'I won't turn him away. Bobby saved my life.'

'Nonsense. You may very well have felt alone when you first arrived and this friend of yours behaved considerately. I appreciate that. However, you are not obligated to let him, or anyone else, sleep in your apartment, and I will not stand for it. Do you hear me?'

'I'm staying in New York.'

'We'll see about that.'

'Let's change the subject.'

'Very well. But let me remind you, this matter is not settled.'

'Oh God. Oh God,' said Ruth.

'Suppose you tell me about this drama class. Has your application been approved?'

'I thought I mentioned last time I wrote.' She paused to light another cigarette. 'I audited some classes and they were just unbelievably dreary.' She brushed her hair away from her eyes. 'Steve insists I have a natural talent for free verse. It's very challenging.'

'Oh? Who is "Steve"?'

'Steve Cook. I wrote you about him. He's ad manager for *Houyhnhnm*. He's marvelous. Perfectly marvelous. I really felt terribly presumptuous showing him my things. He's met Auden and all those people and knows something about simply everything on earth. But anyway he said they showed unique promise and originality, and he's taking them to the poetry editor. I really am terribly excited. Appearing in *Houyhnhnm* would be absolutely tremendous – you have no idea!'

'Well, fine, fine. I hope something comes of it. Now, Ruth, I have no intention of belaboring this subject, but one thing must be clearly understood. You are not to permit this man to stay in your apartment overnight again.'

'If one of your friends needed help would you turn him away?'

'My friends happen to be men and women I have known and respected for many years. They are not odds and ends of humanity. They are not homosexuals, thieves, gangsters, or any of the rest of it. They are fine people whose friendship your mother and I value greatly. They are people we enjoy having in our home. They are people we are not ashamed to introduce to anyone.'

'I am not going back with you,' she said almost musically. 'I am not. I am just not.'

'Suppose we have dinner,' he said and snapped his fingers at the waiter. He was not satisfied with the conversation. The situation had not been resolved. He was puzzled as well as exasperated because Ruth always had seemed more pliable than Carolyn, less temperamental and obstinate, certainly much less quarrelsome, yet now she was behaving in a way that Carolyn would never dare. He thought of Douglas – stubbornness in him like the grain in wood – and knew that these characteristics of his children were his own. None of this came from their mother. Her qualities were of another sort, and she was predictable. He noticed Ruth looking at him with amusement, but he saw no reason to smile.

93 The jeweler's son

During dinner she suddenly remarked: 'Guess who I ran into? Harvey Glatz.'

Mr Bridge lowered his knife and fork. 'The devil you did! What was he doing here?'

'He lives here now.'

'He does, does he? I didn't know that. What sort of business is he in?'

'He's a furrier.'

'Is he! Well, let's hope you haven't taken to buying furs,' he laughed. Then he continued: 'I wasn't aware you knew young Glatz. If I did, I'd forgotten. He was some years older than you.'

'I didn't know him. I was at the ballet last Tuesday with Steve when he came up to us at intermission and told me his name and said he was from Kansas City.'

'So! How is he doing?'

'Brooks Brothers suit. Shoes by Florsheim. Pergolesi tie. He's lost most of his hair. How old is he?'

'I'd have to think. I suppose Harvey must be thirty by now, or, if not, he's close to it. He's a nice young man. He's all right. His father was a nice man, too. Every member of that family is decent.' He paused a few moments with a thoughtful expression. 'Well, that was quite a coincidence. Glatz Jewelry is still at the same location on the street floor of my building. How many years they've done business there I have no idea. They occupy a larger floor space than any other company in that building. Great God, I couldn't begin to estimate how much money that firm makes. There were four of those men originally. They were Lithuanian Jews. One of them died several years ago and another one, I understand, is in Germany. I expect his people must be quite worried. He went over there to try to get some relative out, and I don't believe they've heard from him. Lord knows what could happen, the way things are these days. Then there was Harvey's father, Milton, who was the one I knew best. He was a fine, upstanding man. I was sorry when he passed away. The fourth one of those brothers is the man who runs the business now. I see him occasionally. He has a daughter.'

'Harvey thinks quite a lot of you.'

'Oh?' Mr Bridge said, and reached for his wine glass. 'Well, I'm glad to hear that. I always liked young Harvey.'

'He told me something about you.'

'He did? What was that?'

'He told me you once did some legal work for him.'

'Yes, that's so. I did. Quite a while ago.'

'Did you send him a bill?'

'Why do you ask?'

'He told me that when he didn't get a bill from you he called the office, and Julia said "Forget it".'

'I told her not to send him a bill.'

'You never charged him?'

'No, I didn't. He was a nice young fellow who was in the midst of some difficult times. I believe he was having personal problems and at the same time was attempting to set up a little business in Kansas City and needed every penny he could lay his hands on. He sent us quite a nice basket of cheese and candied fruit that Christmas. You may remember it.'

'You're a strange person,' Ruth said. 'You're my father and all that, but I really don't know what goes on inside your head.'

Mr Bridge laughed uncomfortably. 'Well, Ruth, I'm afraid I don't know what to make of that statement.'

'You're so hard and so cold and so humorless. Then you do a thing like this. And for a Jew.'

He stopped eating. In a controlled voice he said: 'I do not know what you are talking about. The fact that young Glatz was Jewish had nothing to do with it. I would – in fact, I *have* done the same thing for other people who were not Jewish.'

'Your charity work?'

'If you wish to call it that.'

'That's what Julia calls it.'

'And just what else has Julia told you about what goes on in my office?'

She reached across the table and rested her hand on his. 'Now don't go home and fire Julia. She isn't giving away secrets. She assumed I knew about it. Sometimes you treat us all like strangers.'

'When you say I treat you all like strangers, whom do you mean?'

'Douglas. Cork. Me. There are times you treat Mother like you never saw her before.'

'I am not aware of that,' he said, and began to wipe his fingers on the napkin. 'If so, Ruth, that certainly was the last thing on my mind. I believe you must have misinterpreted something I said or did.'

'No. It's the way you are. Everybody who knows you knows it. Dr Sauer said you were a consummate Puritan.'

'I am not sure I understand.'

'Oh Christ, let's forget the whole thing.'

'I will not. I want to get to the bottom of this. If I have done something wrong I wish you would tell me. Your mother, your brother, your sister, and you yourself mean more to me than anything in the world. I hope you are aware of this.'

'Will you please quit? I may be about to cry.'

'I intend to get to the bottom of this matter.'

She hid her face in her hands and whispered, 'For once in your life can't you let something go?'

He was embarrassed and puzzled. He looked around to see if anyone was watching. Then he said, 'I seem to have upset you without meaning to. I'm sorry. I do not know what this is all about and I am trying to find out.'

'Let's not quarrel.'

'We are not quarreling, so far as I know. You have made a statement which is most disturbing. I am attempting to discover what it is that I have done wrong.'

'Listen, I'm exhausted. I'm terribly tired. I really must go back to the apartment and get some sleep.'

'Wouldn't you care for dessert?'

'No. No. No! I don't want dessert. I don't want any God damned dessert. Will you please let me alone?'

'As you wish.'

He beckoned the waiter to bring the check. Then they rode back to her apartment without speaking. He could not understand why she refused to explain. He wanted to ask again, but he was afraid she would become hysterical.

94 Jussi Bjoerling

Before saying goodnight she asked if he would like to attend the Bjoerling recital.

'Whatever you wish,' he smiled, and took out his wallet and gave her twenty dollars, saying, 'I have no idea what the tickets are, but this should be sufficient.' Then he asked where it was to be, and at what time. The recital was in Carnegie Hall the following night at eight thirty.

He got there at eight o'clock and waited at the top step with his arms crossed. The number of people arriving for the concert surprised him. Presently he saw Ruth get out of an expensive foreign car. She found him at once, as though she knew where he would be standing. She waved as she came up the steps, and then for a few minutes they remained outside while she smoked a cigarette. She was smoking too much, but he wanted this evening to be pleasant so he did not mention it. He gestured at the crowd.

'Great Scott, you'd think it was a movie premiere. If this fellow gave his concert in Kansas City he wouldn't draw anywhere near this many people.'

Ruth dropped her cigarette, stepped on it, and took him by the arm. In the lobby he bought a program and after they were settled in their seats he opened it, read about the artist, and contemplated his picture. Bjoerling had somewhat fleshy features and dark hair.

As for the songs, none were familiar. Having seen what he wished to see, he gave the program to Ruth.

As soon as the singer appeared from the wings there was an enthusiastic ovation. He was short, dignified, rather portly, and for some reason his feet looked uncommonly small.

The lights dimmed and the concert began.

Before the end of the first song Mr Bridge was thinking about other matters and the music sounded far away, as though the man was singing in a different hall.

95 The lecture on El Greco

Two days later, Saturday, Ruth suggested another cultural excursion, this time to the Metropolitan Museum where there was to be a lecture on El Greco by a famous art historian. Again he agreed. He had visited the museum once before, about ten years ago. Since then he had made a number of trips to New York and several times had thought of visiting the Metrpolitan again, but for one reason or another had not done so. He did not particularly like El Greco pictures he had seen because the figures were distorted; however, it might be interesting to learn something about them.

During the talk he found himself dozing, and when he blinked and straightened up he was unable to concentrate on the information. He remembered only a few phrases. He remembered 'the eyes of the demented have an exalted look', and he believed he heard the lecturer say that El Greco used to paint the insane people of Toledo, which was curious. Otherwise it was a wasted hour. Then Ruth wanted to see the pictures, so he followed her around without saying much. The pleasure of the afternoon was in being with her.

She stopped in front of the portrait of Cardinal Don Fernando Niño de Guevara, Archbishop of Seville and grand inquisitor during the reign of Philip the Second. The tense, elderly churchman in his cherry-red robe and red hat sat like a burning pyramid in the wooden chair. A document lay on the checkered floor near his feet. Behind the dark-rimmed glasses a shrewd pair of eyes bent suspiciously to the left. His elongated right hand lay relaxed on one arm of the chair, but his left hand convulsively clutched the other arm.

She asked what he thought of the portrait. He replied that he did not know much about painting, but it seemed to be well done and was probably a good likeness of the man.

Staring at the face of the cardinal, she said, 'I bought a print of it. He reminds me so of you.'

96 Equality

While wandering around on the second floor of the museum they met Steve Cook. He was a tall, impeccably dressed Negro with aquiline features and pale blue eyes. Mr Bridge shook hands and then stood by with his arms folded while Ruth and her friend chatted about Spanish painters and various other matters. Finally Steve Cook announced that he ought to be getting back to the office. He turned to Mr Bridge and smiled, and remarked that it had been a pleasure to meet Ruth's father and that he hoped they would meet again.

'Thank you,' Mr Bridge said. After the Negro walked away he asked if this was the man who had escorted her to the ballet, and she said it was.

'You are begging for trouble,' he said.

She threw the hair out of her eyes and said, 'Oh, dear Christ!'

'Where did you meet this person?'

'In the subway.'

'I see. What does he do for a living?'

Ruth was not sure. He was the advertising manager for *Houyhnhnm*, but this was merely because he was kind enough to help out. He was not getting any salary for it. She thought he had a part-time job as a public relations man, maybe with one of the airlines. He used to work for an advertising agency. Maybe he was still there. He was writing a play. He had appeared as a guest on a radio program, but she did not know why he had been invited.

'Actually,' she said, and tossed her hair again, 'Steve is a Renaissance man. He's so out of his element in our era. He told me he would much rather have lived in Florence at the time of Leonardo or else in centuries to come when the potential of the human mind will be fully appreciated. He's unbelievably talented, you know. I mean, really! And his I.Q. is just incredible!'

Mr Bridge did not ask any more questions. He judged from her attitude toward the Negro that she had never been intimate with him. Because of their mutual interest in art exhibits and plays and so forth they had attended one or two of these things together. That was all. Yet they had gone together, they had been seen together, probably they had eaten together. Perhaps this intermingling of the races was inevitable. In centuries to come it might be all right. But not now.

A few days after returning to Kansas City he noticed a story in the *Wall Street Journal* about the factors responsible for success in business. It was headlined 'All Men Are Not Created Equal'. He clipped out this headline and saved it.

97 Jews

The conversation about Harvey Glatz continued to trouble him, and soon after his return he attempted to explain in a letter to her that she was wrong if she believed he felt any animosity toward the Jews. He wrote that he had always believed a person ought to be judged not by his background or his race but by the sort of person he was, by the people with whom he associated, by his actions, his speech, and his appearance.

Then he went on to other matters, saying that she looked fine although a few pounds underweight, that he had been pleased to learn she was getting along all right in her job, that he liked her apartment – which was not true, he did not approve of the location, though the rooms had been cleaner and neater than he expected – and that if she needed anything she should not hesitate to let him know. In New York he had not asked if she needed money; she was wearing new clothes, the apartment was adequately furnished, and she had given no indication that she was having a hard time. If she was underweight and somewhat pale this was probably because she considered it fashionable.

He summarized the news from Kansas City. The weather had been very warm. Douglas slipped and fell while running around the swimming pool and knocked himself out. They had been afraid he might have a brain concussion, but Dr McIntyre reported that he had the skull of a gorilla. Carolyn was spending almost every day on the golf course. She was getting very good, beating nearly everybody who played against her. There had been a series of robberies in the country-club district – the Ralph Porters' home had been looted and Mrs Porter lost a ruby necklace inherited from her grandmother. Virginia Catlett, whom Ruth might or might not know – the family lived in the large English stucco next door to the Montgomerys – had become engaged. Downtown traffic was getting so bad that he was giving some thought to hiring a chauffeur.

This seemed to be all the news worth mentioning and he was about to close the letter, but after reading it he felt he had not satisfactorily answered her accusation that he disliked Jews. It seemed to him she had treated him unfairly, and he could not get over a sense of shock at the realization that she considered him prejudiced. Apparently she had thought this for a long time.

He continued writing: *I am acquainted with a number of fine Jewish people. I am sure you know Mr and Mrs Jacobson, who have been friends of ours for a number of years. In fact, your mother and I were invited to their daughter's wedding. The Jacobsons are fine, upstanding people. Naturally I cannot know their private opinion of me; however, I would be most surprised to learn that I had ever said or done a single thing which offended them. If so, the error was inadvertent. Mr Jacobson also happens to be an attorney, with the result that I have had a number of occasions to deal with him. I can honestly state that to my knowledge he has never in any way whatsoever reflected discredit upon his race. You may also know the Lepkoffs, who have lived in that enormous Tudor home on Verona Terrace for a good many years and whom we see occasionally. They, too, are fine people. He is a top executive at Burstein-Morris. They are a credit to the neighborhood. I believe your accusation is totally unfounded. I do not know what has given rise to this impression that you have of me, but I think you ought to go over your thoughts 'with a fine tooth comb'. It appears you are not being objective. As I mentioned to you in New York, I had the greatest respect and liking for Milton Glatz as well as for his son Harvey. When I knew them they were both decent, hard-working men. If I did not send a statement to Harvey this was in no way connected with his Jewishness. I merely wished to be of some assistance. If I have done something wrong I am sorry, but I do not feel I have committed a crime. You state that Harvey Glatz thinks highly of me. (I was gratified to hear this.) I believe if you were to inquire whether I have under any circumstances given him or his father cause for believing I dislike the Jewish people he would respond in the negative.*

He closed the letter as he always did, with love, and signed it. Then he recalled a bit of good news about the du Pont stock he had given her for her birthday, so he added a postcript telling her that an extra dividend had been declared.

He read the letter through. It was not all he wished to say, but he felt he had clarified his position. He enclosed the headline he had torn out of the *Journal*, with no explanation. He thought she would understand.

98 Bernice

'My daughter. My most valuable jewel,' Isaac Glatz said, squeezing her plump arm. The girl's black Mediterranean eyes narrowed with pleasure.

Mr Bridge touched the brim of his hat and replied as he invariably replied when introduced to a woman: 'How do you do?'

The elevator doors clicked shut, locking them in together. The cage began to descend. He heard himself talking to the jeweler, who had inquired about Mrs Bridge and the children, and he knew he was responding normally, but he was conscious only of the girl. She resembled Ruth, but with a swarthy skin and the bent Semitic nose of her father. She was stockier than Ruth, with heavy bones and the eyebrows of a man. Her thick, masculine body gave off a strong odor as if she had been outdoors picking walnuts.

The elevator stopped. The doors slid apart. He stepped to one side so that the girl could leave first, followed by her father. Outside the building he said good afternoon to them, touched his hat again in deference to her, and went on his way. As he walked toward the garage it occurred to him that he was not attracted to the girl as he had supposed he was. It was not Bernice Glatz he wanted. Desire for his own daughter had surged from the depths where it must be concealed.

99 Jade pig

Crossing Tenth Street on his way to the Muehlebach one rainy Wednesday he knew suddenly that he wanted to eat in some other place. Almost every day he had gone to the Terrace Grill. He decided to try the coffee shop at the Continental.

It was crowded, and he looked about for an empty table. Then he saw Grace Barron. He did not want to have lunch with her, but it would be embarrassing to pretend he had not noticed her, so he went over.

'Hello, Mr B,' she said rather mournfully. 'I thought you were planning to ignore me as usual.'

He took off his raincoat and hung it on the rack with his hat and his umbrella and sat down across from her.

'What have you there?' he asked, indicating a curious little stone object lying on a paper napkin. She pushed it toward him and he picked it up. The stone was cool and surprisingly heavy. He saw that it was a carving of a pig with pointed hooves and a sharp snout.

'He's jade,' she said. 'I think he's jade, and he's ancient. The catalog says he's from the Han Dynasty. I got him at an auction this morning.'

'Jade, you say?' He turned the pig around, inspecting it critically. 'I was under the impression jade was of a greenish hue.'

'Green, blue, yellow, white almost any color. This little guy was in somebody's tomb. That's why he's brown, he was buried in the earth for such a long time.'

'Do you plan to have it authenticated?'

'Do you enjoy finding out you've been swindled?'

'Well, perhaps you haven't been "swindled", as you put it. Of course, I have no idea—'

'Oh, do stop,' she interrupted. 'I hate to think of what I paid. If Virgil finds out he'll be furious. I can just see him!'

Mr Bridge smiled. 'I won't inform on you. I hope you didn't get stung. I expect a great number of these so-called antiques are in fact fraudulent, but naturally there is a chance of it being genuine.' He continued to inspect the carving. It seemed to be well done, but he could not see why anybody would want it. 'I wasn't aware you were an art collector.'

'I saw him and I had to have him. I was terrifed somebody else would get him. I was ready to spend everything. Sell the house, Virgil's golf clubs, the Cadillac, everything. Everything. Everything!'

'If you're pleased with your purchase, all right,' Mr Bridge said neutrally, and set the pig on the napkin. 'Let's hope the thing is worth whatever you paid.'

'You're not as cold as you pretend to be,' she said. 'I think your doors open in different places, that's all. Most people just don't know how to get in to you. They knock and they knock where the door is supposed to be, but it's a blank wall. But you're there. I've watched you. I've seen you do some awfully cold things warmly and some warm things coldly. Or does that make sense?'

'I'd have to think about it,' he smiled, and picked up the menu. 'What do you recommend?'

'Turtle soup.'

'Turtle soup?'

'Never mind, Walter, there isn't any. I was being foolish again.' She sighed, and with a dejected expression she began stroking the pig. 'Tell me, Walter, have you ever ridden a bicycle?'

'A bicycle? Of course. When I was a boy. Why do you ask?'

'Suppose the four of us get bikes and go for a ride in Swope Park? Virgil would if you would. You're such an influence on him.'

'I'm afraid I must doubt that last statement. Virgil is his own man.'

'What a nineteenth-century figure you are. Honestly!'

This was the sort of remark she made, affectionate and yet insulting. He did not like it. He watched her stroking the snout of the pig and it occurred to him that she was lavishing on a stone animal the affection which perhaps she denied her husband. She was a lost, unhappy little woman. He thought he should feel a sense of pity, but he did not. She jeered at too many things.

'Virgil says the country is going to hell in a basket. Is that so?'

'My opinion of Franklin Roosevelt is pretty well known. If somebody does not put a stop to this New Deal socialism it's my conviction that the country will find itself in serious difficulty, and soon.'

'Virg says you wouldn't give a Communist the time of day.'

'I have no love for Communism. None whatsoever. Let me tell you, if the Communists once obtain a foothold in this country they will stop short of nothing. Those people, if they ever get started, will divide up everything we have, make no mistake about that. Now you may not be disturbed by this prospect. You may not mind "sharing the wealth". But I, for one, have worked too hard for too many years to surrender lightly what I have earned and regard as my own.' He stopped talking. She already knew his opinion of Communism. He could not understand why she had brought up the subject.

'I find it one of the world's loveliest thoughts,' she said. 'Christ asked us to love each other. Marx is asking us to be sure everybody has enough to eat.'

She was attempting to start an argument. 'If so, it has been a singular failure,' he said. 'And let me remind you that Winston Churchill addressing the House of Commons stated recently: "If I had to choose between Communism and Nazism, I would choose Nazism." '

'That son of a bitch.'

'Grace, let us not become any further involved in this. Seldom does an argument of this nature serve any constructive purpose.'

'Virg won't talk to me either. He says I'm a woman and women have no grasp of politics. Nobody wants to talk to me. I feel like I'm living on an island.'

'What sort of talk is that?' he said with a deprecatory expression, and crooked a finger at the waitress, who had approached and was standing nearby.

As soon as he had given his order she resumed: 'Tell me, are we getting into this European horror?'

'Let us hope not. Let us hope we remain uninvolved until it blows over.'

'Can we?'

'The prospects are not encouraging.'

'Alex says this is the first time a rotting civilization will be able to diagnose itself.'

Mr Bridge took a sip of water, wiped his lips on the napkin, and said, 'Alex presumes a great deal. Civilization may not be rotting. My personal opinion is that if Roosevelt and his left-wing advisers do not undermine the freedom and security of this nation we should see advances in many fields of endeavor which will literally stagger the imagination.'

'Jesus, Jesus,' she muttered with an affected Irish accent, 'would you be thinking so, Walter Bridge?'

'If teasing me amuses you, I don't mind.'

'Now could you guess who I saw just the other day, Walter Bridge?'

'I'm afraid not. Whom did you see?'

'Your friend Avrum Rheingold.'

'The man is scarcely a "friend", as you well know.'

'Ah, but he thinks he is.'

'As far as I am concerned he is a jackal.'

'He admires you.'

'I would sooner hear one courteous word from a man I respect than a barrel of fulsome garbage from such a man.'

'He's taken to wearing a diamond ring as big as a cube of sugar on his pinky.'

'That is his privilege.'

'He dyes his hair.'

'Why do you tell me all this? You know perfectly well that what the man does, or is, is a matter of absolute indifference to me.'

'He may be moving into your neighborhood. He wants to buy the Edison house.'

'As far as I know, the Edison house is not for sale.'

'He says it is. He's put in a bid for it.'

Mr Bridge was silent. The thought of Avrum Rheingold living in the Edison house enraged him, but he was careful to hide his anger. He reached for his glass, took another sip of water, and cleared his throat. He did not like the feeling that swept through him, or the urge to say aloud that he approved of the pogrom in Germany.

'You really are, aren't you,' she said as though she could read his mind. 'I always suspected it.' And she began to cry.

For his birthday Ruth sent a copy of *Houyhnhnm* together with a card announcing that he had been given a one-year subscription. It was published in Greenwich Village, which was to be expected. On the front cover was a drawing of a laborer and on the back were weakly printed photographs of contributors to the magazine, all of whom were young, three of them wearing turtleneck sweaters. He leafed through the magazine and did not much care for what he found. A portfolio of photographs of jazz musicians. A one-act play. Poems. Stories. Some pen-and-ink sketches. Several articles which looked as though they were trying to be controversial. He laid the magazine aside. However, because Ruth had given it to him he knew that sooner or later he must read a few pages. She might never know, or ask, whether he had read it or not, but because it was a gift from her he felt an obligation. In his next letter he thanked her for the subscription and said that while he had not yet gotten around to reading the first issue of *Houyhnhnm* he planned to do so.

Finally he could not avoid this chore any longer. He set an hour for it and when the hour came he walked into the study, shut the door, flattened *Houyhnhnm* on his desk, and began to study the table of contents with a dissatisfied expression. The first article was some sort of critical appraisal of a Brazilian poet. The second was a satire on Hollywood movies. Next was an interview with a former convict. Since poetry was out of the question and he already had seen the pictures there was nothing to do but look at the stories. They sounded unpromising. The first was titled 'Zoo', next was 'Pipeful of Dreams', which presumably was about narcotics, and the last, set entirely in lower-case without any punctuation, did not have a title. He considered throwing *Houyhnhnm* in the wastebasket. But he had promised Ruth he would read some of it, so there was no way out. He contemplated the authors on the back cover. The author of 'Zoo' was a boy supposedly named Herman Hermann, who had wild eyes and a straggling beard which gave him a singular resemblance to a goat. He was so unusually repellent that Mr Bridge decided to find out what he had written. He crossed his legs, leaned back in the swivel chair, and began.

The story consisted of a description of the houses and citizens of Sheridan Square. After finishing it he considered whether he had read enough or whether he was obligated to try something else. In another three months he was going to receive a second issue and ought to read at least one piece in that, and two further issues would follow before the year of purgatory ended. So he placed *Houyhnhnm* high on the bookcase where he would not come across it again by accident, and, very much relieved, went downstairs to the kitchen to fix himself a drink. Mrs Bridge was in the kitchen preparing dinner because it was Harriet's night out.

'Where is Douglas?' he asked.

'He went tootling off somewhere. His friends came by and he couldn't resist. He did promise to be home by nine thirty.'

'And where is our daughter?'

'Still at the club. She phoned a little while ago. She should be here any minute.'

'This family is flying off in all directions,' he said, and sat down at the kitchen table with a drink in his hand. 'Well, I tried to read that magazine.'

She was peering into the oven at the roast. 'You did what?'

He repeated what he had said, gave a summary of the story, and went on: 'What I don't understand is why in the name of all that's holy these young people can't write about anything except the gutter.'

Mrs Bridge was opening a can of succotash.

'This young fellow goes on and on about torn window shades, drunks, prostitutes, and I don't know what-all. A little bit of that goes a long way, but he just wouldn't let up. He insists on rubbing your nose in it. I thought the darn story was never going to end.'

'Well, I suppose,' she murmured, and slid a pan of rolls into the oven.

'Kids today say "That's life!" but I tell you there's more to life than the sort of existence people lead in Greenwich Village. I don't mind saying I've seen enough of life to know a bit about it. Years ago when I was a young man I lived in a slum district and I didn't like it and certainly never was foolish enough to consider it romantic, and I never want to go back to it. But these young people nowadays sound as though they're attracted to the trash cans and every other sort of filth they can find. I don't understand what they're up to. Frankly, I was tempted to hand the thing over to Alex Sauer to see what he could make of it.'

'Oh!' she said, and stopped work. 'Guess what. Madge called this afternoon. Dr Sauer and Genevieve are getting married. I was simply floored.'

'More power to them,' he said, lifting his drink. 'For a wedding present I just might send them a year's subscription. I suspect it would be right up their alley.'

'Now, that's not very nice,' she said.

A few minutes later Carolyn came home, and he asked what she had been doing all day. As usual she had been playing golf. Most of her summer was being spent on the Mission course. It was a waste of time, he thought, but at least she was not mixed up with a Greenwich Village crowd.

101 Billy Jack Andrews, pro

Billy Jack was the golf professional at Mission Country Club. He had been there as long as anybody could remember, he was at least sixty-five years old, and only children called him Mr Andrews. The day was not far off when Billy Jack would retire. That was what people said. But they had been saying it since he was fifty, and now, seeing him on the course, it appeared he would still be the pro when he was eighty. He had taught Carolyn how to hold the clubs when she was eleven, but after her first few lessons he quit being a genial instructor and became a relentless coach. A year later he insisted she begin playing in the annual tournament. He told Mrs Bridge that Carolyn could become a champion, which naturally was reported to Mr Bridge. Both of them were bemused and waited to see what would happen.

Unfortunately, Billy Jack told Carolyn the same thing, no doubt to encourage her and give her the confidence to play against older girls. Carolyn's game improved much faster as a result of this compliment, but after a while she began talking as though it was his fault she had not yet won the championship. He took these remarks with good humor and continued to coach her, but his grandfatherly affection was cooling.

Then one day after she had played the course against the Mission women's champion, losing by two strokes, they were walking up the path toward the clubhouse, followed by their caddies, when they met Billy Jack on his way out with another student. He stopped to inquire about the game and he congratulated Carolyn for having played so well. She replied that if he had not instructed her to use a six-iron across the water hazard on the fourteenth hole she would have tied the match.

Billy Jack told Carolyn she was insufferable. He told her she had not paid any attention to his advice about the water hazard and he informed her that in general she had a great deal yet to learn about the game, as well as about common courtesy. In his years at Mission he had encountered plenty of temperamental golfers. He did not intend to be pushed around by this one.

Carolyn was too astounded to speak. Nobody had ever spoken to her like that, so she did not know how to react; she glowered helplessly as Billy Jack and his student walked on down the path to the course.

But as the minutes and the hours went by she began to know how she felt; what she wanted more than anything on earth was to have Billy Jack fired. She wanted the head of Billy Jack Andrews on a platter. His flayed skin she would nail to the wall just as her brother once wanted to nail a squirrel to the wall, and his reputation she would grind into the dust. And because she did not have the power to accomplish this she went to her father, who had been a member of the club for a long time, who had paid dues for years, who surely would be in a position to destroy the pro. She argued her case and waited, confident that he would rise up in rage. But for some reason he did not. She was puzzled because he appeared to be thinking it over.

Mr Bridge was acquainted with the pro. Years before, he had taken a few lessons with the idea of getting some exercise, but a round of golf used up half the day – which seemed wasteful – so he had quit. Since then he had run into Billy Jack now and then at the club, and the pro remembered him, which was a bit flattering. Mr Bridge liked Billy Jack.

Carolyn tried every device she had used on her father in the past.

Nothing worked. He told her that even if her resentment was justifiable, which he doubted, he did not think that a single incident was sufficient cause to demand that the pro be dismissed. He inquired if other golfers were complaining about Billy Jack. Carolyn replied that everybody was complaining; but as soon as she had said this she realized her father would ask for the names of people who had complained and he would call them up, so she went on quickly: 'Don't you care if an employee of the club insults me?'

Mr Bridge understood that nobody else had complained and he understood that she was attempting to divert him. He replied that perhaps she deserved what she got.

Carolyn's hands trembled as though she was about to seize something and throw it. The freckles on her face stood out like measles.

'You listen here, young lady,' he said in a warning voice, 'you simmer down.'

It might be true that the professional had spoken out of turn, and it was true that despite his status, which caused him to be treated by the members as an equal, he was, after all, one of the employees. Nonetheless, Carolyn's arrogance could not be tolerated. He told her that she was not to adopt a superior attitude toward Billy Jack nor toward any other employee of the club, nor toward anybody else, for that matter, anywhere, at any time, under any circumstances. If she did, she was going to find herself in hot water. Was this clear? And to emphasize the seriousness of this message he dropped his forefinger on the desk – in the silence of the study it sounded like the tap of a bird's beak against the window.

Carolyn gave him a sudden, stark look and retreated. Her eyes told him all he needed to know: she would behave more considerately from now on. Or, if she did not, at least she would be aware of what she was doing.

102 Peggy

Another employee of the club that summer was a cheerful little waitress with heavy breasts and a mole on the tip of her nose, who carried trays of sandwiches and cold drinks from the coffee shop to the swimming pool. About a week after she started to work Douglas was observed to be quite friendly with her, a fact which Carolyn reported at home. Nothing was said about this until a second report suggested that Douglas and the waitress were seeing each other elsewhere.

Mrs Bridge was alarmed. She did not like Carolyn reporting on her brother, neither did she like the thought of him going out with the waitress; and so, after hinting to Douglas that she was aware of his activities, and getting no response, she took the problem to her husband.

He listened to the details. He felt more or less the same, although slightly more irked with Carolyn and somewhat less concerned about Douglas.

She asked what he thought should be done.

He suggested they ignore the matter. It was a summer romance, and the petals would turn brown pretty rapidly in September because the girl lived halfway across the city and attended a different high school – one more bit of information from Carolyn. But then he reconsidered. Douglas was not yet old enough to drive, so the threat of the automobile could be ignored; however, he had reached an age where a girl from a lower-class family might seem like fair game. This attitude could cause trouble. It was not apt to, but it might. He said he would have a talk with Douglas.

He did not like questioning his son, but having committed himself, he did. Douglas was invited into the study, the door was shut, and without wasting any time Mr Bridge asked how much he knew about the girl.

Douglas slumped in the witness chair. Not much, he said.

They had met at the club, was that correct?

At the swimming pool.

At the swimming pool, all right. Where did she live?

In a big apartment building near Menorah Hospital. Her mother worked at Menorah, he thought.

Menorah? Was this girl a Jewess?

Douglas didn't know. He had never thought about it. He guessed she might be Irish.

What was her name?

Peggy O'Hara.

Was it true they were seeing each other away from the club?

Yes.

How many times had they seen each other?

He sighed. Three or four times. Maybe five times.

Where did they go on these occasions?

Bowling. Movies. Sometimes walked around.

How did she get home?

Took the bus, transferred to the streetcar, walked the rest of the way.

Had he gone home with her?

Once. Her mother didn't like it.

Douglas was sliding lower and lower in the chair. His mouth hung open and his eyes rolled toward the ceiling with a look of anguish.

Mr Bridge said he was sorry, he did not enjoy asking these questions, but it was easy for a boy to find himself in an awkward situation with a very young girl. And please sit up straight in the chair.

There was a long pause. One particular question must be asked. Had he been intimate with this girl?

Douglas coughed. He scratched his nose. He took a deep breath. Finally he murmured no, not very much. Just a little.

Did he like this girl? Or was she merely an available girl?

Well, yes.

Well yes, what?

He liked her.

Did he think he was in love with her?

No.

Mr Bridge asked if there were not some girls from his own high school or some girls who went swimming at the club that he would not like to take to the movies.

Not especially. He liked Peggy pretty well.

Why?

She was different.

In what respect?

Most girls were stuck-up. They thought they were hot stuff.

Not all of them, surely.

Most of them. The other ones were ugly. Anyway, he liked Peggy. She gave him a free ice-cream cone.

And here, completely unexpected, was the clue. Mr Bridge leaned forward. So she gave him an ice-cream cone, did she? Why did she do this?

Well, one day she brought him an ice-cream cone, that was all. He hadn't ordered it, she just brought it down to the pool and handed it to him. No other girl ever had given him anything.

Did he expect presents?

No. No, he didn't expect anything.

Then Mr Bridge was silent for a while. At last he said: All right, but be careful.

103 Venus of Mission Hills

As he was passing Carolyn's room he glanced in. She stood naked on one foot in front of the long mirror, arms poised as if she were about to dance.

In the study he dropped his briefcase heavily on the desk. He wondered if she had seen him as he walked by. He looked down the hall. Now the door to her room was shut, so she knew. The fault was hers, he thought angrily. She should know better than to leave the door open when she undressed. He sat down at his desk, unzipped the briefcase, and started to examine the papers he had brought from the office; but he saw her nubile body as she posed before the mirror. He reminded himself that she was his daughter, but the luminous image returned like the memory of a dream, and although he dismissed it, soon it returned. He stopped work and held his head in his hands, wondering how much time must go by until he could forget.

Dearest Ruth:

Your mother and I are planning a short vacation in Europe. I had hoped it might be a lengthy trip insofar as there are many famous cities we both would like to see, but the pressures of this office apparently will not let up. If anything, they grow worse from year to year. Consequently, we expect to be away from Kansas City approximately five weeks (six weeks if I find that I am able to arrange my schedule accordingly). We arrive in New York by train — as your mother does not like to fly — on or about the sixth of August. I will let you know the exact date as soon as the travel agent has confirmed our various European hotel reservations. We expect to spend two days in Manhattan, and hope you will have some time for us. This trip is partly a vacation for myself, but it is also a fulfilment of a commitment I made to your mother many years ago. I promised her that one day we would visit Europe. She does not yet know about this trip. I am saving it as a surprise and intend to give her the news on her birthday, hence I sincerely hope you will not mention this (or allude to it in any form) when you write to her.

The family is in good health as usual. I am very grateful for this. Except for the usual childhood illnesses and the occasion when Douglas sprained his ankles jumping off the garage roof we have escaped serious injury and sickness. Few families are so fortunate. Let us hope our luck continues to hold. (Julia, too, remains in good health. What I would do without her I do not know.) Your sister Carolyn we have seen very little of this summer as she evidently prefers to spend as much time as possible on the golf course. The club professional repeatedly states she 'has the makings of a champion' — but I am positive your mother has written you about this. We shall wait and see. Your brother is greatly relieved to have the braces off his teeth once and for all.

Is there anything you need or want? I do not, of course, know how the money is holding out. I trust you are not spending the sum that I put into the bank for you recklessly. Money does not grow on trees. I worked very hard for many years to acquire what I have. Buy whatever you need and enjoy yourself, but remember there is much more to a successful life than playing around and indulging various fancies to no constructive purpose. My condition remains — you shall expect no more money from me as long as you remain in New York (except in case of emergency). If you enjoy living there, as you seem to, I sincerely hope you will prove capable of supporting yourself. Therefore you should strive for advancement and not squander your salary. If so, you will regret it. But as I say, if you should abruptly fall ill or some other emergency should arise, do not hesitate to get in touch with me. After all, that is what fathers are for.

A number of young men have telephoned the house to ask your whereabouts. Your mother is taking care of the situation. Neither of us is in favor of giving out your address unless we know the person, or unless you specifically request us to do so. Now that you are no longer a child but are 'on your own' in one of the world's largest cities you should take care. I am sure you are aware that carrying on with strangers can prove perilous. You will discover that old friends are best (something I learned after much heartache).

I doubt if I have much news to interest you. One of the men with whom I have lunch at the Muehlebach, Dr Alexis Sauer, who I know you remember, recently returned from a flying visit to the Orient and India with his second wife, who is very much younger than himself. I gather they had a 'close call' at one point in the plane. His descriptions of the beggars and suffering and local color, such as elephants with painted foreheads, were fascinating, but I doubt if I care to visit that area. There is suffering everyplace on earth — I have witnessed enough first and secondhand and have little desire to travel halfway around the globe for a glimpse of leprous beggars. It is my opinion our European tour will prove more rewarding. However, as the French say, 'Chacun à son goût'! I trust you recall enough of your high school French to be able to translate this expression.

In regard to news closer to home we read in the Star that one of your classmates, Sue Ellen Stubbs, who is the niece of a friend of your mother, Margaret Hockaday, is engaged to a West Point man whose name escapes me at the moment. They are being married in the autumn at West Point. October, if memory serves. Should you wish to attend the wedding, I am sure it could be arranged. Let your mother know and she will telephone Miss Hockaday. I do not know how close you and this girl were during your schooldays, however it seems to me that a West Point wedding ought to be very colorful.

I do not believe there is much else. Mrs Barron and your mother are planning to visit the Nelson Gallery this afternoon. Mrs Barron spends a great deal of time visiting art galleries of all sorts. It is too bad you and she did not get to know each other better. I suspect the two of you have much in common.

Our weather has changed for the better. We have been reasonably comfortable the past several days with moderate temperatures, thunderstorms, and showers.

Love,
Dad

105 Art of India

Finding himself a few minutes ahead of schedule, he decided to walk to the federal courthouse instead of calling a taxi. On the way he passed a bookstore, and in the display window stood an expensive volume on the art of India. He stopped walking. Elephants with painted foreheads, cribs of women, moaning beggars, funeral pyres, ancient red-stone forts, leprosy, children infested with lice, and quite a lot more of what he found in India had been described by Dr Sauer while eating lobster bisque at the Terrace Grill. Among the spectacles he described were the temples of Konorak and Khajuraho, whose walls were decorated with erotic sculpture – thousands of men and women in fantastic positions and groups of people performing as though they were animals – and this was what first came to mind when Mr Bridge thought about India, because it represented an attitude toward life very distant from life as he knew it in Kansas City. Children dying of starvation on the streets of Calcutta were easier to imagine than the existence of temples covered with swarms of copulating figures, perhaps because poverty in some degree was common. Everywhere in the world one could find sick and hungry people. In Europe there was filth, hunger, and squalor, and this could be found also in Kansas City; but nowhere else was anything comparable to these Indian temple displays of licentiousness.

He walked into the store and asked to see the book. It was filled with handsome, colored photographs of painting and sculpture. There were no pictures of the scenes Dr Sauer had described; however, there were a good many photographs of impossibly voluptuous, dreamily smiling dancers with almond eyes and bells on their ankles.

He bought this book and at home he placed it on the coffee table in the living room. Mrs Bridge promptly exclaimed over it, but then she began to look through it, and after that she did not have very much to say.

Days passed. She did not mention the book again. Douglas frequently looked at it, Harriet was found with it in her lap when she was supposed to be vacuuming the carpet, and Carolyn looked at it when nobody else was around. But the book was never mentioned. Mr Bridge considered the situation, and one evening without a word he picked it up and carried it into the breakfast room where he made a place for it on the top shelf between *Ben-Hur* and a leather-bound copy of *Who's Who in Kansas City*.

106 Publishers' graveyard

That the only large bookshelves should be in the breakfast room had always seemed curious; nevertheless, that was where they had been built, so there most of the household books eventually were laid to rest. There lay the old Agatha Christies and Erle Stanley Gardners he had employed as soporifics after the tension of the day. There stood several abandoned cookbooks, the dictionary, *The Rubáiyát*, *The Sheriff of Chispa Loma*, the travel adventures of Lowell Thomas, Dr Foster's little volume of essays titled *Thoughts at Eventide*, *Hammond's Illustrated Nature Guide* and *Northwest Passage*, and various school textbooks which for one reason or another had not been exchanged at the beginning of the new school year. There rested, all forgotten, those diaphanous novels penned by ladies with three names which Mrs Bridge had hurried out to buy because everybody that season was buying them, or which she had won as a prize at an afternoon card party. There, too, like a warped tombstone, leaned a gaunt volume of Currier and Ives prints, and *Thirty Days to a More Powerful Vocabulary*, and *The Magnificent Ambersons*, and a biography of Marie Antoinette. And there were others. Unreadable Christmas gifts and birthday gifts. In the dappled sunshine of the breakfast room, arranged solemnly side by side or piled one atop the other could be found an almanac with humorous drawings, books about gardening, *A Treasury of Best Loved Poems*, a short history of the Civil War, the collected lyrics of Sara Teasdale, *Great Wines of France*, *The Santa Fe Trail*, *Of Human Bondage*, *Bambi*, and numerous others – undisturbed by any hand, unless it might be Harriet indolently dusting the shelves with a wand of peacock feathers.

107 Good luck

En route to Europe they stopped three days and two nights in New York, but Ruth spent only one evening with them. While they were finishing dinner at a Chinese restaurant she offered a confused and apologetic explanation as to why she could not see them on the second evening, immediately adding that when they came through New York on the way back to Kansas City she would have more free time. To conceal his disappointment Mr Bridge picked up his fortune cookie, broke it, and pulled out the paper.

'Good luck who wait,' he read aloud. 'This must be a misprint. I suppose it means "Good luck to those who wait".'

Ruth snapped her fortune cookie apart and straightened the crumpled paper. ' "Your new affairs will turn out well," ' she read, and laughed.

Both of them turned to Mrs Bridge, who looked at them blankly. There was no fortune cookie on her plate. She had eaten it.

'Mother,' said Ruth with an incredulous expression, 'did you eat the paper?'

With as much dignity as possible she said, 'I thought there was something odd inside.'

After a long silence Mr Bridge said, 'Do you mean to tell me you never saw a fortune cookie before?'

She smiled stiffly.

'Well,' he said, 'I'm not sure just what we do now. Would you like another?'

'No, thank you, I don't believe so,' she replied, and she touched her pearl necklace as if it were a talisman which would protect her from everything strange.

In the days that followed this remarkable incident he found that it affected his feelings toward her, reawakening his desire to guard and shelter her. He had nearly forgotten her extraordinary naïveté because he had grown accustomed to it. He began to remember astonishing remarks she made in pure faith, and attitudes which touched him deeply because they were born of genuine innocence. She had never smoked a cigarette, and never had he heard her use a vulgar expression. She believed that women should refrain from saying or doing anything coarse, just as she believed most people to be generous, well intentioned, and trustworthy. He wondered again, as he used to wonder when they were first married, how she had managed to live this much of her life with such simplicity, unaware of treachery, suspicion, malice, guile, and so many other means whereby life is lived; and he realized more clearly how he himself was responsible. He had taken her from the home where she had been sheltered as a child and substituted himself for her father, so she knew nothing she had not been permitted to know. Now she must refuse to believe everything which contradicted her beliefs. As long as she lived she would be like this.

While she wandered around the deck of the ship studying the ocean and chatting with other tourists, he observed her with a sense of amazement. She was forty-seven years old and this was the first time she had seen an ocean. Of course it was natural, because they lived so far from the ocean, yet he could not get over his amazement. Once he had taken her to Chicago; there she saw Lake Michigan and was greatly impressed. In forty-seven years she had seen Lake Michigan and had viewed the Rocky Mountains a few miles west of Denver, otherwise she knew of nothing larger than Lake Lotawana. Several times she had mentioned how much she would like to see the Grand Canyon.

He often thought about this; it saddened him and filled him with grave wonderment, and caused him to feel obscurely guilty. Perhaps they should not have waited so long to take this trip. They could have visited Europe sooner, seen and done many things. Now it was almost too late. She was passing through life with a neutral and pleasant expression, utterly failing to recognize the world in which she lived: a desperate, harsh, remorseless world where everybody knew there was a piece of paper inside a Chinese fortune cookie. This was more than merely odd. It was more than strange. It was a bit grotesque. Perhaps they should have gambled at Las Vegas and flown to India. There were sights and sounds and experiences far beyond the limits of Kansas City which perhaps they should have shared before this.

And yet there had been so much to do at home. She had been busy with the children. He had been occupied with his career. They had lived reasonably and logically, with fine practicality, and it had come to this. Over halfway through life, possibly much closer to the end than they knew, this was where they found themselves.

108 Foul weather

Three days before they expected to reach England the ship began to roll as though some immense weight in the hull was sliding from side to side: water sloshed across the portholes, pencils rolled off tables, passengers grabbed for support when they tried to walk, closets creaked, the staterooms grew dark and then light again and dark, the sky was brindled gray, canvas chairs on the promenade deck flapped emptily, and not many people came to lunch. Mr Bridge, though, had never felt better and was on his feet at the first note of the steward's gong; and after a big meal he strode around the decks and climbed the ladders and stood with his nose pointing into the wind while he appreciatively sniffed the icy spray. The previous days at sea had been all right, he had enjoyed them too, but this was more to his liking.

The weather got worse. The ship plunged like a wild horse, foam spewed across the bow and crossed the decks with a rushing, spattering hiss, water trickled inside the portholes, bottles and vases fell over, and Mr Bridge decided he was feeling thirty years younger. He thought it might be fun to play shuffleboard, so he descended to the cabin where he had left his wife with a copy of *Reader's Digest*. Now she lay on her bunk. A washcloth was spread over her face and a bottle of medicine stood on the table. He regarded her with silent disapproval and climbed back up to the lounge – steering himself along the tilting corridor with an amused expression – lunged like a fencer at the door, managed to get inside without cracking his head, and looked about hopefully for a shuffleboard opponent. But in the lounge there were just five passengers, every one of them more dead than alive, staring at nothing as though they were made of wax.

And the weather got worse. Several members of the crew entered the lounge and strung ropes from pillar to pillar. The ship heaved and rolled and buried itself in the waves as though it intended to dive for treasure. The horizon sank dizzily. The deck shuddered. The passengers sagged in their chairs as if their bones were pudding. Mr Bridge observed them with disgust. He found the motion of the ship invigorating.

At the first note of the supper chimes he hurried down to the cabin once more. Possibly by now she had recovered. But when he inquired if she was ready to eat she feebly turned her head to the wall. He asked if he could bring her anything. A bowl of soup? – an orange? – a slice of cake? She did not respond. He climbed the ladder again, whistling. He had not whistled for many years.

He marched into the dining salon rubbing his hands with anticipation. He sat down alone at the table, which seated eight, and without hesitation he devoured everything the steward put in front of him.

109 On the morning train

One rainy morning before dawn they landed at Southampton and in sleepy silence rode through the orderly English countryside toward London. Somewhere along the way a middle-aged Englishman wearing a sweater and a tweed jacket stepped into the compartment, seated himself, and began to read a newspaper. Mr Bridge was dozing when the door opened and he caught only a glimpse of the man before he disappeared behind the newspaper, yet in that instant he saw something which disturbed him, and he waited for a better look. At last the Englishman folded the paper, then Mr Bridge saw his face. The face was that of his grandfather.

Later in the day at their hotel in London while she was unpacking the suitcases he studied the timetable of the Southampton train. He was certain he would never again see this man, who had vanished in the crowd at the station as mysteriously as he appeared, and he had no intention of trying to locate him, but he wanted to know the name of the town where the Englishman got aboard the train. So he shut his eyes, trying to recall the announcement of the stop; then she asked if he had a headache. No, he said, and put away the timetable.

During their five days in London he realized that he was

searching for the man – in the hotel lobby, on the street, in restaurants, art galleries, and theaters. If he had encountered the stranger he would not have spoken, nor offered the slightest sign of recognition, yet all the while they were in London he found himself hunting for that face.

110 Petra

They spent their first evening in Paris with a young art student from Kansas City named Morgan Hager whose parents had informed him that Mr and Mrs Bridge were touring Europe. He therefore was expected to entertain them, if they wished to be entertained. Hager called the hotel, suggested an apéritif, and volunteered to come by for them in a taxi. Mr Bridge, suspecting that Hager might be existing on very little money, told him the taxi was unnecessary, and they arranged to meet at a sidewalk café called Le Petit Lapin.

Here, after a second apéritif, Mr Bridge expressed a desire to see something of the Bohemian life. Hager thought this over. He scratched his head without removing his beret, he plucked at his beard, and finally he suggested they have dinner at a restaurant called Henri's on Montparnasse. Artists and models ate there.

This sounded fine. Mr Bridge paid for the drinks and they started up the boulevard in the direction of Montparnasse.

They walked past the Comédie Française, they walked around the Luxembourg Gardens, crossed Raspail, went up one alley and down another, and eventually, having walked for more than half an hour, they arrived at Henri's. It was extremely small, with sawdust on the floor, very dirty and very crowded.

For various reasons this meal was memorable. Mrs Bridge was unable to cut the beefsteak without help, the wine resembled cherry soda with flecks of cork floating about on the surface, the bread was like stone, one of their neighbors, whom Hager introduced as Claude, had not bathed in a month or two, and Claude discovered a spider in his salad, although this did not trouble him very much. Still, as Hager promised, it was something of the Bohemian life, and the bill for three came to less than coffee and croissants at their hotel on the Champs Elysées, a fact which Mr Bridge did not intend to forget.

Yet what made this experience memorable for him was neither the execrable food, the dirtiness, the extraordinary customers, nor the remarkable price, but a mention of the fabulous city of Petra, whose intricately carved cliffs echoed the tinkling bells of camel caravans a thousand years before the birth of Marco Polo. He paused with a slice of tomato in mid-air and began to recite: ' "It seems no work of man's creative hand by labor wrought as wavering fancy planned, but from the rock as if by magic grown, eternal, silent, beautiful, alone!" '

'My word!' Mrs Bridge exclaimed. 'What was that? – if you please.'

' "Match me such marvel save in Eastern clime, a rose-red city half as old as time." That was by John William Burgon. It was quite a celebrated bit of verse during my school days. As a matter of fact, I believe it won some sort of important prize. We were required to commit it to memory. So you have been there, have you?' he said to Hager. 'I was under the impression the place was virtually inaccessible.'

'I must admit I'm altogether at a loss,' Mrs Bridge said. 'What on earth are you talking about?'

'Morgan? Would you care to answer?'

Hager said, 'You probably know more about it than I do. You answer.'

Mr Bridge laughed. 'If you have been there you should be the authority. However, I suspect I might be able to answer the question. I became quite fascinated with Petra as a consequence of memorizing the poem. The poem, of course, consists of a number of stanzas, and there was a day I was able to quote it in its entirety. I doubt if I could do so now. At any rate, as I say, I became quite taken with Petra in consequence and visited the library in order to find out more about it. Let me see what I can recall.'

He cleared his throat. 'Petra was constructed – or I should say, carved out of the cliff – by Nabataean Arabs during a period of some five centuries commencing about 300BC. It is located approximately two hundred miles south of the Dead Sea. For a number of centuries it was a wealthy and celebrated city with a vast caravan trade, but declined in importance with the rise of

Palmyra. The Nabataeans were astute traders and competent engineers, digging wells, building cisterns, and terracing arid land so that the surrounding desert would produce sufficient grain, fruit, and vegetables to feed the people. Their kingdom – if such it may be called – at one time extended as far north as Damascus. I seem to recall that a Nabataean governor ruled Damascus when St Paul was converted on the Damascus road. In any event, Petra was annexed as a Roman province and later was conquered by Moslems and still later by Crusaders. It was then abandoned and "lost" to the world. Even the knowledge of its existence was lost until a Swiss explorer, whose name escapes me at the moment, discovered it early in the nineteenth century. Now it is considered one of the world's most rewarding and adventurous travel experiences. The ornately carved façade of a building referred to as the "Treasury" is reputed to be a never-to-be-forgotten sight. And I believe this pretty well summarizes my skimpy knowledge of Petra. Morgan, I'm sure you must have a great deal to tell us about it. We certainly would be interested in hearing. I have, in a manner of speaking, often dreamed of visiting Petra.'

Hager looked uncomfortable.

Mr Bridge went on: 'The encyclopedia states that the rock is stratified in a magnificent profusion of color – the famous rose color, as well as crimson, purple, saffron, and various other hues intermingled with black and white. Now tell us, is it as beautiful as the encyclopedia would have us believe?'

Hager said it was, and once more scratched his head.

'So you've been to Petra, have you!' Mr Bridge remarked as though reluctant to believe it. 'The rose-red city half as old as time – and you have been there!' Gazing at Morgan Hager he wondered how an insignificant, fatuous boy had managed to do what he had merely dreamed of doing.

111 Good night, good night!

As they were leaving Henri's restaurant Hager pointed to a hotel further down the street, and putting on a droll face he said it was a very famous hotel. Mrs Bridge promptly wished to know why.

Because, he announced with a theatrical gesture, Mademoiselle Susy used to live in that hotel. Mrs Bridge confessed she had not heard of Mademoiselle Susy. Hager appeared rather startled; he glanced uncertainly at Mr Bridge, but finding no comfort there, in fact no response whatever, he looked again at Mrs Bridge and opened his mouth to explain, but changed his mind and suggested they wander toward St Germain des Prés for a cognac. Mrs Bridge, however, would have none of this, not until she heard the story of Mademoiselle Susy. Hager pulled off his beret and turned it inside out as though he expected to find the answer inside, and then he put it on again.

Mr Bridge, studying him with frank curiosity, guessed that the reference to the hotel and the woman was intended as some sort of a joke. Probably she had been a notorious prostitute who conducted her business there. But the joke failed because neither of them had heard of her, so Hager had talked himself into a cul-de-sac.

'A cognac,' he said, 'sounds to me like an excellent idea, Morgan.'

Mrs Bridge suspected something was being kept from her; she repeated that she was not walking one more step until she had heard all about Mademoiselle Susy.

'She had a pony,' Hager blurted, and gave Mr Bridge a stark, desperate look.

Mrs Bridge, more bewildered than ever, shook her head helplessly. Hager tugged his beard and rolled his eyes.

'Let's get that cognac,' said Mr Bridge.

Mrs Bridge stamped her foot. 'Both of you stop right where you are. I insist on knowing what this is all about. Morgan, why did she have a pony? Did she like to ride?'

Hager said breathlessly, 'I don't know, she had an Alsation dog, too. Listen, I've got to be going. I'm late. I got to meet somebody. Good night. It was sure swell meeting both of you. Good night.' He was backing away.

Mr Bridge nodded. 'Good night, Morgan.'

Mrs Bridge was completely confused. 'If you're late, Morgan, we certainly won't keep you. But—'

Hager was nearly staggering in his haste to get away. 'Good night! Good night!' he cried.

'Good night, Morgan,' she answered, waving to him. 'It's been awfully nice. We enjoyed the evening so much.' She was still waving to him with a bewildered and hurt expression when he turned the corner.

112 J'ai faim

The next day they got off to an early start and by noon had visited Montmartre and the church of Sacré Coeur, been to the top of Notre Dame, and spent several minutes in the Invalides peering down at Napoleon's tomb. Then after a ride to the top of the Eiffel Tower and a tasty luncheon of lobster and chilled white wine they proceeded to the Louvre. Mrs Bridge had been looking forward to this. First on her list were the Mona Lisa, the Venus de Milo, and the Winged Victory of Samothrace. They located the first two without much difficulty. But after wandering about for some time in search of the Winged Victory, meanwhile stopping to inspect vases, tapestries, paintings, mummies, and other relics, Mr Bridge proposed to wait outside while she continued through the Louvre alone. The Louvre held an impressive and invaluable collection, but in London they had spent almost three hours at the National Gallery, to say nothing of five or six other galleries and museums, and there were more coming up in Florence and Rome. Enough was enough.

So he left her in the corridor beneath an enormous painting of some half-naked people struggling on a raft, picked up the camera from the entrance where he had checked it, and went outside and sat down on a bench in the shade of a tree. The day was very hot. He took off his linen coat and folded it across his lap. He observed the French children in blue smocks playing with hoops and balloons, old women knitting and chatting, and he felt pleased with the trip so far. He considered what they had done and thought about what was next on the itinerary. The Riviera. Italy. Switzerland. Then home again. Germany and Spain, unfortunately, must be excluded. Maybe in another few years when the children were grown and these countries stabilized themselves a more comprehensive tour would be feasible. He thought about the children, about Harriet's drinking, and the work at the office. He thought of sending a wire to Julia to find out if everything was in order. But she had a copy of the itinerary and she was sensible. She would be in touch if necessary. He thought again of how important this trip was for his wife. He had felt the emotion she herself felt at the first sight of Notre Dame. This moment alone was worth the expense, the preparation, and all the annoyance of travel. He reflected that they should have done more traveling. However, there was still time. In the years to come they would visit other countries. The Orient. The Middle East. When it was not so difficult they might arrange to see Petra.

Finally she emerged from the Louvre and he knew at once that it had been everything she hoped. He asked what she wanted to do next and she wondered if they might walk around awhile in St Germain, which they had not visited because of Morgan Hager's extraordinary disappearance. He doubted if there was much in St Germain except some more Bohemian artists, and they had encountered plenty of those the previous night; however if that was where she wished to go that was where they would go.

He flagged another taxi. They rode across the Seine, got out of the taxi and walked around, and finally they settled in a café to rest and discuss what they had seen.

Presently a little girl about nine or ten years old stopped at the table and held out her hand. She was dressed in a rag and did not have any shoes. Her face was streaked with dirt. She had been crying. She stood beside the table, her eyes fastened on Mr Bridge, and she murmured, 'Monsieur, j'ai faim.'

He reached into his pocket for a coin. Then he paused without knowing why, and he exclaimed harshly: 'Go away! Go away, child! Get away from this table.'

The little girl coughed. In her soft, pleading voice she repeated, 'J'ai faim.'

He waved at her. 'Off! Off! Allez-vous!' he cried, brushing at her. 'You may as well leave right now, because I will not give you one red cent. Not one cent will you get from me, do you understand?'

'J'ai faim. S'il vous plaît, monsieur,' she whimpered. She wiped her nose. She coughed again. Her beseeching eyes stuck to him.

Mrs Bridge said, 'Walter! For Heaven's sake!'

'You let me handle this,' he replied. He shook his finger at the child. 'Allez-vous vite! Run away, child. You will get nothing here. Go away!'

'J'ai faim,' whispered the little girl, and clutched her stomach in case he did not quite understand French.

He gestured furiously because she was attempting to humiliate him. 'Leave us alone,' he said, aiming his index finger straight between her eyes, 'or I will send for the police. The police. Comprenez-vous?'

She pretended that she did not, but he was sure she did. Very sadly she wandered away.

'Oh, Walter,' Mrs Bridge gasped after the child was gone. 'I know how you feel about giving to people in the street, but goodness, there are exceptions! I haven't been so embarrassed since I don't know when.'

'That child was attempting to take advantage of the fact that we are tourists,' he said, and he was still angered.

'The waiter should not have allowed her to molest us. Nor was she begging, she was demanding. I will not be coerced. I contribute a reasonable percentage of what I earn each year to various charities. In addition, I do occasionally give money to street beggars. However, I refuse to be taken advantage of. That is all there is to it. The subject is closed.'

He knew she was ashamed of him, and it was an unpleasant way to end the afternoon, but he did not see how he could have behaved differently.

Half an hour later they left the café to return to the hotel. They stood on the corner while he waved at taxis, but it was the rush hour and none would stop. They decided to walk a few blocks toward the hotel in the hope of catching one along the way, and as they crossed a narrow side street opening into the boulevard he caught her arm and pointed. On the curb with her feet in the gutter sat the little girl. She was not coughing and crying, she was counting money, stacking coins in neat rows with the casual ease of a professional. She was a fake who preyed on tourists, there was no doubt about it. She had several dollars' worth of francs.

'I thought so!' he remarked to his wife as they continued along the boulevard. 'Something told me to beware of that child. I was suspicious right from the start.'

113 Moulin rouge

He had frequently reminded her that in Paris the one thing they were going to see if they saw nothing else was a cancan. He always laughed when he said this, while she, pretending to be somewhat scandalized, always protested but ended by saying that if he was determined to go she certainly intended to go along as a chaperone.

So to Pigalle they went for dinner and a revue, and afterward in the taxi while they were returning to the hotel he joked about the cancan girls. He announced that he was planning to send a dozen roses to the one who had caught his eye; she replied that if he dared he would never hear the last of it.

But in their room after she had fallen asleep he lay awake with a somber expression. He remembered how the girls danced on one leg in time to Offenbach's music and how they waved their skirts. The cabaret was filled with tourists and the sexuality of the spectacle was false, contrived for effect in every detail, like the black elastic garters stretched across their full young thighs; yet he had been astounded. What he had expected to see he had seen, and therefore it was not exciting, it was more in the nature of a confirmation; but he had been unprepared for the lascivious screams of the girls — screaming while they waved their skirts, as if their bellies were afire. Again and again he could hear those obscene cries in the musky silence of the Parisian night.

He turned his head on the pillow to look at his wife; she lay motionless in a deep, exhausted sleep. He thought of her affectionate embrace, which was invariably the same, and he felt resentful, for something which rightfully belonged to every man had been denied him.

114 Les sabots de Millet

Among the famous attractions in the environs of Paris which she was most anxious to visit were the Bois de Boulogne, the cathedral of Chartres, the palace of Louis XIV at Versailles, and the forest of Fontainebleau where the celebrated artists of the Barbizon school had worked. So he arranged for a limousine and a driver.

She enjoyed them all. Perhaps she enjoyed Versailles and Chartres more than any of the other sights because she so often mentioned the palace grounds and the tapestries, and the rich stained glass of the ancient cathedral. What he himself could not forget was the simple hut where Millet had lived. He could not understand why a man would endure such poverty unless it was inevitable, and in Millet's case it was not inevitable: he had elected to live that way so that he could spend all of his time painting.

Mr Bridge continued to think about this, and the more he pondered the indignity of living in a hut the more it annoyed and puzzled him, so that one afternoon as they were strolling on the Champs Elysées he suddenly remarked: 'I do not insist a person has to live in a place like Versailles or anything of the sort. Far from it. But it beats me how that artist Millet could be indifferent to ordinary comforts. Lord, there wasn't a toilet in that place, there wasn't any heat, there wasn't anything. If the fellow liked to paint pictures, all right, but if there was no public for his pictures why didn't he get a job like everybody else? He could have done his art work over the weekend. If I'd been in his shoes that's how I would have handled the situation.'

115 Cannes

It was raining when they left Paris. The rain dropped straight down, warm and windless, and continued most of the day so they were not able to see much of the French countryside, but by the time they reached Lyon the sun was shining. There they spent the night, next morning they went to Avignon, where they visited the bridge, and after a few hours in Marseille they took the train to Cannes. They arrived very late, had dinner, and went to bed. Mrs Bridge was asleep instantly, but for the second time in three nights he found himself restless and reluctant to close his eyes.

An hour or two went by. He could not lie in bed any longer. He got up and walked to the window where he stared at the Mediterranean and at the people sauntering along the esplanade and loitering in the cafés. Some of them were tourists, so it did not matter what they did; but many of them were French, many of them had to get up for work in the morning, yet there they were enjoying themselves as though nothing else mattered. He was mystified. He had observed very much the same thing in Paris, and to a lesser extent in London. Evidently these people managed to hang on to their jobs and conduct a certain amount of business while spending three hours at lunch and playing around half the night. In the United States that would be impossible.

He decided to go out. He looked at his wife. She appeared perfectly at peace, and was not apt to be disturbed to wake up and find him gone. He dressed, took the elevator to the lobby, walked out of the hotel, and crossed the boulevard to the esplanade. The branches of the trees were rustling in a warm sea breeze and a globular white moon hung like a Japanese lantern above the harbor. The indolence of the people was troubling. He walked to the edge of the water, where he folded his arms and tried to assess the mood that had come over him.

Presently he discovered a woman seated on a bench in the shadows. She was watching him. She got up and approached and spoke to him in French. He could not quite understand what she said, but it sounded as if she had invited him to have a cup of chocolate at a café. He ignored her. She spoke again, but now he understood her even less, and he stared over the top of her head at the water as if she did not exist. She shrugged lightly, and with that faint intake of breath Europeans sometimes used, she wandered away.

When he returned to the hotel he found his wife asleep in the same position. He undressed and once again put on his pajamas. He sat on the edge of the bed with his chin in his hands and he thought about the woman, whose eyes reminded him of black cherries. Although he had not known exactly what she said, her voice was that of a sensitive and cultured woman. He concluded he had been wrong to assume she was a whore. Possibly she had left her sleeping husband and stepped outside for a little while just as he had done. She must have recognized him for what he was, and there had been nothing improper about her invitation. He thought of getting dressed again and going out to search for her, but now it was too late. He reflected that there were many things he had not done because for one reason or another they seemed unsafe – too many, perhaps.

116 Darkness at noon

From Cannes they proceeded to Monte Carlo, which they agreed was one of the most picturesque and attractive places they had seen. Mrs Bridge mailed a number of postcards to friends in Kansas City and they visited the casino where Mr Bridge played roulette until he had lost the ten dollars he set aside for this purpose. They hired a car with a driver who took them around some of the nearby villages, and they were very well satisfied.

They had lunch at a sidewalk café. While they were eating they began to notice people shielding their eyes and squinting at the sky. The light was changing. The earth was darkening. A black disc was moving across the sun. By the time they had finished lunch the marble table top was cool, as if the sky had filled with clouds, and stars were becoming visible. A planet glowed in the west. The sea was black and ominous and the sun was a flaming red crown burning with unimaginable ferocity. She suggested they return to the hotel and he agreed, and there they relaxed until the bright rim of the sun reappeared and the Mediterranean landscape looked familiar.

He continued to think about this experience. He had not been out of doors during an eclipse since he was twelve or thirteen years old and he was surprised that it should still affect him in the same way. He had recognized the feeling instantly – the sense of being in the presence of something monstrous. He did not like it, and he was

416

puzzled that a man such as himself could feel ill at ease when the phenomenon could be explained so simply.

117 Another one

From Monte Carlo they went to Genoa for a night, then to Pisa for a look at the tower, and from there they went direct to Florence which they liked immediately. It was hot and cloudy, but there was so much to see. The church of Santa Croce, the Ponte Vecchio, the Medici chapel, the doors of Ghiberti, the Piazza Michelangelo, and much more.

The second afternoon, exhausted by the size of the Uffizi Gallery and the humid weather, they decided to return to the hotel for a nap. As they were getting out of the taxi in the Piazza della Repubblica a toothless old woman came hobbling up mumbling something and holding out her hand. Mr Bridge waved her away.

In the room he drew the shades and began to undress. The air was suffocating, and his feet felt like bricks from tramping the corridors of the museum. His wife had enjoyed the Uffizi, he was sure of that, so the afternoon was worthwhile. Even if she had not enjoyed it, at least they had been there. Tomorrow they could take in Michelangelo's house and the Campanile, she wanted to do some shopping, they needed more film for the camera, and the Buca San Giovanni had been recommended for dinner. The following morning they would be off to Rome.

Mrs Bridge, lying motionless on the bed with a damp washcloth over her face, said, 'Walter, couldn't you have given her a little something?'

For a moment he was puzzled, then he realized she meant the beggar, and he said: 'Those people are all alike. You remember that child in Paris. They'll take advantage of you every time, whenever they think they can, simply because we are American tourists. I've never known it to fail. They assume we are million-aires, and I am sick and tired of it. These people can smell a dollar a mile away. That old woman doesn't have much – I am not implying she is well off. But this is supposed to be a vacation and I don't intend to have it spoiled. I've had enough requests for money since we left home. Everywhere I turn somebody has got his hand out. If you think I'm stingy, so be it. I plead guilty. But I want to have a good time on my vacation. Nor do I wish to be nagged about it.'

She lifted the washcloth from her face and said, 'You're right, I suppose. I simply couldn't help feeling sorry for her. The poor old soul.'

'I feel every bit as sorry for her as you do,' he said, and he paused for a drink of water. Then he went on: 'But it's like pouring sand in a rathole. My Lord, I'm not able to feed everybody on this earth.'

118 The Etruscans

No sooner had they walked out of one gallery or museum than she mentioned another. He concealed his boredom as much as possible. Occasionally he came upon a picture or a statue that he liked, but for the most part he accompanied her patiently and silently while thinking about what he must do as soon as they got back to Kansas City. London alone would have been sufficient, or the Louvre. Then there was Florence, and still she had not gotten tired of art exhibits. He could no longer count the number of museums and galleries, old and new, large and small, which they had visited. And now in Rome there were more. The Vatican treasures he did want to see. The Sistine Chapel, of course, and the famous Laocoön ought not to be missed. Of the hundreds of masterpieces they already had looked at he could remember only a few. The one he remembered most vividly, excepting the Mona Lisa and the Venus de Milo, was an Etruscan statue of a man and a woman reclining on a couch. They were smiling not at each other but into the distance, as if they might be entertaining company in their home. One of the husband's hands rested affectionately on her shoulder and this casual gesture somehow proved that they were married. He was impressed that the artist had been able to present such a convincing embodiment of marriage and he had stayed to examine this piece of sculpture while she wandered along to something else. The figures were natural, almost commonplace, yet there was great distinction to them. They possessed a certainty which he understood, which he had not experienced in his own life until he married. The assurance of the reclining man pleased him because he had felt this strange, soft power himself, never more than when his wife was beside him; but he was more absorbed by the figure of the woman because of the confidence and trust she expressed. She did not doubt that she was loved, or that whatever she did while her husband was nearby was as it should be. He thought he had never observed such nobility shared by the men and women he knew.

119 Mi piace la banana

She greatly enjoyed the cafés along the Via Veneto. There she was content to sit for an hour or more sipping lemonade or iced tea while chatting with English-speaking tourists; but he could not sit quietly for such a long time, and because she was safe in a respectable café they agreed that whenever he felt restless he would go walking and come back for her when it was time to return to the hotel. The plan worked nicely. Five days were allotted to Rome, and each afternoon at the conclusion of a sight-seeing tour they relaxed for a while at one of the cafés, then he got up and disappeared among the side streets. He walked rapidly, seldom pausing to investigate anything, because he was less apt to be accosted if he walked as though he was in a hurry to get someplace and he disliked these all-too-frequent encounters on the street. He strode past monuments, fountains, antique shops, galleries, and other attractions as if they did not exist, though he was aware of them, sometimes recognizing them from a previous sight-seeing trip. Walking invigorated him and helped him to think, and there was much to think about.

On his way back to the Via Veneto after one of these excursions he was hailed by a small, curly-haired boy with impudent black eyes and a shoeshine box. The hotel porter took care of his shoes, but the boy had such an engaging face that he stopped walking. The boy promptly crouched at his feet and went to work. Mr Bridge was amused by his cheerfulness. He did not seem to feel deprived; apparently he did not mind polishing shoes.

'Giovanni,' he said, grinning, and tapped himself on the chest.

'You are Giovanni?'

He nodded vigorously and Mr Bridge laughed.

'You marry?'

'Yes. Oh, yes indeed. I have been married many years.'

'You like?'

'Do I like marriage?' Mr Bridge asked with a smile. 'Why, yes, of course. And when you grow up, Giovanni, you too will get married.'

Giovanni laughed.

'You like banana?'

'Bananas? Why, yes, I like bananas. In fact, I like bananas very much.'

Giovanni hopped to his feet and beckoned, and all at once the conversation became intelligible. Mr Bridge marched back to the Via Veneto with one shoe polished.

120 From Rome

Dear Carolyn and Douglas:

Your mother is suffering from another of her sick headaches this afternoon, hence I am writing to you in her stead. I hope you will not mind this substitution. I am not much of a letter-writer. However I shall do the best I can. As you no doubt have observed from the postmark on the envelope we are at present in Rome. I believe Mother has kept you informed of our travels up to this point, so I shall not summarize.

The weather here is muggy and cloudy. Our itinerary calls for us to leave for Naples and Sorrento the day after tomorrow, and we are hoping to find some sort of breeze at these places. It would be a welcome relief. Otherwise our stay here thus far has been pleasant. We have walked through the ruins of the Colosseum, have been to the Borghese Gardens as well as the museum there, also to the baths of Diocletian and Caracalla, as well as numerous other sights. Rome is comparable in certain respects to Paris and London. The Via Veneto is a major boulevard and is your mother's favorite spot. Recently we chanced to be seated at a café when an American couple inquired if they might share our table as no other tables were available. Naturally we said yes, and were very glad we did so, as they turned out to be Mr and Mrs Marvin Dunn of Kansas City! This is indeed a small world, as the saying goes. The Dunns are acquainted with the Montgomerys and the Koeppels, as well as several other couples we know. They were returning from a trip to the Holy Land and had much to say about it (having visited the Mount of Olives, Bethlehem, Nazareth, Sea of Galilee, etc.). They say the Jordan River is about the size of our Blue River at home. I was under the impression the Jordan was considerably larger. Your mother and I have discussed the feasibility of altering our itinerary to enable us to see the Holy Land, but have concluded there is insufficient time, as I must be at my office on the sixteenth.

Unfortunately, preparations for war continue on all sides. I regret to inform you of this. It is apparent that 'people never learn'. Many of us believed the World War would be a war to end wars, yet this does not appear to have been the case after all. It is disillusioning. Evidence of a forthcoming confrontation cannot be overlooked. No one knows where or when it will commence, but it will. Everyone is saying so. Mr Dunn says that only in the Holy Land did the threat of another world-wide war appear to be remote. He is of the opinion that certain nomadic sheepherders in their Biblical costume are totally unaware of the existence of Adolph Hitler's Nazi organization. This is extremely difficult to accept, but Mr Dunn claims this is so. In any case, I am very glad we have taken our European trip this year instead of postponing it until next as I had considered doing. I do not know what this part of the world will be like next year. Benito Mussolini is a troublemaker. Let us hope America will not become involved.

Your mother has, if I am not mistaken, kept you up to date and will be writing to you again when she feels better. The clerk of our hotel has a cousin in Manhattan. (We have met this sort of thing frequently.)

Not much else of interest. Have visited many museums, fountains, and various other tourist attractions. Consequently, we are a trifle worn down and will be glad to get home. The schedule calls for us to sail from Genoa on the fifth. Both of us are looking forward to the ocean voyage in order to rest and recuperate, although your mother hopes the crossing will be quieter than the east-bound trip. The ocean was unusually rough. Many passengers suffered 'mal de mer'.

In brief, we have all but fulfilled a long-standing dream and expect to arrive in New York in approximately two weeks. There we shall see Ruth before catching the train to Chicago, where we are obliged to transfer before continuing to Kansas City. I have never understood the necessity of transfering

421

in Chicago. It is a great inconvenience to travelers. I do not for the life of me know why the railroad people insist on alienating customers.

    I enclose a small check for each of you to spend however you choose.

    Wishing you both happiness. Trust all is well at home.

Love,
Dad

P.S. I hope you have not neglected the lawn, which requires more water during the summer months. Also, as you know, the Frigidaire has been 'on the blink'. Has the repair man attended to it? If he has failed to show up, you should telephone my office and inform Julia of the fact. She has his number and will handle the situation.

121 Intimations

The day after he wrote this letter the Nazis invaded Poland. Two days later he and his wife were aboard a French ship en route to the United States.

One night near the middle of the Atlantic they were sitting in their deck chairs waiting for the moon to rise. The night was so dark that although they were side by side they could scarcely see each other. They had not spoken for a long time and Mr Bridge had been meditating on the war, when all at once a remarkable idea entered his head: he became convinced that the ocean was not what he thought it was – the ocean was not a limitless dead lake which was the home of billions of fish, weeds, and protozoic organisms; it seemed to him instead that the ocean possessed a life of its own, and furthermore the ocean was conscious that he, Walter G. Bridge, and his wife were traveling upon it. This conviction was so extraordinary that he sat up and looked over the rail. Phosphorescent waves rushed past with a threatening, sibilant hiss. Horrible black forms were boiling out of the darkness and obscuring the stars. Uneasily he leaned back in the chair and groped for his wife's hand. As soon as he found it her fingers tightened convulsively around his own. Then he realized that she was weeping. Very much amazed he bent toward her and wondered if he should ask what was wrong, but he decided to wait;

possibly she was weeping for no specific reason, as women do. In a little while she withdrew her hand; he heard the snap of her purse opening, and guessed that she wanted a handkerchief. She blew her nose. He heard her draw a deep breath. Then she patted his arm.

'Everything has been just lovely,' she said.

She had been crying from happiness, which was something he had never done in his life and which was incomprehensible to him. Thoughtfully he contemplated the fearful blackness surrounding them, for there was no light anywhere beyond the rail of the ship, and he wondered if this was how it must be, if this was how they would end their lives, accompanying each other so closely, loving each other, touching one another with affection and sympathy, yet singularly alone.

122 Wedding present

She wept more often, he noticed, and seldom for a specific reason. He disapproved of this; it embarrassed him and made him feel helpless. He did not know what to do about these emotional fits, so he ignored them and hoped she would get over them. Fortunately, she did her weeping at home instead of breaking down in public.

One evening at dinner not long after their return from Europe the gravy boat tipped over again. Nobody knew how many times this had happened. The gravy boat had been a wedding present. It was a curiously shaped thing of heavy silver and came with a gracefully curled ladle and a tray etched with flowers. She loved it. Nearly every night it was on the table. He disliked it because it was impractical, and each time there was an accident he wanted to tell her to put it in the attic and buy one which would not tip over. Obviously the thing was impractical, she admitted this, which meant that if he suggested putting it away she probably would agree. She would agree, but she would be hurt. So, year after year while helping himself to the gravy he focused his attention on this odd silver vessel and never relaxed until it was out of his hands. Every member of the family except Douglas knocked it over at one time or another, and on each of these occasions Douglas shook his head very slowly with an expression of disgusted amazement. Mr Bridge could not understand why Douglas, who frequently bumped into doors and tripped over cords and cut himself and dropped everything else, never spilled the gravy, but he never did.

This night it was Carolyn. She caught it before it went all the way, but the tablecloth was spattered and Harriet was summoned from the kitchen to mop up. Then Douglas remarked, as though he had been recommending this for a long while, that he still did not see why they did not have the boat soldered to the tray.

Everybody turned on him.

He paused with a fork full of beans almost in his mouth and glanced around the table uncertainly, surprised by the effect of his suggestion.

'Mother,' Carolyn said, 'You know, he's right.'

Douglas, sensing that nobody would correct his table manners at this moment, reached halfway across the table for a handful of biscuits.

Mrs Bridge was considering the gravy boat, and she appeared ten years older.

'Suppose we leave it as it is,' Mr Bridge said. 'The thing was not meant to be soldered. All of us can be a little more careful.'

Douglas said, 'It'd be a cinch to fix. It'd take about two minutes. I could fix it myself at school.'

'You could?' she asked.

'Sure. In metal shop we do soldering.'

'If it's going to be done it will be done professionally,' Mr Bridge said. 'I know you could do the work, Douglas, but this was a wedding gift and your mother thinks a great deal of it.'

'Suit yourself.' He shrugged. 'If Mother wants me to, I can. Otherwise, okay. It's no skin off my tail.'

'Sharpe's does awfully nice work,' Carolyn suggested.

In a choking voice Mrs Bridge said: 'I want Douglas to do it. If he thinks he can do whatever needs to be done I want him to do it. Nobody else is going to touch it!' She began to cry.

'What in the world is going on around here!' Mr Bridge muttered, and flung down his napkin like a gauntlet.

123 Football

Tryouts for the team began soon after school opened in September. Douglas approached his father for permission and confidently held out a mimeographed sheet of paper.

'They don't issue uniforms to the guys until they get this signed at home.'

Mr Bridge accepted the paper, scanned it, and gave it back. Douglas gazed up at him with a stricken expression.

'You are not playing football.'

'What do you mean? What do you mean I'm not playing football?'

'Just what I said. I won't have you breaking an arm or a leg.'

'You're kidding!'

'That sport is dangerous. I have heard too many cases where some boy has been injured.'

'You've got to be kidding.'

'I mean it.'

'Everybody in creation is going out for the team.'

'You are not.'

'Who did you ever know who got hurt? Name one. I mean, really hurt? Just name me one.'

'There have been a number of instances. And every year or so some boy is killed playing football. You may as well make up your mind to it. I will not have you run the risk of serious injury, or worse, for anything as insignificant as football.'

'Vandermeer's father signed the permit.'

'What has that to do with you?'

'It's pretty obvious. I mean, what am I going to say when Coach asks for my permit?'

'You tell the coach your father did not give you permission to play.'

Douglas clutched his head. 'Oh. Oh, sure. Sure. Sure, I can just see that, all right. In front of all the guys.'

'Nonsense. You are not going to be the only one.'

'If Rodney Vandermeer can play, why can't I? He only out-

425

weighs me about fifteen pounds. And David Griffith got his permit signed. And so did all those guys who made the team last year.'

'We are not going to get involved in a discussion.'

'I just want to try out for halfback. I don't want to be a tackle or guard. I probably can't make the team anyway because they got Nichols and Kurtz, and then there are a lot of other guys that didn't graduate so I probably haven't got a Chinaman's chance anyhow, but I don't see why I can't even at least try out.'

'Well, you are not. And that is that.'

'But why not? I mean, how come? I won't get hurt. I never broke a leg yet, did I?'

'You can play basketball, or you can play tennis, or you can try to make the swimming team. These are all fine sports. There should be several athletic teams you can try out for. Swimming is an excellent sport.'

'I want to play football.'

'You play some after school, do you not?'

'That's only touch. You can't play tackle without equipment. You need helmets and shoulder pads and all that stuff. Touch isn't even real football.'

'I'm afraid "touch" will have to do. I don't want you being tackled by some boy twice your size.'

'You sound like I was made out of porcelain or something.'

'You are flesh and blood. It might be a good idea to start getting used to the idea. As you grow older you will discover that you have certain limitations.'

'Yuk.'

'I realize you didn't come here for a lecture, but the fact remains that having lived a good deal longer than you I have learned a few things that you have not.'

'Oy, oy, would you let me play if I weighed two hundred and fifty pounds?'

'When you grow to that size we'll discuss the matter again. Now is anything else on your mind? If so, I'll be glad to talk about it with you, but I have no time to discuss football.'

Douglas waved the sheet of paper. He said with as much sarcasm as possible, 'I might as well toss this in the wastebasket.'

'As you like.'

Football was not mentioned again for almost a month. Then an item appeared on the sports page of the *Star* about a boy in Ohio who died of a broken neck after a school football game. Mr Bridge pointed to the article.

'Have you read this?'

'Oh, yuk,' Douglas said wearily. 'Do you always need to prove you're right?'

124 Square peg

Both of his sisters had pledged a sorority soon after entering high school, yet Douglas, for reasons his parents could not understand, refused to join a fraternity. They knew he had been invited by at least three fraternities, but the weeks were going by and he appeared totally unconcerned. Once he remarked that a group of Sigma Deltas had stopped him on the way to Civics and told him they wanted to have a talk, but that was all he said. His parents decided not to press him, and so the wait continued. He seemed unaware that they were waiting, and apparently he did not care that his two closest friends Tipton and Vandermeer had joined a fraternity.

By the end of November it was advisable to investigate this matter. One evening while the three of them were in the living room his mother inquired as casually as possible whether he was still trying to make up his mind which fraternity to join. Without looking up from his book he answered that he had not thought about it. She said, after a respectful pause, that she believed most of his friends had already joined a fraternity. He went on reading.

Then Mr Bridge, who had been listening carefully, asked if he still saw as much of Tipton and Vandermeer as he used to. Douglas turned a page, and shrugged.

'Old friends are best,' his mother observed.

He nodded, and went on reading.

Mr Bridge concluded the time had come to bring this problem to the surface. 'Are you going to accept one of those invitations, or not?'

'I doubt it,' he murmured without raising his eyes.

'May I ask why not?'

'Why should I?' he countered, still reading.

'Because these contacts will prove valuable in later life.'

'I'll take your word for it,' Douglas answered in a flat voice, but with no animosity.

'Well, then,' said his mother, laughing, 'won't you let us know what you've made up your mind to do?'

'Is there any huge rush?' he asked.

'We would like to know why you object to joining a fraternity,' his father said.

Douglas hung the book on his knees, hunched his shoulders, and spread his hands. 'So who's objecting? Who's got objections? Tipton wants to join a frat, it's his business. It's okay with me. The same goes for Vandermeer. What's it to me?'

'These boys who have invited you to join their organizations have gone out of their way to be nice to you. You should remember they have been under no compulsion to invite you.'

'I imagine any number of boys would snap at the chance,' Mrs Bridge added.

'One day these boys are going to be stockbrokers, insurance agents, physicians, corporate executives, and so forth. It will pay you to know them. It's time you recognized the fact that in this world nobody, no matter how independent – and this goes for me as well – succeeds altogether by his own efforts. We need to help each other. Just as I assist certain people, so they assist me.'

'Who's arguing?'

'They seem to be awfully nice boys, and I'm sure they must think quite a lot of you if they've invited you to join. Isn't Paul Battenhurst a member of Sigma Delta?'

Douglas nodded.

'Well, then. You don't want people to think you're a misfit, do you?'

'I don't mind. Who cares what they think?'

'I do not understand this,' his father said. 'When I was your age there was no such thing as a high school fraternity. I was unable to join a fraternity until I was at the university. The men I became acquainted with as a result have been extremely useful to me on a number of occasions.'

'We don't want you to do anything you wouldn't enjoy. It's just that we suspect you haven't quite realized what a good time you might have.'

'Does that mean I've got to?'

'Oh, goodness,' she said, and turned despairingly to her husband.

He hesitated. In college the choice of fraternity was important. Some had excellent reputations, and the alumni were influential men. Others were little more than social clubs whose alumni did not amount to much. When it came time to select a college fraternity the matter ought to be discussed thoroughly. A high school fraternity was less important; even so, it was good preparation.

'In my opinion, it would be a mistake not to.'

'But does that mean I've got to?'

'You are not listening. The choice is yours. Your mother and I have already told you what we think.'

'Okay,' Douglas said, 'as long as it's up to me I'd just as soon skip the whole business.'

And there, for the time being, the problem rested.

125 The dancing master

At the middle of the school year, having skipped a semester, Carolyn graduated from high school and was enrolled at the University of Kansas, which was in the town of Lawrence about forty miles from Kansas City. Many of the students had cars and there was frequent bus service, so one way or another she occasionally came home for a night or for the weekend.

Late Saturday night Mr Bridge was lying in bed reading a mystery novel when he heard the front door open. Mrs Bridge, who had been dozing, immediately sat up. They heard Carolyn come upstairs, go into her room, and slam the door. Mrs Bridge got out of bed, put on her robe, and went in to see what was the matter. Half an hour later she came back. He peered at her inquiringly over the top of his glasses.

'She's terribly upset. There was some sort of a scene with Gil.'

'Who is Gil?'

429

'She's mentioned him. Gil Davis. They've been running around together. He sounds like a nice boy.'

'What's the problem?'

'It's a long story. There was a dance at the university this evening and apparently Arthur Merton was there.'

'The fellow who operates those dancing schools?'

'Yes. I'm not sure how it happened, Carolyn is still too distressed to be very clear, but it appears he invited her to dance and she refused. I understand one of his studios is opening in Lawrence. I suppose that's how he happened to be there.'

'Now just one minute. Let me get it straight,' Mr Bridge said. 'This Merton fellow asked Carolyn for a dance?'

'As I understand it, yes.'

'Why?'

'I find nothing odd about Mr Merton inviting Carolyn to dance,' she said resentfully. 'Carolyn is quite attractive.'

'I am wondering why he happened to pick her.'

'I didn't inquire. It doesn't matter,' she replied, holding her head with her fingertips. 'I'm afraid I'm getting another of my spells.' She walked into the bathroom and began to hunt for something in the medicine cabinet.

The conversation was becoming disorganized; he had a feeling that if he asked any more questions it would get worse. She drank a glass of water, shut the door of the medicine cabinet, and went on explaining.

'Carolyn turned Mr Merton down because she didn't realize who he was. She assumed he was simply some strange man. And now, of course, she's just sick.'

'Ah ha!' he said. 'I begin to see. But what does that have to do with the boy?'

'Gil? She's furious with him. I don't blame her in the least. I would be, too. He recognized Mr Merton, but for some reason he thought it would be amusing not to tell her.'

'This is all very peculiar,' Mr Bridge said, and turned the book upside down in his lap. 'This Merton fellow was in Lawrence and showed up at a university dance. He invited Carolyn to dance but she refused because she didn't know who he was. This boy she was with recognized the man but did not tell her. Is that the story?'

'As nearly as I can gather. I think Carolyn is perfectly justified. I don't blame her one iota for being upset. She'll never have another opportunity like that. It's a shame.'

'Well,' Mr Bridge said after thinking about it, 'that is too bad. And if you ask me, this boy she's running around with is a little cracked. However, I don't suppose it's important. Two weeks from now she'll have forgotten the entire business.'

'Walter Bridge,' she said, walking out of the bathroom with both hands pressed to her forehead, 'for once in your life you are as wrong as a man can be.'

126 Hot number

Two days later Carolyn reappeared just long enough to get some clothes out of her closet and have a glass of milk and a sandwich. Arthur Merton may not have been forgotten, but he was not mentioned. The sorority was planning an 'Arabian Nights' party, and this was all she talked about. A feature of the party was to be a belly dance. She was trying to decide whether or not to be one of the belly dancers. The idea of putting on the costume and dancing for a crowd of fraternity boys obviously excited her, but at the same time she was reluctant to expose herself. She announced that she might do it if they promised to let her dance in the back row. Then, whoever was driving her to the univeristy was in front of the house honking urgently. She swallowed the remainder of her sandwich, drank the rest of the milk, grabbed her clothes and ran for the door.

127 Socrates

Observing that his son looked shaggy, Mr Bridge suggested a haircut. Douglas replied that he could not get a haircut, he could not possibly get a haircut because his external being would not then be in harmony with his inner self.

For a few moments Mr Bridge considered this. Being unable to make any sense of it, he requested an explanation. Douglas was not merely willing to explain, he was eager to explain, and Mr Bridge

431

discovered that in the course of miscellaneous reading which seemed to spring from subject to subject with no apparent pattern Douglas had come upon the wisdom of Socrates. Specifically, the inner man should correspond to the outer man.

'This is a commendable philosophy,' Mr Bridge said. 'However, I suggest you visit the barber.'

Douglas repeated that he could not. It was impossible.

Mr Bridge repeated that it would be good thing to pay a call on the barber, not next month or next week or the day after tomorrow, but tomorrow, preferably in the morning, before school. Otherwise there was not going to be any allowance next Friday, or the Friday after. No allowance until the external being appeared more harmonious to the eye of the spectator. Douglas answered disdainfully that he could get along without an allowance. In fact, rather than accept an allowance any longer he would get a job after school. He would become independent. Mr Bridge said this was a splendid idea.

A week passed. Douglas began to look remotely Byronic. He had not found a job because he had not looked for one, and because he did not get any allowance he did not have enough money to go bowling with Tipton and Vandermeer, which he wanted to do very much. But still he would not get his hair cut.

Friday afternoon of the fourth week, after school, he borrowed fifty cents from his mother and got the haircut.

After inspecting him that evening Mr Bridge handed him his customary allowance. Neither of them said a word. Integrity had been defeated, there was no question about it.

128 Eagle scout

Much to the astonishment of everybody, possibly excepting his mother, Douglas finally managed to become an Eagle Scout. He had started off rapidly, almost spectacularly. Soon after becoming a Tenderfoot at the age of twelve he had passed his test and been promoted to Second Class. But then he began to slow down. He had difficulty passing the first-aid examination required for promotion to First Class; after failing twice he gathered himself for a major effort, passed it, and was then seen on Tuesday nights dressed in his khaki uniform and white neckerchief with the big First Class badge pinned to his breast pocket. The next rank was Star. The insignia was smaller and simpler than First Class, with greater dignity, and represented a sharp advance and separation. The examinations were more detailed. Five merit badges were required. Douglas earned five merit badges without much effort, and his mother sewed the little felt emblems on his sash. To become a Life Scout, privileged to wear a brilliant red metal heart, an additional five merit badges were required; and here a familiar problem came up because these five were not optional and one of them was First Aid. The consequence of this was that he remained a Star Scout for almost a year, with nine merit badges on his sash.

His mother encouraged him. She was sure he could do it. He was not so sure. He pointed out to her, as well as to anybody else who cared to listen, how difficult it was, how practically impossible it was to earn the Merit Badge in First Aid. For instance, one had to demonstrate preparations for transporting a person with a compound fracture of the forearm. Prepare and apply a splint to a broken thigh. Demonstrate control of bleeding from a varicose vein in the leg. Control arterial bleeding on wrist and calf of leg simultaneously. Show what to do in case a person chokes from drawing water or food into the windpipe. Tell the dangers involved in transporting an injured person when the extent of injury is not known. Demonstrate what to do if a companion dives into shallow water, strikes his head, staggers ashore, and falls unconscious. Demonstrate treatment by covering, position, and heating devices for severe shock.

And all of this, Douglas claimed, was only the beginning. But his mother said she was sure he could do it. Finally he believed her, and he became a Life Scout.

Eagle Scout, the culmination, required twenty-one merit badges. Thirteen of these were mandatory, including Bird Study, Cooking, Personal and Public Health, Pathfinding, Pioneering, Physical Development, and Civics. But the bête noire of First Aid had been vanquished. One colorful little emblem after another was sewn to the khaki sash, which was beginning to resemble a flower garden, until he had nineteen of them. But again he became discouraged. He had been a scout for more than three years. It would be a fine thing to become an Eagle Scout, and only two more merit badges were necessary; but he had gone through the list of requirements in the handbook again and again looking for two easy ones and had not found any. He doubted if he could make it. His mother said she was sure he could.

He qualified just in time to receive his badge at the annual Boy Scout Roundup in the municipal auditorium. Scouts from all the troops in Kansas City and nearby towns were to be there, and more than one hundred Eagle badges would be awarded. The mother of each new Eagle Scout was invited to accompany her son during the ceremony. When Douglas somewhat diffidently inquired if his mother would be interested in this she told him she would not miss it for the world.

So on that night one hundred mothers, each with a red rose pinned to her breast, were seated on folding chairs on the floor of the arena, and beside each mother stood her son. They listened to speeches, and the audience enthusiastically applauded every speaker. Then the Scouts were summoned to the front of the auditorium where they filed across the stage, received their Eagle badges, and shook hands with the mayor. After this they marched back to stand at attention beside their mothers. Next came the moment Douglas had been dreading. At a signal he was expected to bend over and kiss his mother on the cheek. The idea of one hundred Eagle Scouts bending over to kiss their mothers at exactly the same instant gave him a feeling of extreme discomfort. What was wrong with this public act of devotion he did not know, but something was wrong. When the signal was given and the band struck up 'America the Beautiful' he pretended to be confused; he remained standing more or less at attention, turning his head from side to side. He hoped his mother would believe he was attempting to discover what was going on, and presumably by the time he found out it would be too late.

Mrs Bridge sat quietly with her hands in her lap, an expectant smile on her face, but nothing happened.

High up in the huge auditorium Mr Bridge observed this. He was so far from the floor that it was difficult to distinguish individuals, but when ninety-nine Eagle Scouts leaned over to kiss their mothers, and one did not, he recognized his son. He surmised that Douglas was embarrassed. It was not that Douglas did not

434

love his mother, simply that he had reached an age where he was unable to kiss her in public. The only puzzling thing was why Douglas took the problem more seriously than other boys in the same situation. Mr Bridge could not understand this. It annoyed him. However, he did not intend to talk to his son about it. What concerned him more was the effect on his wife. She had been hurt, he knew. She did not say anything about it after the Roundup while they were driving home, but he knew.

As they were getting ready for bed he said to her, 'Let me make up for that,' and with no other word of explanation he put his arms around her. Then she began to cry, and she was still crying a little when at last she fell asleep in his arms.

129 Locking up

Each night before going to bed he locked the downstairs windows and doors. Robberies in Mission Hills were rare, and a watchman patrolled the neighborhood; even so, there was always the possibility. Through the years he had tried to impress upon the children the necessity of locking up, because one day they would have homes of their own, yet he was not sure they had taken the lesson seriously. Perhaps Carolyn did. But he worried about Ruth and Douglas. Many times he had pointed out that it took only a few minutes to check the doors and windows. This was a small investment to make in return for security. They listened, but if he asked whether or not they agreed, they agreed with no enthusiasm as though they only wished to avoid a lecture or an argument. He worried particularly about Ruth because she was living alone in New York, and usually when he wrote to her he reminded her to bolt the door before going to bed. As for Douglas, the only thing to do was to remind him continually that carelessness could be costly; and since he was almost sixteen years old, old enough to assume more responsibility for the house, Mr Bridge decided to turn the job over to him.

Douglas, being informed that henceforth he was responsible for locking up, instantly replied that he would forget.

Mr Bridge responded that for this very reason the job was his, so he would learn never to forget.

Most unwillingly Douglas accepted the role. Every night he made the rounds protesting and complaining while Mr Bridge followed him from window to window to door, examining each latch to make sure the job was properly done. After they had locked up like this for about three weeks Mr Bridge felt he had been sufficiently trained, and quit following him. However, the knowledge that he himself had not checked everything afflicted him so that he did not sleep very well.

For a few nights he resisted the urge to get out of bed and find out if Douglas had done what he was supposed to do, but finally he could resist no longer; he lay awake until he thought Douglas would be asleep, then he got up, put on his slippers and robe, and walked through the house feeling the locks. And there came a night when he discovered an unlocked window in the breakfast room.

After snapping the lock shut and testing it he hurried into Douglas' room and shook him awake. Attempting to control his anger he said: 'I have told you at least one dozen times to make absolutely certain those breakfast room windows were locked. Somebody could get in there. You have not been paying attention. Somebody could have stolen your mother's silver. How many times am I expected to tell you! I will not stand for this. I have worked many years to provide us with a comfortable home and I am not going to have you throw it away. Do you understand?' Douglas' eyes were open but his face was asleep; he groaned and rolled over.

Mr Bridge was too exasperated to go back to bed. He paced through the house examing the doors and windows again. He thought of how often he had told his son to make certain the house was locked. It had been a waste of time. He returned to the bedroom, reached under the mattress, and pulled out the pistol. He had planned to give it to Douglas on his twenty-first birthday, but now he decided not to. He shifted the gun from one hand to the other, weighing it in his palm and fondling the knurled grip and the icy barrel. Twice a year he cleaned and oiled the gun, and occasionally he lifted a corner of the mattress to see if it was where it belonged. There was always a chance Harriet would steal it. He did not like the fact that she knew about the gun. If she did take it and sell it or give it to some Negro in the North End there could be a great deal of trouble. It could very well be used in a holdup. She had been warned never to touch it, and each time he looked he found the gun in the same place; yet he could not forget that when Douglas was a child she had shown it to him.

The clock in the hall struck three times. He was surprised. An hour had passed since he went downstairs. He shoved the gun into the holster and slid it beneath the mattress. He hung his robe in the closet, stepped out of his carpet slippers, and lay down in bed carefully so as not to disturb his wife.

130 A pal of Morrie

Carolyn was home for the weekend, and a few minutes before the beginning of 'The Bell Telephone Hour' while Mr Bridge was settling himself in his chair beside the radio she asked if he knew any gangsters. No, he replied, he was not on friendly terms with any gangsters; but then he remembered something that had occurred years before and he added that he had once met a man who ought to qualify. Carolyn wanted to know what he was like. There was some purpose to the questioning, but he could not guess what it was. However, there was no apparent reason not to answer, so he told her about the experience. He had gone to North Kansas City to visit a client, and afterward as he was about to return to the office he happened to meet a man he had not seen for a long time. This man had been a detective on the police force but was obliged to retire because of a scandal. They decided to have lunch together at a spaghetti parlor near the bus station, and while they were eating they were joined by a friend of the detective.

At this point in his story Mr Bridge paused and smiled. 'Carolyn, you may not believe me when I tell you what occurred next, but this is the truth; after I had been introduced to the fellow he slipped into the booth with us and slapped me on the knee. He said he had heard my name and – these are his exact words – "a pal of Morrie is a pal of mine". Then he asked – and again I am quoting – if there was anybody I wanted him to "take care off". That was the expression he used. Was there anybody I wanted him to "take care of"? I said there was not, and let it go at that.

However, after the fellow got up and left I inquired about him and was informed that this man was a member of a mob. He was a professional murderer who was known to have accounted for at least six people. Now, how do you like that for a gangster story?'

'Introduce me to him.'

Mr Bridge laughed.

Carolyn said, 'I mean it. I want you to introduce me. Daddy, I've got to talk to him. I really do.'

'I'm afraid that's impossible. In the first place, as I've already told you, this was some years ago.'

'You could find him. You know you could.'

'If he is still alive, which I doubt.'

'I've got to meet him.'

'You might just as well get this idea out of your head, because you are not going to meet him. Assuming I could locate the fellow, I most certainly would never introduce you to him. Now, suppose you tell me just why you have suddenly acquired a taste for gangsters.'

Carolyn explained that her journalism teacher had instructed the class to write a feature article on somebody engaged in an unusual and provocative line of work. She was supposed to interview such a person. 'Please,' she begged, 'I've just got to meet him, Daddy. I really do. Nothing could conceivably happen to me. Besides, Kansas City is so corrupt, and if I could interview this man I could expose this terrible corruption, don't you see?'

'What I do see is that it could result in more problems than either you or I are prepared to handle. You steer clear of men like that. You stick to your journalism class. Don't you get any wild ideas about fooling around in the North End.'

'But that's what journalism is. Can't you see? No. No, naturally you can't.'

'I have seen enough, believe you me! Those Italians and Jews on the north side of Kansas City are dangerous, and don't you ever forget it.'

'Italians and Jews, you say?' She reached for a cigarette. 'Why "Italians and Jews"?'

'Because that is what most of those hoodlums happen to be. I am not expressing prejudice. I am reporting a fact.'

'A fact, you say? Would you define "fact"?'

'We won't go into that,' he said. She was behaving foolishly. She had picked up this absurd manner from somebody at the university.

'If that's how you feel, I can but acquiesce,' she shrugged, and puffed on her cigarette with a look of superior understanding.

'You stick to the things you know about. Find somebody else for your journalism assignment. If you are looking for somebody in an unusual line of work I can introduce you to a bail bondsman. How would that be? I know a man with an office not far from City Hall. I expect he would be willing to discuss his business with you. That should be unusual.'

'Oh, God,' she murmured, and she sounded like Ruth.

'I am not forcing this on you. I am trying to be helpful.'

'It's sweet of you. It really is. But I mean, honestly, you don't begin to have the faintest conception of what journalism is all about. Not really.'

'So be it,' he replied. 'But let me warn you. You are not to go poking your nose into affairs that do not concern you, and what goes on in the north end of Kansas City has nothing to do with you.'

He turned to the radio. He adjusted the volume and the tuning to his satisfaction. The Telephone Hour was beginning. He leaned back in the chair and crossed his legs.

'Now,' he said, 'suppose we enjoy the music.'

131 Crime and punishment

Not long after this the body of a young girl was discovered beneath a clump of bushes on the mud flats bordering the river. The coroner's report stated that she had been criminally assaulted and murdered. Mr Bridge, reading the account of this in the *Star*, decided to save the paper and show it to Carolyn the next time she came home. And because his wife had not yet seen the paper he read the story aloud. Then he commented: 'When they find this fellow – if they ever do – I can bet you my bottom dollar he will have a record. They pick some fellow up for perversion of one sort or another, and after a while these psychologists and social workers insist he's all right, so the parole board turns him loose and he goes right on doing it and eventually kills somebody. It happens time and time again. I'm sick of it! I'm sick and tired of it, I tell you!'

Mrs Bridge had continued with her sewing while he spoke, only registering enough expression to prove that she was listening. She knew almost exactly what he would say as soon as he got started. He had stated his opinion many times. She was not expected to agree or disagree; however, some sort of acknowledgment was necessary, so she remarked when he paused: 'You just wonder what drives people to do things like that.'

'I don't know and I don't care,' he retorted. 'But I do know one thing. I know there is only one method of stopping these people. Great God, even the streets in this part of town are not safe any longer. It wasn't six months ago that the Koeppels' daughter was molested right up there on Stratford Road.'

'I know,' she said, shaking her head.

'But listen to these professional do-gooders and what do you get? Treat these sex maniacs like human beings and let them out as soon as the law provides. Then the same business starts all over again. That's what you get. I've said it before and I intend to keep on saying it until somebody pays attention!'

'It's a problem, there's no doubt about that. I guess it must be awfully difficult to know just what to do.'

'I'll tell you what to do. The same thing I've told you before. Do away with these people. Do away with them once and for all!'

'That sounds awfully severe. I'm not arguing, of course, and goodness knows something should be done with people who can't seem to control themselves. But I just wonder if you can resort to capital punishment in every case.'

'You do, do you?' he replied grimly. 'Well, let me tell you, I hope this fellow's next victim is not somebody from our family. You might have a different attitude if this girl whose body was found out there by the river had been Ruth or Carolyn. You might not feel so lenient if you had seen a few of the things I have seen and talked with the police about it.'

She did not answer. She continued sewing.

He knew he had spoken harshly to her. He went on insistently, but in a more moderate tone: 'There are decent people and there are people who cause nothing but trouble, and don't tell me I don't

440

know what I'm talking about, because I do. I've seen enough of both kinds. I do not know what makes men behave like this while the majority of men behave decently throughout their lives. I do not pretend to know and I do not believe anybody knows. It is fashionable nowadays to blame the parents, or a childhood accident, or Lord knows what else. Maybe there is some truth in it, I don't presume to know. However, I do know one thing: there is one way and one way only to put a stop to this sort of business. You get rid of these habitual criminals. Treat them like human beings and this is what you get! This is your thanks!' He struck the newspaper with the back of his hand.

'Perhaps you're right,' she said.

'I know I'm right,' he said, and turned the page looking for something else to read.

132 Autumn

That night he was sleeping when he realized his heart had stopped. Instantly he opened his eyes, and just then it resumed beating. He laid both hands on his chest, licked his lips, and waited for what would happen next. But his heart pumped along, and after a while he dropped his hands on the blanket and shut his eyes and tried to sleep, but sleep would not come. He could not stop thinking about his heart. He did not think there was anything seriously wrong, yet these seizures were occurring more and more often. He resented the fact that his heart was not in perfect order; and because he was unable to sleep or to forget about it he got out of bed and sat down in a chair beside the window where he plucked at his wrinkled pajamas and meditatively observed the dark street. Leaves were dropping from the maple trees, fluttering like butterflies in the night wind. He watched them and it occurred to him that they were trying to tell him something. A leaf flattened itself against the window beside his head and leaped away into the darkness, and a feeling of profound despair came over him because everything he had done was useless. All that he believed in and had attempted to prove seemed meager, all of his life was wasted.

133 Black pledge

Mrs Bridge walked into the study with a worried expression. Carolyn had just telephoned from the university to announce that she was planning to quit her sorority. A Negro girl from a small town in western Kansas had been pledged with the full consent of the chapter, but as soon as the news leaked out there had been objections from alumnae. A group of women from Topeka had driven to Lawrence and talked to the girls, urging them to reconsider, pointing out that it would damage the sorority's reputation. Now more pressure was being applied. Some of the girls were receiving calls from their parents. National headquarters had been notified. The president of the alumnae assocation was flying up from Dallas. The routine of the sorority had been completely disrupted. Most of the girls were frightened by the criticism and were in favor of telling the Negro girl they were sorry, it had been a mistake, the pledge must be renounced. But several members of the sorority were defiant. They wanted the girl to remain. Carolyn was one of these.

'I believe she really is on the verge of quitting,' Mrs Bridge said. 'She was almost in tears she was so distressed. She asked me what to do, and Heaven knows I hadn't the slightest idea. I was wondering whether you might speak to her.'

He asked if she was still on the telephone.

'No. But I promised to call back as soon as I'd talked it over with you.'

He frowned and rocked around in his swivel chair. 'What in the devil am I supposed to tell her? She got herself into this mess.'

'I know, but I did promise to call.'

'Well then, call. Tell her whatever you please. I don't want to get mixed up in this business. Lord knows it isn't any concern of mine.'

'I feel so sorry for everybody. That poor child – the Negro girl, I mean. It's such a tragedy.'

'I wouldn't waste much sympathy on her.'

'You don't mean that.'

'I do mean it,' he said irritably. 'I do not know one single thing about that girl other than the fact that she is colored, which is all I need to know. That girl knew perfectly well that by attempting to join a white sorority she was going to create a problem. Don't tell me she didn't realize it, because she did.'

'I'm sure she did.'

'All right, there you are. This girl deliberately and willfully set out to cause trouble.'

'We can't assume that, Walter. You're not being fair. She may not have had the least inkling it would start such an uproar. I imagine she wanted to join the sorority, and apparently the girls liked her.'

'She knew what she was doing. I know the type. They're all over. They are setting out to wreck the underlying foundations of this country. This business at the university is not accidental. It is not a case of an individual wanting to join a sorority. It is part and parcel of a calculated plan these people have. Whether you care to believe it or not, that happens to be the truth. I know it for a fact. And as time goes by you'll see I'm right.'

Mrs Bridge sighed, and laid a hand to her forehead. 'I sometimes don't know what to think. It's a shame these things happen.'

'Those girls in the sorority have nobody to blame except themselves, and I include Carolyn. They ought to have sense enough by the time they get to a university to realize they can't do everything they want to. It's their own fault. If they didn't realize what they were getting into they are not mature enough to be making decisions. I have no sympathy for any of the parties involved in this mess.'

'I'm sure none of them imagined it would go this far.'

'I am not so sure. It wouldn't surprise me if they did. I don't know what gets into kids these days, but they can't let well enough alone. They ought to have let the girl know she wasn't welcome as soon as she tried to butt in.'

'Now, Walter, that's not right. That's not right at all. Carolyn was very clear about it: they wanted the girl.'

He lifted his hands in a light gesture of surrender. 'Have it your way. I've given you my opinion.'

She stood up and wandered toward the door, but paused with a vague expression and said while toying with her beads, 'I just hope Carolyn doesn't carry out her threat. No matter how strongly she feels about it I can't see how quitting the sorority would accomplish much.'

'I agree. I hope she doesn't. But if she does it won't be a tragedy. She can live in a dormitory or a private home. Quite a number of those people in university towns rent rooms to students.'

'I spoke with her on the phone last week and she sounded so happy.'

'Well,' Mr Bridge said indifferently as he resumed looking through the papers on his desk, 'it's too bad.'

'Then you won't talk to her?'

'If you insist, I will. Frankly I don't consider it any of my business, and sooner or later she'll have to learn to face these problems by herself. She might as well get started right now.'

'I suppose,' Mrs Bridge said. 'Oh, dear. Well, I did promise to call, so I'd better. I honestly don't know what to say to her.'

'That woman flying in from Dallas may be able to straighten them out. I hope so. I hope so for everybody concerned.'

'Then you think the best thing would be for the girls to admit they made a mistake?'

'That is not what I said. My opinion on this matter is irrelevant. The decision is theirs. I wash my hands of the entire affair.'

134 Gil Davis

One morning less than a month later Carolyn arrived from the university in midweek with an opal ring on her finger, located her mother in the breakfast room staring out the window at some chickadees in the garden, and announced that she was engaged to Gil Davis. This news was not received with much enthusiasm. Mrs Bridge asked if she had told her father. Carolyn had not. Mrs Bridge suggested it might be a good idea to let him know as soon as possible. Carolyn responded that it might be better to wait until he got home, and then, after dinner, if he was in a good mood, that might be the time to tell him.

They discussed the situation a while longer. Carolyn suggested that her mother telephone the office in order to let him know about the engagement. Mrs Bridge countered by saying that since it was

Carolyn's engagement it was up to Carolyn to break the news.

After about an hour, very reluctantly, Carolyn telephoned the office.

Mr Bridge, on learning that she thought she was going to marry some individual by the name of Gil Davis, informed her that he was too busy to listen to this sort of nonsense, if she did indeed have a ring from this boy she was to give it back, and furthermore she was to return to school at once because he was not paying her tuition in order for her to skip classes and come trotting home whenever she felt like it. He had never heard of any Gil Davis, he said, which was not true – he remembered Gil Davis as the boy responsible for the Arthur Merton fiasco – but he said this in order to let her know that he considered Gil Davis too insignificant to remember. And even if he had heard of this boy, whatever his name was, it did not make any difference because there was not going to be any marriage, nor any engagement, not now, not this year, not until she had finished her education. That was all there was to it. He was busy. He was not going to waste any more time discussing it.

Carolyn began to cry.

Hearing the familiar and unpleasant female noise, Mr Bridge announced that he had no intention of leaving the office to drive home and straighten this matter out. She was to get hold of herself at once.

Sobbing with rage, Carolyn slammed down the telephone receiver. Somewhat later, after lunch, having had time to mull over what had happened, she started back to school with the opal ring in her purse.

Mr Bridge came home earlier than usual on the chance that she might still be there, because the longer he had thought about her so-called engagement the angrier he got. But she was gone. Harriet told him she had left soon after lunch. He strode into the hall, took off his hat, his gloves, and his coat, laid his briefcase on the table, and went looking for his wife. He found her in the bedroom seated before the mirror at her dressing table. She did not appear to be doing anything. He had a feeling she had been there a long time not doing anything. He was puzzled that she could squander so much time this way. She did it often. He himself could not sit still for more than a few minutes unless he was occupied. He had never understood how she was able to spend thirty minutes or an hour in a trance. However, if that was what she chose to do it was all right. Harriet took care of the house and the cooking, and Douglas made no demands. There was not much else to be looked after. Possibly that was why she sat around.

He asked if Carolyn had returned to university. Mrs Bridge said yes. He wanted to know how she was feeling when she left. Mrs Bridge said she had seemed terribly unhappy but was no longer crying. He asked who the boy was. Mrs Bridge told him as much as she herself knew about Gil Davis, which was that he came from a town called Parallel in southern Kansas near the Oklahoma border, he was a junior at the university, studying business management, and he worked three afternoons a week in the dean's office. There was one other thing, but she did not mention it: his father was a plumber.

Mr Bridge asked what fraternity Gil Davis belonged to.

Mrs Bridge was not sure; she thought Carolyn had mentioned that he did not belong to a fraternity, but it would be best to ask Carolyn about that.

How long had she been acquainted with this boy?

Mrs Bridge was not sure.

Mr Bridge announced that he was not going to have his daughter running around with every Tom, Dick, and Harry.

Mrs Bridge said, 'Goodness, you're behaving as though it was my fault!'

He said, 'I don't know whose fault this is.'

'The boy is probably all right,' she said.

'You may think so, but I do not,' he said furiously. 'These state universities are jam-packed with opportunists. Now, I am not wealthy, but one day what I have will belong to you and the children, and I do not intend to let some no-account get his hands on it. I have worked too hard for too many years.'

'Well, I do think you're being unreasonable. You've never so much as laid eyes on the boy.'

'Nor do I intend to. Carolyn promised me she would give back the ring.'

'I was listening. I could hear every word. I wouldn't be surprised if half the neighborhood heard.'

446

'Never mind that. Did she say anything to you about giving this fellow back his ring?'

'Not in so many words. But she promised, so I'm certain she will. I believe, though, she did mention something about waiting until tomorrow.'

'Tomorrow! Why does she have to wait until tomorrow? Why isn't she returning it as soon as she gets back to school? There's something funny going on here, and I don't like it.'

'I imagine she's simply too overwrought to speak to him right away. Honestly, Walter, you could have been a little more understanding.'

'I don't know what has gotten into Carolyn,' he said as though he had not heard. 'It's costing me a considerable sum of money to put that girl through school. I sent her up there to learn something, not fiddle around. Does she think I'm made of money? Does she think I'm paying the bills so she can chase around day and night with this whatever his name is? Either she straightens out or I'll know the reason why. I will not put up with this much longer, believe you me!'

'I'm sure she's doing her best. Her grades are quite good, really.'

'They should be better. She ought to be at the head of her class in the university just as she was in high school. She has the brains for it.'

'She certainly does.'

'There is no excuse for her behavior. If there is one thing on this earth that exasperates me it is seeing some person fail to make use of his or her natural ability. She is five times as bright as most of the kids in that university and she is not making use of it. Instead, she spends all her time chasing around with somebody we never heard of and know nothing about.'

'I don't believe she spends all of her time with him.'

'Who is the boy?'

'Don't glare at me, if you please. I'm not responsible.'

'I don't know the first thing about that boy. Where did she meet him?'

'Why didn't you ask her instead of simply giving her the dickens? She would have told you if you had asked. All you did was shout at her. No wonder she was upset.'

'She is too young to think about getting married. Young people today have no idea what they're getting into. They think they can go ahead and marry as soon as they feel like it. It isn't as simple as that. There are children, for one thing.'

'You needn't tell me,' said Mrs Bridge.

'What in God's name does the boy think he's going to do after he gets out of school. Does he expect me to support him?'

'Walter, really!'

'How do we know? If she cares for this boy why is she afraid to bring him here so we can have a look at him?'

'You're not being fair. Carolyn says he works in the dean's office when he's not in class, and it's an awfully long drive here. Besides, you can't expect her to march the poor boy into the living room for your inspection.'

'If she expects my permission – now or any time in the future – that's what she is going to do. Young people today have no sense of responsibility. It wasn't like that when I was a kid. I was attracted to several young women before I met you, and I made it a point to meet their parents. I didn't go skulking around behind their backs.'

Mrs Bridge smiled.

'I don't know what amuses you,' he said querulously, 'but I didn't, and that is a fact.'

'I've never seen you this way.'

'I would be a very poor father if I allowed my children to do whatever they pleased. I am looking out for Carolyn's welfare. When I was a boy I used to think I was entitled to do as I wished, and I resented the authority of my parents. Now I realize they were correct.'

'Let's not talk about it anymore,' she said, and patted his cheek. 'Carolyn will keep her promise to return the ring, and perhaps that will be the end of it.'

135 Guess who?

The next afternoon Mr Bridge was at his desk studying the mail when the door to the outer office opened as if it had been hit by a windstorm and there stood a gaunt, ugly college boy with tangled hair and protruding yellow teeth. He was breathing like a horse. Apparently he had run up the steps instead of waiting for the elevator. The brown-and-white saddle shoes, the sweater – he could not be anything except a college boy. Julia, greatly excited, was tugging at his sleeve with a frantic expression, but he was not paying much attention to her.

Mr Bridge considered him for several moments. Then he said: 'I believe I have a fairly good idea who you are. I do not intend to talk to you. Not today and not tomorrow. So you turn around and high-tail it back where you came from. Do you understand? Because if you do not, I shall send for the police.' To emphasize this he placed one hand on the telephone.

The boy did not move.

'Get out. Get out of my office,' Mr Bridge said. 'I will not tolerate such behavior.' But as he looked into the narrow blue eyes he could see that the boy was difficult to intimidate.

'Julia,' he said, 'you may leave us alone. I'll take care of the situation.' He waited until the door closed. Then he put down the letter he had been reading and he leaned forward, pointing at the boy.

'Yes, I know who you are. Furthermore, I know your type. Universities are jam-packed with opportunists. Well, let me tell you something, young man. If you think for one minute that you are going to marry my daughter you'd better think again.'

'I'll make her a damn fine husband,' the boy said. He was getting his breath back.

'I don't like anything about you,' Mr Bridge said. 'But if you want to sit down for a few minutes, you may.'

The boy settled himself in the chair beside the desk. 'I haven't got any money,' he remarked as though it was something of a joke. 'I guess she's already told you.'

He had nothing to recommend himself, except the fact that he was unafraid. This, and the idea that he loved Carolyn. He was homely and he was poor. Nor did he appear to be the sort who cared a great deal about earning money. He was not unintelligent, but on the other hand he was not exceptional. He had the curious shaggy quality of a boy from a small town. This could wear off after twenty years, or it might mark him forever. That would depend on the boy himself. But it was plain enough now, and while there was nothing shameful about coming from a small community, still it was no asset. How would he look at the country club? He might be ludicrous. At the moment, with his teeth and his farm-boy hair and his conviction that he and Carolyn were meant for each other, he was as naïve as a Kansas boy could be. What was there to recommend him as a husband for Carolyn – who was highly intelligent, attractive, and who would eventually inherit some thousands of dollars. What could this boy offer in exchange? Love? Perhaps. It was too soon to tell. Neither of them could know if they were in love until many years had passed. What else had he? Nothing except the desire of youth, which could be found on any corner, together with the fact that he was not easy to frighten.

'You seem to be under the impression that whatever you want, you are entitled to have,' Mr Bridge said.

He grinned and shook his head. 'No. She's all.'

'Young man, you presume a great deal.'

'We're going to get married, Mr Bridge.'

'Not without my permission you are not.'

'You can't stop us.'

'We'll see about that.'

'I'm going to have her. One way or another.'

'Carolyn is too young to consider marriage. She will complete her education before she does anything else. As for you, your time is up. I have been more than lenient with you. Now you make tracks out of here.'

'I didn't come all the way from Lawrence just so you could kick me out, so don't pull that stuff on me.'

'You have three seconds to start moving.'

'One, two, three. Bull!' the boy said, lifting three fingers. 'Cork told me your folks lived in Sugar Creek.'

It was after dark when they left the office. Gil Davis said he ought to be catching the bus to Lawrence, but Mr Bridge invited him to spend the night at the house. There was room enough, and it was time he met Mrs Bridge.

136 *Legal secretary*

Julia had worked in the office from the beginning, and he had never forgotten how attractive she was when he first saw her. She had seemed much too young to be an experienced legal secretary, but there was nothing wrong with her references so he had taken a chance. Through the years she had done her work well and every night she rode home on the bus to the crumbling, stone apartment building just off Valentine Road, unless they had worked late. Then he drove her home.

Once in a while they stopped across the street for a drink before going to the garage to get the Chrysler, and because he knew she enjoyed these visits to the cocktail lounge he was careful that they did not become a habit; she ought not to regard these moments as one of her rights. Perhaps if she lived a more varied personal life there would be no harm in treating her to a drink more often, but night after night as punctually and obediently as a child who has been ordered to come straight home from school she took the bus to the apartment and was met by her crippled sister. He had never inquired how she felt about this. It was easy to imagine, just as it was easy to imagine the interior of their apartment – cluttered with potted plants and lace doilies, cheap glassware, enameled trinkets from the dime store – all the junk two unmarried sisters would collect to prevent themselves from admitting the truth. No doubt the place smelled of medicine. Tokens of poor health littering the rooms like a bird's nest sprinkled with broken eggshells.

One evening when they had finished their drinks and he was anxious to get home for supper she touched him. He had been about to reach for his wallet when she caught his hand. He was very much surprised. He wondered what could be wrong. She fixed him with an imploring gaze. Her eyes were moist, she was breathing uncertainly. It occurred to him she might be sick; he asked if she felt all right, but evidently she did not hear the question. He disliked her hand resting on his. During the many years they had worked together she had not once touched him deliberately, and almost never by accident. He found the touch of her hand unpleasant. He looked at it and saw the usual slender, weak, unimpressive feminine hand with tapered fingers. It was no longer the hand of a young girl. It was creased from work, and although the skin had remained soft and the fingers were still delicate the shape of it had subtly changed. This was now the hand of a middle-aged woman. It was speckled with brown liver spots.

Julia, seeing him observe their hands together, gave a gentle squeeze. Mr Bridge could not tolerate this. For twenty-five years only one woman had been so intimate. Gradually, without saying anything, as though unaware of her grasp, he pulled his hand away.

Julia suggested they have a second drink.

He consulted his watch although he knew to within five minutes what time it was. She had never before asked to have a second drink. However, because he had asked favors of her – sent her on minor errands which probably hurt her dignity, and called her to work on Sundays and holidays – because of all this, because she was Julia on whom he had depended for such a long while, he agreed.

That a mature and sensible woman could get drunk on two bland cocktails seemed impossible, yet she was not half through the second glass when the signs became apparent. He had never seen her like this and he said in a low voice, hoping nobody would overhear, 'Julia, pull yourself together.'

Julia sobbed.

He looked down at her severely. 'I am taking you home. Get your coat.'

She did as she was told. He put on his hat, his topcoat, his gloves, picked up his briefcase and the *Wall Street Journal*, and held the door open for her. They walked out of the lounge and started toward the garage, but they had not gone five steps before she did something else which shocked him; she took hold of his arm as though they were man and wife. He did not try to dislodge her, but he said to himself while they marched toward the garage that he would not treat her to any more drinks. He reminded himself that this was his own fault, he never should have indulged her. She had been working hard, she was fatigued, and this might be one of those days when women lose what slight self-control they ordinarily have. Now the only thing to do was to get her home without any further embarrassment. Hopefully she would be all right by tomorrow, she could apologize if she felt like it, although this was not important, and they could go on with their work.

While they were driving through Penn Valley Park she had a weeping fit. He ignored it, but he was displeased. He avoided looking at her. He thought of how she had aged. A broad gray streak ran through the middle of her hair and she had begun wearing horn-rimmed glasses. Her waist was thick. Something had gone wrong with the circulation in her legs, so she had bought a pair of black orthopedic shoes.

By the time they reached the apartment she had almost recovered. She was still sobbing now and then, but more from exhaustion than grief or whatever it was that started her off. He was disgusted by the shameless display of emotion, but he was also concerned. He wanted to help her, if possible; however, he did not want to say or do anything which would set her off again. Already he was late for supper and had not called home because he did not want to try to explain the situation. So, with the motor idling, he gripped the steering wheel and waited for her to get out of the car.

Julia finished wiping her eyes with a little handkerchief.

She tucked the handkerchief into her purse and, as if it were the most natural thing in the world, she invited him up to the apartment.

Mr Bridge was astounded. 'I believe not, Julia. Thank you,' he said. He expected her to get out, but she did not.

Then she asked if he realized what day it was.

The simplicity of the question exasperated him. He cleared his throat and kept both hands on the wheel.

Julia nodded. 'I guess I should have known. I'm an idiot. I told myself you weren't like that. Not really. Not at heart. You are, though. From your Homburg to your expensive gray gloves.' She puffed out her cheeks and made a small popping noise. 'Dear Miss Lovejoy, respectfully yours, et cetera. Such a laugh. So much for indispensable Julie.'

'If you're not feeling up to par maybe you ought to stay home tomorrow. I won't need the Loomis brief until Friday.'

453

'Right,' she said. 'Stay home. Get a good rest, old girl. Feel better Monday. Don't know what I'm talking about, do you? Do you?'

'I must admit I don't.'

'Okay, here goes. Listen, Mr Walter Bridge who lives in a lovely home on Crescent Heights. Cling to your wheel, old sport, because here comes one true confession. I've given you the best years of my life – the very best years. You never used them. You never wanted them.'

He looked at his watch.

'Don't remind me,' she said. She opened the door of the Chrysler. Still she did not get out. 'You never forget a thing, so ask yourself this. How many years ago today did I walk into the office for the very first time? Good night, Mr Bridge. I think I will stay home tomorrow, with your permission.'

He drove home greatly shocked. It had never occurred to him that she regarded her association with him as anything more than a job. He did not want to lose her; he hoped that after a day away from the office she would have recovered her sense of values so they would be able to continue as before. If not, the only solution would be to let her go.

137 In the vault

It seemed to him that a good many people he knew were disintegrating as unmistakably as Julia. He himself was having difficulty with a stiff neck in the mornings, and the time had come for stronger reading glasses, and he was worried about the irregularity of his heart. However, it was a comfort to observe how rapidly his friends were aging. Virgil had gotten so fat that his lower lip protruded. Lutweiler was completely gray, though he played tennis and went swimming so often that he had retained a youthful air. Alex smelled like a tobacco warehouse and appeared to be turning yellow from the nicotine. Mrs Bridge, he thought, did not look as old as most of her friends. She had not changed very much. She was thoroughly girdled now, her lips were faintly puckered, and her hair was set by the beauty parlor with an eye to practicality; but in contrast to her friends she was in good shape. Lois Montgomery was wrinkling around the neck like a stalk of cauli-flower. Madge Arlen, evidently suffering from some kind of disorder, walked stiffly, rather like a turkey. Grace Barron was withering and shriveling like a plant in dry soil. Ultimately they were all going to go. They were going to vanish like the elm in the yard: grass now grew over the place where it stood for fifty years, and the people who would someday live in the house, whether they were Douglas' children or an unknown family, would not even be aware that a stately tree was gone.

In the privacy of his cubicle in the basement of the bank Mr Bridge waved his hands at nothing, as if he might brush away these unhappy meditations forever. He began to think about Harriet. She was drinking too much, it was no longer possible to pretend that she was not. She kept a bottle hidden in an empty carton of soap flakes in the cupboard beneath the sink, and sometimes she tried to hold her breath while serving dinner. Something had to be done.

He thought about Ruth. He could not understand why she permitted a homosexual to spend the night in her apartment, or why she wished to associate with Greenwich Village bohemians and Negroes. What she was doing did not make sense.

Nor was she alone in the pursuit of folly. The grandiose projects of mindless pundits rolled out of Washington as regularly as doughnuts, and at the apex of this insane pyramid sat Roosevelt, dispensing fireside affability and panaceas as foolish as his hat, meanwhile packing the Supreme Court with socialists and an-archistic 'liberals'. Father Coughlin called him a great betrayer and liar. The priest was not far wrong.

Progressive educators, so-called, were at work in the schools. Subjects taught for generations were being demeaned and aban-doned. Psychologists, social workers, and various other apologists of lawlessness were excusing the criminal for his crime, blaming each daily outrage on those who committed no outrage. Soon enough nobody would be considered responsible for anything. What would happen next? It was violently unjust that such things could come to pass while a man spent his life and all of his energy working to achieve some degree of security for himself and his family. There was so much change, so much absurdity, so little respect for the traditions and the ideals upon which civilization was founded.

Wearily he resumed examining his stock certificates and bonds. Once more he read through his will. Everything appeared to be in proper order.

138 Winter

At first the snow appeared tentatively, sifting down from the clouds like flour through a screen; gradually the frozen earth was covered, and the leaves beneath the maple, and the lower corners of each windowpane were rounded. By the time Mr Bridge left the house to drive downtown the evergreen boughs were sagging.

Snow fell all day, hushing the noise of traffic. Lights stayed on in offices and stores.

Late in the afternoon he instructed Julia to call the garage and tell Mr Buckworth to put chains on the Chrysler because it was apparent that the residential streets were going to be treacherous, and when he started home an hour later it was still snowing. He drove cautiously, stopping at each intersection, and it was six o'clock before he reached the Union Station. He turned on the radio for the six o'clock news. The Italians were advancing in North Africa. John L. Lewis was threatening to shut the mines again. Fire had destroyed an apartment building in the Negro district of Kansas City. A liquor store on Linwood Boulevard had been robbed and the proprietor was shot.

By the time he got to the Plaza the snow was falling thickly. Automobiles, telephone poles, shops, all were capped with snow. The tennis courts were level white rectangles. The black iron posts of the nets resembled fence posts in a farmer's field. At the intersection of the streetcar line there had been an accident; people were gathering, and an ambulance with its red light flashing was moving slowly through the traffic. In the shopping district the stores were still open and bright with Christmas decorations and the roofs of the buildings were strung with lights as they were each year. He considered driving around to enjoy the spectacle, but the snow was getting deep.

He crossed the Brush Creek bridge and a few minutes later started up the Ward Parkway hill. After every snowfall somebody tried to go up Ward Parkway without chains. Before he came to the crest of the hill he saw what he expected: a car had skidded off the road.

At the top of the hill some children had built a snow fort, and a barrage of snowballs rose toward him but fell apart in the air.

Huntington Road had been cleared. In a little while he reached Crescent Heights, turned in the driveway, and allowed the Chrysler to coast into the garage.

He paused on the back steps to stamp the snow from his shoes while Harriet waited just inside, and as soon as he was ready she opened the door. He was puzzled by the expression on her face. He hesitated, then he asked if anything was wrong. Harriet replied in an unnatural voice that Mrs Bridge was at the Barrons' house. His wife spent a great deal of time with Grace Barron, there was nothing unusual about this. He glanced at her impatiently. She backed away and began stirring a kettle of soup on the stove.

'Come, now,' he said. 'This has been a long day for me. I am in no mood to drag information out of you. What is going on? Is Mrs Barron ill?'

Harriet touched her lips as though she was afraid to speak. She murmured. He was not quite certain what she said. Then very clearly he heard her say that Grace Barron was dead.

'She is what?'

'She is dead?'

'You say she is dead?'

Harriet nodded vigorously and started to cry.

Mr Bridge placed his briefcase on the drainboard but immediately picked it up because he had laid it in a pool of water. He reached for his handkerchief but realized that Harriet had a dish towel and was trying to pull the briefcase out of his hand.

'Here, let me attend to that,' she was saying.

He gave it to her, and she dried it while he gazed out the kitchen window. He noticed that snow was piling up on the ledge just outside the glass and it occurred to him that the weather forecast had been correct. The snow was heavy and looked as if it was going to continue all night. It must be snowing throughout the Midwest.

'Mr Bridge, you all right?' she asked.

457

'Yes. Oh, yes,' he said. 'I'll be all right, Harriet. This is startling news. You are positive, are you?'

She handed him the briefcase without saying anything and resumed stirring the soup. He walked out of the kitchen and went upstairs. In the bedroom he discovered that he had forgotten to take off his hat and coat. He put them on the bed, undressed, and went into the bathroom to take a shower, but presently he saw that the tub was almost full. He did not remember turning on the water for the tub; however, it did not make any difference, so he stepped in and sat down and shut his eyes. He thought about Grace Barron. He recalled the rainy day he had eaten lunch with her and how she had insinuated that he was sympathetic to the Nazis. Perhaps deliberately and maliciously she had misinterpreted what he said. He reflected that he had never liked her very much. If she had not been such a close friend of his wife he would have avoided her. She had always been contentious and unstable. She was a lost, unhappy woman. Virgil had given her whatever she wanted. She had been given too much, which might be the reason she was critical of people, critical of everything which did not coincide with her own prejudices. In fact, she had seemed critical of her own pampered existence. She was spoiled and disagreeable. She had not known enough to appreciate her good fortune, the security Virgil had provided, nor whom to thank for it. Her death was a shock, but each death is a shock, whether it is a person who dies or whether it is something as inconsequential as a gray squirrel or an old elm tree, and he concluded that he felt no particular regret.

He began to think about the snow, which would make it difficult for his wife to get home. He remembered how dark it had been all day and how the snowflakes were swirling past the streetlights when he drove through the Plaza. The flakes were as large as moths, floating and sailing everywhere in silvery profusion.

He heard what he thought was the peck of a bird at the bathroom window, but then he knew it must be his wife tapping at the door. He sat up, realizing he had gone to sleep, and saw his dripping hands, which for an instant he could not recognize. They had been lying under the water for so long that they were shriveled and wrinkled.

'May I come in?' she asked.

'The door is unlocked,' he said.

She stepped into the bathroom. She looked tired and subdued. He asked how Virgil was feeling and she answered that Dr Foster was there.

'Dr Foster,' he said. 'If you want my opinion, Virgil is more in need of a sedative than any spiritual consolation.'

She replied vaguely, 'Oh? I suppose. I was on the phone most of the day. So many people called.'

'Was it a heart attack?'

'We're afraid it was an overdose of pills. Lois and Madge have been there. We're telling callers we don't know the cause. We decided it wouldn't do any good to disturb the men at work. That's why I didn't call you.'

'Sleeping pills,' Mr Bridge said. 'I suspected as much. Sleeping pills!' The idea of suicide exasperated him. Now her children must suffer, and she had hurt her husband in the cruelest way a woman can hurt a man. Rather than go on living with him she had wilfully destroyed herself. She had shown her children how little they meant. She had left her husband to endure every ugly speculation. He knew he had been correct to feel nothing at the news of her death. What she had done was cowardly. What such a woman deserved was scorn and contempt.

139 The volunteer

The news from Europe got worse. Chamberlain, of course, was responsible; Roosevelt, too, because he had concurred with the British capitulation at Munich. Much of the world soon would be at war, there was no longer any doubt about it.

I warned you, he said to his friends, for he remembered very clearly predicting what was going to happen as a result of the Munich appeasement. A policy of firmness could have deterred Hitler, but the appeasers in London and Washington had been given their way. What Hitler already had done, and what he would do, was disastrous; consequently there was no choice, the German organization must be defeated. Hitler was insane, and this was unfortunate because some of his ideas were sensible.

Douglas asked for permission to join the Marines.

Mr Bridge refused, pointing out that the United States was not at war.

Douglas argued that he was going to be drafted when he was eighteen, whether the United States got into the war or not, and if he waited until he was drafted he would no longer be allowed to choose the branch of service he wanted. He went on to say that he knew there was not much difference between the Army and the Marines, because in either case he would be a foot soldier. Just the same, he wanted to become a Marine.

Mr Bridge took off his glasses and rubbed his eyes. 'You are getting ahead of yourself. You will not be eighteen for quite a while. If you are still anxious to join the Marines at that time we will discuss the matter further.'

Douglas thought the war would be over by then.

'That would be wonderful,' Mr Bridge replied.

Douglas asked if he could volunteer for the Navy and become an underwater-demolition expert.

Mr Bridge said he could not.

It was not dangerous, Douglas insisted, because he would get very good training.

Mr Bridge waved impatiently.

What would happen, Douglas persisted, if the Nazis invaded America?'

'Should that occur,' Mr Bridge said, 'you may volunteer for anything you like. For the present, however, you will continue your education. When the government requires your services you will be notified. Until that happens we are not going to concern ourselves.'

Douglas had spoken somewhat windily in order to demonstrate his fearlessness. And apart from proving to his father that the idea of being punctured by a bullet or blown to pieces by a grenade did not frighten him, there were other reasons for joining the service. He was bored with school. He suspected that he was about to fail Spanish, and he was not doing much better in Public Speaking; if he could get into uniform before the end of the semester he would not have to worry about these problems. Besides, it should be exciting to be in military service and get to travel around, see some things, and meet older women. Furthermore, while wearing a uniform he would be treated with some respect.

He said to his father: 'You sound like you hope the Germans win.'

Mr Bridge told him to stop talking nonsense.

'You hate Jews.'

'Never have you heard me make such a statement.'

'When Mr and Mrs Arlen were here one night you said you hoped the British didn't stop Hitler too soon.'

This was true. He had been joking because he knew the Arlens felt as he himself felt about the Jews. He could not imagine how Douglas had overheard the remark.

'I do not like that,' he said. 'Not one bit. You are never to say any such thing again, do you understand? I will not listen to any more of it. I have had enough for one evening. More than enough.'

After a long silence Douglas asked if he could have permission to join the Army Air Corps.

Mr Bridge said no.

140 Death ray

Douglas remained in school, but he was excited by the war. Several of his friends had gotten permission to enlist. Others spoke of running away from home and buying false birth certificates in order to get to Europe while the fighting was still going on. Radio broadcasts and newspaper reports were full of accounts of air raids and of naval battles. At dinner he talked about an article he had read in a scientific magazine which suggested that beams of light could be used to kill.

'According to this article what they probably will try to do is throw these beams several miles and focus them. They don't think anybody can figure out a defense, because if you get caught in these rays you just sort of evaporate.'

'I hope the scientists never succeed,' his mother said firmly. 'We have more than enough dreadful weapons. I'm so opposed to all these bombs and guns.'

Douglas spread his hands. 'I'm telling you what I read. It isn't my brainstorm. Also, they figure the German scientists must be working out these same scientific principles, so it means it could turn into a race to see who figures it out first. The English sure better win or we'll be duck soup.' And he drew his finger swiftly across his throat.

'Honestly, what gets into people,' she said with a helpless expression. 'It just makes you sick.'

'Haw!' Douglas said, and reached for the biscuits. 'Who started this war?'

'Oh, I suppose you're right,' she answered. 'I don't even like to think about it. Everything is in such a state. You wonder why people can't learn to get along together.'

'Ask Herr Schicklgruber, the Dummkopf.'

'You are absolutely right,' Mr Bridge said. 'Ask Hitler. And may the Lord help us if the Nazis win this war, because life will not be worth living. I don't mind telling you, if any new weapons are invented I hope the United States invents them.'

141 Joy to the world

Every few months, acceding to the wishes of his wife, he found himself in church. Usually he agreed to go on Easter because that day seemed appropriate, once around Christmas, and once or twice more during the year whenever she became insistent. In church he behaved very nearly as she hoped he would. He waited inexpressively through the sermon, held the hymnal, and more or less pretended to sing along with her, contributed a dollar when the plate came down the pew, and lowered his head enough to remain inconspicuous when Dr Foster summoned the congregation to prayer – although he refused to shut his eyes. And he often consulted his watch, as though by this he could bring forth the welcome notes of the recessional.

He attended church on these occasions partly because he had no wish to attract attention by abstaining completely, but principally because she wanted him to. She needed him there not merely to demonstrate for the benefit of the neighborhood that her husband was not atheistic, but as actual bodily insurance against possible recrimination by God for such sins as he may have committed. In her heart she did believe God existed – He was a bit larger than a normal man, perhaps seven feet tall with a shaggy white beard untainted by cigar smoke, who dressed in a sort of white nightgown similar to the one He wore on the ceiling of the Sistine Chapel.

So it was that on a crisp, snowy, Sunday morning just before Christmas they were lodged in the first row of the balcony of the tidy little Congregational Church. Dr Foster was hard at work and Mrs Bridge listened attentively. Mr Bridge was thinking about other things while he waited for the end of the service. The air in the balcony was stale and his head felt congested, but he did not like to sit on the main floor where he was obliged to look up at the minister. He scratched his ankle and thought of how much he would rather be at home in front of the fireplace with the Sunday paper.

He sighed, louder than he had intended. He blinked, yawned, and looked around. There was not much to look at. Everything about the church was passionless. He remembered Chartres – the chill, somberly echoing nave, the stone effigies, the ominous shadows and crude colored-glass windows. The Congregational Church was bland, as innocuous as the man in the pulpit. This was a different kind of religion. It was more comfortable, and the minister's sermon was no doubt more comforting than the stark admonition of the Middle Ages. Here one never heard a warning from the man in the black robe. Here was no funereal sculpture in the niches, no blood-red windows. It was all quite pleasant.

He considered Dr Foster discoursing on biblical events and wondered how a man could retain such innocence through the vicissitudes of life. It was as though the minister never worried or doubted. He resembled a stout, pompous little druggist, the sixty-year-old face as vacant as a melon – a trifle sleek and epicene, almost shiny. Time was not darkening or blemishing the surface of the man, nor had years disturbed the liquid flow of his faith. Imperturbably he stood in his pulpit and perpetuated a vision suitable for children. He stood so securely and lectured with such powerless conviction because he knew nothing else. He was a truly virtuous man, if not truly good.

It was time once again to sing.

Mr Bridge got to his feet reluctantly. He opened the book and held it for his wife, who sang in a pure, slender tone. The congregation sang 'Joy to the World', and he sang a few phrases because he enjoyed the Christmas carols.

Yet while he was singing he reflected on the word 'joy' – the archaic sound of this odd word, and its meaning. He reflected that he had occasionally heard people use this word. Evidently they had experienced joy, or believed they had experienced it. He asked himself if he ever had known it. If so, he could not remember. But he thought he must have known it because he understood the connotation, which would be impossible without having experienced it. However, if he had once known joy it must have been a long time ago. Satisfaction, yes, and pleasure of several sorts, and pride, and possibly a feeling which might be called 'rejoicing' after some serious worry or problem had been resolved. There were many such feelings, but none of them should be called 'joy'. He remembered enthusiasm, hope, and a kind of jubilation or exultation. Cheerfulness, yes, and joviality, and the brief gratification of sex. Gladness, too, fullness of heart, appreciation, and many other emotions. But not joy. No, that belonged to simpler minds.